Come Innocent Leave Understood

Come Innocent Leave Understood

Shannika Crawford

Warrior Princess Nation, LLC

First Printing, 2021

Published by Warrior Princess Nation
North Las Vegas, NV
For information email admin@warriorprincessnation.com

Dedication

You ever noticed when you met someone with a mental illness, they are bluntly honest? Well, that was my best friend. She died in 2003, and that was a very sad day in my life! She was very understanding, and she looked at me as a prize, not a problem. She listened to me, gave me great honest advice, was very intelligent. However, she took a wrong turn in life, and it got the best of her. She was mistreated and judged by many for her drug addiction & mental illness, but she had so much insight. I'm speaking of my mom. I rarely heard the good about her, but I knew she loved me. I look at people who are supposedly "normal" sometimes as posters. They think they have it all together; good on the outside, but some are so empty inside. The world may think I didn't matter to my mom, but we mattered to each other. I will miss my best friend!

ACKNOWLEDGEMENTS

First, giving glory and honor to God in Jesus' name for pulling me through.

I thank my two God-sisters, Jenise and Loretta, for always being there, and my God-mom, Ms. Norma Jean, who believed in me and never gave up on making this happen. Ashley, thanks for loving me and lifting me up.

Of course, I have to acknowledge my 2 young adults. Mom will always love y'all through it all. I also want to thank all the foster parents who took me in and Mama Jewell, who always made me feel welcomed. To Aunt Karen, thank you for the good advice.

To all my foster siblings who love me as if we are blood, I love you dearly!

To my biological brother, thanks for combing my hair for school and being there when we had no one.

To my biological sister, we have a weird kind of closeness but don't test us. Thanks, little sister, for reading the first 55 pages and waiting patiently for the rest.

I can go on and on, but you will make the next go around, for sure!

1

Isaac walked down the long street in the sun with his white t-shirt, blue jean shorts, tube socks, and sneakers that were not good enough for school but good enough to go outside and play. His hair was in multiple braids, and he had a smile that could light up a room. He had 2 balls his mom and stepdad bought him earlier from the $.25 machine when they went to the local grocery store. Finally, Isaac got to the sign on Broadway, where he usually met his best friend. They had to meet at the end of the street every time they played because, for some reason, their parents were against them playing together. Finally, he saw his friend, David, with his golden silky straight hair. He walked, waving and smiling the rest of the way. David wore a white t-shirt, green sweatpants, and white sneakers in the same condition as Isaac's.

"Hey, Isaac!"

"Hey, Dave, you ready to play ball?"

"Why you didn't tell me, now I have to go back and get one then sneak back down the street to play."

"No, you don't, look!"

Issac snatched two balls from his pocket with a smile. David removed one of the balls from Isaac's hand.

"Ooh, cool, these are the ones we wanted with the high bounce."

David bounced it high and jumped to catch it. Isaac smiled, knowing he made his friend happy.

"Hey, Dave, you wonder why our parents don't want us to play together sometimes."

"Well, my mom said we are just not the same."

"Well, what does your dad say?"

"He just looked at me and told me to eat my dinner and stop asking questions."

"Well, my dad said my mom's mother worked for people like your mom, so that's good enough reason to stay away and that it might start uh, 'confusion.'"

"Confusion?"

David stated the word just as baffled as Issac had.

"Yeah, I wanted to know what it meant too, and my mom said sometimes confusion starts trouble."

David smiled and stuck out his leg, danced, and wiggled it around.

"Oh, well, I listen to my mom and dad, but I think we are the same."

Isaac looked down at David's leg and stuck out his own, and wiggled it around too.

"Yeah, our legs wiggle around, and we both have two, huh?"

"Yeah!"

So, Isaac and David continued to play with the bouncing balls until they noticed the streetlights were almost on.

"Well, I better get home."

"Yeah, me too. Hey, Isaac, what are you eating for dinner?"

Isaac listed the menu.

"Greens, cornbread, baked chicken, oh yeah, and some red Kool-Aid!"

David rubbed his belly; he knew about greens and cornbread because his auntie took him somewhere, and they ate that.

"Ooh, your dinner sounds good! I'm having sweet peas, tuna casserole, dinner rolls, and lemonade!"

Isaac loved to eat, and he liked the combination, so he rubbed his belly as well.

"Ooh, your dinner sounds good too! Hey, Dave, that's something, huh?"

"What, Isaac?"

"We both like to eat; that's the same, huh?"

David smiled, excited about something else he had in common with his friend.

"Yep, and there is nothing wrong with that!"

Isaac and David laughed, as they often did, gave each other a high five, and headed their separate ways.

"See you tomorrow, Isaac."

"Okay, Dave."

Isaac got home and bathed before dinner. He was quiet the entire time, wondering would he ever get to eat dinner at Dave's house and would Dave ever get to eat with him and his family. Brenda, Isaac's mom, stood over him with a bowl of greens in one hand and the other on her hip.

"Boy, now I know I didn't slave over that hot stove, so you can stare in space, go ahead and finish eating, son."

Isaac looked up at his mom, not having far to look up. His mom was only 5 feet tall, heavyset with her hair in a ball, and dimples showed when she smiled.

"Okay, mama."

Isaac looked at his plate again as Brenda smiled at him, then she went to the other side of the table where her husband was sitting. She looked down at Samuel and smiled.

"Do you want some more greens, babe?"

"Well, if my boy will have some more with me, I will. Is that okay with you, little man?"

Isaac looked over and smiled at his dad. Even though Samuel was not his biological dad, he was a hard worker and treated them well.

"Yeah, daddy and I can probably eat more greens than you now!"

Isaac stuck his chest out far as he could. Samuel looked at Isaac proudly; he never looked at Isaac like he wasn't his real son and didn't treat him like he wasn't either.

"Oh, so you big man instead of little man now, huh?"

Brenda shook her head at both of them, filled their plates, and sat down to finish her food as well.

In the middle of Isaac eating, she saw the fullness on his face.

"Alright, big little man, you proved your point. Now it's time for bed, school tomorrow."

Isaac sighed in protest.

"Aaaw, mama, you said I can watch T.V. for thirty extra minutes tonight."

You could hear the disappointment in his words. As if she remembered saying that, and it just slipped her mind, Brenda gave in.

"Okay, I did say that. You sure didn't forget that, well how come you can't remember to take out the trash."

Brenda and Samuel laughed, and Isaac shrugged his shoulders.

"I don't know."

He rushed over to the television.

David and his family finished their dinner. His dad, Steve, prepared to go off to work. He worked graveyard and was the lead at a warehouse. He looked at his son and rubbed his head.

"Alright, goodnight, son, give me a hug."

David hugged his dad and rushed back to the television.

"Well, something has your attention."

Steve walked over to see what David was looking at.

"I want to make a go-kart, like that one on T.V., dad."

"Well, we can go in the garage on my days off and do that, son!"

"Dad, not to be mean, I want to do this one, you know, like my own thing."

David looked up to see if his dad agreed, cause in reality, he wanted to make his go-kart with Isaac, but that "confusion" word popped up in his head. He was not ready to tell his dad he wanted to do it with Isaac, not wanting that long lecture before his dad went to work on why he couldn't make a go-kart with Isaac. Steve looked over at his wife first.

"Well, okay, my little carpenter and mechanic, go ahead."

David looked at his mom as she cleaned the table from dinner; David knew he could ask questions now that his dad was gone. He would ask 99 questions, and she would answer 100 because she loved her son.

"Mom?"

"Yes."

She already felt questions coming along. She sat, pulled her hair back, and crossed her long slender legs with the dishtowel in her hand.

"You think I, uh, I can make a go-kart with a friend?"

David stared right into his mom's face and waited for the answer he wanted to hear, which was yes. Samantha frowned.

"Didn't you tell your father you wanted to do it yourself, young man?"

"Yeah, but I just remembered that my friend knows where to get go-kart wheels."

"Well, what's wrong with you and your father making them?"

David hoped he could reach his mom with a kid's point of view.

"Mom, that's not cool; I need wagon wheels; they look better. She wanted to agree even without knowing which friend it was. But, she better not ask him another question because it could turn into 99 questions for her.

"Well, your father and I would love to see the outcome of your own creation, so go ahead, and I'll let him know.

"Now go to bed."

David jumped up and hugged her; he was so happy and couldn't wait to bring the go-kart idea to Isaac tomorrow.

"Cool! Thanks, mom; I love you."

Samantha kissed his forehead.

"Okay, I love you too. Goodnight."

2

After school, David quickly changed into his play clothes and asked his mom if he could go outside. His dad was asleep from working all night; that was who he usually asked. David huffed and puffed.

"Mom, can I go outside?"

Samantha remembered David asking last night.

"Oh yeah! Oh, wait! No homework?"

She looked at David, waited for the answer.

"Mom, today is Friday!"

Samantha slapped her forehead.

"Oh yeah, go ahead, David. I will let your dad know you are outside."

David rushed out and down the block.

Isaac was getting out of his school clothes. He had to clean his room because he had left it dirty the night before. He quickly cleaned so he could go outside and get David.

"Mom!"

There was no answer.

"Mom!"

Still no answer, so he yelled loudly.

"MOM!"

She finally answered.

"Yeah, Isaac."

"Are you taking a nap?"

Brenda noticed he was by her bedroom door, so she answered Isaac sarcastically but not in a mean way.

"Well, I was."

"Oh, I'm going outside."

Brenda sat up and disappointingly shook her head.

"Isaac, come here."

Isaac knew the firm voice, so he went right to his mom.

"Yes, momma?"

"Now you are a smart, productive boy, and you know you ask me can you go outside, you don't just tell me you are going!"

She looked to see if he understood.

Isaac's eyes got big.

"Oh, I apologize. Can I go outside?"

He hoped his apology got him off the hook in the productive whatever kind of way she spoke of.

"Yeah, but be in before your dad gets off work so we can play a game or something."

Isaac rushed off, almost running.

"Okay."

"HEY!"

She yelled as if she was going to fuss. Isaac stopped so quick his play shoes screeched on the hardwood floor. He thought she looked over and saw he had missed something in his room.

"Oh, huh?"

Brenda held open her arms.

"I just wanted a hug."

She smiled and laughed at the same time; she often did that. She loved to joke with her son to let him know there was more to life than seriousness. A time to play and a time not to play.

"Momma, you always get me like that."

He was relieved and happy all at once. He rushed over and gave her a big hug. Brenda embraced Isaac with her comfortable chest, one he remembered falling asleep on at 3 years old.

"I love you, mom."

"You better, all that pain I put up with when I was in labor."

She laughed.

Isaac kinda knew, now, that meant when she gave birth to him. He would often hear her tell stories over and over again of him being born, and that word, labor, came up often. So he laughed too.

"Okay, I'll be in before dark, momma."

Brenda let him go and smiled, knowing her son was growing up. But, she didn't want to let go, like any typical mom who saw their kid growing up.

Isaac rushed outside and made his way down to Broadway Ave. to meet his best buddy. They played with other kids in the neighborhood, but no one clicked with him like his buddy Dave. David had waited and did not see Isaac, so he was back at the house in his garage going through his dad's materials. He grabbed nails, wood, and a hammer. David held all the materials by himself and made several trips. When he finally saw Isaac, he was exhausted. So, he dropped all the materials in front of Isaac.

"Hey, Isaac!"

"Oh hey, what's up, Dave. What are you about to do?"

"No, not just me, us. I saw on T.V. a commercial that had a go-kart, and I know we could make one better than that one. I just need to get the wagon wheels your cousin let you have."

Isaac remembered he still had the wheels. His cousin comes to visit every year from deep down south, in Georgia. His dad just threw the wheels in the backyard yesterday when his mom and dad were spring cleaning. Isaac thought fast, hoping that the wheels were still back there and not thrown away.

"Man, that's a good idea! Let me run home and get them out of my backyard. We are going to have our own car!"

Isaac smiled at David, and he smiled back, glad to see his friend was as excited as he was about the go-kart.

"Yeah, while you go, I'll sort out the wood till you come back."

Isaac rushed off and got home as fast as he could. He went through the yard and saw six wheels. You would think four would have been enough, but one wheel was always the steering wheel with old school go-karts. So, Isaac grabbed all six; now, they both would have a steering wheel. He slammed the gate behind him. Brenda looked out the window because she heard the gate bang and noticed Isaac had the wheels and was running down the street. Then she saw David as he sorted out wood. Brenda looked surprised.

"Lord have mercy! I told that boy to play with him every blue moon. I know David's parents don't know they're playing!"

She could see Broadway's corner from her porch, but she placed on her slippers and stepped out to see Isaac better but hesitated to call him back home. She saw the excitement on her son's face. She didn't hear Isaac say anything was going wrong, so she stepped back into the house, kicked off her slippers, and tip-toed to the window.

"Lord, they just kids, but I'm going to have the curtain open, that's for sure."

She went back to baking her grandmother's famous apple pie to block negativity out of her mind on what could happen. She was not worried about the boys; she was mostly concerned about how David's parents and her husband would feel if it ever hit the fan. She just prepped her ingredients, shook her head, and sat down to cut her apples. Isaac made it back to David, who was excited Isaac still had the wheels.

"Yep, that is just what we need, six wheels!"

Steve woke up from his sleep and stretched. His wife was on the other side of the bed, reading her book.

"Hon'?"

Samantha placed her finger in her book.

"Yeah, sweetheart?"

"Where's David? It's too quiet; I don't hear the T.V."

"Oh yeah, he went outside at first, then I heard him in the garage rambling through stuff, then he rushed back outside."

Steve smiled, remembering that his son was in the go-kart-making mode. Steve stood up, stretched again, and went outside. He walked to the third house opposite of his and looked down the street. Because their block curved to Broadway Ave., Steve had to do that, but Isaac's house was straight down where Brenda could easily see. He saw his boy laughing and hammering the wood and nails. Steve's smile went upside down, and he grew hot with anger. He went back into the house and slammed the door.

"I'LL BE DAMN!"

Samantha jumped up and almost dropped her book. She got to the living room to see what was bothering her husband. She looked at him but didn't say a word because she knew he would say what was troubling him.

"Do you know David is making a go-kart with that NIGGER BOY! Oh, that's why he wanted to make the go-kart on his own, huh?"

Steve mocked David.

"No, daddy, I have it. I want this to be my own thing. And David has my wood and other materials too; that boy might steal it. I'll call him in the house to get my stuff right now!"

Samantha tapped him on the shoulder.

"Steve, I don't approve that much of him playing with that boy either, but you have been asleep for hours, and nothing's gone wrong yet. I know Isaac is different, and I'm shocked, but nothing may go wrong at all."

Samantha had a few wrong views herself; however, she was the type of person that was open-minded and tried to look at the big picture. Steve was still upset but listened somewhat to his wife's advice for a change.

"Well, alright, but I'm going to say something to David. This is my house, that is my hammer, and I'm going to say how I feel."

Steve stormed to his garage to see what other tools were out of the house.

Samuel got off work early and got dropped off on the other side of their house. Samuel didn't bother to look down Broadway; he went straight into the house where his wife was almost done preparing the apple pie. He smelled the aroma.

"Ooh wee, babe, what's on your mind?"

Brenda jumped up from grabbing a pot she needed from the cabinet. She was now nervous and wondered why Samuel was home so early.

"Uh-uh, what you mean, babe?"

"No, it's just every time you worry or get nervous, you make your famous pie. Like that Golden Girls show my cousin and you would watch; they have a problem, they would talk it out over cheesecake."

Brenda looked at him and slightly smiled because Samuel knew her well, but she didn't reveal what she was upset about.

"So how was work today? You are home kind of early."

"Babe, it was nice! Hard work, but the day actually went smooth for a change. We kept up with production at the bottling company, and that is always good; we are intact for the week."

"Good hon', maybe that's why I made apple pie; I probably felt your success."

She giggled.

"Yeah, right Brenda."

He went to hang up his coat, and she continued to handle business in the kitchen. Brenda had never kept a secret from her husband, so she yelled out to Samuel from the kitchen.

"You know kids still have an imagination in the two-thousands."

Brenda threw that statement in there and waited for him to say, 'what do you mean?'

"Yeah, I know,"

Brenda snapped her finger and whispered.

"Dang!"

A little nervous, but she continued.

"Yeah, because some kids still build go-karts!"

She paused and waited for a response.

Samuel sat up in his recliner with the biggest grin on his face.

"GO-KARTS! You took me back now, Bren. I don't hear too many kids making them like when we were coming up. If they do, they better not have a big motor and go all the way old school the way gas prices are now."

Brenda and Samuel laughed, but Brenda gave herself away when she laughed a little too long.

"Okay, so what kid you know building a go-kart because that laugh wasn't quite genuine."

Brenda mumbled.

"Isaac and David."

"Babe, speak up. I can't hear you. Who?"

Brenda was glad he didn't hear her the first time but forgot about the mumbling and went ahead and spit it out, not lying but giving only a half-truth.

"Isaac."

"Oh, my son is making a go-kart! Oh, I am in on that!"

Samuel jumped out of his seat.

"Where my boy at?"

Samuel went straight to the backyard, but he didn't see Isaac. He ran to the front window.

"There goes, my boy! He wanted to...."

There was a pause, and the excitement went away. Samuel moved from the window to look back at Brenda.

"I still want that apple pie but now are you going to explain why you made it instead of ignoring the question. What's up with Isaac playing with that?"

"It's David."

"I KNOW!"

"Well, I knew you would be upset, but I didn't know he was about to build one with him until Isaac ran in the backyard and grabbed the wagon wheels Lema left before she went back down south. I started to stop him, but he looked so excited, and I didn't want to steal his joy, you know."

"Yeah, whatever, well, I'm still opening up this curtain."

He went to open up the curtain that had already been opened, but he had just closed. Brenda replied.

"Well, I had it open, but you closed it."

She tried to make Samuel laugh like she usually did.

"Yeah, I guess so, Ms. Apple Pie!"

Brenda knew this would not be it; her husband was the type to get his point across when you least expected it. Samuel would speak out in the middle of nowhere, whether you liked it or not. So Brenda went back to the kitchen and tried to cook her best as she did on the holidays to clear the atmosphere of what she knew would occur.

3

Isaac hammered one of the wood pieces so hard he broke through one.

"All man! Shoo, I always mess up!"

He put the hammer down.

"I do too, but my dad has this stuff in our garage; it's called wood glue; it might fix it. I will go get it,"

Isaac had the biggest smile.

"Thanks because I was going to give up."

David thought of something else that would make Isaac smile.

"How can you give up? We are NASCAR brothers!"

David jumped up and danced side to side. Isaac jumped up and did the same silly but fun dance. They made their new NASCAR dance up along with their car. David took off to get the glue, and Isaac put the broken piece to the side and started on another part.

David went into the garage and heard his dad. He tried to do a good job of being quiet because he didn't want to disturb Steve and refused to tell his dad he was making a go-kart with Isaac. He decided, however, to use his manners and spoke.

"Hey, dad!"

"Yeah, Hey,"

Steve did not speak with much enthusiasm.

"Dad, can I use some of your wood glue?"

Steve was ready for the approach.

"NO! So you can take it with you down there to that Nigger Boy!"

"But da...."

"I said, NO, and that's final! You are going to learn playing with him."

David was almost in tears, and his voice shaky.

"All we doing is...."

"I don't care what you two are doing. Oh yeah, you making your own 'thing,' your own creation, huh? Just go ahead and play with the nigger boy but don't say I didn't warn you."

Steve turned away from his son and continued looking through his tools to see if more were gone.

David ran down the street until he got to Isaac; tears unfolded all the way there. Isaac was singing a made-up song theirs.

"*Here comes my NASCAR brother ready for the chase; my NASCAR brother ready for the race.*"

Isaac stopped singing.

"Hey, I sing that bad I made you cry?"

David yelled out.

"WHY? WHY? WHY?"

Then balled his fist and swung at the air.

"Why what, Dave?"

"My dad won't let me use his stupid glue."

"Oh well, that's okay, we can tape it. Your dad may not have too much left and,,.."

"NO, Isaac, you don't know, okay!"

"Well, it's okay, friend. I don't know what?"

David yelled, not at Isaac, but about what was said.

"HE SAID NO BECAUSE I AM MAKING A GO-KART WITH THE NIGGER BOY!"

David and Isaac plopped on the curve and sat quietly. They had seen racist movies, and they knew that word did not mean the nice boy down the street. So they sat, and silence prevailed as they looked at each other, wondering what to say next. Finally, after ten minutes of saying nothing, baffled and upset, Isaac sought to change the subject to make things better. He was good at that and got it from his mom. The laugh now and cry later syndrome, as she called it.

"Well, Lema is a tomboy, and I saw her tape some wood on one of her tree houses when I went to visit her one summer."

Isaac looked at his friend to see if that cleared the air. David gave a big smile. He knew Lema. She was a strong-minded, bossy, but friendly girl with a lot of free speech, whether you wanted to hear it or not, and she was a tomboy. She was willing and capable of fixing almost anything.

"Yeah, I bet she did."

David looked over at Isaac.

"Isaac, I'm sorry, I am."

Isaac knew why he was saying sorry, but he disagreed.

"For what? For what your dad said? Just tell me you're the same friend I knew yesterday, and there's no sorry needed."

"Well yeah, of course. You are a boy, and I am a boy, and we're the same, so I don't know why my dad has to say that nigger boy like you are from outer space!"

David was agitated at the thought of what his dad said. Isaac was not bothered by it one bit. His parents had the wrong interpretation of David and his parents. All he knew was Dave was his friend no matter how either parent felt.

"Hey, man, the way your dad and my parents think gives me a good idea."

David jumped up, eager to know.

"What's that!"

"What color is the NASCAR flag?"

David's eyes light up like the streets of Las Vegas.

"BLACK and WHITE!"

"So, are you thinking what I'm thinking?"

David nodded yes in agreement, but no words came out.

"Even though your color is white and mine's black, our car can be about us, and we can get over that word, that dumb word, confusion. So I'm going to find out what that means to."

"You said your family said that word meant trouble. You think you should ask?"

David was concerned about his friend. If Isaac's parents found out he was playing with him, Isaac would not get a pat on the back in good faith.

"Well, we need to know."

David changed the subject because he was getting teary-eyed again.

"We need to save money for some paint, and I only have $6.00 from my allowance."

"Well, I have $5.00, and when I get another dollar, we should have enough."

David and Isaac are only 9 years old, so their combined money was extremely valuable at the age of no bills and worries. They shook hands like they usually did and said their goodbyes. As Isaac walked away, he stopped and turned around. David was dragging what they completed so far home.

"Hey, you think you should take that home knowing how your dad feels about me, and we've started on that together?"

David put part of the go-kart down, disgusted because he knew his dad would disapprove.

"That's right, huh? Well, you said your parents felt the same way. So we can't leave it at your house either."

Isaac nodded his head in agreement, so they stood there thinking. David thought of Ms. Opal. She was a Caucasian elderly woman who loved kids but never had any, only nieces and nephews. Ms. Opal would go out of her way to help any child, no matter their color or physical abilities. She lived between Isaac and David in the middle of the block.

"What about Ms. Opal?"

Isaac ran to Dave, picked up one end of the yet-to-be-completed go-kart.

"Yeah, because it's almost time for my dad to come home, so we better hurry!"

David picked up the other end.

"Now I don't have two drag it home."

They got to 113 Broadway Ave., where Ms. Opal lived. They opened her iron gate and went up three steps to knock on her door. A sweet old voice rang out.

"Well, who is it?"

They looked at each other happy she was home, but they knew if she wasn't, she was either at church or the store.

"David!"

"Isaac!"

"Hey boys, you're having a fundraiser at your school. Let me go get my checkbook."

David stops her.

"No, Ms. Opal."

He made eye contact with Isaac because he was about to fib and wanted Isaac to agree.

"Our parents don't have room at our houses, so can we leave our go-kart we're making in your yard, and when we want to work on it, we can come in the yard to get it."

Isaac was scared to blow it, so he just shook his head in agreement.

"Sure, why not? Maybe I can send you guys on a run to the store for me when you finish making it, and I can bake you some cookies to take home."

She thought about what she was saying because even though these boys had more respect than most nowadays, she still let them know she was fair with the adults.

"Oh, if it's okay with your parents first."

Isaac spoke up, remembering his friend's tears and not wanting David to get yelled at again.

"Yes, Ms. Opal, it is."

Ms. Opal smiled and glanced over her yard until she found a spot that was just right for the go-kart and where the flowers in the garden wouldn't get crushed. She pointed to the corner of her yard.

"How about right there, boys?"

"Okay!"

"Okay!"

As they put the go-cart in the corner, Ms. Opal watched to make sure they put it away safely. That was how she was; she forgot all about her garden and made sure they were safe and didn't fall.

"All right, now if I'm not here, go ahead and come in, okay?"

They smiled and agreed with appreciation.

"Okay, Ms. Opal."

David looked at Isaac and nudged him to say something too. Isaac was happy but nervous because he knew they should've spoken the truth.

"Oh, yeah, thank you, Ms. Opal!"

She closed the door slowly.

"You boys are quite welcome."

David and Isaac left as they jumped up and down; when Isaac went down, David jumped up.

"Yeah! Yeah! Now we have a place to keep it."

David stopped jumping.

"I know. I'm glad I thought of Ms. Opal."

"Why you think of her?"

David tied his shoe while he answered Isaac.

"Remember about six months ago she kept Megan's birds?"

"Oh yeah, that cry baby girl with the big glasses that used to live around the corner."

David laughed.

"Yeah, and as much as she whines, Ms. Opal kept her birds until they moved, with no problem. She fed the birds and cleaned the cage. She just likes us kids."

"Yeah, well, all I can say is good thinking."

David bragged and brushed off his shoulder.

"Yeah, I know, I'm the man."

"Aww, please! Well, see you tomorrow, David."

Isaac walked away towards his end of the block. David walked off with a cool walk; proud he thought of a go-kart parking space at Ms. Opal's house.

"See you tomorrow."

Isaac waved bye as he ran home.

Isaac saw his stepdad's work boots outside and wondered what he was doing home so early. As he walked in the door and the smell of good food and apple pie hit his nose. He looked around the living room, but no one was there.

"Hey, mama? Where are you?"

Brenda stepped out of the kitchen into the living room and straight to the T.V. She hardly got to watch it, between taking care of the home, her son, and her husband.

"Hey there, your dad is home already."

"Yeah, I know. I saw his work boots. Where is he?"

Brenda Lu grabbed the remote.

"He's in the kitchen."

Samuel stepped in the doorway of the kitchen, licking his fingers, getting ready to jump in the conversation he was waiting to get into. That was his character. Whether you liked it or not, he will say how he feels.

"Aye, little man, this apple pie tells me how worried your mom is. You know that is the only time she makes it?"

"Yeah, that's true."

Isaac was still standing there with his hands in his pocket. Looked at his mom, who was watching television. Isaac hoped she would say what was wrong, but there was complete silence. Then his dad went right into it.

"I heard you making a go-kart. If you ever have a fight with your so-called friend, I will go ahead and make one with you."

Samuel wondered why Isaac was so quiet. Isaac was not even facing him but looking off in the air.

"Dad, what do you mean, so-called friend?"

"A person who you think is your friend but is not."

Samuel was glad that he could be bold and relatively honest with his son. Isaac was furious; how could his dad say that. He was not out there when David ran home to get wood glue and was fussed at by his dad about the 'Nigger Boy.' The way David had cried, he knew that a 'so-called friend' would not have cried like that.

"HE IS NOT A SO-CALLED FRIEND!"

Isaac stuck his chest out with no fear; however, he realized he said it with too much emotion, so he puts his head down; he knows how grown-ups feel about that.

Brenda spoke up, "baby, there's nothing wrong with saying what you want to say, but watch how you say it. Isaac, you have to remember we are still your parents."

Isaac listened, but now since they are talking, he wants to know what that word confusion means. He was a smart boy, but of course, there were some things he just didn't know at nine years old.

"Okay, daddy, mama, I apologize."

Samuel, posted at the dining room table, smiles; even though Isaac raised his voice, he loved the boy more than life itself.

"Okay, son, you just have to learn one day about some kinds of people." Isaac was furious now and felt his dad was talking as if David was some kind of animal. Isaac ignored it, but it still hurt him. He decided instead to get right into his question.

"Dad, what's confusion?"

He just wanted to know this word once and for all since it had to do with him and David.

"Oh, well, let me start with confused."

Isaac hoped his dad would give him an excellent example to remember and relay to David so they both could gain some kind of understanding.

"Okay, I have a prime example...."

Brenda already knew that Samuel would be rude and sarcastic, so she turned the television off and sat at the dining room table.

"Isaac, come sit over here, baby."

"Okay."

"Okay now, son, this is the deal. Can you see how making a go-kart with your friend, no that's not good enough.... David's father and I could argue because we know we just don't get along. We tell you, kids, not to play to prevent misunderstandings and arguments. That's what confusion mostly is, something that will start arguments, you understand?"

"Well, yeah, so when you told me that it would start confusion when I play with my friend, you were saying that all of us are going to argue?"

"Yeah, I guess, something like that. You may not argue with David now, but you will later. That is why I just don't want you to play with him that much. Okay?"

Samuel waited for his son's response but noticed that he didn't have his son's approval at all but could care less. Since Samuel was a little boy, he could not stand his aunt's husband, and everybody knew it was because he was white, and David was no exception. Isaac had his head down, sadly wondering why grown-ups can't get along. He had to just deal with listening to his parents, so he acknowledged his dad, not wanting to be considered disrespectful. Brenda tried to cheer up her son. She wanted to go through the entire history, explain how black people were treated, and let him know some white people died caring about us and sticking up for black rights. Isaac and David reminded her of all that, but right now was not the appropriate time. Her son's face dragged on the ground so low it looked as if only a mop could get it up.

"Baby, go wash your hands so we can eat dinner. Then, we can think of a game to play afterward."

Brenda noticed that cheered him just an inch, so she left it at that.

"Alright, can I eat some apple pie first, then my dinner?"

Usually, nine times out of ten, that answer would be no, but he looked so sad; she figured letting him do something harmless wouldn't hurt.

"Okay, sweetheart, just this time, but don't make it a habit."

"Thank you, mama. I knew there was something I loved about you."

Isaac walked toward the bathroom and looked back, giggled, and teased his mom like she did all the time.

"Ooh, so I have to give you what you want for some love, huh?"

She stood up with her hands on her hip and waited for an answer. Isaac stopped before he got out of her sight.

"Maybe."

He laughed as she chased him.

"Come here, boy!"

Isaac ran into the bathroom, knowing he beat his mom and slammed the door. Samuel looked at them and laughed.

"Brenda came on and let that boy get cleaned so he can eat."

"Yeah, Golden Girls on anyway."

Television was usually 50% Samuel, 40% Isaac, and 10% herself.

She hoped since Golden Girls was on, she could get her 10% in. Samuel loved his wife and her little traditions.

"Go ahead; it's your world."

He was a typical man and knew he held the remote like Eddie held the cup in the Golden Child.

Isaac got a scoop of apple pie, the biggest scoop he can get. Then, before he said his prayer to bless it, he asked his parents a question he wanted to ask before washing his hands.

"Oh yeah, momma? Daddy? I have another question."

His dad turned around, "go ahead, just ask."

"You know Ms. Opal seems nice all the time, is she confusion."

He slapped his forehead.

"I mean confused?"

Samuel laughed; out of everybody on the block, she was the sweetest woman.

"No, that's a good person. She wouldn't hurt a flea."

They all laughed, knowing it was true. Isaac prayed and ate his pie.

4

David's dad was in the garage, and his mom was on the phone with his aunt. Steve heard David come in 5 minutes ago and was trying to find a way to call his son in the garage since he was so upset. David was tremendously hurt and resentful.

"Uh, uh, David, what uh, what are you doing?"

David was glad he came up with the idea of leaving the go-kart at Ms. Opal's.

"So, do you want to come in the garage and hang out with me?"

Steve felt guilty that he yelled at David, but not one bit about what he said.

"Of course, dad," he sighed.

"What's with the long face, son?"

David was scared but tired of holding it in, "I would say, but you are just going to put me on punishment or spank my behind."

"What, what do you have to say? Is it that bad?"

"NO, not to me!"

Steve knew where his son was going with the conversation, and David went right into it.

"Okay, dad, it's just not fair. Out of all the other kids I play with, they do not like to do the same things I do with Isaac. I like to play ball, he likes to play ball also. I like NASCAR; he also does. I tried to please everybody else you and mom picked for me to play with, and they just say, 'that's dumb!'"

Steve cut his son off before he forgot the point he wanted to make.

"Well, I kind of understand how it is when you have a friend that likes what you like, but he may steal or try to have you wearing all that jewelry they wear."

"Well, what about the guy who fixes your car, dad? You said that he is the best mechanic you ever had, and he is the same color as my best friend, Isaac."

Steve was now looking like that word 'confusion.'

"Well, well, I would not invite him over our house. I, I, don't worry about me, you just don't be his friend for too long, now help me straighten up my tools."

Steve's tone of voice let David know the conversation was over. Even though he did not understand his dad's ways, he loved being in the garage with him. David was happy he got some of his frustration off of his chest.

"Dad, is this a flat screwdriver?"

"Yes, son, it is."

David and Steve worked until they got tired.

Steve went to bed, but the situation with David and Isaac still bothered him. His son was building a go-kart with Isaac, and that especially ticked his nerves. Samantha looked over at her husband's unusual behavior.

"Okay, sweetheart, how many times are you going to fluff that pillow?"

"Honey, I know our mechanic is black, but that's not my friend. I just want our son to hang out with the right people."

"Where did that come from, about our mechanic?"

"In the garage, David mentioned that if I don't like Isaac so much, why did I say our mechanic is the best."

Samantha placed her hand over her mouth and giggled very hard.

"Well, he does have a point. You know Steve, the other day I was thinking. I'm starting to change my view about other races. You can't count one bad encounter against a whole race. They all don't act the same, and just because one person out of the race does something wrong does not mean the whole race does something wrong."

"Well, is this coming from a woman who says all black women have attitudes?"

"You know, the other day I was at the clothing store, same-store as Isaac's mother. My entire basket tipped over, and not one employee helped me at all. They just looked at me and rolled their eyes, 90% of the employees were white, but Isaac's mother ran over to help me. She helped me with no strings attached."

"So one good deed, and you think I'm going to change my views. Just cut the light out Sam, I'm going to sleep. Good night!"

He slammed his hand on his pillow and turned his back to his wife. Samantha shrugged her shoulders and cut the light off, and went to sleep herself.

5

Two days have passed, and Steve took his son and wife places to avoid David and Isaac playing. Samuel was doing the same thing with his family. Neither one could do this all the time; they both worked. It was Friday, and David was glad his family wasn't going anywhere. He finished all his chores, and of course, asked to go outside. Samantha looked at Steve, with the wife's look, as if she was telling him it is not fair to keep his son in the house.

"Go ahead, son,"

Steve's tone of voice was low and unconvincing. David was excited.

"I'll be in before dark!"

Samantha smiled.

"I know you will, young man."

David rushed outside, and at Broadway Avenue, he looked towards Isaac's house, but he didn't see their car; he even passed Ms. Opal's house where their go-kart was. David was the type of kid that did not like to do things alone, especially when he had a best friend.

"Man, I wonder where Isaac is at?"

He stood there for 30 minutes, waiting for their car to pull up. Then, finally, he figured maybe Isaac's dad was at work, and Isaac and his mother were home. David looked back to make sure his parents weren't looking for him or peeking out the window, then he dashed down to Isaac's house as fast as he could. He knocked on the door three times but no answer, so he ran back where he was.

"I know my dad is happy; I guess I will have to play with Jerry for today."

He threw rocks all the way to Jerry's house, which lived next door to his. He was agitated because he missed his buddy and was anxious to finish the go-kart. David was not mean to Jerry; however, Jerry only liked to collect bugs, which David and Isaac didn't like. He knocked. Jerry came to the door. A cute chubby Caucasian and Hispanic kid with short blonde hair. He always carried some kind of bug, insect, or reptile. When he came to the door, he had an iguana inside a case. Jerry had on some jeans, untied sneakers, and a shirt that was a little too small for him.

"Hey, David, look how big my iguana is now!"

Jerry held up the cage to show David who was not interested, not even a little bit. David tried to be friendly. He acted as if he was excited but couldn't hide the truth.

"Uh, yeah, okay, that's nice. Ask your mom if you can come out."

Jerry's mom was a single parent. She worked very hard to provide financially and spoiled Jerry. Asking his mom for permission was very rare.

Jerry yelled.

"Mom, I'm going outside."

Ms. Sinclair replied.

"Okay, Jerry, just let me know when you come in. I am on the phone handling business."

David just shook his head. He knew if he just told his parents instead of asking, he would just be sitting in the house for a week.

They sat on the porch. Jerry just talked about bugs, reading about bugs, and catching bugs.

"You want me to go inside and get my net? I think I have an extra jar we can catch butterflies!"

He looked at David and hoped he would say yes.

"No, hey, I have an idea. Let's see who can make the best car sounds!"

"That seems boring and noisy."

David looked at Jerry, puzzled; how could Jerry say that. David and Isaac did it all the time, and that's one of their favorite games. Jerry was focused on his iguana. He tapped the cage and talked to it as David looked in the air and rolled his eyes.

"Now, can I get the net?"

David slapped both his hands on the side of his face.

"Yeah, get the stupid net."

Jerry heard what David said but was hoping he heard wrong.

"Huh?"

David had never been the kind of kid to hurt people's feelings, so he didn't repeat it.

"I said go get the net and jar."

"Okay, we will have fun; you will see."

Jerry went to get them and took his iguana into the house. David sarcastically responded as Jerry walked away.

"Yeah, yeah, fun."

Right now, David wished he was a butterfly and could fly away himself. Finally, Jerry brought 2 jars, 2 nets, and a hat with different bugs and butterfly print. David looked at Jerry's hat weirdly.

"What's with the hat?"

"This always gives me good luck to catch more than one bug!"

David shook his head and reached out to receive his jar and net.

"Oh well, okay, I guess, let's just do this."

Jerry was excited, walked off the porch at a steady pace. He looked back at David, who moped off the porch slowly. As soon as David got off the porch, he spotted two butterflies, one white and one orange and black. He made a car sound and tried to catch the butterflies in his net.

"Vroom, Vroom!"

The butterflies took off from the flower they were on. Jerry was mad.

"NO! NO! NO! You cannot make those sounds; you will never catch an insect!"

David could care less.

"Oh."

"Let me show you."

Jerry got his net ready to catch the butterflies that flew onto another flower. He eased towards them with his net, quiet and steady. Jerry set the net right on top of the butterflies with ease, and they went right in. He used his other hand to close the net, whispering.

"Open the jar, hurry, please!"

David opened the jar, and Jerry placed the butterflies in and closed the lid.

"Hey, you're really into this, huh?"

"Yeah, how could you not be?"

David thought since he was not into it anyway, it's easy not to be.

"I don't know? What are those holes doing on top of that jar."

"You mean to tell me you don't know?"

David answered back sarcastically.

"Uh, no?"

"That's so the bugs can breathe."

"Oh, okay."

Even though David wasn't having much fun, he learned something new to share with Isaac.

Two hours went by, and David's dad came on the porch. Steve was excited to see his son playing with Jerry instead of Isaac.

"Hey, son, just checking on you. You can stay outside as long as you want; it's not dark yet."

"WHAT! That boy like Lema? As bossy as she is, she thinks she's the next president. So, I guess he would be the first man instead of the first lady."

She laughed out loud, and Isaac joined in.

"Ah, man, that slipped. I didn't mean to tell you that, momma, please don't tell David and definitely not Lema, please."

Brenda pointed to Isaac to sit down as she looked down the hallway to see if Samuel was coming.

"Child, I'm not going to say anything but listen between you and me; I think David is a sweet boy. I know you don't understand your dad and me completely, but to be honest, I see nothing wrong with you playing with David, besides your dad and his dad disagreeing. You were so happy when you came to get those wagon wheels. So, when you're finished with the go-kart, let momma know. I will make sure to come on the porch and watch you two speed in the new wheels, okay?"

That was music to Isaac's ears. He jumped up and hugged her as hard as he could.

"Okay, momma! Okay!"

He hugged her again, and Brenda laughed.

"Alright boy, I know I need to lose a few pounds, but you about to squeeze them off!"

"Sorry, momma."

"Oh, that's alright. I'll take hugs from you anytime, son. Let me go and take my bath."

Isaac was still smiling because, for once, she understood David was his NASCAR brother. Like Samuel and Brenda, he felt David was heaven-sent as well.

"Okay, momma."

6

The next day Samuel sat at the dining room table reading the paper, Brenda was writing more of her book, and Isaac finished his chores and just had his bath. The house was quiet as ever. Isaac stood between them.

"Uh, daddy, momma?"

Both parents looked up at the same time.

"Can I please go...."

His stepdad cut him off.

"Outside? Yeah, but you have to come in a little early, we have to go to the second service at church today, and we have to pick up Lema."

After Samuel finished, he turned back to his newspaper. Isaac looked over at his mom and smiled, remembering what they talked about earlier. She smiled back as she read the connection, then went back to writing her book.

"Okay, I will."

He ran out his door, out the gate, and down to where he usually met David with no hesitation.

David had been in the garage all morning with his dad, and they started to watch a little T.V. together. Then, finally, David was ready to go outside. It was as if he felt Isaac was out there already. David sighed and stretched.

"Ooh, boy, it's early and daylight."

Steve got the hint and knew his son wanted to go outside, which he was happy about. He thought David would be playing with Jerry.

"I get the hint son, go outside and play. Your mother and I need to spend some quality time together anyway."

Samantha was puzzled.

"Uh, we... do?

They spent so much time together, all day when Steve was home; if they spent any more time, they would hate each other, and she knew he felt the same way. Steve looked up and gave her the wink.

"Yes, babe."

"Oh, okay, yes, go have fun, David. We will see you when you get in; it's Sunday anyway."

Samantha shrugged her shoulders at her husband and looked at him like, what is going on. David went right away while his parents were acting so weird before they changed their minds.

"Okay, Steve, what was all that about, and when have you gotten so excited about David going outside. Don't think I haven't noticed you trying to keep him from going, and now you have the same 32 teeth grin as yesterday. So, what's going on?"

"Oh, go on. I just want David to have fun outside."

He looked up at Samantha and noticed her raised eyebrow.

"What!"

"Alright, I may be a little excited because I went on the porch yesterday and saw him playing with Jerry."

Samantha frowned in disappointment.

"Oh, okay, no wonder. Jerry! He's into bugs and insects, and you know our son is not into that. Just last year, we had to stop him from making a living out of killing ants and burning their trail every time he went outside. Remember?"

"Yeah, yeah, I remember. Well, David may have had a change of heart."

Samantha walked towards their kitchen to the backyard.

"Yeah, okay, I think when you saw Jerry, you had a change of heart for the both of them. I'm going to do laundry."

Steve got upset; to him, it seemed his wife was betraying him.

"Well, you know what, go do the laundry. Okay! This is not about me. You are making it seem like I put David up to playing with Jerry. I told him he could play with that Nigger Boy, just not so much."

Samantha was frustrated with Steve. She remembered how sweet Isaac's mother was to her in the store. She looked back at Steve before she walked out of the screen door.

"It's Isaac honey, David's friend's name is Isaac."

She closed the screen behind her. Steve was now furious; he snatched the T.V. remote and slammed himself down on the couch, flicking through channels. He sarcastically mocked his wife.

"'It's Isaac honey, his name is Isaac.' I don't give a hoot!"

David ran towards Isaac as Isaac was running towards David. They gave each other a high five, then fell down.

"Hey, man!"

"Hey!"

When they ran towards each other, they ended up right in front of Ms. Opal's house. As if reading each other's minds, they proceeded to open the gate. When Ms. Opal heard the gate open, she peeped out the window and saw it was the boys. She waved, and they waved back to her. They dragged the materials down the street to the spot they were making their go-kart.

"Once we finish, we need to take our money and buy the paint."

David looked over at Isaac to see if he was paying attention since Isaac was busy sorting out the wood and nails.

"Yeah, I know. Oh, Dave, I have to go in early today."

"Why?"

Isaac grinned.

"Oh, nothing bad, we just have to go to church like your family, plus we have to pick up Lema."

Isaac didn't understand David's expression because Isaac still thought girls were stupid.

David sighed with a cheesy grin on his face.

"Ooh, I understand now."

"Well, speaking of understanding, found out what confused means."

David snapped out of his love trance.

"Oh, uh, my bad, yeah, what does it mean?"

"Well, check this out. My dad said that by me playing with you, that would start confusion, and we will all argue."

"Who is, 'we all?'"

"He's talking about my parents and yours because they don't want us to play together. Then my dad started talking crazy about how I should not play with you because I think you're my friend, but you're not. Then I yelled at him and told him that you are my best friend."

David checked Isaac's arm and face, legs, and hands. Isaac moved David's hands.

"What are you doing?"

"You mean to tell me you yelled at your parents, and you are still alive?"

"Yeah, I know, my mom told me to watch it! I was almost dead. But you are my real friend and not a so-called friend, as my dad put it."

Dad was glad to know that Isaac felt the same anger he felt when his dad talked about Isaac.

"Don't worry, I'm going to ask you what you asked me? So just tell me you're the same friend I knew yesterday, and we're cool!"

Isaac had a sneaky grin.

"You know I am, LEMA!"

"Oh, no, you DIDN'T!"

They wrestled and shared laughs, then started back to work on the go-kart.

The boys finished, and the only thing left to do was the steering wheel, paint, and make the doors open up. It was 3 hours later, so they grabbed everything and dragged it back to Ms. Opal's yard.

"Well, Isaac, I can't come outside until Tuesday. I have homework before the end of school to make up in Ms. Geneva's class."

"Yeah, I heard about her; she lives to give homework. Well, I will see you Tuesday then."

"Okay, see you Tuesday."

"You mean you will see us Tuesday."

David had a huge smile.

"Yeah. Oh, yeah."

Isaac and his family got out of church at 5:30 p.m. and rushed straight to the airport getting there at 6:00 p.m.

"Oh, that was a good sermon today."

Samuel agreed.

"Amen. Shoo, hit me with a few pointers. So much so I thought he was talking straight to me a few times."

Isaac was in the back and looked out the window, eagerly waiting for his favorite cousin to arrive. He had a few other cousins on his mom's side, but his dad's family was a bunch of dead beats. He knew those cousins wouldn't know if he even existed. The 7:00 plane finally arrived at 7:15, so they waited for Lema to come down into the airport lobby. Other people passed by, and then here came Lema. She was a thick redbone girl with long hair, pretty brown eyes, sandals, and a summer dress. She is 2 years older than Isaac with a southern accent

"Hey, y'all!"

Brenda rushed to hug her and squeezed her tight.

"Ooh wee! How is auntie's baby, and how was your plane ride?"

Samuel laughed. He already knew that Lema's answer was going to be interesting. He grabbed her suitcase and headed towards the car. Lema and Isaac hugged as they caught up with Samuel.

"Auntie, that plane ride was fine, but I guess they stingy. They only gave me peanuts. So I ask 'em where the collard greens. No cornbread or nothing!"

Brenda and Samuel laughed. They knew that she really asked, and they could picture it.

"Don't worry, cousin, you know my mama is really from Georgia, so she knows how to cook like your mama."

"Thank God! I'm hungry. Peanuts! Shoo, I ain't no monkey; next time, I wanna catch the bus so my mama can pack me some food, shoo."

"That's enough, Ms. Grouchy, now put on your seatbelts."

"Okay, Mama."

"Yes, Ma'am."

All the way home, Isaac and Lema laughed, talked, and caught up from the last time they saw each other. Brenda and Samuel were engaged in a conversation; however, they got a kick out of Lemma's accent. Especially Brenda Lu, that took her back to when she was a little girl. She had been in Cali so long now her accent was gone.

They went straight to the table to eat dinner, later than usual, of course, because they had to pick up Lema.

"That's what I'm talking about auntie, you still got it. That's why I don't get homesick when visiting my favorite cousin; you cook just like my mama."

"Yeah, well, back then, we learned how to cook, clean, and you had to learn social skills."

Samuel cut right on in.

"Yeah, now you kids got it made. You all get to watch T.V. or play these video games most of the time."

"No, Uncle Sam, I got to clean up. Now my mama making me

cook too! I think the only thing I don't have to do like y'all had to do is pick cotton, shoo."

They all laughed. That was the Lema, sweet, loud, and outspoken. It would seem to some adults that she was just a smart-mouthed child; however, her family overlooked a lot. They just knew she was a grown-minded kid.

"I ought to give you two one of my big, squeeze the life out of you, hugs, but I'm tired tonight."

"Well, I guess I will join you Tonight; the T.V. was watching me; I'm not watching it. Isaac, don't forget you have school until Thursday, then your summer vacation starts."

As Samuel walked away, Isaac smirked his mouth. He wished school was out already like Lema.

"Yeah, I know. Come on, Lema, you can watch T.V. but let me get your covers out for the bottom bunk."

In the room, Isaac cut on the radio instead of the T.V. Lema felt bad her cousin still had school for a few days. She tapped him on the shoulder while he was making the bottom bunk up for her.

"Isaac?"

"What's up, Lema?"

"You know what, it's my first day here, so go climb up on the top bunk, and I'll go ahead and lay down so we can talk each other to sleep. How about that?"

Isaac knew his cousin had a big heart, and he knew what she was trying to do, make him feel better since he had a few days left in school.

"Okay, Lema, that's cool!"

Isaac went to the bathroom to put on his pajamas and let Lema get dressed in his room. By the time he got back, Lema had sat on the bed and brushed her hair while she counted.

"51, 52, 53...."

"Why do you girls do that?"

"Do what, boy!"

"What you doing right now; brush their hair and count."

"Cause we get rid of the old hair and make room for the new hair, that's why my hair so long and folks think I got a weave. Everywhere I go, 'is that a weave.' Black people and white people always think that. I be wanting to say, 'all black people ain't ball-headed,' and if I was, it's just hair!"

Lema started to sing her favorite song from Indie Arie.

"I am not my hair. I am not your expectation, no!"

Isaac danced while she sang, being silly, but he loved his cousin's southern church voice.

"Lema, I'm getting tired. I better go to sleep for school."

"Okay, big-head."

"Oh, big-head, huh?"

He grabbed a pillow and hit her, but she blocked her head.

"Okay, don't start nothing, won't be nothing!"

They both laughed and went off to sleep.

7

Samantha had her sister over for a while since Steve had gone fishing with some co-workers. This was David and Isaac's last day of school, so David went into the living room with his mom and aunt.

"Hey, Auntie Linda!"

"Hey, Nephew! Wow, how tall are you going to get?"

"My mom said if I keep eating my vegetables, taller than this."

Samantha and Linda laughed. The same line was used on them by their parents, and it is convincing generation after generation.

"Yeah, well, that is true, sweetie."

David looked over at his mom. He loved to see that same smile she got every time Auntie Linda came over.

"Oh, mom, now can I go play?"

Before he got the answer, knowing his mom was extremely happy, he bombarded her with another question.

"Mom, how come dad gets mad every time I play with Isaac? That's my best friend, and he didn't do anything wrong to anybody he...."

Samantha cut him off because she saw Linda wondering what was going on.

"Look, David, go ahead and play with Isaac; just be careful, please."

He hugged his mother and auntie then ran straight out the door.

"Now, what was that all about!"

Samantha knew she had to explain, anybody would be curious family or not, and Linda knew her brother-in-law well.

"You know how Steve can get sometimes, and he's just concerned David will get hurt playing with Isaac, that's all."

"When are you and Steve going get off your high horse? It's 2006, and you two are still prejudiced?"

"Now wait a minute, Lin! I didn't say Steve didn't want him playing with Isaac because he was black or anything!"

Samantha was a supportive wife, and she often took up for her husband, even though she knew how wrong he could be.

"Come on, sis! As many bad statements, he makes when we go places, he was always prejudged of that particular race, and I really don't like that. I have friends of every cultural background. It's just not right! All prejudice is ignorance to me."

Samantha placed her head down. She was like her husband 100% until she encountered a few good situations with black people that changed her stereotypical viewpoint.

"Yeah, I can say you are right, sis; my views are getting better slowly but surely."

Linda was relieved that her sister was not as stereotypical as she previously was.

"Yeah, I noticed you let him play with Isaac. I am proud of you, sis."

"I just have to get ready to get chewed out by my husband later. It may take a tragedy, but he will come around one day."

"Well, let's just hope he comes around. Let's just hope so."

David was outside anxious for two reasons: his NASCAR buddy and Lema. Since his dad was gone fishing, he walked all the way to Isaac's house. David's heart pounded from the fear of his parents if they found out and his reaction after he saw Lema. At the door, he heard talking and laughter. Isaac, Lema, and Brenda were making a surprise gift for Samuel. Brenda Lu found a picture of Samuel's mother, who passed, so with the use of modern technology, they could put the image on a quilt. Brenda was trying to make Samuel smile because every year in the month she died, Samuel cries and plays 'For the Good Times' by Al Green. David knocked on the door, then looked at his shoes and straightened his shirt. Brenda was not expecting anyone, so she was puzzled as to who it could be.

"Who is it?"

"Uh, it's David."

Brenda and Isaac smiled at each other. Nine times out of ten, David would wait down the street. They knew what that special knock was about.

"Isaac, get the door. And Lema, it's your turn to sow on a pattern now, you ready?"

Brenda Lu stopped the work on the quilt because she realized that if Isaac was going outside, he was most likely taking Lema. Isaac opened the door and tried to hold his smile.

"Hey man, what's up, buddy?"

David passed up Isaac and stuck his head in the door.

"Hi, Ms. Brenda. Hi, Lema."

David smiled at Lema, and Isaac giggled. His friend always spoke back, but he was too focused on talking to Lema. Isaac laughed at the thought of David's crush because he thought it was goofy. Brenda saw the nervousness in David, so she tried to break the ice.

"Hey, there, David. You look really nice today, and you have really nice shoes on too."

David blushed, looking like cherry Kool-Aid.

"Oh, thank you so much."

Lema noticed David was taller than when she saw him last year. She did not have a clue about his crush, but she always considered David, a good friend. In her eyes, he was not 'fresh,' as she would call the other boys who tried to kiss her. Lema walked to the door on the other side of Isaac.

"Boy, you got tall! You been eating yo' Wheaties, huh?"

David was somewhat speechless.

"Uh, oh, uh, well yea, yes."

Brenda and Isaac looked at each other and giggled; however, they did not believe in spreading innocent things like this and blowing it out of proportion. Isaac saw his friend was mesmerized right then, so he waved his hand over David's face.

"Uh, hello! I will just ask my mom could I come outside today."

"I heard you; yeah, go outside."

She bent her finger for Isaac to come closer to her so no one else could hear them.

"I think you have to help your friend walk down the curb."

"What you mean by that momma?"

"Because the way that boy is floating on air, he may not walk but glide down the street like a Spike Lee movie."

Brenda and Isaac laughed very hard; they couldn't hold it. Lema turned around being her curious self, as David just stood and waited for an answer.

"Isaac, Auntie Brenda, what's so funny?"

"You know my momma keeps me laughing."

Lema laughed too because she felt her aunt should have been a comedian a long time ago.

"Yep, me too."

Now, David started to laugh because he wanted to fit in, but he laughed so hard, a little too loud and way too long.

"AHHHAAA, Ha, HA, HAAAA, Ha."

Everybody stopped laughing and stared at him, so he stopped out of embarrassment.

"Oh, can you come? I mean, can you two come outside?"

Brenda gave them the okay. She had had her fun for the day. She needed to get back to cleaning.

"Yeah, we can."

"Can y'all wait until I get my jacket?"

"Yeah, Lema, we will wait on the porch."

While she went to get her coat, Isaac turned to tease David about his crush.

"Now you can close your mouth, Dave."

"Oh, shut up! She is getting prettier and prettier.

He let out a sigh at the thought of Lema which made Isaac grab hold of his stomach as though he was going to be sick. He hadn't started to like girls yet.

"Yuk, that's gross."

Lema ran past them with her jacket.

"Come on, y'all, let's go!"

Isaac and David walked down the street, then right past Lema, headed for Ms. Opal's house. At the gate, the boys got ready to go right in. Lema wondered what they were doing. She remembered how nice Ms. Opal was, but they were not raised to just walk into anybody's gate even if you knew them.

"UH, UN!"

"What?"

"I know y'all not finsta just walk in Ms. Opal's gate. What's wrong with y'all. I'm not about to get no whippin'!"

David tapped Lema softly on the head. He had wanted to touch her ever since he saw her.

"Don't worry, your pretty little head. We already asked her if we could come in her yard."

"Move, boy! I don't see her out here."

Isaac was frustrated that Lema wasted time.

"No, Lema, we asked when you were still in Georgia!"

"Oh, well, what's that box thing?"

David went to answer, but Isaac gently put his hand in front of David's face as if he was saying, I got this.

"This is our car, our trip to the stores, our first set of real wheels, Lema."

Lema was a tom-boy. She was always ready to climb a tree or build something, and she wanted in on this too.

"Come on, you and David got to let me help. Let me in on that, shoo, this going to be so fun."

The boys grabbed the equipment, and Lema jumped right in to help.

"I should have known this was a car. There goes the steering wheel. I'm so silly!"

"No, you're not, and I'm glad you will help; three heads are better than two."

"Thank you, David. You so sweet; you always so nice to me. You not like most stupid boys!"

David grinned so hard you would think he had 33 teeth instead of 32. He was mesmerized by Lema's attention and compliment and could barely speak. Isaac shook his head in disgust.

"Oh, boy! Let's go finish the go-kart. PLEASE!"

David snapped out of his trance and got back on task. They got to the end of the block where they usually built. Isaac and David talked to Lema about how they would put their money together to paint the go-kart.

"I have an extra dollar, so we should have enough, right?"

"Yeah, my money right here, Isaac."

The boys put their money together and counted it up. Lema pulled a twenty-dollar bill out of her sock.

"DANG!"

"Where did you get that money from?"

"Before I came out here, I babysat my neighbor's bad 2-year-old girl. She should've gave me forty dollars, that girl worsen!"

David scratched his head.

"Worsen?"

"Yeah, BAD!

"Oh."

"Lema, you can go ask my momma if we could go to the store; it's 8 blocks away. She always says you grown, plus you 2 years older than us."

David agreed with a head shake, then he wondered about himself.

"Yeah! Lema, while y'all go to ask, I'll go home to ask my mom too. My auntie here, so my mom is in a good mood."

"But who is going to stay here with the go-kart?"

They all looked at each other. Then they saw Jerry coming down the street with a jar of worms and a net. David smiled and came up with a plan. Something like his dad would do.

"Jerry! Just the person I wanted to see."

Jerry was happy and thought David enjoyed the bug-catching the other day. He hoped Isaac would like it just like he did.

"Oh, you told Isaac about the bugs?"

"What bugs?"

David whispered to Isaac.

"I will explain to you later."

David turned his attention back to Jerry.

"Jerry, we have to go ask our parents if we could go to the store. Could you watch over the go-kart, and if they say yeah, you'll watch it while we go?"

Jerry was an easy-going kid even though he was spoiled materially by his mom. He pushed his glasses up.

"Well, okay."

Lema remembered Jerry from playing with him in the neighborhood.

"Oh, I kind of remember him. That's David's neighbor, huh? Hi Jerry."

Jerry looked up at Lema, wiped his hand on his shirt then reached out to shake Lema's hand. Lema shook his hand, but David snatched Jerry's hand and somewhat sat Jerry down on the curb.

"Just watch the go-kart, please!"

"What was that for David?"

David thought fast and tried to come up with something. He was shocked by his reaction too. He knew his feelings but remembered Lema was still in the dark.

"Oh, uh, because we don't have that much time, that's all."

"Come on, Lema, let's go ask. We will be right back, Dave."

They went their separate ways.

David got home, and the first thing he saw was his auntie's famous lemonade with the slice lemons in it. David loved when he got a lemon seed in the cup, and he remembered his mom telling him it was because it was homemade. He noticed his mom was playing Yahtzee, the game she always played with his aunt. His taste for lemonade overpowered his question about the store.

"Are you okay, David?"

David caught his breath from gulping down the lemonade.

"Yeah, since I had some of Aunt Linda's lemonade. I'm really good!"

He poured another cup. Aunt Linda looked over and smiled at him, happy to see her nephew enjoyed it.

Lema yelled loudly.

"AUNTIE BRENDA!"

Brenda ran into the living room to see what was going on and why Lema was so loud.

"GIRL! I heard you. I know you are just naturally loud coming from the south, but I bet my sister heard you in Georgia too!"

"Auntie Brenda, you so crazy, but that's a good one, shoo."

Isaac stood with his hands in his pocket, eager to spend his paint money. He hoped Lema would hurry up with the conversation.

"May we go to the store?"

She wasn't sure which store it was, so she looked back at Isaac.

"Is that the store or a hardware or...."

Isaac cut her off. He was eager to answer, so his mom would know exactly where they were going so she would be more likely to say yes.

"Lema, it's a store, but they have a fabric part, grocery store, and everything else."

"Oh yeah, that is right; my mind is just going."

Brenda shook her head. She knew that girl was only 11-years-old but when she talked you forgot her age sometimes.

"Yeah, you two can go, but be careful crossing that crazy street up there on Main. People drive so stupid on that street!"

Lema looked back at Isaac, and they both smiled so hard.

"Now, take these five dollars and get me some bread; you two can keep the change."

"Yes, ma'am! We will bring the bread right back, auntie."

Brenda loved when Lema came to town. It was like being with her sister, except her sister wasn't as headstrong.

"Okay, sweetheart, okay, son. Lock the door behind you, please."

They ran out of the house excited. They laughed as they made their way to where Jerry was.

"David not back yet?"

"I don't know. You don't see David, and I don't either."

He ignored the fact that Lema was looking for David and rambled on.

"Hey, Lima, you like bugs, you know insects and stuff?"

Lema put her hand on her hip and raised an eyebrow. Isaac just sat back and braced himself because he knew Lema.

"Boy! Look! I'm looking for David. We got to go to the store, and another thing, my name is Lema. Not Lima, like lima beans!"

Jerry pulled down his shirt that was always too small, then he pushed up his glasses.

"Well, sorry, I know now, Lema, and whenever you like to play with me, you can help me catch insects, that's all."

Lema sat on the curb by Jerry but not too close. She felt a little bad now. She remembered David told her that Jerry's mom bought him whatever he wanted just to get him out of her face even though she loved him. Lema was taught that most spoiled kids lack hugs. Some spoiled kids didn't even know what it was like to be cared for emotionally or have a supporter for real-life issues. They mostly looked at their parents as an A.T.M.

"I apologize, Jerry. I'm just anxious to go to the store. I love to shop, shoo. Well, I will play with you before the summer is up. I can tell you about the red ants in Georgia; they bite too!"

"Really?"

"Yeah, really!"

Now it had been about five minutes. That was a long time for a child when they were ready to go. Isaac tapped Lema's shoulder.

"Do you think his parents said no? It has been a few minutes."

"Well, the only way to find out is to go down there since everybody at his house is home."

Isaac's heart pounded. He remembered that harsh 'nigger boy' comment by David's dad, as well as the meaning of that 'confusion' word from his own dad. Isaac's voice was shaky. He didn't want to cause confusion and have his dad and David's dad arguing.

"Let's just wait down here, okay?"

"Boy, that's your best friend. Why you act like you scared to go to his house?"

Isaac was scared, but he wouldn't dare tell Lema what had happened. She was the type to ask grown-ups why they act like that under any circumstance. When it came to racism, she had a racist couple loving her down south because she was so outspoken and headstrong. In California, you can hardly tell who is racist, but down south, whatever race don't like each other, they just don't speak. Lema talked that racist couple to death until they talked to her.

"No, it's not that, uh, I can just stay with Jerry and uh...."

Lema cut him off. She snatched his shirt and pulled him in the direction of David's house. She was determined to get her way.

"Come on, cousin! I will not walk down that street by myself, plus it's your best friend, shoo."

Isaac sweated, and his heart beat faster the closer they got. Lema knocked 3 times very hard. David jumped up. He remembered that he came to ask if he could go to the store. All the lemonade had sidetracked him. He knew if his dad got home, he would not be able to go.

"Mom? Mom? Can I go to the store with Isaac and his cousin?"

"What? Slow down! What are you asking me? Well, wait, let me get the door first, then say what you have to say, so I can understand you."

Samantha opened the door and saw Isaac. She looked over at Lema, who she had never seen before but remembered hearing about Isaac's cousin. The way she smiled at the two kids, you could tell her racist ways were just picked up and not permanent. Isaac was really scared now. He knew Lema was going to open her mouth first. That's why he figured she could have just gone by herself.

"Yes?"

"Hi, Ms., uh, Ms. What is your last name, ma'am?"

Linda walked to the door and stood by her sister. She heard this young southern accent girl who spoke respectfully, and she was curious to see what was going on.

"Mrs. Smith."

"Okay, uh, Mrs. Smith, can David go to the store with us? I watch for cars, and I look both ways. I don't talk to strangers. I...."

Samantha politely cut her off then looked back at her sister. They got a kick out of Lema.

"I don't mind as long as he lets me know when he is back, and he can look out for cars and things too. I hope."

She looked back at David and smiled, but she and Linda noticed a grin on David's face. The face you only saw when a boy had a serious crush on a girl.

"Yeah, mama, and I'll let you know when we get back."

Isaac finally got enough courage to say a word. He had been standing behind Lema, hoping that everything would go ok and that they wouldn't start 'confusion.'

"Thanks for letting him go with us."

"No problem."

As David walked out the door, she stopped and whispered in his ear.

"Hurry back before your dad comes home from fishing. He really doesn't say too much of you being at the end of the block, but the store, I don't know."

David smiled at his mom for being understanding but was disappointed at his dad's stupidity.

"Okay, mama. See you later, Auntie Linda."

"See all of you, be safe."

"Yes, ma'am, nice talking to you."

Samantha closed the door, and they laughed.

"Now, was that not the cutest little southern girl you ever saw, Sam?"

"How you know Isaac's cousin is from the south. Did I tell you about her?"

"You don't have to tell me. I can tell by her accent. And how many kids in California say yes, ma'am?"

"Oh, yeah, huh. Did you see the smile on David's face when that little girl spoke?"

"Ooh yes! I want Steve to change completely, but you better let him come around and change 100 percent before you tell him about that grin we just witnessed."

"I know, huh. Oh, by the way, did you hear what David wanted before I opened the door? He talked so fast."

"I'm pretty sure it was the same thing the little girl, Lema, asked you. Could he go to the store. I know I heard store for sure."

Samantha was satisfied and glad it wasn't too serious. He asked so many questions she sometimes ignored him.

"Well, come on, Lin', so I can finish beating you up in Yahtzee."

"Whatever, sis, whatever!"

8

Samuel got off work exhausted but happy. He got an entire week off to spend with his family and niece-in-law.

However, slightly changing the lyrics, Samuel jokingly sings an Usher song.

"Where is my baby!"

Brenda was cleaning the restroom, and when she cleaned, she was in a zone and rarely answered anyone. This time she wanted to get straight to the point about the store run before Samuel asked.

"Lema, Isaac, and David went to the All-in-One store."

Samuel looked very upset, but he knew his wife had a reason behind everything she did.

"So, you feel they will be safe?

"They will be okay. Lema is very responsible, you know that."

Samuel could not disagree with that, but he knew she was trying to overlook what he really meant. He did not want Isaac and David together. So he decided not to make too much of a fuss about it.

"Okay, babe. I'm going to use your favorite line, 'prayer changes things,' right? You better pray. I'm not feeling this."

"Uh, huh, Samuel."

Brenda went back to cleaning. She did not want to continue on this topic. She felt it would end if she didn't say much at all.

Lema, Isaac, and David got three blocks from the store, and Lema called out a fun game that her parents at home played with her often. Her parents are not together; however, they thought of fun games to keep her happy when they were in her presence. They always wanted her to know that she was not why they broke up; they just had irreconcilable differences.

"Hey y'all, let's play a game I play at home with my momma and daddy. It's called my car, your car."

"How you play that, Lema?"

David had such a crush on Lema he just stared at her face like he had never seen her before. He was so baffled he forgot cars were even in the game. Isaac remembered the game, sighed, then tried to help his helpless friend out.

"David, you know, we play it all the time when we see the few cars that come down Broadway, goodness!

Isaac spotted a Chrysler 300.

"That's my car!"

"Boy, that's rude; I didn't even get to explain the game to David, shoo!"

"He already knows, but if it makes you happy, explain it to him. I know it will make David happy."

David nudged Isaac.

"Oops."

Lema still didn't know about David's crush.

"What you talking about? Anyway, David, when you see a car, you have to yell real fast, 'MY CAR!' Then the other person cannot pick that car because you called it already, okay."

David stood up straighter than usual with his chest out, trying to impress Lema.

"I got it, and I'm ready! Are you ready, Isaac?"

Isaac was so ready he had picked 10 cars in his head while Lema explained.

"Yeah, like 10 minutes ago. Let's do this!"

They played the game, and it helped them get to the store faster. The store was crowded; however, kids always made their way through a store when they needed to.

Steve arrived home from fishing; he took his tackle box and fishing gear right in. He saw his wife and sister-in-law playing Yahtzee and laughing about old times. He got along with his sister-in-law, Linda, on most occasions.

"Hey, Sam, honey. Hi Linda."

He mumbled his half-hearted greeting to Linda but went over to kiss Samantha. Linda loved to tick Steve off; she felt he was too arrogant and her sister too timid. She hated his ways and made every attempt to show him she was not like her sister.

"Hey, Trout, oops, I mean Steve."

Steve was glad she was being sarcastic so he could say something back.

"Yeah, I came home early because I smelled your presence, fishy, or better yet, heard it, you big mouth bass!"

He looked over at Sam, who just shook her head. She knew if they were not barking at each other, something was wrong. That was their way of showing a bit of love towards each other.

"Anyway, honey, as I was rudely interrupted, "Where is my boy?"

Linda grinned; she couldn't wait to see his expression. She felt his racism was ignorant, and he would never explain and cared less when the subject came up.

"Yeah, Sam, where is David?"

She moved closer to the edge of her seat and waited for Sam's answer. She wanted her sister to toughen up and tell him how irrational he was. Samantha, however, just grew anxious.

"Honey, let's go to the room and talk."

Steve figured it was his house, and he could talk wherever he wanted to.

"I can talk right here! This is my house. Now, where is David so I can show my son what I caught?"

Linda gave her sister a look to reassure Sam that she would not let anything happen to her. Linda's daughter had been killed by a drunk driver who was Caucasian. If anybody could have hatred in their heart, it would be her. However, she had a big heart and had chosen to forgive the driver and pleaded with him to get help. In court, she stood and said as much, which made everyone cry their eyes out. That was why she felt Steve's hatred was nothing but stupidity. Sam mustered a bit of courage while her sister was there and proceeded with her head held high.

"Well, I allowed him to go to the store."

"You let our son go to the store by himself?"

Linda felt sorry for her sister, knowing what was coming, so she butted in. Usually, she would be rude; however, she calmed down her tone for her sister's sake.

"Oh, Steve, you know your wife is smarter than that she...."

"Who asked you, Linda!"

"1, 2, 3..., can I finish, please!"

Steve was puzzled because Linda did not give him a foul answer. Samantha was nervous and braced herself for the fallout.

"David went with two kids, a handsome boy and a cute little girl.

"Oh, him and Jerry. Well, which little girl, because the girl they used to play with, Meagan, moved."

Samantha took a deep breath looking for faith and courage to tell Steve who David was really out with. She glanced over to Linda for reassurance.

"No, Steve, he went with.... He went with Isaac and his cousin from Georgia, Lema."

"HOW IN THE HELL COULD YOU LET MY SON GO WITH THAT LITTLE FUCKER! AND I HEARD ABOUT THAT BIG MOUTH COUSIN OF HIS!"

Both Samantha and Linda got into it with Steve. Samantha was bold and expressed her anger like never before.

"OH, COME ON, STEVE!"

"How could you think I'm not capable of keeping our child safe from anything!"

"Yeah, and it has been 30 minutes, and they are just fine. I am so sick of your prejudice; it makes no sense at all!"

Steve had been stuck in his ways so long he thought nothing was wrong with it.

"Oh, come on, Linda, you don't have anything better than that. You keep saying I'm prejudiced, yeah, yeah, think of something else!"

"Well, we were, as of today, I totally choose not to be! I was just following my mom and dad's wrong views from a couple of bad experiences with another race. We felt every person in that race was like that, which was dumb."

Samantha badly wanted to mention how the guy who destroyed their lives and killed her niece was Caucasian. However, she saw how upset her sister already was. Every year on her niece's birthday, she had to console her sister and didn't want to open that wound today. So, Samantha decided to just keep quiet. As she slammed her body down into the chair, she saw Linda grab her purse.

"This is my cue to leave. I can't stand this anymore!"

She left without saying bye to anyone, thinking of her own child, and almost shed a tear. Then, they heard Linda's car screech off. But, Steve had no remorse. He loved his wife, so he calmed his tone down a bit but was still harsh.

"I'm sitting my chair right by this window, and my son better not come home with even a paper cut!"

"Well, when 'our' son does come home with not even a paper cut, you let me know!"

"Yeah, and if something does happen, it's all your fault; how about that!"

Steve laid the guilt trip on Sam. He waited for a response; however, Samantha ignored him. He moved his chair closer to the window and turned toward the TV, flicking the remote repeatedly.

Isaac went right to the paint aisle, and Lema and David followed. Isaac knew the store like the back of his hand; his mom shopped there often.

"So, here we are. What color did you guys want to paint the go-kart?"

Isaac thought this was his chance to override Lema. She always had her way since she was the oldest and bossy too.

"Oh, wait a minute, since this creation is David's and mine, we get to come up with the colors first. Isn't that right, David?"

He reached out his hand to give David a high-five like they always did when they agreed. David looked down at his hand then back over to Lema, who had her hand on her hip. David looked into Lema's pretty eyes and almost forgot Isaac was even there.

"Well, since Lema is a young lady, we will let her pick first."

"OH MY GOD, YOU SOLD OUT!"

"Oh, hush boy, at least somebody got some manners around here. You could learn a lot from David."

"Well, whatever, what color you choose, Lema?"

Isaac ignored her previous comment. He was just ready to get back to paint the go-kart. Lema looked at all the colors and spotted a metallic gray that she instantly picked

"Ooh, Ooh, I like that one; that is flossin'."

David smiled; he loved Lema's accent and southern slang. Isaac liked it too but hated to admit it. He always said something smart-mouthed, but Lema always had a comeback.

"What you mean flossin'? You in Cali girl, and the word is, 'that's tight,' if you mean you like it, okay!"

Isaac popped his collar up, trying to impress David but David was too busy looking over the paints.

"Oh, you trying to jones, boy? 'That's tight,' don't even sound right either; only thing tight is the paint on that lid!"

David laughed hard, partly just to get Lema's approval. Isaac laughed also. He was the spitting image of his mom; he could dish out a joke and take one in return.

"That is a good one, cousin!"

"Yeah, it was. Well, let's get that 'tight,' 'flossin' gray metallic paint. Is that okay with you, cousin?"

"Of course, let's get it!"

"What about that blue paint? It rocks!"

Lema and Isaac looked at each other and back at David. Now it was time to tease him.

"So now, we have 'tight,' 'flossin', paint that 'rocks'! We need to enroll back in school for the summer, all of us."

They laughed so hard a store employee came to see what was going on. He was 5'11", slim with thick glasses, and had a slightly bad attitude. He was the type that felt all kids were disruptive, good or bad.

"May I help you three?"

Lema could hear the attitude in his voice, so she approached him in her own way. Not trying to be disrespectful, more bluntly honest.

"Do you really want to help us, or do you feel we are doing something wrong, sir?"

The employee pushed up his glasses, a bit confused on how to answer her. For one, he never heard a kid in California say sir to an adult; and he never had a kid question him with a question so fast.

"Uh, well, uh, yeah, you three were a bit loud, and uh, well, uh, you called me sir."

He pointed to his name tag.

"The name is Lionel; when you say sir, I feel old."

"Well, sir, I see 20 gray hairs. How old are you?"

Lema asked politely. However, Lionel noticed that with this little girl, it would be a long debate for sure. His glasses fogged up from being highly aggravated.

"Never mind my age, just keep the noise down and shop, please!"

Lionel walked away so hard his penny loafers screeched. Dave gave Lema props. He knew he would not have had the courage to say anything to Lionel.

"You let him have it, Lema!"

"Have what?"

Isaac shook his head, not understanding. His parents and others they've been around claim Lema is so smart; how come she doesn't catch on fast.

"No, Lema, he said you got him good when you kind of fussed at that Lionel dude."

"Oh my god! I didn't mean to fuss at him. I should go and apologize."

Isaac was ready to just get the go-kart materials they needed. He knew his cousin. Lema would search high and low just to apologize to Lionel. Instead, he decided to remind her of what she was there to do.

"Lema, we don't have time. We have to get the bread, plus the extra five dollars is going to be ours, remember."

Lema loved having responsibility and did not want to do anything to lose trust with her aunt.

"Ooh, yeah!"

She grabbed the paint. David was a step ahead of her and came around with the shopping cart.

"Load the paint, my dear!"

They got the rest of the paint, the bread and waited in line.

9

Samuel was a little upset that Brenda talked through the movie like a woman that sought his attention.

"Excuse me, babe!"

"Well, excuse me, babe, I was just going to ask you if you needed anything!"

"Yeah, and if I said yes, you were going to talk through my entire movie too. You know I know you!"

Brenda smiled. She loved the way Samuel knew her. Although she had gotten his hint, she still wanted to talk.

"Okay fine, I just cleaned this house; I always cook, and I can't get 30 minutes of your time, fine!"

Samuel thought it was cute at times when she tried to act bratty. He knew that she was spoiled by no one else except him.

"Come here, mama; what's wrong?"

Brenda tried to hide her smile as she walked over to Samuel and slumped down next to him. They both laughed

"You don't know if I had something important to tell you, shoo."

"Well, what's important? I'm all ears, spit it out."

Brenda loved talking with Samuel. She explained everything to Samuel about her day and David's secret crush on Lema. He was puzzled about how anybody could end up liking that bossy little girl.

"There goes the new female lieutenant. Lema will not allow anyone to care about her unless it is at her command. Now, who you say had a crush on her? I couldn't hear that part."

"I said David, sweetheart."

Samuel laughed so hard he knocked the television remote off the table.

"Come on, you serious?

"Yep!"

"That boy's parents already can't stand us. Liking Lema, well, that makes David an official nigger lover."

"Now that is enough, Samuel, come on!"

"What? I'm just saying. To be honest, I feel sorry for David. We know who's going to wear the pants if they do have a relationship. Lema would snatch poor David like in the caveman days if he didn't make it down the altar fast enough."

"How could you say that about Lema? She does have a big heart."

"Now, I am not saying she doesn't have a big heart, just bossy. But, in reality, I have to admit I think it's cute and innocent; I can see the silly grin on David's face. But, you have to realize, Brenda, I'm a man. I know the dumbfounded look when we like somebody."

Brenda laughed hard, remembering the look on David's face.

"What's funny now, Bren?"

"I just pictured David's face when he came down here to pick up Lema and Isaac. He had that dumbfounded look you were just talked about."

Samuel looked at his watch, wishing all the kids would come back soon, and wondered how David could go to the store with them in the first place. Samuel and Brenda had some prejudice but nothing like Samantha and Steve; however, neither family's prejudice made any sense.

"Yeah, speaking of the kids, they have been gone about an hour and forty-five minutes."

"You know how kids lag when they get freedom, plus Lema has her phone."

Samuel grabbed the remote and continued watching his movie.

"You prayed, right?"

Since Samuel had been with Brenda, she told him to pray so much that he automatically did it.

"I'm married to Ms. Praying Lou; you know I did."

Steve dozed off but decided to apologize to his wife. So, he knocked on the door, which was rare for him. He would usually just walk in because he had the "this is my house" syndrome. But, with his knock, Samantha knew he was coming with a surrender flag. So, Samantha opened the door then sat right back on the bed to read her book. Steve knew this would not be easy, so he made a joke to break the ice.

"Hey, uh, it's hard living with an old trout, as Linda would say?"

Samantha looked at Steve for half of a second, then back in her book. Steve just kept talking until Samantha responded back; however, her words were short and sweet.

"Look! I know you've had a change of heart toward "people," and that's fine, but I'll change when I want to, babe. Maybe I won't ever change. It's my life, my thoughts, and my opinion. If I were that harsh of a person, you would not be with me. Right, Sam?"

"You know what, Steve, you're right, it is your opinion, your life, and I do have reasons why I am still with you. Since you want to talk, let me ask you a question. Have you ever seen the look on your son's face and how delightful he is when he plays with his friend? Let me rephrase that, his best friend?"

"You are jumping the gun. I wouldn't say Isaac is his best friend. What about Jerry?"

"No, Jerry is not his best friend; you picked Jerry to be his best friend; you know insects and bugs are not David's thing. He is just polite to Jerry, who is a good kid, a spoiled one, but a good kid that everybody gets along with."

They are interrupted by a knock on the front door. Steve went to answer it.

"Speak of the devil, look who it is, Jerry! How are you, Jerry?"

Jerry was not good at conversing with adults.

"I don't know, I'm okay, I guess? But, hey, I was supposed to watch the go-kart for David and Isaac, but can you watch it?"

Samantha wanted more answers, so just like her son, she asked questions.

"Do you have to leave, Jerry, and go home?"

Jerry pushed up his glasses and held up a caterpillar in a jar.

"No, I need to get some more of these right quick."

Samantha jumped back, looked at Steve, then headed toward the bathroom.

"Ugh, I will be right back."

Steve grinned; this was his chance to talk to Jerry alone.

"Hey buddy, listen up...."

"My name's not Buddy; it's Jerry."

"Yeah, whatever, listen, wouldn't you like some more nets, bugs, and insects?"

"Sure! You know a new spot where I can get some around here?"

Jerry hated to walk far, so if Steve had a place close by, he was all for it.

"NO! But, I can give you twenty dollars to put that go-kart in your backyard."

Jerry's eyes lit up like a Christmas tree. Even though his mother spoiled him with money, he was excited he had another source now.

"SURE!"

"Shh, now do what I ask and get back so I can give you your money. Okay?"

Steve looked back to see if Samantha was coming. Jerry gave Steve the jar with the caterpillar and his net.

"Here, you hold these; I will be right back!"

Steve grabbed them and placed them on the floor in disgust. He wiped his hands from the dirt on the jars.

Samantha came back and saw the dirty jar with the caterpillar in it, and Jerry was striking down the street.

"Ugh, why you have his bugs, Steve, and where is Jerry going without them?"

Samantha was no fan of insects and bugs, only her books.

"Oh, well, uh, he is going to put the go-kart in his yard. He's going to help the kids instead of asking us to watch it."

"Oh, that's nice of Jerry. Knowing Jerry, he's probably helping so he doesn't have to walk anywhere; he could ask for a ride in that go-kart later."

She laughed.

"I'm wrong, true, but wrong."

Steve laughed with her. He wanted to distract her from what was really going on. It worked because Samantha headed back to the bedroom.

"Steve, honey, honey, come here."

"Yeah, what is it?"

Samantha smiled at him, thinking he was coming to his senses.

"Don't you want to finish our conversation from earlier?"

Steve wanted to finish the conversation quickly so he could make sure Jerry was doing his job.

"Oh, yeah, uh, as I said, I may change later, and blah, blah, I'm done."

"Blah? Blah? Well, I see you are not in the mood to talk anymore. So what's the rush about?"

"Hey, you know I still have to get in the tub from fishing. So why are you questioning me? Read or uh, watch T.V. Man!"

"Back to the same ole' Steve."

Instead of reading, she decided to get some rest before she started dinner for her two men. When Steve saw Samantha lay down to take a nap, he dashed back to the front door to see where Jerry was. Jerry passed by taking the final parts of the go-kart to his backyard. Steve was satisfied but anxious. He reassured Jerry that he had done an excellent job.

"Alright Jerry, that a boy, come and get your bug and money. Come on, hurry!"

Jerry carelessly threw the last piece of wood and broke another part from where Isaac and David tried to fix earlier, then ran to Steve.

"Thanks! Thanks for the money and holding my jar. Now I can go to the store and get this other net I wanted. I tried to tell my mom, but she is on the phone again."

"Yeah, yeah. By now, you shouldn't be mad about that; now run along."

Steve closed the door and went to get in the shower. Jerry ran home to take his caterpillar in and tell his mom what he was about to do. As usual, Ms. Sinclair was on the phone.

"Yeah? You got to be kidding. Are you serious? Wow!"

Jerry yelled at his mom because she usually didn't hear him.

"MOM, I'M GOING TO THE STORE! YOU KEEP ACTING DEAF BECAUSE YOU ARE ON THAT STUPID PHONE, LIKE USUAL!"

Ms. Sinclair looked over at Jerry and sarcastically waved as if she was saying, "Yeah, just go to the store." Jerry loved to be spoiled materially; however, he wished his mom would spend time with him. Jerry threw on his bug hat and slammed the door as he left headed to the store.

Lema, David, and Isaac finally got to the front of the line. Lema got the money ready while the boys placed the items on the belt for the cashier.

"Okay, that will be $28.90, please."

"Okay, Ma'am, here goes $30."

The cashier smiled at Lema because she said, 'Ma'am.'

"You are from the south, correct?"

"Yes, Ma'am."

"I knew it! I have a niece from the south, and no one says yes, ma'am or sir, around here. Most of the youth here can get pretty disrespectful."

Lema couldn't imagine disrespecting adults, and she knew her cousin wouldn't without getting in trouble.

"Well, I don't know ma'am because of my auntie, his mama. Ooh wee, if he talked smart or anything, he in big trouble too, and he from Cali. My auntie don't play that. Huh, Isaac?"

He was surrounded by a lot of people, and he didn't want the world to know he got in trouble, so he answered quickly then changed the subject in one breath.

"Yeah, she would, now the paint Lema."

"It would be better to say there will be consequences instead of she would get him. People will hear that and run with it."

The cashier smiled at Isaac. He blushed to know the cashier was saving him from embarrassment.

"No, my auntie will get him, shoo."

Isaac just shook his head. David, being a good friend, stepped in, trying to save Issac some embarrassment.

"My mom and dad will get me too if I act up!"

David said it loud enough so that everyone staring could hear. Isaac looked over at David and smiled. Their friendship was strong.

"You will always be my best buddy, David!"

"No, you will always be my brother, Isaac!"

Everyone around them got teary-eyed. The cashier put their items in bags then hurried to take off her necklace, which had two keys.

"I know you three are making a go-kart. My son was making one, but he went to live with his father because of certain circumstances, and now he is almost grown. So I really want you three to take these keys and build the best go-kart on the block, okay."

"Thank you so much, ma'am!"

"We really thank you!!"

"Yeah, we not finished with the go-kart, but keys are perfect, thanks!"

The cashier smiled and waved bye. They grabbed their bags but stopped at the soda vending machine.

"Hush, please, I think I heard my phone ringing. It's in my pocketbook."

She grabbed her phone out of her purse while Isaac and David made car sounds.

"Isaac, this your mom; here, go get the sodas; I will talk to auntie."

Isaac grabbed the change, and he and David went to get the sodas.

"Hello! Hey auntie, how you doing?"

"What are you all up to?"

"Nothing just coming out the store."

"I hear David and Isaac in the back with their car sounds. So, you all just fine, huh?"

"Oh yeah, they still playing, my car, your car. But, Auntie, we got out of that store, the prices rise like gas prices, shoo!"

"Girl, what's rising is your little grown ways. Just hurry back so you can have fun with your friend and cousin before it gets dark. Okay?"

"Yes, ma'am, we on our way!"

Lema put the phone back in her purse and headed over to Isaac and David.

"Come on, we got to get back. Your mama said we need to hurry back so we can play before it gets dark."

"Yeah, seriously, we don't need more things to get us into trouble, huh Isaac.

"Yeah, really!"

Lema didn't know what trouble they could get in; everything they were doing was innocent.

"What trouble? I just got off the phone with auntie; we not in no trouble!"

Isaac told Lema just a little until later, he knew how feisty his cousin was. She lived down south and heard about all the racist stories of the past; however, she still wouldn't go for it. She even changed a racist man, speaking to him every day until he just broke down and spoke back. They have been speaking to each other every day since then. He did not want to explain what he and David were going through. She would go question David's parents on why this and why that.

"Trust me; we will explain to you later. So let's get back to Broadway Street, please, and finish the go-kart."

"Yeah, well, come on, David, let's go."

David blushed and walked along with them.

They got to the end of the store by the garden department outside, and David saw Jerry.

"Hey! Look y'all, there goes Jerry. He was supposed to watch the go-kart for us. What's up with that?"

"Yeah, that's what I'm saying; what's going on?"

"Uh, huh, let's go ask him!"

They all ran towards Jerry.

"Jerry?"

Isaac was the first to call out. Jerry looked up because he always kept his head down and pushed up his glasses.

"Yeah?"

David cut in.

"I thought you were going to watch the go-kart for us; what happened?"

"I just put it in the yard; what's wrong with that?"

David and Isaac automatically thought he was speaking of Ms. Opal's yard. Lema thought that was kind of him.

"Oh, thank you, Jerry. Where are you going anyway?"

"I'm going to buy some more bugs and insect catchers and stuff, well, you know."

Isaac was in a hurry to get back.

"Okay, Jerry, well, we will see you later. We have to get back."

They all waved bye to Jerry and headed towards home.

"Hey, Isaac. Hey Isaac!"

"What's up, David?"

"You noticed we have not seen Ms. Opal in a while. When we came in the gate, she normally looks out the window."

"Yeah, I think she sick, you know we have nosey neighbors, and the lady told my mom Ms. Opal was uh... what's the word. Oh yeah! The lady said she was a little under the weather, and I think that is sick in old people's words."

"We have to finish that go-kart fast, so when she gets better, she can make those cookies for us, and we can get the stuff from the store for her, now that we will have wheels. Remember she said she would?"

"Yeah, she always does. She loves us kids, and we can go take a ride and get her some medicine, too!"

Lema added her two cents.

"Yeah, when she looked at us kids, she acted like she saw angels or something."

"Well, you know I am an angel."

Isaac placed his arms up and made sounds like he was flying.

"Yeah, me too!"

David made the same sounds, flying around also. Lema laughed and joined in with the boys to make it even more fun.

10

Steve stepped out of the shower, still skeptical about Isaac and the big-mouth cousin, as he called her. He checked on Samantha. She was sleeping peacefully, so he headed to the living room. He sat by the window, flipping channels with the remote, and anxiously waited for David's arrival.

Samuel kept thinking about how he and David's family were alike. Even though he did not speak about his racist ways, like Steve, Samuel was just as bad. Some of the things he would say were so harsh.

"Brenda, do you need anything from the All-in-One store?"

Brenda knew where Samuel was going with this, so she went along with it.

"Yeah, I need something, uh, huh, I need some sugar, cotton balls, peroxide, and that's it."

"Wow!"

"What?"

"Your thrifty, you keep peroxide and cotton balls, but all of a sudden, you are out, huh? Let me keep it real because you know what I'm doing. Let's go stake out the kids, Bren."

"Yeah, since you bust me out, let's go. I still want to go to the All-in-One."

"Sure, it figures."

When Samuel and Brenda got to the end of Broadway, they saw an ambulance in front of Ms. Opal's house. They parked, jumped out, and ran over to her. One of the EMTs placed her on a stretcher and got ready to put her in the ambulance. Ms. Opal sweetly talked to one of the EMTs.

"Thank you, sweetheart, now be careful, my purse. It can be heavy due to all my coupons."

She laughed; both EMTs laughed with her. That was Ms. Opal; she could laugh and keep a smile on her face even in serious situations. She pushed a strand of her long gray hair back, looked up in the glare of the light, and glanced at Brenda and Samuel.

"You two didn't have to come see me on the stretcher. I'm always home before dark."

She smiled at both of them, and even though she was being sarcastic, she was happy to see them.

"Well, if that was a way to make us feel bad for not visiting enough, it worked. You are the sweetest lady alive, next to my Bren-Bren; there is no way we shouldn't come see you at least every blue moon."

Brenda cut in, "every blue moon and some sunshine days!"

"Oh, don't mind me, I'm all jokes and smiles, which is probably what keeps my flowers growing in my garden. You know I am proud of the boys. Since they have been building the go-kart, they have not crushed my flowers once. When I told them they could put it in my yard, that was my only rule, and those sweet babies listened. They are going to be two responsible young men."

Brenda and Samuel looked at each other then back at Ms. Opal. She started to hold her heart and squeezed her shirt.

"Call the EMT, Brenda. I better get going; the doctor is supposed to run a lot of tests today."

She reached for Brenda's hand.

"You two are doing a good job at staying together. Stay strong."

Ms. Opal let go of her hand slowly, and as the EMT placed her in the ambulance, Brenda yelled out.

"WE WILL! We will come to see you at the hospital too, or are you coming home today?"

"I will be there three days, sweetheart."

Brenda Lu and Samuel both choked up, so they just waved bye and nodded their heads as if they were saying okay. They did not like to see Ms. Opal in that ambulance. They were only used to seeing her go to church, the market, or working in her garden. So they got back in the car.

"Baby, wait a minute. Ms. Opal said their go-kart was in her yard."

"She sure did. Why didn't they tell us?"

Samuel looked over into Ms. Opal's yard.

"I had a clue, but I wonder if they finished making it because I don't see it in the yard. That's probably what they went to the store in."

"Let's get to the store. They didn't tell us anything. They had no right bugging Ms. Opal; she is nice but elderly!"

"Yeah, let's go talk to them!"

Lema, David, and Isaac started to get tired on their way back, but they were getting there. Lema made a suggestion.

"Hey, boys, why don't we run and take this bread home so we can hurry up and paint. I can't wait. I'm excited, shoo."

"I will speak for David and me when I say, let's do it! We will give you a head start, Lema since you carried the paint when we were almost home. Okay, slowpoke?"

"Get out my face, boy!"

The boys really gave Lema a head start. They held onto the bags tight and tried to catch up to Lema. They finally got to Broadway, where they set everything down. Isaac was still huffing and puffing.

"Lema, you run fast girl, you almost made me fall twice. You play too much!"

Isaac sat on the curve to catch his breath, and David plopped down huffing as well.

"Yeah, how you almost beat us like that?"

"Now I bet y'all will learn next time you try to give me a head start. Thought I was a real slowpoke because I'm a girl. Now, stop being so judgmental!"

She put her head in the air proudly as she pointed in Isaac's face. Issac was tired but sarcastically mocked Lema.

"Yeah, yeah, well, so what, enough with the big words. Don't be so judgmental.

"Oh, somebody jealous, huh? Boy, I'm not studdin' you, no way!"

David stood up. He hated to see his hopefully future girlfriend and his best friend as they argued.

"Let's just sort this stuff out so we can go get the go-kart and start, please!"

Isaac and Lema looked at each other, and both realized they made no sense.

"Okay, well, I will stay here, and you and Lema go get the go-kart. I will sort the stuff out."

Isaac smiled at David. David knew just what Isaac was doing. Isaac sniggled. He was helping his friend and being a brat at the same time. Lema was ready to go, still not having a clue about David's crush.

"Okay, well, let's go, David!"

She pulled David's hand just to rush him a bit. However, David melted inside and looked back at Isaac, grinning. The same grin he had when he had his braces removed last year. Isaac just thought it was the dumbest grin ever because this time it was over Lema.

As they walked, David got nervous and tried to get over it by sparking up a conversation.

"Hey, uh, Lema, how long are you staying out here?"

Lema looked a little confused; he usually doesn't ask that; she is usually gone before she ever saw him multiple times.

"I'm staying the entire summer, well, I hope."

She looked at David and smiled. David smiled and put his head down. He was shy; however, Lema thought she had said something wrong, so she complimented him.

"David, um, you are a good friend to my cousin. Do you feel he's your best friend?"

"Of course! I like Jerry because he doesn't treat anybody wrong, and we have other people we play with around here sometimes. Isaac and I just hang out the hardest! Isaac is the only one like me. Why do you ask?"

"Well, what you told that lady at the store how y'all are brothers, that touched my heart. I can't stand people like that, don't like other races for no reason, it's just dumb."

David thought about the way his dad felt towards Isaac, and he agreed with Lema wholeheartedly.

"Yeah, I agree totally."

He didn't attempt to talk specifically about his dad because he knew Lema would ask more questions. So he instead thought about Isaac and his dad's mechanic.

"Yeah, I know people like Isaac who don't even care about races. They will smile right at you and don't know that who they're smiling at is mean and don't like their color.

Lema broke out in a Norman Whitfield classic.

"Smiling faces, smiling places tell lies, and I got proof!"

David didn't listen to many oldies but goodies, so he was not familiar with that song.

"Did you make that up? I like that song."

"You don't know that song?! Shoo, that song was the beat! And why you think I made that song up?"

Lema was shocked because her family grew her up on oldie but goodies, especially that song.

"Because you sang smiling faces tell lies, and you had proof. I was taught proof means you know about it."

"If my mom or auntie were here, they would say that was cute."

Lema laughed hard, and David joined her.

"Yeah, I can make good jokes sometimes."

They finally got to Ms. Opal's, which wasn't far from where Isaac and David built the go-kart. However, they seemed to have gotten there a little faster.

"I know I'm not blind. I don't see no go-kart in this yard."

David was perplexed; he knew that it had to be there, and why not? That was where they always kept it. So he went to the side of the house to look.

"I know we wouldn't have placed it in too many places because we wouldn't want to crush her flowers. But, you know what, Lema, maybe it's in her backyard."

"Well, if you go back there, I'm staying right here. You know how I ....

David cut her off. He normally wouldn't, but right then, he was worried about the whereabouts of the go-kart.

"Yeah, Lema, I know how you feel about going through people's yards when they are not home. So I will go, no problem."

Lema shook her head in agreement. David went into the yard, but he didn't see the go-kart. He was so upset he ran out of the yard, passed up Lema, and ran to where Isaac was sitting. Lema was running to catch up with him.

"David, slow down!"

He paid her no attention; his focus was on letting Isaac know what was going on.

"Dude! Our go-kart not in Ms. Opal's yard!"

"Maybe you overlooked it. Well, did you look in the entire yard?"

"Yeah, he looked because I was outside the yard, and he went all through it!"

Isaac and David thought very hard and paced back and forth, trying to figure out what could have happened.

"Do y'all think Jerry could have put the go-kart in auntie and uncle's yard?"

"No, that would never happen."

"Well, you don't know, we have to take the bread back anyway, and it wouldn't hurt to look; it's not where it normally would be. So, David, if you don't mind staying this time, we'll take the bread back, and we can look."

David and Isaac were ready for any suggestions on how to find the go-kart.

"Well, yeah, good idea. I'll wait with the stuff. Then, maybe I will see "Bug Boy," come back, and I'll ask him where he put the go-kart!"

Lema tried to calm the situation down.

"It's okay; I'm gone pray like my momma and auntie always say to do."

Typically, David considered everything Lema said; however, buddies are buddies, and David was definitely looking for Isaac's approval on this one.

"Yeah, man, we will find it. It has to be around here somewhere."

David sat on the curb. He started to worry about Ms. Opal because they hadn't seen her in a while. Also, because the go-kart was not where they thought Jerry put it. David thought about everywhere it could be, and an idea popped up in his head, which he spoke out loud.

"No, Jerry too lazy to go farther than the yard to take the go-kart."

He stopped dwelling on it and threw pebbles while he waited for Isaac and Lema.

11

Ms. Opal was in the room talking to the doctor as he walked in. He was 6'2 and 180 pounds of solid muscle, a model's smile, and bedroom eyes. He looked as if he was French, Hawaiian, or Hispanic. A beautiful, surfer type, in shape with a tropical look. The doctor had a reputation of being very professional and polite. He grabbed Ms. Opal's chart from outside the door. Ms. Opal, an 89-year-old lady and very outspoken. She always figured she stayed voicing her opinion, so why stop now. She looked him up and down.

"Well, you're a hot ticket! I know you have female patients sick on purpose!"

"Oh, Ms. Opal, stop."

"You stop looking good."

She laughed, and he grew speechless.

"See, since you can't stop looking good or change your looks, I can't change my opinion, well, facts."

He waved his hands in surrender.

"You won, you won."

He laughed in a way to let her know he was flattered.

"Oh, don't mind me. I am just giving you the compliment you deserve. Now let's get down to the nitty-gritty! What's going on?"

The doctor's smile faded. He hated this part of the job even though he loved being a doctor. When it came to delivering bad news, no doctor was ready or liked it. He looked at the chart, trying to approach the situation as gently as possible.

"I want to say, this is a called, well, you have lung cancer, and you have approximately 3-6 months to live."

He rolled his stool underneath him and sat by Ms. Opal. He looked at her pretty, thick, gray hair and the beauty he could imagine she had back then, and still, the beauty features she has now.

"I am truly sorry I had to be the one to tell you this bad news."

He put his head down and removed his hand from Ms. Opal's shoulder. She lifted his chin and looked into his model-like face.

"Sweetheart, this is not bad news this time. The worst news I ever received was when my husband of 38 years died about 10 years ago from lung cancer; smoking cigarettes. I may have had second-hand smoke all those years. I couldn't get him to stop. I would offer him gifts and trips, but he told me, '*Honey, you just better not smoke these cigarettes, you hear me?*' If he only knew, while he was smoking the cigarettes in the air, I was smoking them the entire time. I'm just glad he is resting in peace, so he doesn't have to hear I have it; then it would be two broken hearts. Baby, I'm just fine; it's just Ms. Opal's time."

If the doctor blinked, tears would have unfolded, so he stood up, gave Ms. Opal the biggest hug, and then laid out a plan.

"Ms. Opal, you can take Morphine, so you won't have to endure so much pain; it is totally up to you."

Ms. Opal opened her purse and held up her bible for the doctor to see.

"I will endure the pain. This all the medicine I need for the next six months. This book has been helping me for 79 years, since when I first started believing in it."

A cold chill came over the doctor.

"Well, okay, I can't argue with that. Still, trust and believe we will help you with whatever you need."

The doctor opened the door to leave, and Ms. Opal looked at herself in the mirror.

"Well, Mr. Marshall, Mrs. Marshall coming on home to join you, my love."

The minute Jerry walked the aisle, he saw what he wanted. As he headed back home, Jerry tried to catch bugs along the way. He looked over and saw Isaac's parents as they drove by. He remembered them from when Isaac was teasing the annoying Meagan, like everybody else before she moved. Isaac's mom was fussing and made Isaac say sorry. Brenda made eye contact as they were driving. She smiled at Jerry, who smiled back but kept walking.

"Hey, Samuel!"

"Yeah, Babe?"

"Wasn't that the kid that Isaac plays with every blue moon?"

Samuel looked out the rearview mirror as he was pulling in to park.

"Yeah, that's him. The one that never ties his shoes. I'm surprised he's never had surgery, all the falls he's had. I guess they're untied so much he now has good coordination to handle it."

"Well, I'm not on that right now. We'll ask Jerry if he saw the kids; he was probably in there with him. Don't you think?"

"You know what, I never thought of that, Bren. When I pull up to him, you ask him; you more familiar with him."

Samuel turned around in the parking lot. As they pulled up on the side of Jerry, Brenda rolled down her window.

"Hey, Jerry!

Jerry looked over at them, stopped walking, and pushed his glasses.

"Yeah, what is it."

Brenda looked over at her husband and sighed. Her kids would never talk to her like that; yes, or at least a "huh," answer. This changed her whole tone from friendly to stern.

"Just have you seen Lema, Isaac, and David?"

Jerry walked away but talked at the same time.

"Yeah, they went toward Broadway to go paint their go-kart. I don't know why they didn't get any bug jars; that would have been more fun. Well, see ya!"

Brenda's motherly instincts kicked in when she noticed the untied shoes AGAIN. She was worried he would fall, so she yelled out the window to him.

"Tie your shoes before you fall!"

Jerry usually ignored adults because he gets away with it with his mom; however, he knew his hot from his cold with some adults. The way she stated her comment, Jerry knew she meant business. So, he dropped down to tie his shoe, and Brenda and Samuel drove off.

Lema tried to open the door, but it was locked, so she called out to the adults with her loud, country voice.

"AUNTIE! AUNTIE!"

Isaac was behind her with both of his hands over his ears.

"Do you have to let the state of California know my mom and dad not home? Dang!"

"Boy, Hush! And anyway, why yo behind not trying to help. You don't have a key?"

"Oh, duh, I just remembered. I could have stopped you from screaming a long time ago."

"Just open the door, shoo, we have too much stuff to do. Plus, we have to find that go-kart!"

Isaac took his time and was being sarcastic while he dug in his pocket for the key.

"Let's see, I have 2 candy wrappers, a hot wheel, an empty chip bag, and oh, look here a key!"

"Now that don't make no sense, all that trash in your pocket."

"Just come on, Misses Clean or Judge Judy, they both fit who you are."

He laughed as Lema barged in the door taking in her part of the bags. She had way too much pride to let the conversation end there.

"Yeah, I got your Judge Judy! At least I will be making all the decisions!"

Isaac had forgotten that his cousin would argue as long as he wanted to. That was one of her strong points, so he had no comeback.

"Well, anyway, whatever, girl!"

Once they placed everything where it went, Lema wrote a note for her aunt and uncle before they went outside. That was a new strategy; he would typically just leave and keep checking in until they get back.

"What are you writing, girl?"

"A note. Auntie and uncle need to know we went back outside, and I'm letting auntie know where the receipt and money are."

Isaac smiled at Lema because certain things she did reminded him of his mother.

"I guess that's why you in charge, huh, smart cookie?"

"Thanks, cousin!"

As Lema finished writing the note, Isaac ran to the restroom, passing the phone as it rang.

"The phone. Well, shoo, I'm right here. I will get it."

Lema answered the phone quickly, thinking it was her aunt and uncle.

"Hello."

"Hey Bren, that's the fastest y'all ever answered for me. I'm on my way over there."

It was Uncle T.J. on the phone, but he didn't tell Lema his name; instead, he started remixing an Isley Brothers' song.

"I'll be on my way to see my family. Ooh, how will they know!"

"Wait a minute, Sir! Who is this?"

"Lawd Have Mercy! Lema?!"

"Uh, yeah, who is this?"

"OH MY GOD! I haven't seen you since you were about 5. I'm really on my way now!"

He hung the phone. Lema looked at the phone, confused. Then she placed the money, receipt, and note down, ran to the bathroom, and knocked hard on the door.

"Boy, hurry up, shoo!"

"Don't you know you don't rush the master?"

"How you the master with that bathroom smelling like that?"

Isaac pulled her into the bathroom with his still wet hands.

"Smell the roses."

Lema ran out of the bathroom, hitting Isaac on her way.

"Yuk, you stink! And you play too much!"

"Now I bet you won't have the last word like my auntie always say you sometimes do. Hey, was that my mom and dad on the phone?"

"NO, it was some strange man. He scarred me, talking about he hadn't seen me since I was five. He kept crying, then said he on his way! I'm not being rude, but he sounded drunk."

Isaac's eyes grew big like headlights. He immediately knew who the caller was as soon as Lema said he sounded drunk.

"Uncle T.J!"

"Who is Uncle T.J.?"

"That's my dad's brother! He is your uncle too. He is a lot of fun. He does drink a lot, but he is smart and has funny stories. My dad told somebody if Uncle T.J. would leave that bottle alone, he could have been a prefessial."

"You mean a professor."

"Yeah, whatever, I just knew it was a smart teacher or something. And my dad said he changed since his wife died or something like that."

"Well, I can't wait to meet him now. I don't remember him too much. I have to see him probably. I can't wait until he comes!"

"Yeah, my dad will be upset, though."

"Why?"

"Well, my mom told me drunk people tell the truth too much, and Uncle T.J. says whatever comes out his mouth. My dad acts like he is embarrassed by Uncle T.J."

"Oh, see, we will get along because everybody in Georgia says that about me! Me and Uncle T.J. have something in common."

"Lema, I don't think that is a compliment. You told me compliments mean something good, right?"

"Yeah, but no one ever said it was wrong yet. Well, let's go.:

They made it down to where David was waiting to help him look for the go-kart.

"What took you two so long?"

Lema cut in as usual. At times she never lets anyone talk.

"Oh, um, I had to write my auntie and uncle a note. They not there, plus Isaac took a dump!"

David laughed and held his nose.

"Yeah, Lema, just tell all my business, why don't you!"

Lema waved her hand at Isaac like she was saying whatever.

"And then the uncle I don't remember name Uncle T.J. called and...."

"Uncle T.J. called?! He rocks! I remember when I first met him, we were playing street basketball, and he made a basket on the light post. When I made the basket, uncle T.J said, "Go ahead, good job Larry Bird, white man can jump!" I didn't know what he was talking about, but with his face and white teeth when he smiled, I knew he was happy for me making the basket!"

Lema was into the story and excited like she was there.

"Oh Yeah?! Well, he said he is coming over!"

David walked over to Isaac, and they gave each other a high-five.

"YES! Well, let's find our go-kart."

"Let's just sit here and think where it may be, and plus, I am not carrying this paint all over the neighborhood! As a matter of fact, this y'all neighborhood shoo! I will stay with the materials and paint, and y'all look. But I still want us to think first."

Isaac sits down on the curve.

"Lema, you talk a lot, but you always have good ideas!"

David sat back on the curve and nodded his head in agreement.

12

Uncle T.J. walked down the street with a bottle in a brown paper bag that he drank from. He was 6'3 200 pounds with clean but dingy pants, a white t-shirt, white Nike's, a long khaki brown trench coat, and a baseball cap on backward. He had a salt and pepper beard that needed shaving; however, he had the whitest prettiest teeth you have ever seen. Everybody was always puzzled how his teeth could be so white as much as he drank. Uncle T.J. sang as he strode, with his hands in the air, dancing with himself.

"Betcha by Golly Wow. You're the one that I've been waiting for, forever. I said, yeah, girl! Forever yeah!"

He continued until he got to his brother and sister-in-law's and banged on the door.

"Bruh?! Sis-n-law, is ya home?'

He got no response.

"Well, hot damn. I know y'all in there. I just was talking to Lil Mama, shit!"

T.J. pulled out a bottle of Thunderbird from his pocket. It was only a swallow left. He took a seat on the stairs to enjoy that last bit.

"Well, I thought I was talking to her. Well, shoo, I will wait. I will wait for some of my sis good cooking too. My brother lucked up on a good cook!"

He pointed in front of him like he was talking to someone.

"That's for damn show, you betta believe it!"

Brenda and Samuel finally saw the kids as they sat on the curb in deep thought. They stopped, and Brenda got out as Samuel followed.

"Isaac, it has been a minute. I was checking to see if you three were okay."

Brenda noticed there was only the paint and some materials.

"Lema, so where is the change and the bread. I know you more responsible than that."

"Auntie, I left you a note, and when you said I can keep the change, I budgeted and still came home with change."

Samuel smiled. He knew Lema had everything taken care of. Isaac and David were relieved as well because Brenda's voice was somewhat firm. Lema passed a piece of paper to Brenda.

"Baby, what's this?"

"A man called, and he said he hadn't seen me since I was 5."

"Yeah, Lema, go on."

"He didn't tell me his name, but Isaac said his name is Uncle T.J.!"

Lema said the name proud. It seemed whenever you mentioned that name, individuals lit up. David and Isaac smiled, but Brenda looked back at Samuel, who was frowning.

"So, what else did he say?"

Samuel hoped he wasn't coming over. Lema mocked T.J.'s singing, although she couldn't remember all the words.

"Oh, he said, 'I'll be on my way, something, something, something, here I come.' So basically, uncle, he said he was coming over."

Samuel headed to the car wanting to beat his older brother to the house. Brenda followed Samuel.

"Girl, you should have told him.... Well, never mind. You three be safe. Come home at 7:00, oh yeah, and Ms. Opal went to the hospital. She said everything okay. Isaac, I will tell you more when you get home, okay?"

"Okay."

Isaac looked at David.

"The hospital? Man, that's why we haven't seen her. I hope she is okay, for real!"

"Me too!"

Lema tried to shine some light on the situation.

"Well, you heard auntie, the lady said she will be okay."

"Yeah, you remember Granny said she was just fine too, so we wouldn't cry that much before she died!"

Lema held her head down. She remembered that incident like it was yesterday.

"Yeah, I remember."

Dave tried to cheer himself and his friends up.

"Well, let's not think bad; let's just hurry up with the go-kart. Then we can go to the store for Ms. Opal like she wanted us to."

Lema saw Jerry coming down the street.

"Wait! There goes the spoiled boy right there."

David and Isaac spotted Jerry also and ran to meet him before Jerry could get to them. Jerry was excited that they were running to him. He wanted to go show off his new bug equipment.

"Hey, look! I have a new bug jar and...."

Isaac cut him off.

"That's cool, but where is the go-kart?!"

David looked Jerry dead in his eyes and waited anxiously for Jerry's answer. Jerry pushed up his glasses.

"Oh, it's safe. Your dad paid me some money to take it to my yard because I was tired of watching it. I asked your dad to watch it, but he just told me to take some money and put it in my yard. I guess he was tired too."

Lema smiled and was ready to go get the go-kart. David and Isaac looked at each other nervously. They knew that if Lema and David's father talked, with her outspoken curious self, David might never be able to see the "nigger boy" again.

Oh, see, it's safe. Don't you live next door to each other? Let's go get it!"

"Oh, uh, well, we can get it another time, right, David?"

"Yeah, uh, we can wait."

"What you two mean? Aren't y'all going to fix this go-kart so we can go to the store for the elderly lady?! Now let's go get it!"

She snatched up Isaac by the shoulder and started to walk behind him. David ran pass Isaac and Lema, trying to beat them to his house. Jerry just hunched his shoulders like, oh well. He looked down and noticed his shoes were untied but kept walking towards home.

Samuel and Brenda pulled in the driveway and saw Uncle T.J., nodded forward, and sleep. Samuel got out and slammed the door on purpose. Uncle T.J. jumped up.

"Hey bro, y'all left me, how dare ya!"

He laughed and reached for a hug, but Samuel passed right by him to open the door.

"Well, I'll be damn. Did I sleep with him last night? Well, I don't think his name is classified because I slept next to my newspaper last night. Hey, it felt like a comforter."

He busted out laughing and slapped his knee. Brenda walked up and greeted T.J., then invited him in.

"Come on in, bro, and have a seat."

Samuel slammed his keys on the table and sat on the couch looking straight at the T.V. T.J. sat down next to Samuel and made a sarcastic remark.

"Well, at least someone welcomed me in the house."

"Well, if you are sitting on the couch, I feel we both welcomed you in, don't you think!" Uncle T.J.: "Praise him, oh, thank you, brother."

T.J. licked his finger and acted like he was writing on a chalkboard.

"That's one point for Sam."

Brenda always let them have their moments; however, she tried to make peace.

"Okay, you two, that's enough. T.J., do you want anything to eat or drink?"

"Drink? That's an understatement!"

Samuel was being sarcastic. T.J. wanted to cry, but he held it for two reasons, he's a man, and men are unfortunately told they shouldn't cry. Secondly, T.J was the older brother, and he did not want to show a sign of weakness to the younger brother. T.J. stared Samuel down, and Samuel did the same back.

"You know what, just because I did not become "College Professor," you know what. I'm not even worried about you. The way you act, I would have put you in my class just to give you an F. How about that? You know you treat me like an unwanted step-child, and Mama didn't raise you like that!"

"You talking about me! Mama didn't raise you like that!"

"Well, let's all clap for Mr. Perfect! Sis, I will have a piece of your wonderful pie or cake if that is okay with Mr. Judge Samuel before he bangs his gavel!"

Brenda wanted to laugh so hard, but out of respect for her husband, she didn't.

"Uh, okay, on that note, I'll bring it in a minute."

Samuel looked at his brother, rolled his eyes, then looked back at the T.V. T.J.'s comment hit home with Samuel. Their mother always told them not to ever judge anyone whatsoever! Furthermore, even though Samuel felt T.J. won the confrontation, hands down, he had too much of a grudge against him to say he apologized.

"Just sit down, man, and wait for your pie, and hush, please, I'm trying to watch T.V.!"

T.J. sat on the couch, took his empty Thunderbird bottle out of his bag, and passed it to Samuel.

"Hey, bro, here, you recycle, don't you?"

"Just sit it on the floor. I will get it later. That bottle smell like your breath."

"Oh, you just hating!"

"Hating on what?!"

"Hey, man, you know what's up! I may reek of the smell of liquor, but when I stand out in front of that liquor store and say, hey sexy Mama, can I have your phone number on my brown paper bag? They say no at first, then I give them this million-dollar smile. They say, ooh, baby, here is my cell, my work, and my home number! Then I made them change up Barry White's lyrics and sing to me. 'My darling, I can't get enough of your smile, babe!'"

Samuel looked down, and even though he did not want to, he busted out laughing, and so did T.J. Brenda heard them laughing like the brothers they are.

"Thank you, Lord! Please let them clear their differences all together one day soon, please! Here you go, bro."

"Ooh wee, homemade pie! Boy, you better not leave her, or else I'm going to be the first one in line like they giving away government cheese."

"Standing in line, my ass! Just eat the pie before you be wearing it."

"Don't mind if I do, I say, I don't mind if I do."

13

Samantha woke up from her nap and headed through the kitchen to the washroom area. She grabbed a basket full of clothes out of the dryer, made her way to the living room, and plopped on the couch.

"What a good nap. I needed that."

She called out to Steve as she folded the laundry.

"Hey, honey?"

Samantha looked up only to see Steve asleep with the remote in his hand.

"Well, I see you agreed with me about taking a nap."

She did not wake him but continued to fold clothes.

Lema, Isaac, and David got to the stairs in front of David's doorstep. Jerry was twenty steps behind; however, he was still walking toward them. David was huffing, trying to find an excuse why he should be the only one who went into his house. Isaac had never come to David's house. David was also worried about his dad being mean to the "Nigger Boy," as he rudely called Isaac. With Lema being there, David felt his father would be mean to the "Nigger Girl," also. David heard Black person, and it was nothing wrong with saying that; however, the way Steve places emphasis on the word made it rude. Really, David just wanted peace, and he cared about his friends.

"Okay, you all wait right here, and uh, I will be right back."

Isaac had no problem with it, but Ms. Noisy Lema had to be curious.

"Okay, but how long do we have to wait?"

David looked through his window, hoping no one was there.

"Oh, well, not long, uh, ask Isaac, not long watch and see."

Finally, Jerry arrived.

"Why are all of you over here? My house is next door."

Lema looked over at Jerry's house.

"Oh, well, we might as well get the go-kart. But wait! I'm not going in your yard, though."

Jerry took it personally and made a rude comment as usual.

"Well, I don't care if you don't want to come in my yard, come on, Isaac. I will bring it out; I need more room for my bugs anyways."

Isaac ignored Jerry and went into the yard. His focus was on the go-kart. But, Isaac looked back at Lema and laughed. You could cook an egg on her head; that's how steamed she was at Jerry with that typical talk to him but rude to everyone else, language of his.

"Boy! You better be glad I'm saved! I would come in your yard, take all your bugs, and sling them somewhere!"

Jerry pushed up his glasses and yelled over at Lema, almost in tears.

"Hey, you better not throw my bugs. Stop being mean!"

Isaac looked over at Lema and gave her the eye, knowing that she was totally wrong.

"She is not going to throw your bugs; stop crying."

"Boy, I ain't going to throw your bugs. You just say things to get on my nerves, that's all."

Jerry forgave her without saying so, then he addressed Isaac.

"I'm not crying! I'm just talking."

Lema had her hand placed on her hip.

"Can y'all just get the go-kart! I'm ready to paint, shoo."

David was relieved his dad was asleep. So, he sat by his mom.

"Hey, mom?"

"Hey, son. Why do you look like you just saw a ghost?"

"I see where I get all the question asking from."

David joked and nervously chuckled. Samantha smiled not one bit.

"Run that by me again, young man!"

David grew even more nervous.

"Oh, uh, mom, I was just joking. But, please, bring your ear over here."

Samantha leaned into David, who began to whisper

"Lema and Isaac are next door. For some reason, Jerry put our go-kart in his yard. So Lema came down and made Isaac come too to get the go-kart."

David looked over at his dad, hoping he didn't wake up. Samantha smiled as she thought about Lema, but her smiles quickly faded. Samantha then understood Steve's sudden case of niceness earlier. Samantha hoped he didn't have anything to do with the go-kart being in Jerry's yard. However, her intuition was 120% sureness that her husband was involved. So Samantha whispered back in David's ear.

"Well, I do remember your dad talked to Jerry earlier. Don't worry, just try to get the go-kart back down the street without waking up the snorer over there."

David paced his hand over his mouth and giggled.

"Okay."

As soon as David tip-toed out of his chair, there was a firm knock at the door. David's heart dropped to his gut. Samantha looked over, wondering who was at the door. Steve slowly stretched and smiled at his son.

"Hey, son! I'm glad you are back from the store safe. We will talk later, okay?"

As Steve put his hand on the door to open it, a big lump came in David's throat. If David had swallowed, it would have felt like a ball of hay. But, instead, Steve opened the door, and to his surprise, there was a cute little girl. He really, deep down inside, wanted to smile at her; however, he held his composure.

"WHO MIGHT YOU BE?!"

Steve looked back at David and Samantha then back at the door.

"Oh sir, I'm Lema, Isaac's cousin. I didn't mean to knock so hard. It looks like you probably was sleep."

Steve was puzzled how Lema knew he was sleeping.

"Well, maybe you're right! How did you know I was sleeping anyway?!"

"Oh, no disrespect, but my mama said when I have a good nap, my hair stick straight up on my head, and that's how yours is, sir."

Samantha and David bust out laughing, and so did Lema, but out of fun. Steve did not laugh at all. Instead, he turned red,

"Well, first of all, I'm glad you think you're funny. Second, if you are coming for David, I don't know why; he comes out when I say he can. Who gave you permission to come to my porch anyway?!"

"Sir, I apologize if I hurt your feelings. I'm really not out to hurt anyone's feelings."

Steve sized Lema up and spoke sarcastically.

"Girl, please! How could you or your cousin hurt me? You people hurt yourselves with no help, now that's funny!"

He laughed hard and looked at his wife and son. There was a disappointment on their faces that he had never seen before. Lema was almost in tears.

"You people?! You know what, Mr.? That sounds like the same racist talk that came out of this racist man's mouth in Georgia a couple of years ago! But I thought it was better out here. Maybe I'm thinking wrong. What do you mean when you say, 'you people?' Is it the same meaning as the man in Georgia?"

Steve got upset. Usually, when he said something rude to adults, that was that, no discussion. But, he had an unusual feeling about this little girl. Steve kept firm, though, because he was stubborn like that.

"Well, I see you're not that dumb, huh? Yes, maybe it is the same because I'm talking about blacks. So, let me see."

He looked in the air, being funny, then back at Lema.

"So that means yeah, you and your cousin."

Steve smiled, thinking it was over. However, Lema was upset, as much as a young child could be.

"You know what, I'm going to pray for you. I found out people who say mean stuff like you don't have a problem with my color; it's just sometimes they have a problem with everybody and don't like themselves neither. That's all, so I will pray for you even though I'm mad right now."

Lema looked past Steve into the house at David and Samantha. Samantha wants to crawl under her seat. However, she was happy that an 11-year-old girl stated things to her husband that she should have told himself years ago. David smiled so hard as if Lema was his hero. Steve was furious.

"Hey, you don't need to pray for me! By the way, David is not coming outside with you, now how about that! And another thing, keep off my porch!"

Isaac was on his way back to Broadway, and even though he was scared of Steve, he was always there when his cousin needed help. Isaac forgot about being fearful and ran right over to Lema. He was upset and protective of his cousin. Lema wanted to cry but didn't; instead, she said bye to David and Samantha).

"Well, bye, I hope to see you two again."

She looked back at Steve as she slowly walked away.

"I hope you get the fear of the Lord in you, Mister, cause I have done nothing to you!"

Steve looked at Lema, puzzled as if he actually agreed with her comment; however, he would not show a sign of remorse.

"Come on, Lema, let's get off this porch!"

Isaac mugged Steve really hard as he pulled his cousin off the porch. Jerry came up clueless and walked with Lema and Isaac as they were coming off the porch. Steve slammed his door.

"She got her nerves talking about how she's going to pray for me, huh. I'm pretty sure she has some relatives to 'pour out some liquor,' as they say."

David cried. He could not take it anymore; first, his best friend, and now his future wife, well at least in his mind. David did not care if the punishment was coming; he went into a rage.

"You know what, dad, you used to be my hero. I used to want to be just like you. But you are mean, and you tell li...stories!"

He caught himself before he said, 'lies.' Steve cut in.

"WATCH YOUR MOUTH!"

"Dad, I don't care if you whip me. But, you should watch yours because you smile in your mechanic's face, and you hate my friends! And they are the same color! You are ooh....."

David stormed to his room and slammed the door. Steve couldn't believe David's tone even though David had some good points. Finally, Steve stood up and took off his belt. Samantha may not stand up for herself, but she was a true mom who would stand up for her son.

"No, you don't! You put that belt away! How dare you get ready to whip our son because he is right. How hypocritical can you be?"

Steve felt the entire house was disrespecting him.

"WHAT! HYPOCRITICAL! Where is all this disrespect coming from in my house, women?!"

Samantha stormed outside but made a sarcastic remark as she did.

"I guess disrespect is rubbing off from somewhere; you take a wild guess! I am going to talk to those kids who have done nothing wrong!"

"Go ahead! I wash my hands with your "good Samaritan" ways.

Everybody wants to do charity work for the black folks and make me the bad guy. My son, my house, my rules!"

Steve went to his room and slammed the door. David, however, was thinking hard, really hard.

"I just have to get in trouble; I feel my butt sore even now. Oh well, I'm out of here! I'll play until just before dark."

David was really a good kid, so sneaking out without permission was new to him; plus, he refused to let his dad keep him away from his friend in any circumstance. So he proceeded to sneak out the window.

Samantha sprinted to get to where Isaac, Lema, and Jerry were.

"Isaac, wait!"

Lema stopped and stopped Isaac by grabbing his shoulder. Jerry just automatically stopped. Samantha spread her arms around them and hugged them.

"Look, I know how David's father is, and that's a misfortune. I really feel one day he is going to come around and accept everyone from all races and walks of life."

Samantha looked to see if they understood. Isaac and Jerry nodded their heads. Lema also understood but had to ask her question.

"I am in no way disrespectful, ma'am, but why is he so evil?!"

Samantha knew Steve had a hardshell with a soft middle, so she took up for her husband.

"I know the way he fussed at you was rude, and he seems like a 100 percent mean man. But, trust me, deep down inside, he really is not."

Lema laid her head on Samantha and hugged her back harder. Samantha got the biggest lump in her throat, and if she had swallowed, tears would have unfolded. Isaac tried to clear the air, quoting something his dad had said to him that was also wrong. However, Isaac felt it would be the right time to share and to get clarification himself.

"Well, my dad, he's not that bad either, and he says bad stuff too.

He said all white people think they are better than us and are all nosey, but not you, Mrs. Samantha. You talk to us like you love us!"

Samantha was a little disturbed by what Isaac's father stated; however, she swallowed her pride and smiled at Isaac for his lovely comment. Everyone looked over at Jerry because he was not saying a word. He just stared very hard behind Samantha. As they all looked back, David walked out of the gate but looked back to ensure no one was looking or coming out of his house. Lema and Isaac looked at each other, and their eyes got big. They knew first-hand David was not supposed to be outside. Samantha raised an eyebrow at him.

"Hello, son?!"

David looked up, and his eyes got as big as headlights. He stuttered.

"Uh, hey, hey, hey, mom."

Samantha waved her hand swiftly for David to come to her. He was not in trouble; she just wanted to know what he was doing.

"Well, um, mom, I was...."

Samantha placed her hand over David's mouth. She bent down and whispered in David's ear as she looked back at her house down the block.

Sshh, you know I'm going to let you stay out here. Try to be in earlier than usual, so your dad won't freak out. When he calms down, I will let him know I let you go out. I will take the raft, okay?"

David looked around at Isaac and Lema's big smiles and Jerry's regular straight face and felt his own face. He smiled so hard his face hurt.

"THANK YOU, MOM. I LOVE YOU SO MUCH!"

Samantha hugged him back, and as she walked away, she looked down and noticed the go-kart, and of course, Jerry's untied shoes.

"Good job, kids, and Jerry, tie your shoes, sweetheart."

David, Isaac, and Lema sounded like a choir.

"Thanks!"

Jerry looked down at his shoes and smiled at Samantha.

"Well, I didn't make anything anyway."

Lema instantly got an attitude.

"Well, you can still say thank you; you helped with something!"

"For what!"

Isaac and David wished Lema would have just left it alone.

"That's okay, Jerry, just have fun too and get to those shoes so you won't fall, please.

Jerry huffed, tired of the constant reminder of his shoes. He picked up a go-kart piece wanting to help now.

"Can we get this to wherever, and do whatever you all want to do with this stuff. I'm getting sleepy."

Isaac smirked, but he was glad Jerry offered to take the go-kart down the street, knowing bugs were really his thing.

14

Uncle T.J. watched an entire movie with his brother. He then decided it was time to walk to the store for a liquor run. T.J. noticed the kids were not around.

"Hey sis-n-law, I knew it was too quiet; where is my nephew and Miss Growny?"

Samuel smiled, thinking about his son and Lema. Of course, everybody knew who "Miss Growny" was, but she is such a sweet girl.

"Samuel and I just left them on the way home. They're on the end of Broadway making a go-kart and...."

T.J. cut Brenda off before she could finish her sentence.

"Ooooooh, Weee!"

Samuel covered his ear because T. J. was so loud.

"Come on, man! My ear!"

"Come on, bro, you know kids don't really make go-karts anymore! That's why I love those kids; they are using their little creative minds. They are so smart! I'm going to talk to them when I'm on my way to the store!"

Samuel did not like that idea at all.

"Now, don't go bothering those kids; come on now."

T.J. stood up, getting ready to go out the door, but he turned toward Samuel.

"Hey, I'm surprised you not down there helping those kids make it!"

"Well, first of all, that man doesn't want me around his kid, and frankly, I don't give a damn because I feel the exact same way about mines.

T.J. was puzzled. There were a lot of kids in the neighborhood, so T.J. needed clarification. He looked over at Brenda.

"Who is he talking about in general, sis?"

Brenda got up. She disagreed with Samuel's views all the way, but she didn't want to get involved.

"Ask your brother T.J. See you. Oh, wait, you coming back?"

Brenda was a sweetheart like that; she did not want T.J. to feel unwelcomed. Samuel gave her a firm look, to which Brenda shrugged her shoulders like, what did I do. T.J. read Samuel's unwelcoming facial expressions but ignored them. Instead, T.J. continued to speak on the situation, acting as a professor, his expertise.

"Well, bro, who is it?"

"The white boy, and his daddy, who drove all the blacks out and destroyed Auntie's house then built buildings."

"Man, please! Auntie's house was about to cave in, and they gave her money to buy a new, improved one. You always feel like somebody white attacking you and everybody for everything."

"Yeah, whatever!"

"Wait, the little chubby boy with the glasses?"

Samuel grew frustrated and tired of talking about it.

"No, man! David, the one he normally plays with!"

"Oh! You talking about my boy, Larry Bird! That's my boy! Wait, his dad didn't have anything to do with that man that was his grandfather, I think."

"Well, that is his bloodline, and they all the same crackers to me!"

"Man, let them kids be kids. If you can't ignore wrong views and have yourself, then you are just as wrong, man!"

T.J. put his finger in his mouth like he was thinking.

"Hmmm, and you say I don't think. Another one for T.J. on the scoreboard."

T.J. laughed and waved bye to his brother as he left out the door. As T.J. got closer to Broadway, he noticed the kids painting the go-kart and Jerry just sitting and holding his bug jars. Uncle T.J. goes right into his song from the Pointer Sisters, however changing the words as usual.

"We are family; I got all my kids with me!"

All the kids looked over. Isaac was the first; his eyes grew the size of the original silver dollar. He and David put their paintbrushes down and ran over to Uncle T.J. Lema looked over at Jerry and whispered.

"That must be who called. Duh, I'm so gone sometimes, they said Uncle T.J."

Jerry put his jar on the curb and stood up. Jerry was rude and weird with all adults; however, all kids loved Uncle T.J. once they had an encounter or two with him. Plus, Uncle T.J was another adult who, when he was around, paid more attention to Jerry than his mom. Jerry just waited for Uncle T.J. to come down, but Isaac and David were not finished squeezing Uncle T.J. yet. Isaac caused T.J. to get emotional.

"Uncle T.J., we missed you!"

"At least somebody missed me."

"I missed you too, Uncle T.J."

Uncle T.J. snapped out of it and stopped thinking of his brother's selfish ways so he could enjoy the kids. Instead, he looked down at David's face.

"You missed me? Are you still on your game, Larry Bird?"

David still did not know who that was but was just glad Uncle T.J. gave him a name. He did know it was a basketball player though, he asked around with his usual questions.

"Yeap! My dunk is better too!"

Uncle T.J. reached to give David a high-five then did the same for Isaac.

"My, man! Well, don't leave me hanging, nephew."

Isaac gave him a high-five rapidly out of being so excited. Uncle T.J. looked down the street towards Lema and Jerry and smiled.

"Girl, the older you get, the more you look like your mama and Aunt Bren!"

Lema was listening to Uncle T.J., but something else was catching her attention.

"Sir, how you get your teeth so white?"

"I may have a lot of things I don't do; one thing is for sure, little one, I always brush my teeth and floss."

He pulled out a zip-lock bag with a toothbrush, toothpaste, and floss inside of it. Then he held it like he was holding a knife or a shank and acted like Zorro, jabbing. Jerry jumped out of his shoelaces and fell to the ground.

"Ah! Oh, My God!"

David, Isaac, and Lema laughed. Uncle T.J. laughed as well, then looked down at Jerry's untied shoes.

"I'm just playing little Biggy."

Jerry got up and pushed up his glasses.

"Yeah, okay. And my name is Jerry. Who is Biggy?"

Lema just looked as Isaac and David sniggled and laughed.

"Come on, you two, don't laugh no more."

Out of respect for Uncle T.J., they stopped. Uncle T.J. kneeled and tied Jerry's shoes.

"No disrespect, little man. I just called you that because you are strong for your size; carrying those bug jars around, you must have strength. You're strong, right?"

Uncle T.J. wanted Jerry to have some self-esteem. Jerry lit when T.J. spoke of his bug jars.

"Yeah! I am strong! Okay, I can be called little Biggy."

Uncle T.J. placed the plastic bag with his toothbrush, toothpaste, and floss back in his pocket.

"By the way, I didn't mean to frighten you, little Biggy."

"That's okay. I wasn't that scared. Some people are scared of my bug jars; when they look inside of them, and they run."

Uncle T.J. looked at Jerry's bug, letting him know he was paying attention to what he was saying; however, he was eager now to go get his liquor.

"Okay, my young ones, I will be back. I'm on my way to the store."

Isaac pouted, putting his head down.

"Uncle T.J., are you really coming back. I know I shouldn't be in grown people conversations, but even though my dad acts like he doesn't want you over sometimes, he brags about how smart you are to his work people all the time. Please come back."

Uncle T.J. smiled in relief. He knew kids don't just make things up like that. T.J. would love to hear that information out of his brother's mouth. He went over and kissed Isaac's forehead.

"Yeah. I will be back, nephew. As a matter of fact, I'll be back for all of you."

Uncle T.J. glanced over at Lema and smiled. She smiled back and placed both of her hands behind her back, and rocked side to side.

"Okay, Uncle T.J., hey, before you go, what's my nickname?!"

"Oh, you want a nickname, huh? Ms. Growny!"

"I like that, hey, I haven't ever been called Ms. before! I always get in trouble if I don't call grown folks Ms. or Mr. at home."

The children happily smiled; they all had nicknames.

"Okay, now, I will be back. Look like you almost finished with the go-kart. I want to be there when all of you strike down the street."

All the kids nod their heads in agreement.

"Okay, uncle."

David chimed in, "yeah, we will be ready for you!"

Lema looked back at Uncle T.J. and smiled.

"Come on, let's paint it!"

"Thank you for tying my shoes."

David, Isaac, and Lema all looked at Jerry, shocked. He just pushed up his glasses.

"What?!"

Uncle T.J. waved headed to the liquor store.

15

Samantha went inside the house a nervous wreck. Not only had she argued with her husband and called him a hypocrite, but she also let her son play against his will. She thought long and hard about how to gain his approval.

"Think, Samantha, think!"

She passed from the living room to the kitchen, then back to the living room, where she sat in her chair. Suddenly, the phone rang. Samantha answered hysterically, hoping Steve didn't come out of the room staggering.

"Hello! Hello!"

It was Steve's fishing buddy Walt.

"Hey there, Samantha."

Samantha was not in a talking mood, so she was very precise.

"Hey, Walt. Yeah, what's up?"

"Well, let Steve know I just caught a 24-pound Sturgeon! I told him he ended the trip too early. Is he awake, busy, or what?"

"Well, he is tied up right now, uh. Can he call you back?"

As she waited for his answer, her phone clicked.

"Oh, I have another call, can I...."

Walt cut her off.

"Well, don't worry, Sam, tell Steve I'll boast later."

He laughed; she shyly did the same.

"Well, okay, okay."

She clicked the phone right over.

"Yes, hello?"

"Man, girly, are you okay?! I hadn't heard you this shook up since you took up for me when I had a boy in the house, and mom and dad said they were coming home early."

The phone call from her sister put Samantha at ease a bit.

"Yeah, sorry Lin, I'm just mad."

Linda braced herself. She knew it could not be good because she had just left her sister's house and knew how Steve could get. But nevertheless, she was sympathetic as she could hear her sister's shaky voice and knew she was fighting back the tears.

"You just what, sis?"

"No, it's just the kids are back and well, David came back by himself, well, they all came together but...?

Linda cut her off. She wanted to cry also, but instead, she reassured her sister.

"It's okay, Sam, slow down."

Taking Linda's advice, Sam told her everything that had occurred. Linda was furious.

"I'm on my way!"

"No, Linda! I'm trying to find a way to tell him I let Dave finish up the go-kart with Isaac and that little princess."

Linda knew Sam only mentioned the kids to get her to calm down. She's so glad her sister isn't prejudiced anymore.

"You know what, sis, I'll stay put. I'm sorry. I know that's your husband, but when is this mess going to stop?!"

"It's okay, Linda, but do not do too much. I need you to hurry; I am all out of ideas."

Once Samantha and Linda hung up, Samantha just sat a while watching T.V. She heard Steve pop open a beer in their room. Samantha was upset that her sister lived so far away. Now she had to come up with a way to deal with Steve. Finally, he came out of the room with a newspaper in one hand and beer in the other.

"Why you look pail like you about to faint? Like the time when I first met your mother."

"Oh, Steve, come on, I just have hot flashes, I guess."

Steve just took her word for it; he did not want to get into the women thing.

"Yeah, well, can you pass me my remote, or am I too hypocritical to have it?"

"Don't start, Steve, please, honey."

Steve was stubborn, but he loved his Sammy as he would often call her.

"Yeah, alright. Well, that son of mine sleep?"

Samantha swallowed hard and quickly lied to throw Steve off.

"Most likely. Here's the remote."

"Thanks! When we were arguing, I wondered what my son was hesitant to call me. That still has me hot!"

She acknowledged stubborn Steve with an apology so he could get off this subject.

"Well, I apologize for calling you a hypocrite, and you know your son is very sad and apologizes to Steve."

"Well, come watch some T.V. with me."

Samantha was satisfied.

Uncle T.J. made it to the liquor store. T.J. was pretty close with the owner. The whole reason the store had a surplus amount of liquor was because of T.J. and his friends. T.J. walked into the store and broke into a song.

"I really miss my, Brandy, ever since you gone away!"

Everyone in the store laughed, including Jabeeb, the store owner. The one person who is very familiar with T.J.'s antics.

"Hey, T.J. man, so that means you want a Brandy today, huh?"

T.J. raised his hand to give Jabeeb a high-five. Then pulled his money out of his pocket.

"Why not, man, why not."

Jabeeb looked at T.J with a sincere smile. He always liked T.J as a person, and Jabeeb was always honest with advice, especially people he highly favors.

"You know what, T.J.?"

"Yeah, what's up Jabeeb, what you know, man?"

"I need someone like you to work in the store. What do you say?!"

Jabeeb placed the liquor in the bag and passed it to T.J. He also pushed T.J.'s hand back, giving him a gesture to keep the money.

"You know, it's people like you that I am glad are here. You see me with not up to par clothes, I only have on new shoes, and I haven't taken a bath in...." He thinks. "Well, hell, I can't remember, we not going there. Anyways, please, don't take this offensive, but I only want to be in public when I'm ready. Working in your store, I may bring people down sometimes. But, trust me, Jabeeb, I'm not always the comedian the neighborhood says I am."

Jabeeb pointed to the worker to grab one of his t-shirts for sale off the rack, a pack of boxers, sweats, and a new hat. He gave them to T.J.

"All, come on, Jabeeb, man, you already let me keep the money for the Brandy, man. At least take the money for these clothes, come on, I insist."

"SShh! Come on now; you want everyone to know I gave you the hook-up?"

"Hook-up, huh! Oh, you getting hip-hop on me now? Thanks, you will get blessed for this. I won't forget about this, but you know how it goes; you get blessed, then a bump in the road happens."

"What do you mean?"

T.J. grabbed his clothes and the paper bag with the liquor in it. He clenched it hard and pointed as if he was pointing to his brother's house.

"The devil is busy. My brother is no devil, but he that bump in the road at times. I wonder how he will act when I ask to shower at his place.

T.J. shook his head. Jabeeb knew the relationship between the two, so he attempted to reassure T.J's heart.

"Oh, just go ask him. I know Samuel as I know you. He is just a bit more hard-shelled but soft in the middle, like a jelly doughnut. Just go, my friend; he will say yes. If not, I am here."

"Thanks, Jabeeb."

T.J. looked over at the worker that passed him the clothes.

"And right on, man. Alright, Jabeeb, I'll be seeing you soon."

Jerry was almost falling asleep on the sidewalk. Lema finished painting up her side of the go-kart, and Isaac and David finished their side. Lema was reading the instructions on the paint can.

"Okay, now listen up, we have to let it dry for at least an hour and a half."

Isaac kicked a small rock across the street very hard. David and Lema looked at each other and back at Isaac.

"What's wrong?"

"No, I'm just ready to drive this thing."

Lema was bossy and a peacemaker all at the same time.

"Well, there goes an extra wagon wheel. Use that one like a steering wheel like we do in the back seat of the car."

Isaac lit up. That was a good idea, something to do until the paint dried. David saw his excitement and passed Isaac the wagon wheel.

"That was a good idea, Lema! Now, since we have time to waste, maybe someone can give Jerry a pillow."

David laughed while Lema and Isaac looked over at Jerry.

"That's dangerous; we have to wake him up."

Isaac frowned, becoming frustrated with Lema.

"Why Lema? Jerry is not bothering nobody."

"Well, this is not a busy street, but cars still come up and down this road, boy! We still need to be alert!"

"Yeah, whatever, but I bet you those cars aren't faster than ours."

Isaac broke out into his and David's song.

"NASCAR, get ready for the race. NASCAR, get ready for the chase!"

David jumped in.

"Oh yeah, NASCAR, get ready for the race!"

Jerry woke up plugging his ears to their singing.

Please! I don't want to hear about no Nascars."

Lema was sarcastic, however glad Jerry woke up.

"Well, look –a- hear, the dead has arisen.

She laughed. Jerry accidentally trips his bug jar checking on them.

"Who died, and who arose?"

Lema had an old soul. She expected everyone to know that saying.

"Never mind, Jerry. Just never mind."

David looked and saw Uncle T.J. walking side to side down the street. He taps Isaac.

"Isaac! Isaac!"

"Yeah, what is it? What's wrong!"

"Nothing's wrong, but there goes Uncle T.J., and he can help us make up some words to our song!"

Isaac, Jerry, and Lema looked down the street and saw Uncle T.J. coming back but walking side to side.

"Yeah, he is coming! Hey, he doing that same dance my mama neighbor, Ms. Frante', whenever she has some special juice. My mama won't tell me the name of the juice. She does this dance."

Lema demonstrated and almost looked just like Uncle T.J. at that moment.

"I can't do it like Ms. Frante' does, though, and my momma popped my hand and told me to stop teasing her. But I like the dance!"

Jerry, Isaac, and David looked at Lema until she finished; however, they were not worried about Ms. Frante' or that dance. They were just happy to see Uncle T.J. Jerry just loved T.J. for paying attention to him more than his mom. It was like the father that Jerry did not have. David could not take it anymore; he yelled out to Uncle T.J. first.

"Hey, Uncle T.J."

Uncle T.J. looked up, and when he waved his hand, he slammed it down so hard he almost fell. T.J caught his fall and continued to walk with his head down. Isaac felt weird. Uncle T.J. usually talks, so Isaac called out to T.J. also.

"Uncle T.J.! Hey unc."

When he arrived, Uncle T.J. did not see Jerry, so he tripped over him and fell.

"Whoa! Timber!"

Uncle T.J. laughed. Jerry's eyes got big.

"Whoa, little Biggy, I didn't see you, but I'm at eye level with you now."

Uncle T.J. laughed again. Jerry slowly covered his nose, trying not to smell the liquor on Uncle T.J's breath. However, Jerry cared about Uncle T.J., too, so he placed his bug jars down.

"Come on, Mr. T.J., I will help you up since you helped me earlier."

Uncle T.J. grabbed Jerry's hand and got up, then Jerry fell. Lema slapped her forehead.

"Oh, brother!"

Uncle T.J. laughed as he lifted Jerry.

"Hey, one hand washes the other."

Uncle: T.J. slapped his knee in hysteria. Isaac and David noticed Uncle T.J. acting a little strange, but they just ignored it because they loved him.

"Uncle T.J., can you help us finish the last part of our go-kart song?"

David looked at Uncle T.J., grinning hard. Uncle T.J. smiled back, and then tears rolled down his face. Lema frowned at David.

"Oh, we can do it. See, you made Uncle T.J. cry! Sing your own song, David!"

"No, No, Ms. Growny, you kids don't make me cry. You kids are so loving. Why my Jade have to go."

All the kids instantly hugged him and gathered around him. He hugged them all back and looked in the air again.

"You loved kids, Jade! You were a good woman. Why you leave me here in this cold world?! But it can get hot with a bottle of moonshine, so I guess I will be fine."

He laughed, and all the kids laughed with him; only Lema knew what moonshine was. The kids only laughed because they were happy to see Uncle T.J. no longer crying.

"Uncle will be back, and I will help, I will help." He started to sing. "With a song, oh yeah, with a song, even when I'm gone."

He walked away towards his brother's house. The kids all looked at each other, happy, however, a little speechless. They were all still a little bit worried about Uncle T.J. Jerry was the first to break the ice.

"I'm going home in a minute; I'm kind of bored."

David, Isaac, and Lema stared at Uncle T.J. as he staggered away. Isaac tried to reassure David but had concerns of his own.

"Don't worry, David, he will be back; I just know it! I wonder whose Jade?"

"I know it is someone who he really must care about."

Lema agreed with them. David put his head down in sadness.

"I lost my cousin. My auntie Linda's daughter got hit by a car. Sometimes she cries in my mom's arms and says, "why Melissa?" And she looks in the air also like Uncle T.J. just did. So yeah, that was my cousin's name, Melissa."

Lema, David, and Isaac all liked Jerry; however, they felt all he cared about was bugs. Jerry rarely showed emotions, so they were surprised to see him console David.

"Hey, I wish your cousin could come back, and is Mr. T.J. going to be alright?

"Yeah, I feel he will. My mama always said when you cry when something is wrong, that makes you not hurt anymore, and you won't be angry later."

Lema's statement made all the kids happy again.

"Well, that's fine. We will just wait until he comes back and helps us sing then."

"Yeah, plus our car will be dry real soon."

Steve was trying to lightweight makeup with his wife with 90% action and 10% verbal. Samantha was on the last piece of clothing to fold.

"Hey, Samantha, now why don't we watch what you want to watch. I always watch what I want to watch anyway."

He passed Samantha the remote, and she slapped both of her hands on the side of her face.

"I got the power! Oh, my goodness, I got the POWER!"

"You know how to make me laugh no matter how much you upset me. I know I can be stubborn sometimes, but wait, why are you looking in the air, Sam?"

"I just don't know where you are going with this. I am waiting for the punchline, that's all."

"Well, there is no punchline! How come when I finally decide to apologize, I have to get all this belittling, certain gestures and comments directed toward me, Samantha, huh?"

"What gestures, Steve? I just looked in the air. You get so uptight sometimes. Honey, maybe you should have stayed fishing a little longer like your friend Walt said."

Samantha cringed. She forgot to tell Steve Walt even called.

"Walt called? You're normally on point with giving me my messages, so what's going on with that?"

Samantha brushed it off like it was no big deal to take the heat off of her.

"Oh, no big deal Steve. We had just started communicating; then you told me to come to watch T.V."

"Yeah, well, anyway, what did Walt say?"

"Oh, he was talking about how he caught a twenty-four-pound sturgeon, and you should have stayed out there, and he will boast later."

"Yeah, that's ole' Walt. He loves to rub his smudgy fingers in my face. If I had caught it, I would have rubbed it in his for sure."

"You men are something else, always in competition. What's so funny, Steve?"

Still laughing, Steve sat right up and turned toward Samantha.

"Now, you need to just stop it, Sam. You and Linda have Yahtzee tournaments like it's a poker game!"

Samantha laughed, shaking her head in denial.

"No. No. No. Linda just doesn't want to admit that the younger sibling is the champion." She poses with her hands on her hips. "So there!"

"Yeah, yeah, just find us something to watch, Ms. Yahtzee of the year!"

Samantha and Steve both laughed. Then, she picked up the remote so she could find them something to watch.

16

Ms. Opal was still at the hospital waiting for her niece, Marie, to pick her up. She saw two teenagers laughing having a conversation. Ms. Opal smiled at them and reached for a peppermint to eat in her purse. She loved kids. She looked out the door as Marie was coming in to pick her up.

"Hey auntie, you ready?"

"Well, I'm ready more than I ever will be. God will prepare me to get ready in a minute."

They headed for the car, but Marie was puzzled. She had never heard her auntie talk like that before.

"Auntie, what you said in the hospital just now, that doesn't sound like my auntie Opal."

Ms. Opal tried to make her niece laugh, not wanting to tell her about the three to six months to live news she had just received.

"Yeah, niece, well, you don't look like yourself when you wear your makeup."

Marie nervously looked at herself in the rearview mirror.

"What's wrong with my makeup, auntie?!"

"Young lady, you went from Marie to Sexy Mingy! You look like an oriental girl when you put on your makeup. The model ones that is."

They both laugh.

"Aww, auntie, you still and always will have jokes. Thank you!"

"You know what, niece, thank you for always checking on me and just being so sweet."

"So sweet? When it comes to you, you are the best auntie. To call you sweet would be an understatement. You took care of everybody's kids. You love all kids of all races; look what you are doing for David and Isaac; they cannot take their go-kart to their houses."

"Oh, they both have a far walk, I understand."

"And who's that other girl, you kept her bird?"

"Meagan!"

"Yeah, Meagan. And that is only a few on the list over the years. We used to rush to the house when I was little. All the kids played tag while you baked cookies."

Ms. Opal sat up a little when she said cookies. She remembered that she was only given six months to live and had promised the boys that she would make them some cookies.

"Hey, Marie."

"Yeah?"

Before Ms. Opal could get what she wanted to say out, they pulled into the driveway. The kids were having fun, and Marie and Ms. Opal watched.

"Look at those kids. The go-kart looks good too."

As Marie was getting out of the car, she noticed her auntie was not getting out. Ms. Opal's seatbelt was on, and she was just gazing out the window.

"Auntie, what's wrong? Come on, you always tell me the truth, and you have been acting a little strange and jumpy, so what's wrong?"

Ms. Opal gave Marie a long stare and started to speak.

"Well, Marie, I have...."

Ms. Opal was cut off by the kids, Isaac and David, first.

"Hi, Ms. Opal!"

"Hello, Ma'am!"

Ms. Opal and Marie looked at each other and smiled when Lema spoke.

"Hey, boys! And hello, young lady! You are Isaac's cousin, right?"

Ms. Opal looked over David's shoulder and saw Jerry behind them.

"Well, hello Jerry?"

Jerry pushed up his glasses.

"Hello."

Lema nudged Jerry.

"I mean, hi, Ms. Opal."

"I see you're growing up, young man; your shoes are tied!"

Ms. Opal giggled, not to tease him; however, he was the kid known for the untied shoes.

"No, Mr. T.J. tied my shoes."

She does not come out a lot; however, she loves everyone, and they love her back the same. She had to think for a moment about who T.J. was. She looked over at Isaac.

"Oh! Your uncle T.J. is on this side of town, huh? He is such a gentleman. Every time I go to the corner market or liquor store, as people call it, right by my church, he always tilts his hat and speaks when he sees me. Oh, T.J. is such a sweet man but judged by many so unfair. So, Mr. and Misses race car drivers, how is the car coming along?

"It's going good, Ms. Opal; almost done, then we can go to the store for you!"

Isaac then brought out another inherited trait from his mother. Sweet but talking out of turn.

"Yeah, Ms. Opal, then we can go and get some medicine for you! My mom said you were sick, and some other people in the neighborhood said it too."

Lema slapped her hand on her face, shook her head, and then

shoved Isaac. Then, she thought of something to say that would clear the air.

"Well, um, hi over there. We didn't speak to you ma'am, what's your name?"

Marie smiled at her.

"You don't have to call me ma'am. My name is Marie."

"Oh, no! I know a lot of people in California don't like that; a few ladies said that makes them feel um...."

Lema was trying to find another word to say instead of old, then she looked right into Ms. Opal's face. Ms. Opal smiled, knowing Lema did not want to say, "old." Then Ms. Opal laughed.

"Old! Go ahead, you can say it, I've lived my life.

"Yeah, what Ms. Opal said. But I have to keep up with yes or no, ma'am or sir because my mom will get my behind with that switch!"

David rubbed his butt, remembering how he was not supposed to be outside. His parents believed in the old school way also. He was thinking and hoping he did not get it when he got home.

"Ouch. Let's change the subject."

"Okay, well, my name is Marie.

"This is my niece her nickname is Ming."

Lema looked back at the boys and smiled.

"Okay, Miss Ming-a-Ling!"

All the kids laughed and started to sing, even Jerry.

"Ming-a-ling, Ming-a-ling!"

Ms. Opal joined in, waving her hands back and forth like she was directing a choir.

"Okay, auntie and kids, I'll accept that one. Thanks for the song."

"Since you all are almost finished with the go-kart, I'll keep up my end of the bargain. I'll make your cookies like I said I would.

Lema and Jerry liked the idea of getting in on the homemade cookies.

"Ooh, I love homemade cookies; what kind are you making, ma'am?!"

"I want three!"

Ms. Opal and Marie laughed really hard. Then Ms. Opal leaned in and grabbed Isaac and David's chins softly.

"I just want to make the cookies since you boys did not crush one flower, that's all."

She did not dare tell those babies she only had 6 months to live. No one wants to face their expiration date, whether near or far; however, she realized how worried she was about it since the hospital visit.

"Little lady, I'm making chocolate chip. And sweetheart, you can have your three!"

Everybody laughed, but Jerry just smiled in agreement and satisfaction

"You can have an extra three, you know why?"

"No, why?"

"Well, I want you to keep those shoelaces tied. It's dangerous, and you can fall and hurt yourself."

She knew Jerry was just a kid who didn't listen, so she made a scenario that she knew he would pay attention to.

"And you could break your bug jars when you fall."

Jerry's eyes grew big; he grabbed his bug jars as tight as he could. Ms. Opal held in her laughter; however, she was glad he took her seriously.

"Alright, kids, let me and Ms. Min-a-Ling get inside here and get things together."

The kids agreed, then ran back to the go-kart.

Marie went to tap her aunt and ask her what she was going to tell her in the car. However, Marie just waved her hand like never mind. She noticed her aunt was rushing fast as she could to get inside. Ms. Opal dropped a paper out of her sweater when unlocking the front door. She didn't know she had dropped her paper, but Marie picked it up and started reading it.

"Auntie, here's your p...."

It was Ms. Opal's release papers from the hospital. *Life-span: 3-6 months. Medication offered: Morphine.* Marie's heart dropped.

"Now I know why she was thanking me for being here and why she was talking so weird. I know she is elderly, but I wasn't ready for this!"

Marie eased the paper in her pocket and walked inside. Ms. Opal was in the kitchen washing her hands to start on the cookies. She grabbed for a pan, and when she came up, it was slower than usual.

"Ooh! Lord is my deliverance now; my bones hurt extremely!"

Ms. Opal grabbed her apron to put it on. Marie comes behind her to help her with the apron. Her voice was subtle, but you could hear the disappointment.

"When were you going to tell me about this?!"

Marie firmly placed the paper down on the counter in front of Ms. Opal.

"Well, I was going to tell you in the car, but when the kids ran to me, I couldn't break the news to you right then; I'm sorry."

Marie broke down crying.

"See, you are just too kind! You have this time limit, and you are apologizing to me! Auntie No!"

Ms. Opal opened her arms to embrace her niece.

"Oh, it's alright, sweetheart, when you get my age, you can talk about all the fun times we had; nothing has changed. I'm the same sweet old lady, right?"

Marie chuckled through the tears. Ms. Opal pulled up a chair for Marie to have a seat.

"Oh, Auntie."

"You just sit here and learn how to make these cookies so you can make for the neighborhood kids."

She made her signature move and lifted Marie's chin.

"Listen, you just keep your word to auntie. You only make these cookies once a year for the children; I don't want them eating too many sweets. And another thing, I don't care what walk of life or color a child comes from; I want you to cherish all the kids and make sure they all get some. So, when I normally make my batches, I can give them to 30 kids. They don't come around like the days of old, so all the kids can get a few extra, okay?"

Marie grabbed a paper towel to clean her face. "Okay, auntie, let me go wash my hands and get ready to help."

"Okay, sweetheart."

Ms. Opal pulled every ingredient out to make the cookies and placed them on the counter. She never needed measuring cups; she just remembered the recipe by heart from so much experience. Ms. Opal sat down, and it felt like an elephant sat on her. She cried out.

"Ooh, Mr. Marshall, I understand this pain; you ready for me now, ooh, God, help me, this hurts so bad!"

Ms. Opal hugged herself and rocked back and forth. Marie ran out because she heard her aunt calling for her uncle. Marie knew she had no choice but to be strong for her aunt right then. Marie grabbed her car keys and Ms. Opal's sweater. She held her composure while placing the sweater on her aunt.

"Come on, Auntie, I have to take you back to the hospital."

"But, the kids. I promised those kids, I don't break promises to children. I should be fine."

Marie wanted to cry. For God's sake, her aunt was dying, and all she was worried about was keeping a promise to the kids.

"No, auntie, we will make them when we come back."

Marie reassured her aunt; however, neither Ms. Opal nor Marie was sure she was coming back. Marie just knew those words would get her aunt to go. Ms. Opal wanted to keep her promise to the kids, but Marie had to get her aunt to the hospital right away.

"Well, okay, sweetheart, okay."

Isaac saw Ms. Opal and Marie drive away.

"Hey, Ms. Opal may have gone to the store to get the other stuff needed for the cookies. So let's surprise her and go to the other store and get her some medicine so she won't get sick anymore!"

Lema was 99% for it; however, they had not asked anyone.

"But we did not ask anyone, Isaac. David's dad doesn't even know he is out here with us. Uncle Sam acts like David's dad too, when we hang out. So, let's just stay here with the go-kart."

David agreed with Lema.

"Yeah, let's just stay here."

Jerry was getting a little agitated.

"Well, you all can wait. I'm going home. Just tell me when the cookies are done."

"It's okay. At least you stayed out here with us this long. David, Lema, and I will all play catching bugs with you next week."

"We will?!"

Jerry was excited. David and Lema looked at each other in disappointment with Isaac's offer. Instead of Jerry walking off, he stuck around feeling like an equal.

17

Uncle T.J got to the door and knocked a melody on the door with his fist. Brenda opened the door.

"Hey, hey, I mean shit! Uh, I wanted to ask your husband could I take a shower, that's all."

Uncle T.J started to cry. Brenda looked back and saw Samuel was in the room, so she gave T.J. a gesture to come on in. T.J. came in and sat right in Samuel's recliner. Now Brenda was nervous; not only did T.J. reek of alcohol, but he was also drunk. Brenda had a little time to talk, and she forgot T.J. was in Samuel's recliner.

"T.J.? You are such a good person. Just talk to somebody one day about what's troubling you. I don't know fully why my husband has this grudge against you. I do know he looks up to you so much! I can tell Samuel based his entire existence on you, and I really feel he shouldn't take whatever grudge for whatever reason out on you. Anyway! On the other hand, you have to tell a person what is troubling you. Maybe if you give a person an inch of what you are going through and how you feel, that may help in some cases. I don't know, T.J., I just see so much potential in you. I always have brother; everybody keeps yelling how you "used to be" or "could have been" this college professor, but you still have intellect."

T.J.'s face was so wet he looked as if he had grease on it. He took his coat and wiped his face.

"See, you're such a good woman. You remind me of my Jade."

"Well, I met her a few times, and every encounter I had with her I loved. So, I am flattered to be compared to a woman like that."

"Yeah, you kind, loving, and a good homemaker. I just wish my brother sees what he has at home instead of judging me on what he thinks I'm doing or what I don't have. And yeah, college professor, I could have been. So what! I lost my best friend! Sometimes, Bren, I wish I could take her place so she can...."

T.J placed his head down and put his hands over his face. Brenda consoled him placing her hand on his shoulder.

"It's okay brother, let me go get some towels and a fresh bar of soap so you can take a shower. I'm going to the back now, go ask your brother if it's okay. I know he will say yes."

T.J stood up straight, just remembering he was in his brother's chair. However, he did not respond to Brenda; he knew his brother's answer would most likely be no.

"You say yeah, but I know my brother. So I will just wait here and...." Reciting the ring announcer's words. "Get ready to rumble!"

Brenda laughed.

"T.J., you something else."

As Brenda went to the back, T.J. looked around at his brother's family photo. Then, he whispers to a photograph of his brother.

"Man, when you going to love me again, little bro? It may take a tragedy, but I know God will reunite us again. Making us close like we used to be."

As soon as T.J. stopped speaking, Samuel walked into the living room somewhat furious.

"Man, what's up?! I thought you saw me enough today! What's up with this shower you need. You asked my wife instead of me?!"

Brenda cut in.

"Samuel, it wasn't like that I...."

Samuel put his hand in Brenda's face like stop talking.

"Just stay out of it and go on, Brenda!"

"Man, you don't even have to get at her like that! Yeah, I asked her. I know what a good woman she is, so I told her to ask you if I could when I first knocked at your damn door! Then I stayed out here and waited for you! Look how you act. Remember, you, my little brother, I know all your ways! Well, wait, I used to know all your ways, so I figured directly asking you, the new you, would say, no!"

Samuel boldly walked closer to T.J.

"First of all, I am the little brother! And with that your, "use to know me comment," speak for yourself on people changing. How you know if I was going to say yay or nay? Therefore, since you think I'm lingering toward no, to make you happy and show you, I haven't changed at all. NO! How in the hell you come down here and ask me to take a shower at my house. All that money you spend at Jabeeb's and everywhere else, you can get a room for a few days and take a shower!"

Samuel turned his attention to Brenda while sarcastically speaking about T.J.

"Look at him, babe, new shoes, white teeth, and ten-year-old pants and jacket. And that shirt."

Samuel shook his head in utter disappointment. Then, finally, Brenda couldn't take it anymore.

"You know what! I refuse to hear you talk about that man, "your brother," this way. This is just wrong, Samuel!"

Samuel can't stand when his wife is not on his side. So, he lashed out a little on Brenda.

"Oh, you don't have to stand there and listen; go in the back then."

Samuel giggled; Brenda was so mad she threw the towels and soap at Samuel and stormed out the room. Samuel looked at the towel by his feet as if it did not bother him one bit. T.J. was furious.

"Let me tell you something! I'm sick of you judging me! Yeah, my wife died; I didn't finish my degree to become this big "college professor." You have not even sat down with me once and said, "brother, cry on my shoulder, or is there any way I can help you!" But before momma died of her heartache, I never threw it in your face how the neighborhood kids would tease you. Call you gay, and you would play in lipstick and things!"

Samuel couldn't believe he remembered or brought up these things. Samuel looked back to see if Brenda was around or heard any of what T.J. said.

"Yeah, look back, but you ashamed of me, right?! Did I ever judge you? No! And when you made your final decision to be back with a woman, I loved you for whatever choice you made back then, and even now, MUTHA FUCKA! And that is what real families do! And you going to deny me a shower! Not only are you heartless, you SCANDALOUS! I have strangers like Jabeeb offering me jobs that I don't need. That's not even my bloodline! Denying me a shower. Something I need just to cleanse my mind and soul. Something as simple as a shower; are you, serious dude. Wow!"

Samuel ignored T.J.'s entire speech except for what he wanted to hear. He still judged T.J.

"Jabeeb offered your ass a job, and you didn't take it?! See that is what I'm talking about; your pride kicked in, huh? What makes you think you don't need a job, but you need to use my shower?!"

T.J. slammed his hat on the floor.

"You know what! You have a diamond on the outside with a cubic zirconia heart! I never thought I would say this about you, but I...."

A phone went off in T.J.'s pocket; the same side he kept his toothpaste on.

"Look at here, a bum with a cellphone."

Before T.J. answered, he looked at Samuel to address his sarcasm.

"Man, fuck you! I will get back at you in 2 seconds!"

Samuel plopped down in his chair.

"Yeah, hurry up. I'm running out of time and patients to kick you out of my house!"

T.J. answered the phone.

"Yeah, hey, sweetheart? Oh yeah, that's fine. No, I may be on my way soon. I may have to take a shower there, sweetheart, okay? Alright, talk to you later."

Samuel, eager to be nosey and kick T.J. out, was happy T.J. got off the phone, so he could argue with him again.

"So, I heard you say, sweetheart, and can you take a shower over some woman's house. If you have a lady friend, why you ask me to take a shower here then?"

"Well, since you so nosey, along with lack of sense, I told you I've been lost since my wife died. You know, like your brain cells! Anyway, since you have this idiotic grudge with me, your niece, oh yeah, you remember my daughter?! Well, she is 21 now and lives independently. Also, you don't have to give her the cold shoulder you give me. She is almost done with college."

Samuel dropped his head low. He missed his niece and realized he let many years go by not being in her life. He was silent with not so much mouthing off this time.

"Now, I will swallow my pride today. The hell with that, can I take a shower here, or do I have to go across town where my daughter is at."

Brenda loved the lack of mouthing off Samuel had now. She was waiting for Samuel's answer also.

18

The go-kart was dry; Isaac and David stood back and looked at it proudly. They gave each other high-five. They did not clap five with Jerry because they knew this was not his thing, and they respected that.

"Yeah, we did it! We did it, NASCAR brother!"

Lema cleared her throat.

"Excuse you, Isaac, what about me?! I painted some of that car too!"

"EVERYBODY, LOOK AT LEMA!"

He sarcastically clapped.

"Okay, yeah, you helped, but I'm talking about putting the whole car together. That was us."

He pointed to back and forth between himself and David.

"You know a man's creation."

Jerry started to laugh at Lema. She looked at Jerry with the stare, and he stopped laughing.

"A man's job? Please!"

David went up to Lema and placed his arm around her trying to butter her up.

"You helped too, sweetheart. You know you get credit to my love."

Usually, David is scared to approach Lema, however, today, the go-kart is finished, and he is a little bold and on top of the world. Lema could not hold it anymore. She noticed David was acting strange, so she called him on it.

"What is up with you? Boy, get your hands off me. You have been acting strange all summer. You have been coming up with all these names for me and just acting weird."

David looked back and smiled at Jerry and Isaac.

"Okay! I'm tired of being scared. I like you, Lema."

Isaac and Jerry both looked at each other and yelled the same thing.

"Yuk!"

Lema was kind of flattered.

"Y'all need to hush!"

Lema turned back to David. Most of her teeth were showing she was smiling so hard.

"Well, David, I'm not supposed to have no boyfriend."

It seems like when you have a crush on someone, you notice all the rejection they may throw. David noticed Lema did not say, "yuk," like Jerry and Isaac. So he felt he still had a future chance with her.

"Well, I am willing to wait for you until we grow older."

Lema just blushes harder; she was at a loss for words.

"Um?"

"Well, if I would have known something made you quiet, I would have told you he liked you last year."

Isaac laughed, and Jerry giggled. Lema shoved Isaac a little.

"Hush, boy! And why you say yuk, Jerry, I thought you were going home?"

Jerry was getting fed up with Lema.

"Leave me alone bossy girl!"

"Ooh! Jerry came up with a better name than Uncle T.J. did!"

Lema rolled her eyes. "Whatever, Isaac! Let's go to the store to get Ms. Opal's medicine. Is it too far?"

"No, it's just a few blocks away. It's before we get to the all-in-one store, you don't remember? It's just by the busier street."

Lema smiled at David. She liked him also.

"Uh, no, I don't remember, David.

Isaac noticed the chemistry. He cut right in because he was getting sick to his stomach.

"Lema, you didn't notice probably because we were playing our car game, but we passed it up. It was just on the opposite side of the street, Lema."

"Well, let's just go and hurry back. This is the first time I feel we may get busted because we are not asking permission. So I just want to hurry up and help Ms. Opal."

"Ms. Opal?"

"What are you thinking about, Jerry?! Yeah, Ms. Opal. Before she gets back."

David and Isaac decided to push the go-kart while Lema steered. Jerry just liked being with the kids.

"Well, I just want to get another bug net. Do you guys think they have them there? I want to come too."

Lema looked down at Jerry's shoes; that was her cue to tell Jerry no. She actually really cared about Jerry; however, she was not into bugs either. She, David, and Isaac didn't know how to tell him that without hurting his feelings.

"Uh, just stay, plus your shoes are untied anyway."

Jerry became a little upset. But, nevertheless, he wanted to hang out with them, even if that meant he was doing something he really didn't want to do, which is walking a lot.

"Well, Lema, I may not know how to tie my shoes. And plus, my mom never says anything so, I'll be fine. Besides, what do my shoes untied have to do with anything?"

"Lema, leave him alone! Just let him come on, he's our friend, and he's been with us all day, so what's the difference now!"

"Yeah, you pretty and all, but I agree with Isaac. So, Jerry, get your jars, and let's go."

"Yeah, she's pretty, pretty ugly."

Isaac laughed hard at his own joke. Then, already upset because she felt outnumbered, she balled her fist to Isaac.

"You got one more time, and I'm going to forget you my cousin!"

They all headed to the store.

As they pushed Lema, they stopped at the busy street corner to wait for Jerry since he was so slow. Once they noticed Jerry made it to the corner, Isaac and David looked both ways and started to push Lema across the street. They ran through so they could get to the other side. Isaac figured Jerry was right behind them, but he looked back to make sure. Lema got out the go-kart, and David looked back for Jerry also. He was in the middle of the street, still crossing. Jerry tripped off his shoelaces in the middle of the street. One of his bug jars rolls in the road; as Jerry went to grab the jar, Lema screamed.

"NO!"

Isaac and David ran to try to pull Jerry to the curb. A Chevrolet Suburban with a husband, wife, and kids tried to stop. The husband slammed on the brakes, the car tire screeched and slammed into Jerry. The hard impact made the SUV turn sideways and knocked Isaac and David slamming them into the curb. The wife and kids in the car scream. Bystanders stopped their cars. Lema was hysterical. Her cousin Isaac was thrown right by the go-kart on the curb, bleeding, and David was also slammed into the curve, crying.

Isaac was screaming, "OUCH! MAMA! LEMA, GET JERRY! GET JERRY!"

Lema was screaming, "GOD HELP US!"

David looked over at Isaac. His voice sounded rough.

"Isaac, you are bleeding! Your entire face is bleeding! I can't move my legs, Isaac!"

The wife of the driver ran to David and Isaac. She looked back and yelled to her kids to stay in the truck. She then grabbed Lema.

"Try to calm down, sweetheart, try to calm down. I'm a nurse, I'm hysterical too, trust me, But I need you right now, sweetie. I need answers to give to the ambulance. My name is Carla, okay, I need the young men to speak as least as possible to help themselves, okay?"

Lema nodded her head but was still shaken up.

"What is your name?"

Lema busted out crying.

"I DON'T CARE ABOUT MY NAME, JUST HELP MY COUSIN AND FRIENDS! NOOO!"

The husband had already called the police. Many innocent bystanders started to place covers and towels under and over Isaac, David, and Jerry. Jerry had broken ribs, so it hurt for him to breathe.

The driver's tears began to roll down his face.

"Oh, GOD! I'm Sorry! Young man, my name is Mike, we are going to help you. Just stay put!"

Of course, Jerry couldn't move; however, the guy was definitely at a loss for words.

"It hurts when I breathe; I'm scared."

Jerry kept looking around at all the people surrounding him. Mike looked in the SUV at his own kids and then at Jerry, which made him cry even more. Carla was checking the pulse of David and Isaac. One bystander tried to attempt to move Isaac and David onto the curve.

"Hey, let's move these kids off the street onto the curb."

"No! Please! My name is Carla. I'm a nurse, do not move the boys. You may fracture or break something else."

She pointed to David and then to Isaac.

"This one can't feel his legs, and that one has fractured his face."

The innocent bystander stepped back and wiped his own face; he had started to cry, wishing it was something he could have done.

"Just stay calm, sir. Thank you for your gesture, and keep praying for everyone; that will help tremendously. He nodded his head in agreement.

19

Samantha sat up fast in a panic.

"Did you hear that, Steve?!"

Steve waved his hand in a careless motion.

"Yeah, I heard it. There are always accidents down the way where that busy street is. You should be familiar with the accidents by now, Sam."

Samantha picked up the clothes basket and threw it to the side. She ran out the door and into the middle of the street, hoping to see David and the other kids. Instead, she noticed everything was gone except their paintbrushes and buckets.

"DAVID!!"

"What is wrong with you?! Why are you yelling like a madwoman?! David is in his room!"

Steve started thinking; that was not a regular yell from his wife. Steve ran into David's room only to see he was not in there. Finally, Steve figured out what that scream was about, so he snatched his truck keys and rushed out the door. He jumped in the truck, rushed down the street, and flung open the passenger door where Samantha was.

"GET IN NOW!"

Steve got to the end of the block, where he clearly noticed the paint bucket and paintbrushes. He made a sharp turn toward the busy street where the accidents usually occur. Samantha sat rocking back and forth.

"O.H., G.O.D.! PLEASE! PLEASE LET IT NOT BE MY SON AND THOSE OTHER BABIES! PLEASE!"

Brenda was the first to notice.

"Did you two hear that?!"

T.J. looked toward the door.

"Yeah."

"Some idiots probably driving fast like usual and crashed. That's why I only let Isaac go to the one-in-all store. That other store, it is too busy and crazy on that road."

Brenda looked down the street; then went outside the door.

"Excuse me, T.J."

T.J. moved to the side.

"Oh, no problem, sis."

Brenda got to the bottom of the steps, looked down the street, and noticed the kids were not there.

"SAMUEL! WHERE ARE THE KIDS!"

Samuel jumped out of his chair.

"What you mean, where are they? They were just down the street!"

He ran out to where Brenda was and saw the confused look on her face.

"Bro, get my keys, now!"

T.J. didn't think twice about it. He got the picture and the frame on what they thought was going on with the kids. He also wondered when Brenda and Samuel saw they were not down there. T.J. hurried up and threw the keys to Samuel. They all jumped in the car. When they got to the place where Samantha and Steve were, near the materials and paint, Brenda had that same mother's instinct as Samantha.

"Oh, Lord, have mercy! Please let these kids be okay!"

T.J. looked at Brenda, knowing only a mother could have the instinct she had.

"Step on it, man! Step on it!"

Samuel was frustrated and nervous.

"Just sit back, man! I'm trying!"

Samantha kneeled down by her son in disgust and crying.

"OH, GOD, IT'S ALL MY FAULT. IT'S ALL MY FAULT!"

Brenda broke down, screaming, and ran to Isaac.

"LORD, NOOO, WHY LORD?!"

"Mama! Mama!"

"Look at my baby's face!"

Brenda glanced around at the entire scene to see if her niece, David, and Jerry were alright. Brenda noticed Lema was shaken up but still at a place where she could talk. So, Brenda started to ask questions.

"How did this happen! HOW!"

Lema was still in Carla's arms, who was attempting to calm her down; however, when she saw her aunt, she felt guilt all over again."

"You get down here!"

Carla and Lema walked a few steps to where Isaac was.

"Auntie, I'm SORRY! I knew something would go wrong because we didn't ask but not this auntie! Isaac and David were just trying to help Jerry. Jerry tripped over his shoelaces in the middle of the street!"

Uncle T.J. was holding Samuel; however, Samuel managed to snatch away in an uproar, using foul language. T.J. was in shock, glancing at the entire scene. He looked in the middle of the street, remembering just a little while ago helping Jerry with his laces. He looked over at his nephew and got choked up. As he glanced at Jerry then at David, he noticed Steve gave him and his brother, Samuel, the dirtiest look. Samuel noticed and gave Steve the same dirty look. T.J. whispered.

"Oh, Lord, I see where this is headed. Please help us. Right now, it's about these kids, and my brother and Steve are being selfish, Lord. Samuel heard T.J., so he snapped.

"What the hell you mean, selfish! That asshole never wanted my son to play with his! It don't matter now, damn it, because both kids are hurt!"

Steve got up, not thinking. He and Samuel were so worried about getting at each other they did not consider the importance of the kids. Steve walked over to Samuel.

"Look here, you jerk! My fucking kid is laid out on the got damn sidewalk! You know why? Because he went against my beliefs, and I allowed him to! But from this day forward, he will not play with your son!"

"Oh, how you think I feel, Punk?! You better get the hell out my face before you regret it!

"My son even playing with your son, I regret!"

"Fuck you, Whitey!"

"And the hell with you, Nigger!"

Samuel and Steve both grabbed each other, tussling and fighting. Uncle T.J. tried to break it up.

Brenda and Samantha both yelled.

"JUST STOP IT!"

Samantha was disgusted with Steve's behavior.

"STEVE, YOU ASS, STOP IT! THINK ABOUT THE DAMN KIDS!"

Carla looked up and saw the E.M.T., so she ran and told them what was going on. Lema kneeled down between David and Isaac. She glanced over at Jerry, then started to ball her eyes out again.

T.J. finally stopped the fight. He was in an uproar because Steve and Samuel were acting so uncivilized.

"WHAT THE HELL IS WRONG WITH THE TWO OF YOU FOOLS?! LOOK AT WHAT IS LYING ON THE GROUND! ALL THESE KIDS ARE DAMAGED! AND LET'S NOT FORGET ABOUT JERRY'S PARENTS, WHO ARE NOT EVEN HERE YET!"

T.J. snatched the both of them up by their collars and grunted his teeth while speaking.

"Now, both of you are supposed to be grown, men. Look at those kids again, and if you tell me there is different color blood over there, maybe I can try to understand your ignorance! Three innocent kids need us. Four when you count that poor baby, Lema. But all you two care about is your hatred toward each other! Think!"

Steve jerked away from T.J.

"Get your hands off of me! I have a half-dead son to tend to. I remember where I saw you before, you drunk! That's all you are!"

Samuel snatched away from his brother as well.

"That's the only thing I agree with Whitey on since I met him. Yeah, let me go too drunk ass!"

T.J. was so angry you could cook an egg on his head. But, he ignored their stupidity and got back to the situation at hand. He introduced himself to Mike before he kneeled by Jerry since his parents were not out there yet.

"Hey, man, I'm T.J."

"I'm Mike. This just should not have happened!"

Jerry looked up at Uncle T.J. panting from broken ribs.

"I'm sorry, Mr. T.J."

"What's going on, little Biggy?! What are you sorry for?"

Mike noticed how familiar they were with each other.

"You tied my shoes, but they came loose."

T.J. looked down, and instantly tears ran down his face. Uncle T.J. pieced two and two together, figured out how the accident happened. He had a lump in his throat.

"Just stay still guy, it's not your fault at all."

The E.M.T. got the stretcher out and politely told T.J. to step aside as they tended to Jerry.

"I want my bug jars, and give them two Isaac and David, please."

T.J. turned around and cried harder. Everybody knew Jerry loved his bugs and bug jars more than life itself, so for Jerry to give them away was a huge gesture for him. It was his way of saying thank you to his friends. As they took Jerry away, Uncle T.J. ran over to Isaac before they took him. He looked at Isaac and David, and his anger grew, but he remained speechless. Carla was still trying to handle the situation when she approached T.J. By this time, he was so nervous and worried he was squeezing the life out of his hat.

"Sir, name please?"

"Oh, yeah, hi, I'm T.J."

"Yeah, I noticed you were with Isaac's family. That's my husband over there that was by the other kid involved in the accident."

T.J. looked back at her husband. He gave a second look since Carla was white and Mike was black. It was not uncommon today; however, T.J. wouldn't have guessed that was her husband.

"Yeah, oh, okay, he's a cool person. He kept blaming himself; Mike must have been the one driving while my nephew and his friends were crossing the street, huh?"

"Yes. And I really thank you for saying my husband is a really cool guy. Did you see the whole thing? And did you go get the parents?"

"Oh, no, I just know that my nephew, niece, and his friends always stick together. And I know their friend, your husband was by, never ties his shoes. I know David and my nephew would have come to Jerry's aid. This is so sad; they just don't deserve this."

"Tell me about it! My husband really tried to avoid all of this from happening. Our entire family is going to therapy after this!"

Yeah, I may go to more than therapy after this!"

T.J. was thinking of A.A. meetings. Carla sized T.J. up. With her experience as a nurse, she could tell he was a drinker; however, she did not judge him.

"Yeah, I hear you."

She reached into her purse and pulled out a card to a good therapist and A.A. drug and alcohol counselor and placed it in T.J.'s hand.

"I'm a nurse, by the way, so I have to get up to the hospital and meet your family and the other young child's family. I saw no one for, uh?"

"Jerry?"

"Yeah, Jerry's family."

"They stay next door to David, my nephew's friend. I'm pretty sure they will get in contact with his guardian. I think he stays with his mom only."

"Oh, okay. Well, my husband and I will see you at the hospital. They are going to St. Medical Hospital over on...."

"Yeah, I know where that is. I'm going home to check on my daughter and let her know about this tragic situation. I have to get cleaned up, and then I'll be over there."

David's and Isaac's families were at the hospital. The bystanders, cops, and ambulance were all gone. T.J. walked away just as Jabeeb pulled up alongside him in his brand new Camaro.

"My friend, get in. I heard of the tragedy! What can I do?! I'm so sorry!"

T.J. looked at him appreciative but was at a loss for words. He was reliving the argument and the tragedy that he had just witnessed.

"Where are you going? Hospital, right? I will take you there. Say something, my friend, just tell me how I can help?!"

"Alright, take me to my house."

"Your house?! Oh, okay, I thought you lived outside; you would talk about the classified you slept under felt like a comforter."

T.J. smiled as he got in the car.

"Yeah, I'm weird like that. I like to sleep with the paper over my head. I love books, so that gives me comfort and darkness. When I'm covered with words, I can sleep better."

"Oh, well, whatever floats your boat, friend. Where to?"

Although they laughed, they were both still nervous about the whole situation. T.J. pointed Jabeeb in the direction of his house.

20

David, Isaac, and Jerry were taken straight into the intensive care unit. Carla gave sufficient information to the hospital about what happened. She then went to assist Brenda and Samantha; they were extremely shaken up. Finally, Carla left the waiting room to go talk to her husband, Mike.

"Babe, I'm so glad your sister decided not to go on her trip out of town and was available to watch the kids. We were headed for a vacation too, just never knew it was going to be a disaster on the way!"

Mike hugged his wife tightly. Carla was hurt even though she did not cry. She was a nurse, so she saw these things all the time; however, it just hit home since her family was involved. It was little children her husband had accidentally hit.

"Yeah, honey, I am a nervous wreck! I am so, so, sorry!"

Carla felt her husband's tears on top of her head. She looked up to reassure his heart and to console hers.

"Honey, is it too much to ask if you could run to Wendy's up the street? We need to put something in our stomachs, and I need to stay here just in case they have further questions."

"Sure, honey. It may take a minute, though, because I'm walking there. I still cannot drive; I'm still shaken up."

Carla felt bad for her husband.

"Okay, my love, I will wait here no matter how long it takes; I understand."'

Mike left to get food. Carla sat down in the I.C.U. room to try to regroup. Steve came to the waiting room to take a breather.

"Excuse me, hey, what's going on?"

Steve remembered her from the crime scene and recognized she was the nurse. Steve was friendly with Carla, trying to show his appreciation.

"Oh, hey, yeah, the nurse!"

"Yes."

Carla thought Steve recognized her; however, she knew there was a lot that went on.

"Yeah, well, my son cannot feel his legs still. I told my wife, see what happens when you hang with the Blacks. It will always be a tragedy! Now my damn son may not walk again!"

Carla was disgusted by Steve's comment; however, she was very professional. She now knew Steve had not noticed her kids and husband. Steve's wife was the one that gathered all details and knew who's who, things women usually do.

"Everybody's entitled to their opinion."

"Opinion my foot, that's a fact! My wife got all the details on what happened from you; you were there. I'm just glad a highly educated nurse was on the scene. I just want my son to get well. My wife keeps crying her eyes out. I hope now she listens to things I say; however, telling somebody I told you so when they are hurting is not right."

Carla was going with the flow of the conversation, even though she was gritting her teeth at his arrogance.

"Well, we women tend to be hard-headed sometimes. However, telling someone I told you so when they are hurting is not right. Isaac ran after Jerry to save him, just like David, did you know that?"

Steve's face showed remorse; however, he did not respond to Carla's comment acting like he did not hear that part.

Yeah, well, listen to your husband, especially when he is giving you wise counsel."

Carla smiled, anticipating Steve meeting her husband. She knew Steve would eat his words once he did.

"You will meet my husband. You two have the same views on that! And I will take your advice and listen to my husband."

"Well, my name is Smith, Mr. Steve Smith."

Carla was disgusted by his cockiness.

"Okay, Mr. Steve Smith, I hate to be the barrier of bad news, but I really need to call that young boy's, Jerry, parents. I'm pretty sure his mom would like to know where Jerry is by now."

Steve folded his arms.

"Huh, please, his mom barely noticed that the go-kart was...."

He stopped himself and placed his head down. He felt bad that he used Jerry for his evil doings. Then Steve started to actually think about his kid that was hurt and Jerry, in addition, Isaac. But Steve was so callous he would not speak on it.

"That was what, Steve?"

"Never mind. Jerry's mom is listed, plus she stays on the phone. Her name is Janice Sinclair. She is loaded with money! Let's just say that's Jerry's A.T.M!"

Steve laughed. Carla grabbed the phone, not finding anything amusing about Steve's comment.

"What do you mean?"

"I say what I mean. Janice just gives Jerry money and sends him on his way. She is alright besides never helping him learn to keep his shoes tied. The entire neighborhood gets tired of seeing it. I was just happy Jerry started to play with my boy again.

Carla ignored his last comment and got Ms. Sinclair's number from the phone book.

21

Samantha looked at her son as he slept so peacefully. Then, she stepped into the lobby to call Linda. Samantha knew by now Linda was at her house. Samantha was shaking, unsure if her son would walk again; however, she could call her sister. Linda was someone Samantha always confided in. She had to let his auntie know, so Samantha dialed.

"Hello!"

"Hey, Linda, where are you?"

"Where am I? Uh, sitting in front of your house, hello! The only reason I am still sitting here is that I'm on the phone with my sweetheart. We were just sweet-talking and girl...."

Samantha yelled, cutting Linda off.

"LINDA, JUST SHUT UP!"

Linda moved the phone from her ear, looked at the telephone crazy, and placed it back on her ear.

"Excuse me?!"

"I put my son in the damn hospital, Lin' when I let him go outside against Steve's will! He went to play with Isaac, Jerry, and the southern girl and, and...."

Samantha got choked up. Linda became instantly nervous and began to cry.

"And what, Sam?! And what! Please, God. Please don't let my sister go through what I went through! What is wrong with my nephew!"

"He's not dead Lin'."

Linda calmed down; however, she was still a wreck since this involved her family.

"He can't feel his legs right now. The nurse, Carla, was nice; she said it may be temporary."

Samantha explained what the nurse and doctors have been telling her and everything that happened."

"You know what?! I am right here in front of Janice's house. You know, time and time again, I tried to stay out of it when it came to Jerry and how his mother brushes him off! I have some words for her! She is not up there with her son! Her damn BMW she loves so much is right here. And let's not forget about her precious phones she cannot part from and...."

Linda was furious and on a roll; however, Samantha cut her sister off. She just didn't want the drama right now.

"Please, Linda, do not go causing a ruckus! Janice Sinclair has not been informed her son is up here yet. Carla said she would call. But, unfortunately, I just don't have the energy."

Linda understood her sister's pain; she just did not want to hear any excuses from Ms. Sinclair.

"Yeah, you think?! Why do you think she doesn't know, Sam?! I betcha Janice is on that phone right now as we speak! After I notify Ms. Sinclair, I'm on my way up there, sis."

Samantha knew her sister all too well.

"Well, there goes the neighborhood. Just do what you got to do and get up here. We need you!"

"Okay, sis, just keep the faith. I will be there shortly."

Linda hung up with her sister and looked back at Ms. Sinclair's door, mugging. She got out, slammed her door, headed to Jerry's front door, and banged harder than usual. Ms. Sinclair walked to the door; however, she was on the phone laughing. Linda was irritated.

"You have got to be kidding me."

Sinclair swung the door open some and glanced out.

"Oh, but I think this is my neighbor at the door, so I will call you back."

Ms. Sinclair hung up, still smiling from her telephone conversation. Linda, however, was not smiling one bit.

"Uh, excuse me, I was wondering where your son, Jerry, is?! My nephew stays next door. I heard you say I was your neighbor, but my sister and her husband are your neighbors."

Ms. Sinclair looked Linda up and down but not in a negative way.

"Wow, you really look like your sister!"

Ms. Sinclair smiled at Linda and reached her hand out.

"Janice, I am Ms. Janice Sinclair."

Linda was ready to cut the small talk and get down to the nitty-gritty. She did not shake Ms. Sinclair's hand.

"Yeah, I have seen you around. Anyway, my question, please?!"

Ms. Sinclair put her hand down.

"Oh, well, okay, uh. Oh, yeah, Jerry is with your nephew, right?"

"Look, you know what?! Your son is in the hospital with broken ribs because his ***shoelaces*** were not tied. Jerry was hit by a car; my nephew and his other friends were victims too! I don't regret the kids helping Jerry, but what I do regret is...."

Linda took a deep breath and sighed.

"Me not coming over here to give you a piece of my mind about how much those shoelaces troubled me. But now those untied shoelaces have caused a tragedy, and the sad part, you don't even know where Jerry is!"

"You know what, don't judge me!"

Ms. Sinclair placed her phone in her pocket, grabbed her keys off the key rack, then she raced out her door, slightly shoving Linda out the way.

"Excuse me!"

"While you shoving people and almost sending me to jail, do you know what hospital he is in?!"

At her BMW, she franticly turned around.

"The way you rudely approached me, I am pretty sure you will tell me!"

Linda felt a little remorse seeing how frantic Janice was. She could not understand how Janice paid no attention to her child. Linda lost her child to a car accident and would do anything to trade places with a parent; however, Linda wanted no parent to go through her experience. Most of Linda's prying was out of concern as she flashed back on her loss. She walked up to Ms. Sinclair and placed her hand on her shoulder.

"Look, deep down inside, I really did not mean to come off so aggressive; however, I will not take back how I feel or what I said. And please pay attention to your son; it is a blessing to have money for your son, but to lose a child is devastating. I have experienced that. Jerry is at St. Medical Hospital. I have to go to the hospital to be with my sister, and we could talk later if you like."

Ms. Sinclair was at a loss for words; however, she gave Linda a nod of agreement. Linda returned to her car. Janice jumped in her car to head to the hospital but first pulled up alongside Linda. She finally found some words to say, and she spoke them softly.

"Thank you."

Linda nodded her head as a jester to say, your welcome. Then, they headed in the same direction toward the hospital.

Ms. Sinclair was almost at the hospital when her cell phone rang. She was in a hurry and expressed a bit of road rage.

"Hello! Hurry up and move, you idiot!"

Carla moved the phone from her ear because of all the yelling.

"Oh, hello, Ms. Sinclair? Is this Ms. Sinclair, Jerry's mother?"

"Yes, yes, I have to go my son was in an accident. I'm on the way to tend to him. I can't talk right now. Is this about his piano lesson? If so, we can talk later, but please, I got to go."

Carla was not worried about Ms. Sinclair brushing her off; she was relieved that Janice knew Jerry was in the hospital.

"Okay, I will let you go. This is the nurse. I see you've heard, good. I will talk to you when you get here."

"Yeah, yeah, okay."

Ms. Sinclair hung up quickly. Minutes later, she arrived at the hospital. She found Jerry's room number and rushed straight to his room.

22

T.J. and Jabeeb spoke of so many things and situations while riding in the car.

"Yeah, now turn left after 5 streetlights on Mayhill Way."

Jabeeb realized this was a hop, skip, and a jump from where he lived himself.

"Uh, is it something you want to tell me, my friend?"

"Is there something you want to know?"

They finally stopped at the destination, 137 Mayhill Ct. The home was immaculate with wide double doors. Jabeeb cut off the car after he parked. He paused and stared at T.J.

"Who knew! Such a humble man; you have a big house, and you stand in front of my liquor store as if you have nothing! Why?!

"Look here, man, material items mean nothing since I lost my wife. She died too young, man. Once she left my life, I tried to stay strong for my little girl, but that woman was an angel. My wife loved me before I was the known professor, and once she became rich, she only enjoyed the good life for a short time."

T.J.'s head dropped so low if he had blinked, tears would have rolled down his face.

"Jabeeb, man, she just wanted to open up a rehabilitation center, and she didn't get her chance."

Jabeeb placed his hand on T.J.'s shoulder.

"You know, you have to enjoy the good times you and your wife had, my friend! I feel she is looking down on you right now. I know your wife is pleased because you both have a place where your girl can call home. However, my friend, do you think your wife wants you to not take care of yourself? If she wants to rehabilitate people, why not start with a person she loves, which is you!"

"Thank you so much."

T.J. pondered what happened between Carla and himself.

"I received my third sign, now that gives me hope for sobriety! Come on, Jabeeb, my daughter, would love to meet you. I tell her about you often, and then I can get ready to go to the hospital."

Jabeeb considered it an honor to meet his friend's offspring.

"Well, that's a plan; come on, let's do it!"

As they enter the house, T.J. starts to sing part of a Prince song.

"Baaaby, Baaaaby, Baaaaaaby!"

In comes this 5'7 slender young lady who was the spitting image of T.J. Jabeeb looked over at T.J. smiling so hard he showed all his teeth.

"No denying that one, my friend!"

They both laughed in agreement. Toni hadn't heard their conversation but politely reached out to shake Jabeeb's hand.

"Hi, my name is Toni. How are you; you must be Jabeeb?"

"Hello, young lady. So, your father has talked about me, huh?"

"Yeah, my dad said your store prices are too high, that's all."

Jabeeb's smile dropped as he looked over at T.J. Toni, and T.J. bust out laughing.

"Baby, you just do not understand I needed that laugh."

Toni looked over at Jabeeb.

"Oh, I'm just kidding. Do you want anything to eat or drink?"

"She looks like you and has your sense of humor too! I will take whatever you have, but something quick, my dear, we have to go back to the hospital."

Toni looked over at her dad.

"Hospital?!"

T.J. sat his daughter down and explained everything to her, even starting from the beginning when T.J and Samuel argued. Toni started to cry, and Jabeed and T.J consoled her as much as they could with kind words of wisdom. Then, Toni got herself together and brought Jabeeb a beverage and a danish. T.J went upstairs to get cleaned up so he could return to the hospital. Toni decided to talk to Jabeed. She liked his character and wise counsel.

"Jabeeb, I feel it's time for my dad and my uncle to come around. I really haven't been around my uncle since I was a teen; now I'm 21!"

She shook her head in disgust.

"Yeah, I feel the same way, young lady. I do not like what happened either. But my grandma would always say, 'everything happens for a reason, no matter of the time or the season.'"

Toni laughed at his hideous voice imitation; however, she nodded in agreement.

"Yes, that is true! And my mom used to always say whenever I leave this earth, look at the light at the end of the tunnel, not the turmoil it takes to get to the end."

Toni put her head down and thought of her mom. Jabeeb noticed the sadness, so he tried to shed some light on the situation to cheer her up.

"We both had some wise women in our lives, right, Ms. Lady?"

Toni remained speechless, giving him a smile. She could see why her dad befriended Jabeeb.

23

At the hospital in I.C.U., one of the doctors spoke to Isaac's father, Samuel. Brenda sat at Isaac's side, reading him a book.

"So, doc, listen, what's the outcome?"

"Come on, sir, let's step out here."

He pointed to the hallway. Then he opened up Isaac's chart.

"Okay, listen up, Mr.?"

"You can just call me Samuel."

"Very well, Samuel. It is not so good. He fractured pieces of the maxilla and mandible. We have to keep giving him Motrin for a few days until the swelling goes down. When the medicine wears off, you will know it. Isaac will be in tremendous pain for anybody, but especially for a 9-year-old. Until then, we will run more tests. I need to get over to the other parents. Isaac's best friend, right?"

He closed the chart and looked up at Samuel with a smile. Samuel didn't smile back, but he agreed verbally.

"Yeah, yeah, uh, that's his friend."

"Maybe later we can have one of you visit the other child. Isaac speaks highly of his buddy."

Samuel felt terrible now and in distress. He dwelt on memories of when he was a kid and his auntie's Caucasian boyfriend, Richard, inappropriately touched him. When she would go to work, Richard was supposed to babysit him. Samuel remembered being outside at the playground, and Richard told him to come into the house. Richard would make him go into his auntie's room, follow behind him and close the door.

Samuel snapped out of his daydream. He goes back into the room with Brenda and Isaac. He sat down and explained to Brenda what the doctor said. Isaac moaned.

"Ouch! Oh! Mama, daddy, help me; it hurts for me to talk or move my face!"

Tears rolled down Isaac's face.

"Where is David? Mama, help him!"

Brenda had the biggest lump in her throat. She turned away for a moment.

"Isaac, please, baby, stop talking, just lay here, baby, please, be still."

Samuel hated himself right then. He clenched his fist, looked at Brenda, then back at Isaac with a blank stare. Brenda tried to make out that look.

"Baby, what's wrong? What's the matter?! I know this is hard for...."

"I will be back, Bren."

Samuel swiftly walked to the door.

"Daddy, please, come back. Where are you going?!"

Samuel held the door so hard that he could've snatched it off. He didn't dare look Isaac's way.

"I got to go get some fresh air, son; I will be back."

Brenda was puzzled. She had never seen him like this. Samuel never left a serious situation in the 8 years she had been with him.

24

Steve was called back into I.C.U. with Samantha. They received the news about David.

"Okay, Mr. and Mrs. Smith, I've never enjoyed giving bad results in my entire career."

Samantha sighed.

"Dr., please, don't hold back. What's going with our son, please?!

Samantha cried as Steve rubbed her shoulders to calm her down. He was anxious about the news as well.

"Well, David is temporarily paralyzed from the waist down."

Samantha's knees got weak, and she almost fell to the ground. Steve held onto her.

"Oh, my God!"

"I know, I'm sorry, but please listen. We have the best physical therapist here that will whip your son back into shape. You two have to keep up the appointments and comply with the physical therapist recommendations step by step, okay?"

Tears streamed down Samantha's face. She just held her mouth and shook her head in agreement. Steve looked at the doctor's name tag.

"Thank you so much, Dr. Andrews. By the way, how much would the treatment cost?"

"Well, if we include the fees and treatment, it will cost about $43,000."

Samantha cried harder and placed her head in Steve's chest. Steve held her, and he thought.

"Okay, we have to come up with it some kind of way. Unfortunately, our savings is only half of that; we may just have to take out a loan on our house."

"Okay, Mr. Smith, I will let you discuss that matter over with your wife confidentially. Then, let me know your family's decision. I know this is hard, so take some time."

The Dr. walked away as Samantha and Steve discussed things.

"Babe, how are we going to come up with this money?! We already took out a loan on our house!"

"I know this, Sam, just go back in there with Dave, I will come up with something, some kind of way!"

Samuel was in the waiting room, rocking in a chair. Carla looked over at Samuel, remorseful, as she thought about all the parents and kids involved. Just then, Steve came into the waiting room. He noticed, so he sat way on the other side. Samuel looked up at Steve and rolled his eyes. Carla noticed the tension. As she looked away, her husband came into the waiting room with the food, passing it to Carla.

"Here you go, sweetheart."

"Thank you, hon'."

Both Steve and Samuel looked at Carla and Mike, and they both huffed. Steve rolled his eyes at Carla. He had no clue her husband was a black guy. Mike was ready to explode when he saw the looks and heard the huffs and puffs.

"Honey, what's that about?!"

Carla whispered to her husband so he could calm down and ignore Steve and Samuel both.

"Not trying to be rude, my dear, but you know we face this kind of judgment all the time from somebody. So, you can figure out what it is, just please, don't bite into it, babe."

"Yeah, you are right, babe."

Linda walked into the waiting room and looked right at Steve. Then looked around at everyone and spoke. Steve's eyebrows were touching; he was so upset at her for speaking to everyone. Linda tapped Steve.

"Hey, which room is Dave in?"

"Room 37."

Linda went to the door and called to be buzzed in to be with her sister and nephew. Once inside, she tried to use humor to not cry, making the matter worse for her sister.

"Nephew, if you wanted auntie to stay and give you lemonade, that is all you had to say. You didn't have to drive to the store and get some."

Samantha smiled, something she hadn't done for a long time. David hugged his auntie as tight as possible, and tears fell from Linda's eyes onto David's shirt.

"Auntie, are you trying to get lemonade on my shirt?"

Both Linda and Samantha laughed; however, they both had crocodile tears. Linda was glad her nephew was in good spirits; this helped her hold herself together even better. Linda and Samantha sat with David, trying to make him as comfortable as possible.

25

Ms. Opal heard familiar laughter. She tried to sit up to hear better, adjusting her oxygen machine in her nose. Ms. Opal's niece, Maria, also known by her new nickname, Ming, is sound asleep next to her. Even though Ms. Opal was in room 31, elderly, she always had excellent hearing. She shook her niece.

"Marie, Marie."

"Yes, auntie?"

"I hear moaning and groaning, and I also heard a kid say, is David okay. When Isaac scrapped his finger, and I bandaged him up, that was the same sound he made but less excruciating."

Marie did not know what her auntie was getting at, having just awakened from her sleep.

"Uh, okay."

"All I am saying, sweetie, is I just really want to know if that is Isaac. Will you go see, please?"

"Auntie, you already have to deal with you. You have the oxygen tank now and other elements. I am not being rude but get you some rest. That can't be one of the kids we just saw on the way back to the hospital; they were just fine."

"Now, I never forget a face or a voice. I just don't remember at times where I place my things. So, I am not delusional, and I have good hearing, plus I know all my babies' voices. So, will you go check, please!"

Ms. Opal looks right into Marie's eyes.

The neighborhood kids are my God-given kids. I just would not live my last days comfortably if I couldn't find out if that is one of mine. I always go with my first mind. Marie, you listen, your first mind is what you should do, and your second thought is what you want to do. Always remember that. Even when I am gone, Marie."

Marie grew a little teary-eyed.

"Okay, okay. For you and the children's sake, I will go check to reassure you, okay."

Ms. Opal nodded. Marie got up and placed the cover over her aunt. Ms. Opal smiled as Marie left. Marie went to the right and walked down the hall. As she got to door number 36, she stopped when she heard talking. Marie stopped because the door was cracked and, low and behold, heard Isaac's voice too. She listened in on Isaac and his mom talking.

"Mom, what did the lady put in that water up there?"

"Baby, that is I.V. solution, not water. The doctor puts medicine in that bag, and it gets to you. That is why you are able to talk a bit better without being in pain."

"Oh."

Brenda was more than ready to share with Isaac how some whites died helping blacks out of love for us. She began to talk slowly as she rubbed his head.

"You know who you and David remind me of?"

"I know, Uncle T.J. told us, is it Wesley Snaps and Widey Allen on a movie he always talks about?"

Brenda laughed, and Marie giggled in the hallway.

"That is Wesley Snipes and Woody Harrelson, but no, not those two, even though I love that movie too. I'm talking about one black and two white guys in 1964, named James Chaney, Andrew Goodman, and Michael Schwerner. They were trying to help the blacks in the civil rights movement in Mississippi, and the K.K.K. killed them. When whites helped blacks back in the day, they were called Nigger lovers. I can't leave Jerry out; he cares for you two also. I don't know when but I am glad you all included him in your project, even though that baby got hurt too."

Brenda put her head down. Isaac looked sad.

"Yeah. Mama, why did they hate us blacks so much?"

"Well, prejudice is a learned behavior. You are not born prejudiced. Plus, not just blacks and whites; other races hate each other. You can have people prejudiced if they do not like someone's size, and different religions argue as well. This confusion is from people being raised a certain way. If your dad, David's parents, and I do not stop, we will be just like those others, teaching our children hatred. The misunderstanding cycle will never be broken, and the world will stay just like it is now, full of greed, jealousy, and hatred."

"Mom, you are not like that! Why did you say if you and dad don't stop?"

"Son, I'm not innocent. I was prejudiced for a while. But, you and David showed me it just don't make sense! You, David, and Jerry were almost killed together, with you two trying to save your friend, Jerry. Not even thinking about color, but that you guys cared for each other like the three guys in the Mississippi killing. Plus, almost losing a child makes you realize what's important. When your dad, David's parents, and I were out there for our kids, trust, color was not the issue because it was all the same red blood you were bleeding."

Brenda leaned over Isaac, crying very hard.

"I'M SO SORRY, S.O.N.!"

Isaac cried as well, mostly because his mom was hurt.

"Mama, don't cry like you told me; God will give you another chance before anybody does! So since God sees you are hurt, He will forgive you, mama."

Marie was also in tears; however, she wiped her face clean and pushed open the door slowly.

"Uh, can I come in, please?"

Brenda was reassured by her son's words, so she cleaned her face and looked over at Marie.

"Yes, who are you?"

"That's Ming, mama!"

Brenda looked at both Isaac and Marie, puzzled.

"Yeah, well, that is a nickname I received from the kids right before I came to the hospital with my aunt. My auntie is Ms. Opal."

"Oh, Lord! What now! Is she okay?!"

"Well, she is being Auntie Opal, humble. However, she is not okay."

Marie looked at Isaac and smiled, then continued speaking.

"But, she knows her neighborhood children's voices. Now, I have to tell her she was right; she said she heard Isaac's voice. And she was right."

Marie looked over at Isaac's I.V. and then back at Brenda.

"Well, I genuinely believe as a mother you do not want to keep re-living your son's turmoil, but may I ask what happened?"

"Well, my son and David tried to save Jerry."

Brenda finished relaying the entire story to Marie.

"My auntie would often tell me about the untied shoes too."

Brenda was not trying to be rude, just being her outspoken self.

"Right now, I don't care what was untied; I just hope my boy and the other two are okay. My niece is shaken up from it all."

Marie nodded her head in agreement.

"I hope everything goes okay with your son and the others. Let me go back and tend to my aunt. I hate to break this news to her in her condition; however, she loves all you children, so I have to let her know."

Brenda's heart dropped, and Isaac looked confused. Every time he talked, his speech was slow, letting Brenda know his medication was working.

"Mama! Ming! We were going to the store to get some cough medicine with the change we had from the go-kart stuff; maybe you can tell the doctor just give Ms. Opal some cough syrup like my mom gives me."

Both Brenda and Marie had the biggest lump in their throats. They both wished it was that simple. But, in I.C.U., it was definitely more than a cough syrup issue. Marie looked over at Brenda and winked.

"I will do that, Isaac."

Isaac closed his eyes as the medicine started to make him sleepy. Brenda whispered to Marie.

"When Isaac is fully asleep, I will stop by and see your auntie if that's okay?"

"No problem! You and your family try and take it easy, okay."

Marie loved the way they all loved her aunt. She went back down the hall to Ms. Opal and explained everything that had happened.

"Well, they won't let me walk, so you can wheel me down there to see all three boys later. It has to be a reason we are all here at the same time and on the same floor. I lived too long, and I know there has to be a reason for this."

"I guess, auntie, I don't know; I just wish I could change all of these circumstances."

26

Linda visited with her nephew and sister as long as she could; however, Linda needed a breather. She also wanted to see where Steve's head was, not to pick on him this time but to sincerely help.

"Well, Sam, I have to go to the waiting room and clear my head for a few reasons."

Linda explains what happened between her and Mrs. Sinclair.

"Yeah, that's you. At least you got her up here for her son."

Linda shook her head in agreement, hugged her sister and her nephew then headed to the waiting room.

Mrs. Sinclair was all situated, and her son was waking up, so she started to rub his head.

"Jerry?!"

"Mama, I am sorry you have to pay the hospital money now. I just didn't want anything to happen to my bugs, but Isaac and David tried to save me though. But they got hurt too."

Saddened by the situation, Jerry placed his head. Mrs. Sinclair tried to make things better the best way she knew how.

"Well, mama is going to make it all better. I'm going to tell those doctors to get you well, and I am going to buy you the biggest bug collection ever!"

Jerry tried to sit up.

"Son, do not try to sit up; lay down."

"Mom, I have to tell you something."

"What is it, Jerry?"

"Do you know why the cell phone you bought me ended up broken?"

Mrs. Sinclair was puzzled why Jerry asked her this particular question; however, she was confident about her answer.

"Yes, because you accidentally broke it. Which is fine, I will just buy you another one. Do you want another one?"

Jerry was hesitant but proceeded.

"Mom, I broke the phone, so I wouldn't be on it as much as you are on yours, and take time away from my bugs like you always take time away from me!"

Mrs. Sinclair placed her laptop on the table and gave Jerry her full attention.

"I never knew you felt that way."

"Well, I do! And another thing, everybody always fussed at me about not tying my shoes, including you, and I was too embarrassed to tell anybody, I DON'T KNOW HOW!"

Ms. Sinclair was hurt by his comments.

"Well, I taught you how to...."

"One time, mom! One time! And I cherished that time so much I left them untied instead and tucked them in my shoe, hoping you would help me again and spend time with me! Now, my stupid shoelaces almost got my friends killed! (Jerry turns his face with a face full of tears): Just go do what you love more than me, on the phone and making money!"

She felt the pain both his and hers. She started to think of Linda and what she said to her. It was pretty similar to Jerry's comments. Ms. Sinclair started to cry and laugh at the same time. Jerry sincerely and softly asked his mom a question.

"Now you are laughing at me?"

"You know what? Now I see how I lost you and your dad. I am doing the same CRAP my mom did to me. Your granny died when you were two, and you know why? She worried herself to death. Your granny told me she was a foster child, and she refused to put me in a foster home. Your granny thought she was saving me from strangers, but I felt like a stranger in my own home, and the same exact thing you are telling me, I told her."

Mrs. Sinclair was extremely emotional. Jerry was tuned in on his mom's entire conversation. He had not had a sincere talk like this with her.

"What, you didn't tie your shoelaces either?"

Mrs. Sinclair laughed hard as she cleaned her face.

"No, son. I forgot how cute you are, but no, I learned to make money like her, and I thought that would make my mom and I close. So, I used to help her and learned the trait of making money."

"Well, your mom taught you, so why are you crying?"

She wanted to explain so much to Jerry about her past; however, right then, she just wanted to make it right.

"These tears, son, are to let you know I hate that it took a tragedy for me to recognize this. I am glad you spoke up. As of today, son, I refuse to make you feel like a stranger in your own house. I love you, son, and I am not going to say I'm sorry; I will just make changes like spending only 4 days a week on my business instead of 7. I can live with that because you are worth more than any black card I have. Instead of sending you to camp this summer, you, your dad, and I are going to Disneyland."

Jerry was overjoyed.

"Hey, mom, I heard they have a bug ride I can get on!"

His excitement faded for a moment, and confusion set in as he thought about her statement.

"Wait, my dad? I thought you said he lived far away?"

"He does. And sometimes men stay away from their kids because the mom stirs up things."

"What do you mean?"

"Well, I snapped on your father very hard just because he told me to pay more attention to my family. I told him if he did not like what I was doing, then to go away. I started to use bad words toward him, so he took my advice and left."

Mrs. Sinclair looked around the hospital room and sighed.

So, now I can hopefully tell your dad how I finally got the picture through this tragedy, and maybe he will forgive me. Your dad is not at all a bad person, Jerry. I am partly the reason your father is not around. I told him to stay gone or else. You are too young to know about how money and lawyers work, but your mom has enough money to pay for him to stay away if I wanted him to, and he just did not want a battle he knew he could not win."

Jerry reached for his glasses on the hospital table and placed them on to clearly see his mom.

"Well, if I can forgive you, I can forgive him too for not being around. Call him, mama."

Not yet. I have to go downstairs to the gift shop and buy you a book and read it to you."

"Wow, mom! The last book you read to me was 'Green Eggs and Ham'!"

"You remember that?! You were only 3 years old! Well, I will be right back."

Jerry yelled out before she walked out the door.

"Mama, I love you!"

She ran to Jerry and hugged his neck, trying not to further hurt the damage to his ribs. She cried.

"I love you too, son. I am so glad I did not lose you completely!"

27

Marie talked to her aunt quietly. She wanted to hear every word her aunt said. Marie sensed her aunt would not be here too much longer.

"Sweetie, help me get my sweater on. You know I have on this ass out, gown."

Marie flung her mouth wide open.

"Auntie!

Ms. Opal got a kick out of it and laughed.

"Well, no other good words for these gowns, plus I am trying to cheer you up. I had my time on earth baby, me passing on is just leaving room in the world for a baby to be born and experience life."

"Huh?!"

"Look, every day someone dies, and a baby is born. Me going to glory is for a reason, and I just want to see my kids for the last time. I just hate it has to be in here. You being sad is going to semi stop me from resting in peace; I'd be worried about you, sweetheart."

Marie smiled, now understanding what her aunt was talking about. She helped her aunt off the bed.

"Okay, okay, no more moping. You can't get mad if I can't help it and cry at times. You taught me tears are to let the bad out and for when a person is happy."

"Ming!" She laughed. "You always were like that since you were a little girl."

"What?"

"You always remembered quotes someone told you when you were ready to win an argument. You are something else, Ms. Lady, now help me on down the way."

Marie helped and strolled her to where Isaac and possibly the other boys were.

Steve was thinking extremely hard, trying to find a way to come up with all that money he needed for the hospital bills. Samuel rocked in a chair, dwelling on everything as well and on how to come up with the money for his family. Linda gave Carla and Mike a friendly smile as she read a magazine she had. Again, Linda felt the tension in the air. Finally, Samuel broke the silence with a rude comment toward Steve.

"People don't want my kid playing with theirs, huh, well the entire time, I felt the SAME DAMN WAY!"

Steve stood up.

"Let me tell you something, LOW-LIFE!"

"LOW-LIFE?!"

"YES! The last time I checked, my son sneaked to the store with your boy!"

"Look here, you ass hole, he didn't have a gun to his head!"

"You sure about that. You pull drive-byes, don't you?!"

"Since you have all the answers, my white sheets are missing. Did you take them, K.K.K. member?!"

The two were so loud the doctors, Ms. Opal, and else everyone heard them. Linda jumped up.

"YOU KNOW WHAT, IGNORANT ONE, AND IGNORANT TWO, JUST STOP IT!!"

"Oh, shut the hell up, Linda. What do you know? You don't even have any kids!"

Tears filled Linda's eyes as she gave Steve the most brutal slap ever. POW!

"YOU DISGUST ME!"

Linda ran out of the waiting room and down the stairs. Samuel spoke up.

"Good! Somebody needed to slap you!"

Steve felt guilty, and his face showed it. He knew he should have never said that, knowing Linda had lost her child. Carla rolled her eyes and shook her head. Carla and Mike were disgusted at both Samuel and Steve.

Ms. Opal made her way past the kids. She wanted to get to that waiting room right away. She took her cane and swung the waiting room door open. Steve and Samuel looked at her as Marie wheeled her in. Ms. Opal, who usually smiled, had the biggest frown when she stared at the guys. Steve and Samuel both smiled at Ms. Opal. No matter how people get angry or hate each other, Ms. Opal had no enemies. Today, however, she was agitated.

"You know I had to pass two children in their hospital rooms just to come see who could say such harsh things to each other."

Ms. Opal pointed her cane at both Steve and Samuel.

I hope it wasn't you two while those poor innocent babies lay in critical condition! You know what?! You two should take out your brains and lay them in the hospital beds because not only are you two acting stupid, your brains are sick!"

Carla and Mike sniggled almost into a burst of laughter. Ms. Opal continued.

"How dare you two smile in my face whenever I see you guys, and you two hate each other all along! Right now, it's not about black and white or whatever. Those kids are in hospital beds. Do you hear me?! And their fathers, of all people, are sick and ignorant!"

Ms. Opal was disappointed and disgusted by their behavior.

"Marie, take me to those kids now! I will be damned to just stand in here and let my heart worry, in my last few days, on how these kids will be treated when I die!"

As Marie turned her around, Ms. Opal continued to speak so that the two fathers could hear her.

"All because two men that I thought were upstanding and civilized hate each other!"

Samuel and Steve watched Ms. Opal roll away before the hospital door shut. Carla and Mike held a newspaper up to their faces; however, they were pleased about what Ms. Opal said. Samuel and Steve looked at each other. Ms. Opal's words hit them where it hurt, so bad that they each just plopped in chairs. As they sat, Steve got a call.

"Hello. Yes, I guess I can come to work for a few days. Oh, and I may need a cash advance. What! Come on, Carl, I have been working for you for over 15 years now! And my son is in...."

Steve was cut off by his boss, which irritated Steve.

"Yeah, well, I have to be there. I have a hospital bill I cannot afford, so I have to be there! Well, by force, that is!"

Steve hung up the phone. Samuel sarcastically jumped at Steve, still holding that same grudge.

"Oh, wow, seems as if you can't pay your hospital bill either. Seems like niggers not the only ones with money problems, huh?"

Carla and Mike became so discouraged and angry they got up to leave. Carla slammed her magazine and newspaper down.

"You know what, let's go, Mike. Any more hatred in here, I would swear up and down the devil himself were sitting in these seats coaching these two!"

Mike looked at Steve and Samuel, shook his head, and left with his wife, grieved by the men's behavior. Samuel looked at Steve, puzzled as to why he did not argue back this time. They kept glancing at each other as the words of Ms. Opal sank in; however, they were so stubborn they still frowned at each other with bitterness. Then, in walked

Jabeeb, T.J., and his daughter. Steve and Samuel were so mad at each other they lashed out at T.J. Samuel looked T.J. up and down.

"Well, what's the suit for?! The kids are not dead, thank God! That suit is not you!"

T.J. rolled his eyes and looked over at Steve. T.J. had felt Steve's eyes on him.

Wow, a suit?! What, you just came from court?!"

Steve chuckled. Jabeeb was irritated at how they could be this rude and especially at a time like this. He hated the way they were speaking to his friend.

"My friend, I must go. I cannot stand to hear this any longer."

T.J. grabbed Jabeeb's shoulder.

"No! You stay; as you can see, stupidity cannot be in the same room with civilization. I need a real person in my corner. So you and my daughter stay."

Samuel jumped straight out of his seat, happy to see his niece after all these years.

"Oh, my goodness! Toni, you are so beautiful!"

Even though she was upset at how her uncle acted toward her dad, she was raised to be polite. Not to mention she was worried about her cousins.

"Thanks. How are you, Uncle Sam?"

Samuel grabbed her and hugged her. T.J. wanted to shed a tear so bad; however, he held his composure. Toni's focus was on her cousin.

"Which room is my cousin residing in, Uncle Sam, please?"

"Oh, your cousin is in room 34, sweetheart."

"Okay."

She patted her uncle on the back then pushed the buzzer to get inside to speak to Brenda and Isaac. Samuel watched his niece walk off before he sincerely addressed T.J.

"I have many reasons why I am the way I am, bro. She has just gotten so big, I missed her and...."

Samuel dashed past T.J. and Jabeeb and ran out of the waiting room. T.J. ran behind his brother and yelled.

"Sam! Sam!"

T.J. looked back at Jabeeb.

"Oh, Lord!"

"Let him go. He will return. He may just need to let off some steam."

Steve looked at everyone and decided to speak what he was thinking.

"One down, two to go."

"You know what?! Man, why don't you worry about that child in that room instead of how disruptive, sarcastic, and callous you could be!"

Steve stood up and realized he'd better go back and check on his son. Steve buzzed to get back in; however, he was not finished with his callous sarcasm.

"Oh, you speak with professionalism, now that you have a suit on, huh? Wow! But I must say I do need to check on my son. Good advice, defendant."

Steve laughed. He was authorized to go inside to where David was.

"See you, defendant."

T.J. and Jabeeb were both disgusted, but T.J. was livid. However, he remained calm for the children's sake. While Steve went in, a doctor came out to speak to one of Isaac's parents. He addressed.

"First, let me say how are you?"

"I'm okay."

T.J. and Jabeeb reached out to shake the doctor's hand.

"And who are you to, uh, Isaac?"

"Oh, yes, I am Tony, Tony Johnson the uncle. Is it okay if you just tell me everything?"

"The doctor looked over at Jabeeb. Will you excuse us, sir? I have to talk to Mr. Johnson privately."

"I totally understand. T.J. I'll be on my way to check on my store. When I am done, I will call you, my friend. Anything you all need, just let me know."

"Thanks for everything. I will talk to you later."

Jabeeb waved and walked away. T.J. and the doctor stepped aside to continue their conversation.

"Now I am supposed to talk to your brother, but just to let you know, the head doctor was going to kick your brother and the other kid's dad out."

T.J. shook his head in embarrassment.

"They were stating racial slurs and rude comments that were easy to swallow. An elderly woman here, who has days to live, must know them. She set them straight and...."

"Wait a minute, was this elderly lady in her 80's, pearl-colored hair, feisty but sweet?"

"Yes, Mr. Johnson. You know her too, I suppose since she knows your bother."

T.J. got all choked up.

"Oh, man. Oh my God! What a damn day. That is Ms. Opal, she's. She's...."

"I am so sorry about all this bad news. However, like I said, this is supposed to be confidential, so please, do not let this spread, especially since it is coming from me. Also, both dads are frustrated because of the very high hospital bills. However, before we proceed with other treatments and care, the hospital has to get paid. Trust me when I say we do have empathy toward all of this for sure. Well, I need to get back to work. Just talk everything over with your family and try to work things out financially. I won't hold you so you can get things going for your nephew. He is in room 34, I think with your daughter or your younger twin, I suppose."

The doctor smiled at T.J., trying to lighten the situation. T.J. smiled back.

Yeah. Hey doc, you know much as I wanted to cuss and fuss at my brother and my nephew's friend's father, I just couldn't. I lost a wife, and if they have a second chance to make their life right.... Well, if my wife were here, she would have made sure everything was right. And she would have me help them make things right. Well, what I am trying to say, doc, is, just let me know how much both of the hospital bills are for my family and David's, and I will pay every red cent."

The doctor's eyes opened wider than a lion's mouth.

"Oh?! What a blessing for both families to have a family member like you!"

"Yeah, I just wish my brother felt the same, but it is not about me now; it is about the children. So please, do not reveal this. I know Mrs. Sinclair, which is Jerry's mom, can pay double-fold for her son's bill; however, I will do something special for them later as well."

"Yes, trust me, we know she can pay also. I agree it is about the children, Mr. Johnson. So, our secret is safe, no worries."

"Cool. Let me go see my nephew and my sister-in-law."

T.J. passed through and noticed Jerry and his mom in the room. He stopped and stared. T.J. wasn't nosey; he was just so shocked to see Mrs. Sinclair. Every time he saw Jerry, he was alone or with friends. T.J. often saw Mrs. Sinclair and knew of her; she was the talk of the liquor store buddies and neighborhood of just being Jerry's A.T.M.

28

Ms. Opal and Marie went in to check on David first. Ms. Opal gave as much wise counsel and love as she could to David. A few seconds later, Steve walked in. Ms. Opal was willing and ready to speak to Steve. She wanted to let him know how brave David was.

"Well, hello Steve. I told this mature young man you have, we all have a lot to learn from him and his friend Isaac. Right, Marie?"

David looked confused. He thought, what possibly could his dad learn from him. He was a kid and always felt he was only made to listen.

"He could learn from me!"

"Oh yes, he sure can. Tell your son, Steve, about your teamwork. You and I know your mechanic, Manzel."

Steve's eyes open wide. He did not know where Ms. Opal was going with this. She continued in a firm voice.

"You remember, you're going to work with Manzel, Isaac's father, and a few others to finish the go-kart, remember. Remember!"

David's eyes lit up like a Christmas tree.

"What, dad!"

Samantha was puzzled at the whole conversation.

"Huh?!"

"Oh, wow! What made you like Isaac's dad now?!"

Steve frowned, smiled, and then shrugged his shoulders in confusion.

"Thanks, dad! Maybe I can heal fast, so I can help! Mom, you heard that!"

"Oh, yeah, I heard it loud and clear."

Steve looked at Marie, upset at how hard she was sniggled.

Ms. Opal started to laugh sarcastically.

"Look at my boy! I am so glad you are happy about the good news! Well, Marie, take me to Isaac's room. I have to finish my job before I go."

Marie and Ms. Opal exited. Steve slammed his hand hard on the table, which made Samantha and David jump.

"What is wrong, dad?"

"Oh, uh, I got a cramp in my leg. I will be back."

Samantha knew how to comfort her husband, so she propped David's pillow before she went to talk to Steve.

"I will be back, son."

"Okay, mom. Love you, dad."

Steve, who was almost in tears, looked back at his son but was speechless. Samantha tried to clear up things a little for Steve.

"I am going to get your dad some medicine out of the car, son."

"Okay. Hey dad? I knew you would like Isaac's dad. Isaac's dad, and you may be just like Isaac and me! That is why his dad will help you with the go-kart; you all are helping each other. You two will be best friends, too; I just know it!"

Steve flung the door open and ran out to the waiting room in a hurry. Samantha trailed behind him.

"Steve! Slow down! Steve! Now, wait just a damn minute!"

Steve turned around toward Samantha.

"Woman, have you lost your mind talking to me like that?!"

"I am sick and tired of this! So you're mad because of what Ms. Opal said to make our son smile?! So what! Besides Linda and Ms.

Opal, we have not been doing a good job keeping our son smiling! That woman loves all our kids. She is about to die, and our kid and the other children's precious lives are at stake! Our kids are heroes! And because they were doing the right thing and she asked people like us to do the right thing and finish the project and stop all this foolishness makes a ton of sense!"

"What do you mean people like us?!"

"GOT DAMN IT, STEVE! Can't you see how much our kids love each other?! We need to learn a lesson from them! They are not worried about a simple color difference at all! And "our" dumb asses. People like us need to come to grips that those babies, including our son, were almost dead! You hear me, Steve?! Almost dead"

Samantha fell to a seat and cried. Steve sat down next to her.

"Look, Sam, I just want to change when I am ready and...."

"So your child and other innocent children have to die before you wake up, Steve, huh?!"

Steve started to cry. Samantha sat up, shocked. She only saw Steve cry once a year, and that was on his mother's birthday.

"Honey, I apologize if I came off a little harsh, but you have got to...."

"Sam! Just hush up and listen, okay?! I am going to tell you why I am the way I am, okay! So please just don't interrupt!"

Samantha shook her head in agreement. She was eager to hear this story.

"Okay, my mom had this long-term significant other named Tim. Well, my grandfather never approved of him because he was a black guy. My grandfather would often tell me not to hang with him, and he would disrespect Tim. So anyway, I went against my grandfather's wishes because Tim was good to me. He took me fishing and spent time with me often. I looked up to him until one night Tim was cursing at my mom, calling her everything in the book except a child of God. Then he slapped my mom around and beat her. This went on for months. I was scared. He was a solid big man, so I called my granddad. I didn't know what else to do.

"Steve, it's okay; this is a healing process. Let it out."

"Okay. My grandfather came over with his shotgun to get Tim."

Steve started to cry again as he talked.

"My mom ran to her dad to stop him. He shot at Tim but hit my mother by accident!"

Sam held her mouth in shock. She then placed her arms around Steve and squeezed him tight. He held on to her.

"Oh, Steve! Wow! I had no idea! So that is why your grandfather has been in prison all this time?! I am so sorry, Steve. Look at me. I cannot possibly understand how you feel, but why, on account of one person, dismiss everyone in that race?"

"Do you understand, Sam? My mother got killed in the process! Not just a neighbor or a person on the news, my mother!"

"I know, sweetheart, but you see how the pattern is going?"

"What pattern?"

"I hate to be the bearer of bad news, but truthfully, out of anger and hatred, your grandfather lost his daughter. I'm pretty sure if hatred was not in his heart against Tim, the outcome would have been different. I know your grandfather was a father in rage, but he would have probably just slapped Tim around a bit and maybe called the police. However, your grandfather's hatred towards Tim's race made the situation worst! Now, babe, you're so focused on your hatred towards Isaac and his family's race instead of this situation at hand. You don't realize all three kids, including Lema, could have been killed! And all because they sneaked to the store for Ms. Opal. They went to the store for her out of love and were almost killed in the process! So they hid from us that they were going back to the store. They were probably scared of asking us supposed to be adults if they could go back to the store because of our hatred! You see what I mean?!"

Steve placed his head down briefly.

"Yeah, yeah. Well, I feel I have been going to church for nothing. I sit there on Sundays, but I do not pray. Why pray when I felt like God allowed my mom to die for nothing. Now, I am sure God is giving me a reality check, letting me know I am following in my grandfather's footsteps when I should be like my son, who is like my mother. My son is so lovable and heartfelt like her. I do not hate those kids. I am going to pray for forgiveness."

"Steve, yes, I want you to change, but I will not let you blame yourself for this entire situation."

Steve cracked a small smile.

"Sam, I'm always thankful that you love me like that, but the truth is the truth, I need to ask for forgiveness! You see, I paid Jerry to leave the go-kart in his yard so Isaac and David would think someone stole it; well, that was my next move."

Samantha was distraught hearing this news; however, she empathized with Steve because of what he had shared.

"Steve, why?! Yeah, well, I understand why you want to pray for forgiveness now on top of everything else. While you pray for forgiveness, I'll go find Linda. I have not seen her in a minute. Steve, she really cheered David up."

Steve looked up at Samantha with a guilty face.

"What now, Steve?! Where is Linda?"

"Well. Well, when I was arguing with Isaac's dad, Linda kind of butted in, and I kind of told her what did she know because she did not have kids anyway."

Samantha stood up quickly and ran to the door.

"Yeah, Steve, you, you pray hard. I may even need to find some holy water downstairs!"

"No need, Linda slapped me so hard water came out one eye, and I saw stars."

Samantha shook her head as she went out to look for her sister. Samantha knew her sister had just stormed off in a rage. Samantha was nervous. If anyone came in contact with her sister, they would get that same slap Steve described. Steve placed his head down, weighted with all kinds of guilt. He picked up his phone.

"Well, Lord, I first need to gather up this money for this hospital bill.

Linda was in her car looking at some pictures of her child from when she was a baby up until she died. She kept them in her glove compartment. Linda's windows were halfway down. She cried and reminisced. Samantha tapped on Linda's window.

"Hey, can I come in, or do I have to beat you at Yahtzee later and piss you off?"

Linda wiped her face and gave a smirky smile.

"Get in here, little sis."

Samantha looked through the photos, missing her niece as well.

"I remember Stephanie calling out to me when she was three. When she wanted cookies, she would always say, "auntie' cocoa, auntie cocoa!"

"Yeah, she was something special! It was so amazing how you figured that out! You don't know how many times I ran to the kitchen and kept grabbing the cocoa and wondering why she was not satisfied."

They laughed.

"Yeah, you know, Linda, I know you are older and think you are too old to have a kid. But, I heard you talk about your new boyfriend from time to time. I met him, and I say he is a keeper, so why don't you try?"

"You always were the little smart nosey one!"

"Hey! I resent that!"

"Trust me when I say I meant that in a good way. Every time I think you are not paying attention, you are. I want to apologize, sis."

"For what?!"

"I just used to feel you always got the easy way out of everything.

I was even evil enough to say why my child died, and my sister got to keep her child. But you know what? I ate my words now my nephew is in the hospital. How dare I wish anything on my family over jealousy! You always needed me just as much as I needed you, and I could not see past that. I am so sorry, Sam!"

Linda reached over, hugged her sister, and sobbed.

"It is okay, Linda. By the way, thanks for slapping Steve. Something I have wanted to do for years!"

They laughed and cried at the same time.

"Well, we need to clean ourselves up and get back to David; he needs us. But, Sam, don't think I hate your husband, that's my brother, and I love him. I just see the good in him, more than he knows. I just hate the outwardly displayed character and actions that are so bad."

"Yeah, that is another story. I will explain it to you later. Let's go."

"Okay."

Linda put her pictures safely away. Then, they got out of the car and headed back. As they got to the elevator, Samantha looked over at Linda.

"Sis, let's take pictures with my niece's favorite cookies and place them on her grave with some flowers for her birthday. How do you feel about that? Is that okay?"

Linda held her head up. Her sister never let her down.

"I would absolutely love that little sis. Thank you!

29

Jabeeb got out of his car headed into the liquor store. He noticed the regular guys who hang in front of his store; however, to Jabeeb's surprise, he saw Samuel standing outside of the liquor store. Jabeeb knew that T.J. would disapprove of his brother, Samuel, drinking like he does. So Jabeeb used some friendly but direct tactics to see what Samuel was doing with the drink in his hand. After Jabeeb checked on his store, he walked back out to see if Samuel was already gone. But to Jabeeb's surprise, Samuel was still there seated out on a concrete ledge, close to the ground, about to have a drink. When Samuel noticed Jabeeb, he tried to place the paper bag with the liquor on the other side of him. Jabeeb sat down on the ledge next to Samuel.

"Hey, my friend, it is pretty cold out here, huh?"

Samuel's speech was slurred; he was already tipsy.

"What! Aww, please, you know you can care less if it's cold outside, okay. You saw my drink, I guess, yeah, tell everybody. I'm not the perfect one; I'm having a drink. I know you saw it, Jabeeb."

"Samuel, last I checked, no one in this world is the perfect one, my friend. We all make mistakes. However, since we are speaking on mistakes, what did your brother do so wrong to make you have such aggression and hate toward him?"

"For the record, let's get one thing straight, I don't hate my brother, okay! I just feel he is too intelligent not to have finished school. And I would not have had to go through certain things, and he could have saved me from certain things.

Samuel was thinking of when he was molested by his auntie's boyfriend.

"Well, is it too deep to talk about?"

"Jabeeb, don't you have some more 7-11's to buy or something?!"

"Well, maybe I do, but you can sit in front of each one I buy; you and your brother are welcome everywhere I reside."

Jabeeb got up and went into the store. Samuel picked up his drink, rolled his eyes at Jabeeb then started to drink again.

T.J finally tried to swallow the big lump in his throat and go see his nephew. He looked in the room and saw his daughter, nephew, and Brenda all speaking; however, they did not see him. Down the hallway and he noticed Marie as she pushed Ms. Opal toward Isaac's room.

"Oh, wow! Now you dress right, so those gorgeous teeth will show. I always see your gorgeous smile and teeth; now you have the outfit to match, huh?!"

Marie smiled.

"Hey, you do have some pretty teeth! Wow!"

"Thank you, sweetheart."

He addressed Ms. Opal, remembering her kindness towards him.

"What are you doing here? Well, what is going on, may I ask? I just hate seeing you here. I remember when I was at Jabeeb's store, and you would always pretend you didn't see my bag, but in my gut, I felt you knew I was drinking. But, you so sweet, you didn't judge me, not once!"

Ms. Opal straightened her sweater and smiled at T.J.

"No, I wouldn't say that. I would judge and say, why is this intelligent young man who has respect for women, seemed like a delight, and all the guys wanted to be around him, just decided to be on this corner. But I just prayed for you and left it in God's hands. And yes,

I knew you were drinking. You used to hide that paper bag and cling onto it, and it sounded like you were crushing a dry leaf."

They all laughed.

"Son, I really appreciate the acknowledgment and respect you have for me; however, no one should be judged. And no one should judge you. You are needed on this earth just like everyone else. But the question you asked earlier of why I am here, well, I am being called to glory. My husband is missing me, I guess. So it's your turn now, sweetheart. Promise me you will help your brother realize there are not a lot of Ms. Opal's out there. Still, we all, let me rephrase that, you all must come together for these kids. You hear me?!"

T.J. was too emotional to agree verbally, so he just nodded his head.

"Marie?"

Marie was just as emotional. If she had blinked, tears would unfold.

"Yes, auntie."

"Alright, I see you two; no tears for me right now. You two just wheel me in to see that chocolate grandbaby of mine that's God-given like David and the rest of them."

T.J. smiled and dried up his almost falling tears.

"Well, I want you to adopt me too! I always heard about those cookies from my nephew and all his friends. So when you get out of here, you can make your ole' son some."

"Well, son, I am passing the recipe to my niece here. She made a vow to me she will keep, so trust me, she will place an extra batch for you; how about that?!"

T.J was thankful to be called son and be involved with the love she gave the kids concerning her cookies. However, just the fact that Ms. Opal was leaving this earth hurt him so.

"Yes. Yes, ma'am."

"Put that head up and show them pearly whites, right now! Now you two escort this sexy lady inside so I can see this young child."

Marie and T.J. laughed and took Ms. Opal inside to see Isaac.

30

Steve was on the phone trying to call around and get loans from everyone he knew for his son's hospital bill. Steve then thought of what Ms. Opal said, then decided to call Manzel.

"Day and Night Auto Shop, this is Manzel speaking; how may I help you.

Steve hesitated.

"Hello? Hello?"

"Hey, Manzel."

Manzel was puzzled because of Steve's shaky voice.

"Oh, uh, hey Steve. What's going on?"

"Hey, uh, if I ever offended you in any way, I uh, I am sorry. My son. My, my son.

"Is everything okay, Steve?"

"No. My son is in the hospital and may be paralyzed from the waist down. Things will get better, and we will have hope only if I can get his physical therapy payment started. The price is pretty steep. So, if I don't get my car serviced for a while, you know why. I want to thank you for your service and...."

"Oh my God! Steve, I want to help truly I do. You are a loyal customer, so for the next four services you need, I will just charge it to you being a loyal customer. We are doing pretty well here at the shop, Steve; that's the least I can do."

Steve sighed. He could never admit it, but Manzel was one person he loved like the brother he never had.

"Oh, and why did you ever think you offended me?"

"Well, long story, but Manzel, I'm not asking for no handouts or no favors. I just was letting you know my circumstance and what I am going through."

"Come on, Steve, how is what I offered you a handout and a favor if I offered?! Please, don't worry about it."

"Thanks, Manzel, from the bottom of the heart, which I just realized I have, thanks!

"Whatever that means, I accept your gratitude. You alright with me, Steve!

31

Samuel was almost finished with his bottle of liquor. He was talking to himself out loud.

"Who cares, who cares? I just don't know why this got to happen to me! I probably can't have kids, and the one son, the one son God blessed me with through Bren, I almost lost! I see why my brother would drink! You can just drown your sorrows."

He took another drink. A guy walked into the liquor store but had been listening to Samuel the entire time. The guy was 5'11, slender, scruffy beard, and looked as if he had just lost his best friend. Samuel looked over at the guy.

"What...in the hell...are you looking at?!"

The guy laughed; he was tipsy himself.

"Well, the name is Rich. And the right thing to say is hello, asshole!"

Samuel stood up, staggering and slurring in words as he talked.

"You know what?! If I was not on cloud nine right now, I would.... Just get out of here. What you doing with a name like Rich, and you look poor as hell?!"

Samuel plopped back down on the concrete and laughed hard.

"Well, from the looks of it, you are not sitting in a nicely furnished living room yourself!"

Rich stepped in and bought his liquor. He talked a bit with Jabeeb.

"Man, what's up with that, Jabeeb?! Me and my boys are supposed to be the only riff-raft in front of your store. So who in the hell is that rude asshole out there?!"

"Jabeeb smiled in agreement but did not speak rudely about Samuel because of the love he had for T.J.

"That asshole would be T.J.'s younger brother, my friend."

"What!! You have got to be kidding me. T.J. always cried about how he disappointed his brother because he drinks. So, what's that about, and where is T.J.?"

Jabeeb got his other customers out the way quickly with their lottery tickets. Wishing them good luck as they headed out and he continued his conversation with Rich.

"You ask a lot of questions that I can't even answer right now. I guess some brothers are like night and day."

"Try midnight and day! That one outside is a piece of work! I only knew him for ten seconds, and I wanted to slap him in the first five!"

Jabeeb shrugged his shoulders and laughed.

"Yeah, well, good night, Rich."

"Alright, Jabeeb. I will get up with you later."

Outside Rich saw Samuel holding his head and still talking to himself. Rich threw him a quarter.

"Oops! What do you know, a quarter for your thoughts."

"I thought I told you to get the hell away from me or leave me the hell alone or something like that."

"Yeah, you did. But the only reason I threw you a quarter and decided to ignore your ignorance was because you are T.J.'s younger brother. And that is the only reason I'm not kicking your ass!"

"Oh, wow! One for T.J. He can save me, whoopty do! One stripe for the "Professor"!"

Rich shook his head, looked weirdly at Samuel, and walked off to where he was going.

Ms. Opal, Marie, and T.J. entered Isaac's room. Isaac was excited when he looked at the door.

"Hey, Uncle T.J.! Hey, Ms. Opal!"

"Hey, nephew!"

A nurse knocked on the door.

"Oh, I see it is getting crowded; I will go get some more chairs. I came in because I am glad there is a lot of love for Isaac in the room; however, we will allow 15 more minutes of visiting time. The doctor wants Isaac to get some rest. Brenda, you and your husband can stay if you like, okay?"

"We understand; thank you."

The nurse smiled at everyone as she left the room to get chairs.

"Uncle T.J., this lady said she is my cousin, and I know it because she looks just like you, with hair!"

Everyone laughed. Ms. Opal looked around for Samuel.

"Honey, where is your husband?"

"He was in the waiting room. Have you seen Sam, T.J., in the waiting room?"

Tony noticed her father's face, so she tried to intervene.

"Well, uh, I saw him, auntie. He was happy to see me and said I have really grown since he saw me last."

"Oh, okay, yeah, you have grown. As a matter of fact, Isaac was one year old going on two when we saw you last, sweetheart."

Ms. Opal chimed in.

"Well, let me cut this short because the doctor is giving us the boot. But, I just wanted to check on you and let you know your father, David's father, and his mechanic agreed to help you and David finish the go-kart."

Brenda coughed out of disbelief.

"Wait, Ms. Opal, no disrespect, but do you mean my Sam?! Are you sure?!"

"Yeah, you mean my brother, Sam, and David's father?! I think you have the wrong ones, Ms. Opal."

"Well, no, I told David, and Steve agreed. So that is my only wish before I go."

Isaac looked peculiarly at Ms. Opal.

"Where are you going?"

Everyone in the room was in complete silence. Everyone except T.J.'s daughter and Isaac knew why.

"Oh, well, uh, I'm going back to my room. I just don't feel good, that's all."

Ms. Opal wanted to tell Isaac the truth; however, she figured no need to worry a child about her dying. Also, Ms. Opal did not want to see Isaac's face if she announced she was checking out.

"Well, my mom now knows why David, Jerry, Lema, and I were sneaking to the store. We were getting you some cold medicine!"

Everyone in the room was silent and close to tears.

"Well, I thank you all, sweetie! See y'all, and I love you all too."

She whispered over to T.J.

"You make sure that you and your sister-in-law get this last dose of medicine for me and get that go-kart request granted. Just get it done, and I want my name somewhere on that ride."

Ms. Opal smiled. T.J. and Brenda both agreed. It seems like good people just go too fast whether they grow old or not. Marie pushed Ms. Opal slowly to the door. Marie was happy there was a lot of love among each other but hated it was limited by days her favorite aunt had left on earth. As they exited, Isaac yelled out for Ms. Opal.

"Wait! When we finish the go-kart, we will ask our parents if they could follow behind us so we can get your medicine, okay?"

Ms. Opal was choked up and speechless. She could only shake her head in agreement, then waved for Marie to take her to her room. As soon as Ms. Opal got into the hallway, her tears unfolded. She placed her head down as Marie pushed her back to the room.

T.J. commented to Brenda as the two of them stood together,

"The good always go fast or first."

"Yes, always."

Isaac didn't know what they were speaking about, but he tried to figure it out. Tony looked around, wondering also, but decided to wait until she went downstairs to see what was going on.

"Hey, uh, dad, auntie, I am going downstairs before Isaac's medicine wears off. I do not wish to see my cousin in pain. I will bring you something when I come back, okay, Isaac?"

"Thank you, cousin! Mom, can you find out where Lema is?"

"Babe, she is fine, but she is not taking all of this too well. You know you two are more like brother and sister than cousins. She is at Pearl and Ron's house."

Pearl and Ron were long-time friends of Brenda and Samuel's neighbors that the two often played cards with.

"Oh, okay."

Brenda could see the disappointment on his face.

"And, your auntie is coming out here to pick up Lema and come see you."

Isaac smiled hard but was a little drowsy. Brenda looked up at T.J., worried about Samuel and where he might be.

"Hey, T.J., can you get your brother and tell him please come on in for me?"

T.J. would not dare tell Brenda that Samuel ran out. He figured Brenda had enough stress going on, so he just agreed to get Samuel.

"I will go get him. I think he went for some air; give me a few minutes, and he should be coming right up."

Brenda grabbed T.J.'s hand.

"Thanks, T.J. Thanks for everything. Your brother doesn't show it, but he needs you also."

T.J. placed his head down in sadness. Then he shook it off and looked up at Isaac.

"Okay, nephew, get some rest now before you get gray hair like your uncle. I cannot promise you will look this good, though, so rest up!"

Brenda laughed. Isaac's medicine had really kicked in, so he was smiling and dosing off at the same time.

"Okay, Uncle T.J."

32

Mrs. Sinclair watched over her son as he slept. She picked up her phone and went through her contacts to Jerry's father's phone number. She sighed as she talked to herself.

"Well, here I go. Saying sorry is never easy. I would rather just pay someone to say it for me, but I have a kid by him, so here I go. Sheesh!"

Mrs. Sinclair dialed the number. When she got to the fourth number, she hung it up. Mrs. Sinclair looked over at Jerry sleeping, looking like her little angel. She then decided to dial again and stepped out of the room. The same nurse as Isaac's walked over to Mrs. Sinclair and tapped her on the shoulder. Mrs. Sinclair jumped, which made the nurse jump too.

"Ooh! You startled me."

"I didn't mean to startle you. I just noticed you are about to make a call, and there are no phones allowed up here. Can you go downstairs to make a call, please?"

"Oh, no problem. If my son happens to wake up looking for me, can you just let him know I went downstairs, please?"

The nurse smiled and reassured Mrs. Sinclair that everything would be okay.

"Sure, I will, my pleasure."

"Thanks a million!"

Mrs. Sinclair rushed downstairs and right outside to call Jerry's father. But, unfortunately, the phone seemed to ring forever.

"Come on, this is hard enough, asshole, pick it up!"

Big Jerry finally answered the phone.

"Hello?"

"Uh, hi."

"Marshana?"

"Yeah, it's me, Big Jerry."

"Okay, what's this about?"

"You know it is hard for anybody to say I'm sorry, but...."

"I didn't do anything wrong but was pushed away from my son and told I wasn't needed by you!"

"Please, Jerry, I know this."

"I haven't heard from you in years. Wait a minute! You admit you were wrong; no wonder it rained up here in my neck of the woods."

"Okay, Jerry, I'll accept that sarcasm, but please just listen! I am up here with your son at St. Medical Hospital!"

Big Jerry got very silent for a few seconds.

"Wow! I was not ready for that, Marshana. Well, I hope it's just the case of Jerry Jr.'s tonsils that need to be removed."

"Oh, how I wish it was that simple. Your son has broken ribs, and the two friends that saved him may be paralyzed, I heard. Oh, wait, one is paralyzed, and the other has a fractured jaw."

"Oh, God! Wait, you said two kids tried to save him?"

"Yes, two kids did save him. Look, the reason I am calling is to apologize, and I should have apologized a long time ago. I am truly sorry for pushing you away. I was so involved with making money; I felt that kept us happy. Don't get me wrong, it pays the bills. However, I made a vow to Jerry that I would only spend four days with my business and not take time away from him. I want you to go to Disneyland with us if it's okay with you."

Well, I have to talk it over with my wife. We have a newborn now."

"I see you have been busy over the years. Well, I just want you involved in your son's life. And maybe he could meet his new sister or brother, I guess."

"Oh, come off of it, Marshana, you know I will be there for Jerry! And tell me, by the tone of your voice, are you jealous or something!"

"What?! Well, I am, but so what, there is nothing I can do about it now!"

"That's where you're wrong! Because for one, I'm not married, and I don't have a kid. I just wanted to see if the old bottled-up Marshana was still there. The one who hides her feelings, but I see you've changed. Don't you want me back, Marshana?! I have been missing you and my son like crazy! I had a few relationships; they never lasted because I was too busy thinking about my family. You have to realize we men are clueless. Unless you say, hey, let's get in the sack, we don't need an explanation for that. However, your emotions and feelings, sometimes you have to express to us, you know. You always were a good woman. When I lashed out and told you to pay attention to us, I just wanted an explanation for my son and me as to why you were more into making money than us."

Tears ran down Mrs. Sinclair's face.

"Hello? Hello? Oh, Marshana, are you crying? I know when you are crying; you get completely quiet."

Mrs. Sinclair wiped her face and managed to get some words out.

"I will explain everything to you later, just please, get up here. And for the record, I have really missed you so much too. I need to see if our son woke up, but I see so many things clearer now since we almost lost our child, Jerry."

"Okay, I should be there in six hours. I'm dropping everything. I'll leave my brother the place, and I am on the next flight out, okay?"

Mrs. Sinclair breathed slow, in relief.

"Okay."

33

Linda and Samantha sat in the waiting room next to Steve.

"You okay, Hon'?"

"Yes, I'm fine, sweetheart."

Steve leaned over and looked at Linda. Linda's head was down, and she was concentrating.

"Hey, Lin'? I know I'm a jerk, and you proved that. I never saw the galaxy until you slapped me. Anyway, I am just going to say it, I truly apologize for everything. Everything I have done since I met you. And it has been hard for all of us since Stephanie been gone, but especially for you."

Linda placed her hand over her mouth and cried as Steve continued.

"Stephanie was your child, and I am only experiencing a touch of that now, and I'm devastated. So, I cannot imagine how you feel. Linda, I am so sorry."

Linda was in complete shock. She looked at Samantha, wondering what had gotten into Steve. Samantha explained the situation of Steve's mom and stepdad to Linda in detail and why he had his prejudiced ways.

"Wow! There is always a reason for everything!"

She stood up, pulled Steve up, and gave him a tight hug.

"Well, brother, it takes baby steps; however, with prayer, we will get through this. We are here for you, okay."

Steve hugged her back tight and cried.

"Thank you so much, sis!"

Samantha was crying in complete happiness that her husband had opened up and was making himself a better person and that Linda and Steve finally saw eye to eye. Now Linda buzzed in so Samantha, Steve, and herself could go back inside with David. As they were walking in, T.J. was walking out. When T.J. passed by, he noticed that Steve was not giving him a look of hatred. T.J. was shocked and curious; however, he rushed out, eager to get to his brother for Isaac and Brenda.

"Man, shoot, where is this fool?"

34

T.J. drove around for 45 minutes, then he pulled over onto a side street. He placed his head on the steering wheel.

"Oh, Lord, please, help me find my brother. Man!"

T.J.'s phone rang, and he answered it.

"Hello."

"Dad, you left. Why?"

"Hey, babe, don't tell Bren', but I am looking for your uncle. He ran off, so I am trying to find him."

"Ooh, that's not good."

"Yeah, definitely no bueno."

"Well, I'm by the gift shop, and I wanted to know what my cousin likes."

T.J. wanted to talk to his daughter; however, he tried to get back to the situation at hand.

"Cars, baby. He likes cars, okay."

"Okay, dad, love you."

"Yeah, me too. I got to go now."

"Oh, but dad, wait! Will I get to meet my cousin from Georgia that Isaac told me about?"

"Yeah, you will meet Ms. Growny very soon."

"Yeah, her name is Lena, right."

"No, Lema."

The line beeped on T.J.'s phone.

"Hold on, baby."

T.J. clicked over.

"Okay, this T.J., speak now or hang up."

"Hey, there it's Jabeeb. I'm guessing you are still at the hospital, yes?"

"No, I'm looking for my brother; he ran off earlier."

"Well, believe it or not, your brother is in front of my store wasted. I saved him from three fights, my friend. Everyone spared him since I told them he's your brother. You may want to come get him now."

"Wait a minute. My brother! Jabeeb, I know you don't wear glasses, but are you sure? You may need them today. You sure it's my brother, Samuel, "Judging," Johnson?!"

"Yes! Yes, that is he, and he is him. Right in front of my store. He always tended to be somewhat rude, but the "courage juice," as you all call it, is making him even worse!"

T.J. remembered his daughter was on the other line.

"Oh, shit! Hold on, Jabeeb."

T.J. clicked over.

"Sweetie, sweetie, Toni, I apologize, love you, and call you back!"

"Okay, Dad, what's going on?"

T.J. had already clicked back over.

"Jabeeb, I'm back. Okay, no matter what you do, do not let him leave. Keep him in front of your store, please, and try to get his car keys!"

"I forgot that he drove here. Okay, T.J., I will try."

"Okay, I am on my way!"

T.J. and Jabeeb both hung up.

Jabeeb went outside and noticed Samuel was still sitting on the concrete, looking into space and talking to himself.

"Sam."

"What man! If you want me to move, just say that!"

"No, no, it's not that. You are so wasted, Sam. Can I please have your keys?"

Samuel pulled his keys out of his pocket and dangled them. Then Samuel stood up, almost falling. But, instead, he caught himself on the wall with his keys still in his hand. Samuel stood up in Jabeeb's face laughing; however, Jabeeb stepped back because Samuel's breath reeks of alcohol.

"You want these keys, don't cha? I'm not going to give them to you! I have to get back to the hospital. Well, hell, I cannot go back to the hospital like this, Samuel; well, I will just go home."

Samuel staggered towards his car.

"Please, just sit down, my friend."

As Samuel staggered towards the car, he fell, and the keys slid out of his hand. Jabeeb tried to grab them, but Samuel beat Jabeeb to the punch. Samuel laughed.

"Yeah, Jabeeb, I am just too quick for you. I am all that and a bag of stale chips in your store. Now what?!"

Jabeeb was serious now and worried; you could hear it in his firm tone.

"I am trying to be nice. Now give me those keys!"

As Jabeeb reached for the keys, T.J pulled up and jumped out of the car. Samuel saw T.J. and looked over at Jabeeb.

"Oh, you called your dog out on me, huh? Woof! Woof!"

T.J. was disgusted seeing his little brother that way, as well as deeply hurt.

"Look at you, man! You wasted!"

"So, what! Does it look familiar?!"

"Hell no! I can stand when I drink!"

"I am so glad you here. Samuel wouldn't give me the keys. I am going to let you handle this now."

"Thanks again, Jabeeb."

Jabeeb went back into the store. Samuel still had plenty to say.

"Handle what?! Nobody can handle me. Just because you are in your suit for one day, ooh wow, you probably still couldn't handle yourself, neither! Just go away, man!"

T.J. leaned over and snatched the keys out of Samuel's hand. Samuel stood up and got in T.J.'s face.

"To hell with you, T.J.! Why the hell did you snatch my keys for?! Now give my keys back right now!"

Samuel tried to snatch them back out of T.J.'s hand; however, T.J. had always been good at basketball, so T.J. switched hand over hand until Samuel gave up.

"Alright, punk, you don't want to give me my keys; how about I sock you?!"

Samuel took a sloppy swing at T.J., who caught his fist. He held onto it tight and made Samuel sit down.

"You ready to calm down now?"

Samuel started to cry.

"No, not until I give you a piece of my mind! You were never there for me! Yeah, the one time the kids called me queer, so what! But, other than that, you weren't there!"

T.J. was furious and tired of taking all the blame from Samuel.

"Wasn't there for what else, Sam?! What else?! I am tired of you blaming me for all your got damn problems! If you don't like me, fine, I will just have to accept that, but what about your wife and son that's in the hospital and need your support now!"

"Shut up! You don't know shit about support! If you did, you would have been there when our auntie's boyfriend was touching me! And auntie didn't have a clue either. When I told her, she got rid of him, but then she used to slap me around like it was my fault. She treated me like a red-headed stepchild all the time and treated you like you were gold!"

T.J. sat down next to Samuel on the concrete, even though he had on his nice suit. That was just how down-to-earth T.J. was. A suit was the last of his worries.

"Man, you know what?! I knew Uncle Robert was weird but damn it! So, that's why you can't stand whites, and you have a grudge with Auntie Fanny?"

Samuel wiped his face, relieved he got the issue of his chest.

"Yeah, bro, that's why."

T.J. placed his arm around his brother. Samuel laid his head on his shoulder.

"Look, man, I uh, I uh, wow. This information is hard for me to swallow. Well, why have you never told me this? I would have listened."

"Man, you were so busy beating people up for calling me faggot and everything else. To be honest, you did not need anything else on your plate. I knew all of that was not easy for you."

"Please! I may be the people person, but sometimes I think that means people-pleaser. I don't know how to be happy unless I am helping somebody else. Now, I think it is about that time, in the process of me helping others, I help myself."

"Yeah, I heard that."

"I know you are the younger brother, but you don't have to follow in my footsteps and drink."

"Man, whatever! Since drinking, just half of the day, I have been able to ignore half of my problems."

T.J. looked down at the ground, upset at himself about his drinking. He wished his brother would stop cold turkey right now.

"Man, I haven't been in my niece's life. I can't even be a good dad for Brenda and her son."

"That is bull Samuel, and you know it! You always helped with bills, saved money for y'all future, and if I didn't know you, I would swear up and down that you were Isaac's father! And you know how mama raised us Samuel when you are raising someone, or you have a

God-given relative, it is not step this or in-law that. Isaac is your son and my nephew!"

"Yeah, well, you go check on them. Nice talking to you, and that's all, folks. I don't even have enough damn money to pay for the hospital bill!"

T.J. just became close to his brother; he wouldn't dare tell him he paid for the bill. He knew Samuel was still Samuel, and he knew his brother would blame him for throwing that he paid the bill in his face. So now was not the time to tell Samuel, so T.J. lied.

"Let's go! You get in my car. I refuse to let you drive, and by the way, I was told by one of the doctors that the hospital bill was taking care of."

"What?! Why? Well, I don't know, T.J., the hospital bill is thousands of dollars! I just don't believe that; you are just trying to get me to the hospital! I have to investigate that!"

T.J. tried to grab the drink out of Samuel's hand. Samuel gave T.J. a dirty look.

"Come on, man, judge not, or thy shalt not be judged or uh, judge not uh, well, just don't take the bottle out my hand. I never grabbed one out of yours!"

"Aright! Whatever! Samuel, just get in!"

T.J. opened the door. Samuel set his bottle and bag in then he got in. T.J. closed the door behind him. T.J. stepped into the store.

"Jabeeb, man, look, can you keep an eye on my brother's car? Please, don't let it get towed. Samuel just started drinking, and I know he likes it too much. He is stubborn and will not stop any time soon. This is all my fault."

"Hey! Don't you say that. Don't you see the sign from God?! This is your chance to help your brother and yourself. Like my grandmother would say, kill two birds with one stone!"

T.J. was still a little frustrated, but he acknowledged Jabeeb because he knew it made sense.

"Yeah, I guess, but...."

T.J. was cut off by a close friend, O.G., that used to drink with him. O.G. yelled in excitement as loud as he could.

"Man! You clean up well! I got to keep you away from my lady. You might cut her while you steal her, you so sharp!"

"All, go head-on with all that, O.G., it's just a suit."

"Just a suit?! Just a suit, my ass! It's a suit, a tie, some Stacie's, cologne, and a shave! You know I am older than you by twos and fews, and I don't miss a beat!"

Jabeeb laughed.

"Yeah, O.G., you sure don't miss anything."

"Yeah, like when your nephew tried to cheat me out of five dollars!"

O.G. waved five dollars in Jabeeb's face. T.J. laughed.

"Come on, O.G., get off the past, man. I'm gone y'all. I have a serious situation to handle."

"Does that mean you not going to come back and hang with your boys later?"

"Oh, trust me, that's going to happen. I will hang with y'all, alright."

Jabeeb had some idea of what T.J. was talking about but not entirely. He looked at T.J., puzzled. T.J smiled at both O.G. and Jabeeb, then walked out of the store towards his car to take Samuel back to the hospital.

35

Ms. Opal lay in her bed having a conversation with Marie while she dozed off at the same time.

"Marie?"

"Yeah, I am here, auntie. But, Auntie, you are tired; why don't you get some rest?"

"Baby, trust me, I am being called to rest whether I want to or not."

Marie choked up, but Ms. Opal continued talking,

"Just listen."

"Okay."

"Okay, when you make the cookies for the kids and the man with the beautiful smile, take your flour about a half cup and shake the chocolate chips morsels around in the flour before you mix it in the dough. That is my secret, so the chocolate chips won't mix together too fast."

"Okay."

"And another thing. I have sixty thousand dollars in my green Bible. I cut a big part in it and placed my money in there four years ago. Marie, please give 10% of that to my church."

Marie nodded her head in agreement. Tears were streaming down her cheeks; however, she was not crying out loud.

"And then save the rest. Every time a person needs, here and there, just give it out until it is all gone."

"Why you... well, I know your heart, but how will I know who needs the money?"

"Just give. Well, for one thing."

She paused and held her chest.

"Ooh wee, that hurts."

"Auntie, what's going on?!"

"No worries, I just heard this is part of the process with lung cancer; my body hurts so bad. I will be okay. I just need you to sit back down and listen to these things, please."

Ms. Opal continued holding her chest.

"Okay, now, just carry one hundred dollars in your pocket a day, and trust me, God will give you the insight on who to give it to. And at times, use your free will judgment and just give."

"Auntie, you are so sweet.'

"I'm just human."

Marie laughed.

"I know that auntie, wait, but what do you mean by that anyway?"

"Well, some people are here for good duties; some are here for evil. No matter how you use it, you have to leave this earth, whether people believe in God or not. Think about it, do you want to rest in peace knowing you did right by most or die nervous thinking you are dying from the dirt you did to people? Plain and simple, it is like this, sweetheart, I am dying now. However, my soul is tired and sick but trust and believe it is not afraid."

Marie's face and tears had dried up. Yet, she pondered on the words of her auntie.

"I never thought of it like that auntie, I hope I'm just as smart as you when I get older."

Ms. Opal chuckled.

"Smart as me, huh? Keep living, and life will make you learn."

"Well, yeah, that is so true."

"Oh, my last and final request before I rest my eyes."

"Okay, I'm ready."

Ms. Opal closed her eyes and hesitated for a minute. Marie sat there and waited. Ms. Opal finally opened her eyes and looked around but then smiled as she looked straight in front of her.

"Alright, look at all the people in front of me, greeting me and getting ready for me."

Marie looked over in the direction that her aunt was looking.

"Auntie, I don't see anything."

"Oh, you don't? Well, I don't think you are ready for this kind of greeting. It is not time for you to understand this kind of greeting yet."

Ms. Opal plopped down, flat line, the monitor beeped. Marie cried out loud.

"NO! NO! NO!"

Marie laid over her aunt. The nurses ran into the room, and one kindly escorted Marie out.

36

Brenda spoke with the nurse that came in to check in on Isaac.

"So, nurse."

"Yes?"

"Okay, so, how is it that my son can speak a little bit out of his mouth, then about an hour later, he has large amounts of saliva and cannot move his mouth?"

"The medicine in Isaac's i.v. We want him to try and talk as much as he can when the medicine is working. Isaac's jaw is fractured in pieces, but his entire jaw is not broken. However, once the doctor finishes his job, Isaac will be fine."

"I'm so glad to hear that news. I can let some of my family know. Thank you for everything."

"Oh, no problem, this is more than just a job to me. I shall return to give Isaac some other pillows. We just want him to sit up a little bit more."

"Okay, thanks."

The nurse left, and Brenda looked over at her son. He looked innocent and slept peacefully.

Brenda went downstairs to call Pearl, check on Lema, and see if her sister had made it into town.

"Hello."

"Hey, Pearl, how are you? Can I please talk to Lema?"

"Sure. Wait, Brenda, are you sure everything is okay?"

"Well, Isaac has fractured bones in his jaw...."

"Oh, my goodness!"

"Yeah, but the bright side is that the entire jaw is not broken. So, everything will be fine; it's just the doctor had to do surgery to remove pieces and whatnot."

"Well, girl, I do not want you to relive that situation. I was just checking on you and your family."

"Girl, no problem. I understand you are just being a friend."

"Let me go get Lema. She has been quiet since she been here."

"Yeah, we both know that's not the neighborhood Lema, poor baby."

"She's okay though, let me go get her."

"Okay."

Lema got to the phone and sadly greeted the caller, not knowing who it was.

"Hello."

"Hey, auntie's baby."

"Hey, auntie! Is my cousin okay?!"

Brenda smiled that Lema got excited, but she was also ready to cry.

"Well, he has fractured pieces in his jaw. But Isaac is like you, strong. So, thanks to the Lord, he will be fine."

"I am so glad, auntie. But, I'm sorry, I was the oldest. I should have told us we shouldn't go. Well, I did, but...."

"Baby, don't you blame yourself, you hear me?!"

"Yes, ma'am."

"All you beautiful kids were trying to do a good thing and get Ms. Opal medicine. You all were doing right, and us adults...."

Her voice began to shake.

"We are the ones who need to say, I'm sorry!"

"Why, auntie?"

"I will explain later. But, baby, did your mom call over there?"

"Yes, ma'am, a few times. My momma said she will be here tonight at 10:30."

Brenda looked around noticed her car was not in the parking lot.

"Uh, okay, uh, love you, Lema. Let me speak back to Mrs. Pearl."

"Okay, love you too."

Lema yelled.

"Mrs. Pearl! Mrs. Pearl!"

"Yes, Miss. Lema?"

"My auntie wants you to come back to the phone, ma'am."

"Okay. Brenda, you call whenever and however many times you need to, you hear? I had Ron thaw out some meat, so I'm about to cook in a second."

There was a long pause.

"Hello, Brenda, are you there?"

"Yeah, I'm here. I just don't see my car. Anyway. So, my sister said she would be there at 10:30, huh?"

"Yes, she said she would call you when she got here. She knew you were already going through so much. But, to be honest, she sounded a little worried herself."

Brenda was preoccupied and not really paying attention.

"Oh, okay. Pearl let me go; I have to find Sam. I don't see my car."

"Oh, okay, talk to you later."

Brenda looked around and saw this sixty-thousand-dollar car coming close to her. So naturally, she jumped out the way. But, to Brenda's surprise, it was T.J. with Samuel in the front seat. Brenda walked over to the car.

"Samuel, Samuel, roll down your window."

Samuel was half-sleep, so T.J. stepped out of the car. He was feeling a little guilty that he left without telling Brenda.

"Oh, uh, hey, hey, Brenda."

"Hey, T.J., what's this about?!"

"Trust me, I should have told you, but Samuel was upset in the waiting room. Then he saw my daughter and was like, I have not seen her in a long time. Well, to make a long story short, Bren, all this is really hard for Samuel to handle."

"I understand where you coming from, T.J., but Samuel knows I need him!"

Brenda put her head down. T.J. felt so bad because Brenda was one person who never judged him. Now her husband was drinking, and he didn't want Brenda to go through that. T.J. placed half of his body in the car and tried to shake Samuel until he woke up.

"Come on, man, get out the car.

Samuel got out of the car, still tipsy. He went to hug Brenda, but she stepped back and covered her nose.

"Ooh wee, baby! You smell like Bevmo after they threw rocks and busted all the bottles!"

Samuel laughed extremely hard, mainly from being intoxicated.

"That's a good one, babe; you should be a comedian. It is so many reasons I am with this woman, I tell you!"

T.J. placed his head down in embarrassment and looked over at Brenda.

"You despise drinking! I mean, you drink here and there, but you don't drink heavily. So what's going on?!"

Brenda was confused, but even more, she was worried.

"Brenda, look at me. I'm worthless. Why do you love me? You and your son deserve better. And I can't even pay for the hospital bill! And..."

Benda cut Samuel off. She was upset at his words, and her tone of voice changed.

"You look here! You are the best man I ever had! Do you hear me?! You are not worthless one bit! Isaac's father called to get back in my life, 90% for me and 10% for Isaac! So don't you ever deny your existence or your place in our lives! You have never been one to cop out;

why start now?! You are too damn strong for this, Samuel! Answer me this, Samuel. Does me not having the money for his hospital bill make me a bad mother?"

"No, Bren, but you have a lot of savings and...."

"Yeah, so what! I have a few thousand saved up, but it's not enough! Just by you not having enough money, that makes you just want to walk out on us when we need you, huh?!"

Brenda was shaking and almost in tears.

"Uh, Samuel, answer me!"

Samuel held her tight to show her he didn't want to leave her or Isaac's life. T.J. wanted to reassure them both so bad and let them know that he paid the bill. However, T.J. knew this was not the right time. T.J. was just glad they made peace. He wanted everyone back upstairs to support Isaac. He walked over and hugged them both.

"Look here, this may be the wrong time to say this, anyhow, everything happens for a reason, no matter the time or the season. My brother and I haven't talked like this in years! And Bren, the way you express how important Samuel is to his family, I know that has to count for something, right?"

Samuel and Brenda nodded in agreement. Then, they walked towards the hospital.

"Thanks, T.J., what you expressed is more than right."

"Yeah, I love y'all. Thanks. Wait. I can't go in there to see my son like this."

"Yeah, I hear you. Brenda, can I go take Samuel to get some coffee at the cafeteria so he can whine down? We'll meet you upstairs in a minute?"

Brenda went over to give Samuel a kiss.

"Yeah, that's fine, T.J. I will see y'all in a minute."

Samuel yelled towards Brenda as she walked away.

"Thanks for always making me feel like a man."

"I can only make you feel like what you really are, babe."

As Samuel and T.J walked to the cafeteria, and since the vibe was good, T.J felt he could convince Samuel to make this first bottle his last.

"Now we can get rid of that first and last bottle, huh, little brother?"

"Huh? Well, for the meantime, but I was on cloud 11 when I was drinking. So I may just use that method instead of having to talk to someone. I will at times just drown my sorrows."

T.J. felt so bad and upset at himself for Samuel's drinking. T.J. got Samuel his coffee and escorted him back up to Brenda. T.J. ran back down to his car and called Jabeeb.

"Come on, man, pick up."

"Hello. Hey, T.J., I was wondering how things are, and you called. Is everything okay?"

"Well, if that's what you want to call it."

"What do you mean?"

"Naw, man shoo, I just feel partly responsible. I know you were saying don't blame myself, but Samuel is going to continue to drink, man."

"Well, how do you know this to be a fact?"

"In so many words, he made it perfectly clear he was going to continue to drink instead of speaking to someone about his problems."

"Oh, wow! Well, what do you want me to help with, my friend? I have the right to refuse anyone at my store. Just say the word, and I will refuse to sell liquor to Samuel at my store for good."

"Good looking out, Jabeeb. That is a really good gesture. If it is not your store, though, it will be someone else's store. And you and I know if he goes to someone else's store who don't know him, with that attitude he has, Samuel will get beat down or ran over or something."

"Well, this is true!"

"You know what, I'm just going to follow your advice and do what you told me a minute ago."

"Uh, what advice? I say so much."

"No, don't worry about that. I'm talking about when you told me how my wife would have wanted me to rehabilitate myself and others. I think I am going to open up a rehabilitation center."

Jabeeb clapped and smiled in excitement.

"Oh, my goodness! That is a blessing! What good news! And thanks for sharing that news with me, T.J.!"

"Yeah, of course. And not only am I sharing the news with you, but I also want you to be the one cutting the ribbon at the grand opening. There is another lady I have in mind I want to be a part of this."

T.J. thought of Carla when she gave him that card offering him help.

"Oh, yes, yes! Your daughter would be perfect!"

"Well, not her, even though my baby girl will, of course, be involved. Anyway, when all this tragedy was going down, and everyone was on their way to the hospital, to make a long story short, this nurse, Carla, gave me this card. She was like a heaven-sent angel. Then you were the last sign I needed with your words of encouragement. Sobriety, here I come!"

"Yes! Yes! Hey, like I say, whenever you are ready, go and grab it! You know, T.J., so many people tell me, 'No, you don't belong in this country,' and, 'you were just given the store.' Someone even gave me a black eye when I got here, as soon as I opened my store! The guy said I am taking all American's money. However, T.J., you know what?"

"What's that, Jabeeb?"

"Over half of the people mad at me could not imagine getting beat and forced to work! I hear complaints all the time about ten dollars an hour. Where I am from, four fifty an hour and hard labor! Sometimes I would get a busted lip for just doing right! So, if I chose to work hard, save money, and come to California to make an easier life for my family, who wouldn't? Well, obviously, people who worry more about me than going to get what's out there. Instead of beating me up, I would help others, but no one gets to know me; they just pre-judge. So when I came to California, and the guy gave me that black eye, I took it with pride!"

"Taking a black eye with pride?"

"Yes, sir. In my country, I was getting bruises for nothing. So, when I worked hard, saved up, and came here to buy what I worked so hard for, which is my store, and got the black eye, I figured, now at least I earned what I have and getting a black eye. Instead of getting a black eye and being sent to bed with no dinner and nothing to call my own! I don't care what people say because me coming to make a better life for my family is common sense."

"I never looked at it like that. Well, on that note, Jabeeb, I will get what I deserve and go after what I want. Thanks for talking to me. I'm going to just go ahead, get in here and check on my nephew and sit with my daughter for a minute."

"Alright. Just know I am just a phone call away."

"Trust me, I know that!"

They hung up, and T.J. walked inside the hospital.

37

While Linda, Steve, and Samantha were in the room with David, Steve thought about the reality of the hospital bill. He tapped Samantha and whispered in her ear.

"Hey hon,' we better go talk to the doctors and come up with a plan concerning David's hospital bill. "

"Yeah, I agree. Lin', we will be right back."

"Okay, I think I can keep this young man occupied."

"Okay, sweetheart, we will be back."

"Okay. Mom! Can you do me a favor?"

"What's that?"

"Can you tell Isaac I said hello?"

Samantha looked at Steve, and he did not have an angry face this time. Samantha looked over at Linda, who gave Samantha a wink. When David did not get a response, he remembered how his dad felt about Isaac. David just wanted his dad's approval so that his mom would agree. So he figured out the parent yes and no team thing.

"Dad, just this one time, can you tell Isaac hello, please?"

Steve looked down and back at his son lying in the hospital bed. Steve thought of the prep talk earlier and how willing and caring Manzel was to help his family. It all popped in his head at once.

"How can I deny you a true friend, sure."

Linda and Samantha looked at each other, and their eyes grew bigger than the bottom of a soda can.

"Thank you, dad! I love you so much!"

"I love you too, son."

Samantha smiled, proud of her husband.

"Hubby, let's go step out and handle our other business, sweetheart."

Steve walked out first. Behind Steve's back, Samantha gave Linda a thumbs up. As the two stepped out into the hallway, Samantha noticed that Marie was down the hallway crying. She headed towards Marie. Steve thought Samantha was going in the wrong direction.

"Samantha, where are you going? The doctor is this way."

Samantha lost her train of thought and went back towards Steve.

"Oh, okay, honey."

The doctor escorted Steve and Samantha to the finance department of the hospital. They both talked things over with the head lady of the finance department, Diane.

"Okay, Mr. and Mrs. Smith, have a seat, please."

They both sat.

"Thank you."

"Okay, we have three options for payment methods. Which we all know are money orders, cash, or credit card. However, it is our mandatory policy that we give you a receipt whenever a payment is made with cash, or we can email you a receipt as well."

"Okay, I have a question. What is the limit you pay on the...."

Steve was interrupted by a phone buzz. Diane held her finger up politely for Steve to hold his thought.

"Hello, Diane Whithers, finance department; how may I help you?"

There was a long pause.

"Okay, are you sure? So, you mean down to a zero balance?"

Steve and Samantha looked at each other.

"Okay. Well, I will let them know. That is most definitely some good news! I love being the barrier of this news. Okay, talk to you later."

Diane hung up the phone and let out a sigh of relief. She closed the file and slapped it down on the desk.

"Well, okay. There is no need to discuss the payment plan anymore!"

Samantha and Steve looked puzzled.

"Well, why not?!"

"I just received a call from my boss who stated someone paid for your son's medical bills in full! Whoever it was also covered the medical expenses so your son could receive the therapy sessions he needs as well!"

Samantha let out high pitch yell in excitement.

"WHAT!!! You have got to be fucking kidding me?! Excuse my language."

Steve jumped out of his seat.

"Now, Ms. Withers, is it?"

"Yes, that's me."

"Now, I have a child in there who needs me, please, no need for games."

"Mr. Smith, for one, I am a professional, and I handle my business that way. Furthermore, I would in no way play Milton Bradley games in these circumstances. Now, on that note once again, your child's hospital bills are paid; in full!"

Steve ran around behind Diane's desk. She drew back, not knowing what Steve's next move would be. Steve picked her up and spent her around, then dropped her back down. She looked at Steve weirdly as she fixed her clothes.

"Come on, Ms. Withers, one of your doctors paid for this bill here at the hospital, didn't they?!"

Diane sat in her seat; still a little shook up from Steve spinning her around.

"I know you are excited, Mr. Smith, but was that gestured called for?"

Samantha patted Steve's chair so he would have a seat.

"I apologize for my husband, Diane, but if I could have picked you up, I would have myself. You have to realize this is shocking to us! But, seriously, I need to know, did you or any doctor here pay this bill?!"

"I would be honored to bestow this gift; however, it is against our policy and regulations to do this. Also, if I knew a staff member or doctor was to do this, I would have to notify the department. That person would be suspended or fired immediately."

Steve was excited but eager to know who paid the bill.

"Okay. Fine. Who is it?"

"Sir, the only information that was enclosed to me was that the bill for your child was paid in full."

Diane leaned in towards Samantha and Steve and whispered.

"Only thing I can say, between us in this room, is that my boss stated it was a he; if that would help any."

"Hmm, he? Well, that narrows it down a lot, but I don't know...."

Steve cut Samantha off.

"Well, we will find out! Thank you! Thank you so much. By the way, even though we did not pay, can we still have the receipt so it will not be any discrepancies or mishaps later?"

"Oh, for sure, I was so excited for you that it slipped my mind. Let me come back down to earth and call over and have them fax that right away. I will personally bring it to you."

Samantha and Steve hugged each other so tight. Diane left her office headed down the hallway. As the Smiths walked down the hallway, Steve noticed T.J. passed by and did not make eye contact like usual. Steve's face dropped in disappointment.

"Okay, honey, you bringing me down. What happened to your excitement?"

Steve looked back at T.J.

"Honey, you think I should apologize to that guy?"

"Only you have the answer to that in your heart. But, it will come a time when you get a chance and bad as I would love for that to occur right now, we need to tell Linda about this good news."

Steve agreed with her. When they finally made it into the room, they had the largest grin ever. Steve stared at Linda without saying a word.

"Okay, Steve, you are scaring me. What is going on?"

Linda looked over at Samantha and saw the same expression.

"Okay, I am really scared now. We have an injured child in here, and you two are smiling like y'all just won the lottery."

Steve ran and picked Linda up and spun her around. She smacked Steve on top of his head with the magazine she was reading to David. Steve put her down.

"Now you had just recently come to your senses in the waiting room; what happened to that?!" Steve clapped his hands.

"Hot damn it! I knew it!"

Linda was completely baffled. Samantha raised an eyebrow as she looked at her sister.

"You paid for it, didn't you?"

"Paid for what?!"

"David's hospital bill."

"I was going to give you two my nine thousand that I have, but I was just going to ask you what else you two needed because I know the bill is way more than that. I don't have a lot of money. So after I gave you what I have, I was just going to pray for a miracle, but I did not pay anything."

Samantha sat down in her seat.

"You know what, Steve?"

"Yeah, Sam."

"We are just too excited and eager to find out who. However, Diane did give us a hint; it was a male, remember?"

"Wait a minute. You mean to tell me someone actually paid the hospital bill?!"

"Yes, but we don't know who."

"Yes, Sam, she did say he."

"Okay, wait a minute, who said he?"

Samantha explained to Linda in full what was going on.

"God is good! I wonder who is that generous, though."

David knew better than to jump in grownup's conversations; however, this time, he could not hold back what he thought on this subject.

"Mom, Dad, I bet you Isaac's dad paid, probably. Isaac shared with me a lot, dad. Ask him, and did you tell him I said hi?"

"Son, we will. It is just so much going on right now, okay. We will talk to Isaac for you."

"Yeah, son, now relax. I know you trust your friend and all, that's fine. I know his dad did not pay that bill."

Steve paused, and Samantha and Linda looked at Steve, wondering what Steve was thinking of was.

"I am going to call Manzel and see if he did this generous favor. I will be back, honey."

Linda watched Steve leave then turned towards Samantha.

"Wow, I wonder if Manzel or just who did that!"

"I don't know, but you better believe we are eternally grateful, I can tell you that! I just could not believe it when she told us that!"

"Mom, can you go talk to Isaac for me?"

Samantha looked at Linda.

"Go ahead on, little sis. You can do it, and you know I am watching over David. He is safe here with me."

Samantha nodded her head and left. She headed towards Isaac's door and noticed Marie in the hallway, and walked to her. Samantha had a feeling Ms. Opal was going, but she was too nervous to ask Marie verbally.

"Is everything okay?"

Marie looked up at Samantha with a blank stare.

"I wish it was; she's gone!"

Marie placed her head in her lap and cried. Samantha grabbed a chair and sat right next to Marie, and put her arm around Marie, and shed tears as well.

"You had an amazing aunt who brought joy to so many lives. And she even kept some alive also."

"Kept some alive?"

"Oh, yeah. There was this little girl named Meagan."

"I remember hearing about Megan. She was the little girl who the other kids always said was weird and a cry baby, right?"

"Yes, that is true. It wasn't Meagan she kept alive, though; it was her mother."

"I saw Meagan, but I never saw her mother."

"I know, there were a lot of people who never saw her mother. You see, Meagan's mother was on a lot of anti-depressants. Megan cried and ran to Ms. Opal's house with her birdcage. I remember this like it was yesterday. I was on my way to the store, and I went to check to make sure things were okay because Meagan was crying so loud. Anyway, your auntie so nice, she told Meagan she would keep her bird, and she and her mom could come down and feed the bird."

"Well, that's strange. Why couldn't they feed the bird at their place?"

"That is how sweet your aunt was. She knew Megan's mom took care of that bird the way she took care of Meagan, which was one of the good traits Meagan's mom had. Ms. Opal knew that that would get Meagan's mom out of the house and into some fresh air. Ms. Opal was the only person that woman talked to."

Samantha got choked up thinking about it. She grew quiet.

"Why are you so quiet. What's wrong?"

"I'm sorry, I was just thinking how the entire neighborhood would look and get quiet when Meagan's mom went to Ms. Opal's house. Meagan's mom was known as the mystery crazy woman of the neighborhood Ol' lovely Ms. Opal. She had a heart of gold and the skin of a porcelain doll for her age. Sweetheart, I know you are sad, but be blessed that you had a wonderful aunt such as her. Ms. Opal changed a lot of lives and David's and Isaac's fathers before she left."

Samantha stood up, and a few more tears came down. She thought of what Ms. Opal would do and how she affected the grown men before she died. Now she knew it would be easier for her to talk to Isaac for David because of the role model and skills Ms. Opal left behind.

"Uh, well, so she passed on her famous cookie recipe, huh?"

"Yeah, let me later surprise the boys and girls with It, okay?"

"No problem. Try to stay strong. We will keep you in our prayers."

Marie hugged Samantha.

"Thank you. You made me feel so much better."

"No problem. You cannot even imagine how your aunt made us feel or what she did for us on a regular basis."

Samantha was about to walk into Isaac's room before Marie stopped her.

"Wait! Whatever happened to Meagan and her mom?"

"Your auntie did so good helping her get into the community and out of the house that she lowered her dosage of anti-depressants. As a result, she received a good job and found her and her daughter a nice home elsewhere. In an even better neighborhood."

"Wow! My auntie must have been an angel."

T.J. talked to his daughter and Brenda since Samuel was still trying to sober up and finish his coffee. T.J. notified Brenda and Toni that he would be back to check on Samuel. Samantha grabbed the door to Isaac's room just as T.J. went out, so they ran into each other face to face.

"Uh, hello."

"You must be the famous Uncle T.J. I heard about from all the kids."

T.J. smiled hard, and Samantha stepped back, a little amazed by T.J.'s teeth.

"Well, I wouldn't say all that, but thanks. David's mom, right?"

"Yeah, that's me."

Samantha shook T.J.'s hand, then looked over at Brenda and smiled, remembering how Brenda helped her before in the store.

"Well, come on in. Are you okay, sweetheart?"

"Oh, go ahead. I have to leave anyway; nice to see you."

"Oh, okay, same here, see you later."

T.J. headed to get his brother but noticed Steve on the phone. Steve was talking pretty loud, so T.J. couldn't help but hear Steve asking someone on the phone if they had paid his son's hospital bill. T.J. continued to walk on to get to his brother, but at a slow pace, somewhat eavesdropping on Steve's conversation. He hoped Steve didn't have a clue that he paid the hospital bills.

"You sure, Manzel? Come on, if you paid my son's bill, I must pay you back. Okay, so it wasn't you? Well, I still appreciate the gesture of you offering help earlier. However, I still need to know who this good Samaritan is. Well, I will talk to you later. Okay, thanks."

Samantha sparked up a conversation in Isaac's room.

"You remember me, right?"

Brenda smiled.

"Yeah, I do."

"You helped me in the store, and our kids helped each other, huh?"

"Yes, this is true. Now we need to pray for each other."

"Oh yes, trust when I say I have been doing that. My son has constantly been telling me to check on Isaac and tell him hello."

Samantha, Brenda, and Toni looked over at Isaac sleeping.

"Yeah, he is sleeping. His medicine kicked in. Now it is time for the doctors to do their job. Anyway, how is David?"

"Well, now that we have the hospital taking care of, we can get the physical therapy our son needs to whip him back into shape and get David walking again."

Brenda was a little disappointed but still happy for Samantha's family.

"It must feel good to have the money you need in times like this, huh? I don't know how that feels."

"Well, I can relate."

"I am trying to sympathize with you here; how do you know how it feels? Did you just not say your hospital bill for David plus the physical therapy is paid for? You cannot relate to our foreign language. We do not know how our bill is going to get paid. Also, we are unsure how we are going to pay for the surgery bill."

"No, well, to be honest, Brenda, we have savings; however, when my husband and I went to talk to Diane in the finance department, she stated someone paid our bill in full!"

"Well, okay, you have good friends, and once again, like I stated, you cannot relate."

"Brenda, please do not make this a personal issue. Trust me, I would have paid my child, yours, and Jerry's hospital bills if I could have. Even though we all know Jerry's mother has the money."

Oh, yeah? Tell me about it? Tell me how you could have helped?"

"We are doing well now, Brenda, and I am sorry you have to find a way with your finances for your child. Look, I didn't come down here to say, 'oh, look, my kid's bill is paid, and yours is not,' okay. To be honest, my son drilled in my head to check on his friend. Also, I realized I never told you thank you for being the only lending hand in that store when I needed you. It is sad it took these circumstances for me to realize so much. I constantly keep our children, as well as us all, in prayer. I thank you, and I am sorry if I ever was rude to you or made you feel some type of way!"

Samantha reached out to Brenda for a hug. Brenda stood up and gave Samantha the biggest hug. They both squeezed each other and cried hard. Toni didn't know the entire story; however, she was glad it was closure to at least one problem.

"We are going to get through this, Brenda. I know it!"

"Trust me, I know it! It is like this tragedy happened for a reason. We all needed to come together!"

Toni passed the box of Kleenex.

"I don't know one hundred percent what's going on, but it truly looks like God's plan for sure! My mom would call it a collaborating to the flower he wanted it to be from the seed."

Brenda took a Kleenex and wiped Samantha's face, and placed the napkin in her hand. Then, she grabbed another one for herself and sat down.

"You're just like your father, Toni; you know what to say, even if it hurts. That was appropriate and needed to be heard. We all miss your mom too."

In the waiting room, T.J. spoke with Samuel.

"How's the coffee, bro?"

"It's doing the job, man."

"Alright, well, I could sit out here with you or go back in there with Isaac before they kick us all out of the room. So, what's up? What do you want me to do?"

Samuel sat his cup down on the table.

"Well, for one, I am a little puzzled. You told me you heard about somebody taking care of my son's bill. I need to check on that. I am going to go upstairs too to pull Brenda out so we can see what's going on."

Samuel looked at T.J. up and down. He remembered his brother dressed like this before his wife died; however, he figured his brother was tax evasion broke now.

"T.J., where you get these suits from? Are they the ones you already had?"

T.J. thought of a quick lie. He wondered why Samuel asked that question right after he said he would check on the paid hospital bill.

"Oh, uh, Jabeeb, was just uh, Jabeeb, bought them for his relative back where he from, and they didn't like the color, so I took over and asked could I have them."

"Oh, okay, I was about to say, my son not dead, don't dress like you coming to a funeral. I know you don't have clothes like that anymore."

T.J. could care less about his rude remarks; he was just glad he threw Samuel off.

"Oh, yeah, I couldn't come up to the hospital smelling, you know what I mean."

"Yeah, I hear you, thanks. It looks like we switched roles. But, hey, man, remember when we were little, we used to worry how shelters got paid."

"Yeah, we were real young and nosey."

"Thanks for everything, man."

"Uh, yeah, wait, what you mean thanks, for what?"

"Just for somewhat bringing me back to reality. You know when a person is angry, they blame the closest person to you. Believe it or not, you are the closest friend I have, and I'm still glad to call you my brother. Anyway, I can pay you back. You just name it."

T.J. was relieved it was not about the hospital bill, once again.

"Well, there is something you can do for me."

"Okay, name it. Spit it out."

T.J. placed his hand on Samuel's shoulder.

"You can let that bottle you had, be your last drink."

Samuel moved T.J. with semi force.

"Good try! Your teeth and smile are not that beautiful to make me change from my new comfort zone! That grin is for the ladies, not for me. Let me go ahead and get up here to do what I'm supposed to do. I have to handle this so I can get to Jabeeb's for some more of my comfort juice; now I'm thinking about it."

T.J. put his head down in disgust and guilt.

"Well, man, go ahead. I have to get some fresh air; I will be back."

T.J. left the waiting room to go outside, and Samuel got buzzed in to talk to the doctors and get Brenda.

38

In Ms. Opal's room, Marie talked with the doctors for the last time before leaving the hospital.

"Well, doc, no need to tell me. I know this is it; I hate those last words."

"Oh, no, don't say that. This is possibly the beginning for you."

The doctor held up Ms. Opal's house keys she brought with her to the doctor.

"Ms. Opal had enough time to write these words for you."

The doctor passed Marie a note that Ms. Opal wrote. The words were scribbled as if her hand was shaking when she wrote it.

"Ming, ha, ha, please take care of my house, Marie. It is yours. Don't forget what I told you."

As Marie finished reading her aunt's words, she clinched the letter and shed a few tears.

"Are you okay?"

"Trust me, I am. Yes, I am sad my aunt is gone; however, I was in the process of looking for another place closer to her to help her, and I almost received it. They were going to give me the answer next week. There are other family members we have; however, she chose to let me have her house!"

Marie smiled and looked down at the keys in her hand.

"Yeah, well, she was an amazing woman, I can say that."

"Yes. Let me get to my new house and finish crying. Thanks for everything, doc."

Marie thought of her auntie's hospital bill. The doctor looked into Marie's face and commented as if he had read Marie's mind.

"Marie, let me let you in on a wise little secret. Eighty percent of the elderly learn, and twenty percent burn."

"What do you mean?"

"Well, I've witnessed this situation all my life, and I am a young 63 years old and just started to save. When we are young, we all feel that a disaster will not happen to us, or we just don't save for emergencies. When people notice the elderly don't become involved with a lot of things that cost money, they are trained to save for situations such as this. What I am trying to say is your bill is paid in full, and your aunt paid for a burial site right next to her husband. So everything will be fine. Enjoy your house, Marie."

The doctor walked away, then stopped and looked back at Marie.

"Just do us a favor and keep her legacy going. Make people happy in this cruel world like she did."

"I could never fill her shoes, but I will keep trying them on until they fit."

She winked at the doctor. The doctor smiled and said his last words as he walked away.

"Nice saying. I'll have to use that one."

Samuel got to the room, and he looked inside. He noticed Isaac sleeping and Samantha, Brenda, and Toni holding a conversation. Then, out of nowhere, it was like Brenda felt Samuel's presence. Brenda looked over at the door, and Samuel waved his hand for Brenda to come out. Samantha looked back and saw Samuel as well.

"Okay, Brenda, I'm going back to the room and let David know Isaac is resting. I'm glad we talked. I will help with your bill, some kind of way, once I've talked to my husband since we were blessed out of nowhere."

Brenda smiled, almost in tears.

"That was a very pleasant thought, but no way. We will not do that to you; we cannot accept handouts."

"Please, Brenda, and remember I said I would try to help. This is no handout. When I talk to my husband and if he says yeah, let me help. We said it was not about us anymore, remember?"

"You are right. Well, let me get out here; my husband is calling me. God bless you, Samantha

"Let me get back to my son and sister. They are waiting for me, also."

Samantha passed by Samuel.

"Hello."

Even though Samuel did not speak back, his sincere smile said hello and a thousand other silent but courteous words. Brenda was walking behind Samantha, and as she was walking away, Brenda grabbed Samantha's hand lightly.

"Thanks for checking on my family. We will talk soon."

Samantha knew they had already said their thank yous and good-byes in the room. But, Samantha caught on quick, and it was pretty clear why Brenda was doing this in front of Samuel. So, Samantha just went along with it.

"Yes, by all means, we will meet and greet again."

Samuel looked at both women curiously.

"What was that all about?"

"We were just having a rational adult conversation. Maturing and accepting responsibility, and all that good stuff."

Brenda noticed Samuel was not staggering like he was earlier.

"You sobered up, huh?"

"Yeah, but don't worry about that right now; look, I'm onto something else. We need to go talk to the doctor."

Brenda looked nervous.

"Why!"

"Come on, Bren, don't worry about yourself or me anymore. It is not a drastic thing, well, a little. T.J. told me, downstairs earlier, that he heard the doctor state that our hospital bill was taken care of. Go ahead, Brenda, you can tell me, babe, your little mad money you saved paid off, didn't it?!"

"Brenda looked confused.

"Babe, trust me, I wished it did pay something or was enough to pay the entire thing off for that matter. Seriously, I have a lot of savings for us, but not like that."

Samuel waved his hand.

"Man, yeah, T.J. just be talking to calm situations down or make people feel good sometimes."

Samuel frowned when Brenda's eyes got big.

"Woman, what's wrong with you? Do you see the ghost from Christmas past?!"

Brenda dwelt on what Samantha had told her.

"Well, wait! Did T.J say the doctor said the entire thing was taken care of?"

Samuel looked up into the air, trying to remember everything.

"I wasn't all the way sober, but yeah, that's what he said."

Brenda was excited, wondering if they would become blessed like Samantha's family.

"Well, where is T.J.? I need to talk to him. I want to know more about what he told you."

"He left. He said he needed some fresh air for a minute."

"Oh, Lord, when y'all men say y'all need some fresh air that is a store run or an adventure."

"Aww, woman, please! Well, if you lightweight believe T.J., I would rather go talk to one of these doctors and ask them for facts."

Brenda thought hard. If this is true, she now believed Samantha how awkward she felt that their bill was paid out of nowhere.

"Come on, babe, what's the holdup? What's wrong? What are you hesitating for?"

"No, babe, it's just, well, I remember when David's mom was in our room, she said something like the bills goes through their finance department. And there is a lady named Diane Withers in the finance department. Honey, Samantha said that woman, Ms. Withers, stated their bill was paid too."

Samuel was not convinced.

"Okay, Bren, and that has nothing to do with our bill."

"Oh, Samuel. No, I am just saying that is the lady we probably should talk to. If you really think about what I just told you!"

"Yeah, well, you on to something. Let's find out where the department is and find out before...."

Samuel couldn't even finish his sentence before Brenda grabbed a doctor.

"Excuse me, Dr.?"

"Yes, I am Dr. Baxter. What can I do for you?"

"Yes, my husband and I were wondering do you have a finance department inside the hospital? If so, where, please?"

"Oh, yes, we do. You would have to speak to Ms. Diane Withers. The elevator is to the right; go up to floor 8. She should be up there in her office."

Samuel and Brenda look at each other and back at the doctor.

"Thank you, Doctor Baxter."

"No problem, that's the least I could do. You two have a nice one."

Brenda and Samuel did as follows, and when they got off the elevator, they both took a deep breath before they went in.

39

T.J paced the floor outside. Then, finally, he decided to call Jabeeb again.

"Pick up, pick up!"

"Hello."

"Hey."

"Hey there, T.J.! Everything smoothing out, I hope."

"If that is what you want to call it."

"Wow, what do you mean? Oh, no, I thought things were getting better, and everything started to somewhat get in control?"

"Just forget it. I needed to call you, but I shouldn't have, I guess."

"How can you say that! I only ask questions so I will not be in the dark, my friend!"

T.J. relaxed and calmed down.

"Man, look, I didn't mean to come off like that, Jabeeb. Seriously, I need to come and talk to you. This over the phone isn't working for me."

"Well, come on down. I will have my nephew take over the store, and we can go somewhere and talk; it's not a problem."

"Cool, I'm on my way."

T.J. made his way out to the car and headed to Jabeeb's store.

Brenda and Samuel entered the finance department. Brenda spoke to the administrative assistant, a very professional woman who looked as if she could be a school teacher.

"Excuse me, is Ms. Diane Withers available?"

"Yes, who shall I say is requesting her assistance? Your name please?"

"Oh, I'm Brenda, Brenda Johnson."

She looked over at Samuel, who had already sat down and was reading a magazine.

"This is my husband, Samuel Johnson. We are here concerning our son, Isaac Johnson, and the hospital bill."

"Okay, no problem."

She notified Diane, who then walked in to greet Brenda and Samuel with a professional smile.

"Well, hello, Mr. And Mrs. Johnson, how are you?"

They both spoke simultaneously as if they were coached by a choir director and were on the same rhythm.

"Hello, to you."

"Oh, okay, well, on that note, what brings you into my office?"

They gave Diane a look as if they wanted to talk in private. So, Diane escorted the couple into her office and gave the two of them the Vanna White from Wheel of Fortune, greeting them to their seats.

"Okay, I do know you two are the parents of Isaac, so how may I help you? Wait. How is he?"

"He's doing. I think once he has his surgery, he will be a lot better. We all hope, shall I say."

Brenda placed her head down. Diane had sympathy for Brenda.

"Don't lose faith yet; he is in good hands with the best doctors. I hope that makes you two feel better and that it counts for something."

Brenda looked up and smiled at Diane.

"I appreciate the encouragement. Yes, it is good for a lot, thanks."

Samuel appreciated all the gratitude and mushiness; however, he started to be his usual self. Which is outspoken with a bit of straightforward arrogance.

"Okay, Diane, check this out."

Brenda and Diane looked at each other, then back at Samuel. Brenda's face was on yellow caution mode, not knowing what he would say and hoping it would be subtle.

"Basically, on my way back up here, my brother said our son's hospital bill was paid for. Well, something like that. He said the doctor said it."

Diane looked baffled, thinking of the Smith's situation.

"Well, did the doctor have a name because we don't have random doctors up here just paying bills? That would definitely cost a doctor their job. But, you know today has been a strange and happy day for some. So, let me call another department and see if your bill has been paid. It won't hurt to see right."

"Well, maybe T.J. just had a misunderstanding. It happens at times, babe."

Diane was puzzled. However, she hoped for the child's sake; this situation is just like the blessing David's parents received. Why would a family member play a game and tell them something untruthful like this? Samuel laughed and waved his hand in disbelief.

"No need to waste your time. Now that is a joke and a dream. No one paid that bill, trust me!"

Brenda agreed with Samuel; however, she did not speak on it. Instead, she just placed her head down in sadness, wondering how they would get the hospital bill paid.

"Well, I do not know your brother; however, if you don't mind, I would like to check. I just don't feel your brother would make something like that up. Especially in this serious situation."

Brenda nodded yes for Diane to check on it.

"Okay, let me call the finance head department."

Samuel threw his hands up.

"Brenda nodded okay, so go ahead."

Brenda sounded hopeless but wanted to know.

"Well, Samuel, it won't hurt, I guess."

Diane made the call. Brenda and Samuel held on for the information but not for the news they thought was never possible.

"Hi, how are you? Oh, well, wow! Well, this is music to my ears and will be a symphony for the parents! I don't know what is going on, but someone is full of generosity and rich! Okay, send the forms so I can have the parents sign and fax them back over to you for confirmation."

Diane hung up and smiled at Samuel and Brenda.

"Well!"

Brenda was excited and nervous.

"Well?!"

"Well, I cannot disclose other patient information. However, I've seen blessings come and go, but in the 20 years of my career, it has been so, so, long since I've witnessed multiple blessings!"

Brenda grew impatient and sarcastic.

"Okay, well, I am. Others are happy and getting good news, but I want to know what good or bad information ours is."

Samuel intervened. He noticed the frustration in Brenda's voice.

"Well, since what my brother stated was a myth, is there just a payment plan we can be offered for our son, so we can get the ball rolling?"

Brenda looked at Samuel in relief since he stepped in and asked what she had already asked more assertively.

"How about if I told you that the ball rolled down the court and jumped into the hoop!"

"What?!"

"Yeah, well, for some reason and a good one, someone paid for your son's hospital bill in full!"

Brenda and Samuel's eyes grew big like Susan B. Anthony's.

"Well, I'll be damn, my brother wasn't lying! But, Ms. Whithers, do you think that one of the doctors here paid her, well, our son's hospital bill?"

"Well, like I said before, we would love to help in different situations, but when it comes to people's financial status with their families, we are not allowed."

"Like you said before? You never told us that before. This is our first time meeting with you."

Diane flashed back to when she told David's family the information.

"Oh, yes, excuse me, it has been a long day. I tend to get my conversations mixed up from time to time."

"Oh, okay."

"So, what's the next step? We need to, well, just uh."

"I see you are speechless, Mr. Johnson, so I will step in. What happens is I will get a copy of the receipt for your records that the bill was paid. Then we can proceed to give your son all the care he needs for his surgery. The stay in the hospital and all other fees are taken care of as well!"

Brenda jumped up, shouting and praying out loud.

"Oh, Lord, you are worthy to be praised! Even when I have done nothing, you always do something, Lord!! For I am nothing without your love, mercy, and grace!! Thank you, Lord! Thank you!!"

By this time, Diane's hand was over her mouth, and tears rolled down her face. Samuel had tears of joy. He placed his hands on Brenda's shoulders and escorted her out of the office.

"We thank you so much!"

Diane was speechless and wiping her eyes.

"Diane, Diane, can you hear me?"

Diane trembled when she finally spoke.

"I will send down the receipt when I receive it."

Diane got up and opened the door to her office to escort Samuel and Brenda out. Brenda turned her face. Diane was not rude. She was just overjoyed with both families' news and tried to stay professional and not get choked up again. Brenda continued whispering as she walked out of the office with Samuel escorting her.

"Yes, Lord, yes!"

T.J. made it to Jabeeb's store. He opened his glove compartment and took out seven dollars. T.J. walked in and spoke to Jabeeb's nephew, Ahkili.

"Hey, nephew."

"Hey, T.J., how are you, man?! You look good in your suit!"

"Yeah, well, thank you. Let me get some brandy."

"Okay, no problem."

Ahkili took T.J.'s money and handed him the brandy. As T.J. reached for the brandy, Jabeeb came out and looked at his nephew, then looked over at T.J.

"Hey, there, friend. I will be out there in a minute."

T.J. wanted to hide and felt a little bit embarrassed even more because Jabeeb never judged him, but T.J. did read Jabeeb's concerned face when he saw the bottle.

"Alright, man, I will be waiting in the car."

Jabeeb smiled and waved in agreement. T.J. opened the bottle but did not take a sip. He just sat there for ten minutes with the bottle opened; he was just sitting and thinking. Jabeeb got into T.J.'s car.

"Hey, what's on your mind, T.J.?"

"Well, first off, I want my brother to think and not drink!"

"Oh, come on, he is a thinker, just like you!"

T.J looked offended, thinking Jabeeb was sarcastic.

"No, not like that friend! When you used to stand outside my store and drink, I saw everyone come to you for advice."

"Yeah, but that was just it. My brother just released twenty-three years of turmoil on me! My brother is not going to change overnight! You see how he acted when he drank, Jabeeb!"

"Oh, yeah, you are right about that one."

"Then you know I paid the bill for David's family and my nephew out of love. So why don't I just understand that."

"Come on, T.J., you know you love people no matter how they treat you! You have a heart! With you, it's about those kids! I know that is the main reason for your acts of kindness."

"That's just it! You see the way they talk, my brother and David's dad?!"

"So what they don't! Well, not yet! Trust me, humble man, their hard hearts will soften."

"Humble man, what you mean, now?"

"Any man that can pay thousands of dollars, walk away, and not leave a trace of information that they paid nor wait for a pat on the back, a thank you, or care to receive praise; that is humble pie!"

"Thanks, man. I just figured those kids had enough going on. Especially the way the parents act towards each other."

"Yeah."

"I haven't come to grasp that those kids are in the hospital in that condition. Now, my brother with this new drinking problem. At times, I even wonder if my daughter knows I really love her. Then I saw the sweetest woman in the world, I didn't think could leave, Ms. Opal! She looks like she is on her way out Jabeeb and...."

"Oh my God! You mean Ms. O?!"

"Yeah, man, that sweet older woman who used to always buy the semi-sweet chocolate chips from your store."

"Ah, I remember when she would say, 'Oh, no one has the kind of semi-sweet chocolates I use except your store. I guess that is why you are so sweet and treat everyone in the neighborhood well.'"

"Yeah, that was her. She always had a kind word to say. I just hope she has a speedy recovery, but the way she was talking, she was ready to go."

"Why would you say that?"

"Anytime you are giving up your homemade recipes to another family member. When I talked to her, she told her niece to make cookies for the neighborhood kids after she was gone. And she didn't sound enthusiastic when I asked her when they made the cookies could she join me.

"Jabeeb lost his composure and slapped his hands down hard on T.J.'s dashboard.

"I just hate this, my friend. It seems like the good are only here for days!"

"I understand your pain, but you have frustration built up, I see, besides this situation. You are strong; watch the dashboard."

"Oh, I am so sorry, truly."

"It's alright, man, I just, I.

T.J. gripped the bag of liquor in his hand. Then, finally, he just laid back in his seat and sighed. Jabeeb looked down at the bottle and tried to speak to T.J. in a nonjudgmental way that would stop him from drinking.

"Yeah, so uh, T.J., have you anything else you wanted to talk to me about?"

T.J. knew what Jabeeb was trying to do, so he looked over at Jabeeb and gave him the biggest smile with his pearly whites.

"You alright with me, Jabeeb. You know what?"

"What?"

Most men use 25% words and 75% actions, so T.J. just summed up what he had to say in a few words.

"Just know that you are 100 grand."

T.J threw his hands up to give Jabeeb a high five. T.J then looked down at the bottle while still talking to Jabeeb.

"I don't need this liquor like this. I just cannot let something control me like this, you know. Man, I had too many signs, and my boys I hung out with need me."

"I agree, yes they do!"

"Yeah, and my wife wouldn't want me carrying on like I don't care. Do you know how she died?

Jabeeb was excited that T.J. was pouring out his problems, but he held his composure.

"No, I don't think you shared that with me; however, I didn't want to bring that up when you told me your wife died. I know that is a touchy situation for anyone."

"Yeah, but it's a reason for our communication season right now."

"Well, okay, I'm all ears, speak."

T.J. put the bottle in his lap and started to speak.

"Jabeeb, this woman had the biggest heart. She helped everyone and their kids on birthdays that she could. She randomly took a hundred dollars out of the bank and just gave it out."

"Wow!"

"Yeah, and she had a big family, but they were not close, so she worked her ass off, man! Anyway, she finally got her house, money, and everything she needed. You know, well-deserved blessings. You should have seen how her family tried to flock back into her life when they were not even worried about her like that! Then, I stood by her side. I told her, man! Tears filled T.J.'s eyes and started to flow.

"I told her, you don't have to cater to no one; this is your life you built. You doing right; you don't have to kiss nobody's ass! You know?"

"Oh yeah, I totally understand."

"And Jabeeb, she did good listening and following my advice and kept away from the haters and people in her family that just wanted to use her. Anyway, I guess I should not have pushed the issue on how her family was so bad. I mean, she kept drinking and drinking; she died with cirrhosis of the liver! I lost my woman because of my advice. I should have just told her to stay around them if she could handle their ways. And I should have just not dealt with them."

T.J. laid his head on his steering wheel and just cried. By this time, Jabeeb had a few tears himself.

"You know, you may get upset, but I am going to give it to you straight as I can! You helped your wife; you did not harm any situation!

T.J.'s head was still down, and he was rocking back and forth. Jabeeb yelled.

"Hold your head up and listen!"

T.J. had never heard Jabeeb use that tone of voice, so he held his head up and listened.

"Now, for one, you helped give her a child, a gift of life. I know she was appreciative to the Lord she had a beautiful daughter with you! That was an experience in life that you two shared that I know made her happy! And yes, so what you told her that. It was good she stopped dealing with the fake family members and did not kiss their butt! Yes, it may have hurt her. Suppose you were not there to encourage her, T.J. I truly believe she was a nice woman and would have given all her money and every inch of energy. She would not have a beautiful home for your daughter and you to finish her legacy on! T.J., you need to save souls! There are people out there holding a bottle or maybe doing drugs for a similar reason! I know it's that saying you cannot blame your addiction on others but BULLSHIT!"

T.J. jumped and looked at Jabeeb, surprised. He had never heard Jabeeb use profanity.

"If you do not have the support of family, who is supposed to love you. Especially if you are giving all of your energy, sometimes you end up grabbing negative things that cannot talk back, judge or poke you, pull, and just use you! Look, I read a lot, and when I read about addicts, the first thing addicts lack when they go to treatment is support. They said it was because most family or friends say, yeah, right, they'll be back. Yes, I may sell liquor, and it is up to an individual if they drink too much; therefore, who am I to judge?! That is like a person on the cliff, and I push them off! Trust me, I used to beat myself up and say I am the cause of alcoholics because I have a liquor store. Then I sat back and thought, food chains are getting blamed for children being overweight when their parents are in control of how much food their children consume! I am pretty sure no restaurant places a gun to parents' heads and says, you buy your kids extra fries now and give your kids diabetes or else!"

T.J. busts out laughing. Jabeeb smiled in relief he was getting through.

"So, you see, T.J., I cannot stop making a living because I have a store, and people overindulge for whatever reason. All I am saying is, take all your experience and what your wife went through, and learn the good from the bad. And please, open up that rehabilitation center like your wife wanted you to. Save other lives, T.J., like you did hers before she left this earth. Your wife died with a satisfied soul that you and her daughter are okay and can build from each other."

T.J. looked at Jabeeb.

"Hey, I think I agree with everything you said, Jabeeb. Thanks for being heaven-sent, seriously!"

Jabeeb got out of the car, closed T.J.'s car door, and leaned in the window.

"I wouldn't say all that about me. You are the one who saved lives right out here in front of my store, time and time again. You are the one with the wings; you just need to learn how to use them and fly. Now let me go in my store; you know how Ahkili can get with my customers."

T.J. laughed. He was relieved he had something to laugh about through all his emotions. Everyone knew Ahkili was totally the opposite of Jabeeb.

"Yeah, I know, tell me about it! Well, my head is held high now because of you. So go on in there. I don't want you to file bankruptcy when Ahkili gets through!"

"Seriously!"

Jabeeb glanced at the bottle and gave T.J. some small advice.

"Well, just relax and clear your mind before you go to the hospital; remember everything we talked about, my friend."

T.J. knew Jabeeb didn't judge him; however, he saw Jabeeb glance at the bottle.

"Thanks, man, but trust me, I will be alright."

Jabeeb went inside, and T.J. sat back and thought for a minute, then headed home to get some rest. He called to let his daughter know that he needed to rest his head and be back at the hospital in the morning. Toni decided to stay with Brenda.

40

Marie was at Ms. Opal's house having a meeting with some of Ms. Opal's church members. They put together plans for Ms. Opal's funeral services. Marie decided to go back to the hospital and let her auntie's neighbors know. She only felt it was right to tell the others at the hospital this important information. Marie knew this was sad news, but they would want to know. She got teary-eyed, reliving the situation and when she thought about her aunt.

Marie pulled into the parking lot. She took a breather before she went inside the hospital. When Toni and Brenda got back inside the hospital, Brenda told Samuel it was his time to go get some rest.

"Hey, sweetheart, good morning."

"Good morning, baby. Hey, little lady, good morning. Thanks for being by our side. You are strong just like your dad and...."

Samuel paused. He did not know how she felt if someone brought up her mother's name.

"It's okay, Uncle Sam, you can say my mom. I love when people mention her, especially in a good way. It makes me feel good."

"Oh, okay, well, your mom as well."

"Thank you, Uncle Sam."

Toni, Brenda, and Samuel looked over at Isaac sleeping.

"He seems like he is really sleeping a lot."

Toni looked back over at Isaac with concern. Brenda and Samuel sat down.

"Yeah, I know. The doctor said the more rest, the better, and he'll have surgery today."

Samuel was deep in thought.

"Speaking of that, I have some homework to do."

Brenda caught on to Samuel instantly.

"Oh yeah, I was thinking and calling people all night. I have not come up with a conclusion or person yet. And you know what, Samuel?"

"What's that, Bren?"

"Everyone kept saying, yeah, that's such a blessing. Someone is not telling the truth, and all I want to do is show my gratitude and say thank you."

"Well, I will figure it out for the both of us, don't worry. I will see you all in a minute."

Samuel left out the door. As he got close to the waiting room, he reached for the door to leave out and swung it open. Marie yanks forward. She was already holding the door, getting ready to get buzzed in. Marie jumped as she was yanked forward.

"Ooh, wee!"

"Oh, my bad, I'm sorry. I was just leaving out the door."

"Excuse me, but you look like another guy who was talking to my aunt before she passed, except he was a little taller and he had a beautiful...."

"Smile?"

"Yeah, how did you know I was going to say that?"

"Well, yeah, we look alike because that is my brother. And who is your aunt that passed? I don't think I know her."

"Oh. Yeah, I am sorry for assuming you knew my aunt. Her name is, well, everybody knew her in the neighborhood as Ms. Opal."

Samuel looked at Marie astounded as if he had just seen a ghost.

Then there was a long pause. Marie looked at his expression with concern.

"Well, did I say something wrong?"

"Oh, my God! I didn't know.... She was just... Me and David's... Never mind, I have to go. I have another reason to drown my sorrows, now."

A few tears fell from Samuel's eyes as he walked away. Marie was still confused and hoped Samuel would be okay. She carried on with what she felt she needed to do. Marie knocked on Isaac's door softly. She looked in the window of the door and saw Isaac sleeping, so she waved her hand for Brenda to come out the door so they could talk. Brenda stepped out.

"Hey, sweetie, are you okay? Your face is red!"

Brenda grabbed Marie's face and rubbed it softly.

"Hey there! Yeah, uh, this guy with beautiful teeth...."

"T.J.?"

"Well, yeah, I guess he is known by the smile and teeth. When I made the batch of cookies for the neighborhood kids, my aunt said to make sure I made some for him. "

Brenda looks a little confused.

"Well, let me cut the small talk. My aunt has passed on."

Marie choked up, and Brenda held her mouth as tears rolled out.

"And she told me to help several with some money she left and...."

Brenda cut her off, excited and lightweight, yelling.

"I knew it was someone special! She paid for it, didn't she?! Ms. Opal paid our son's hospital bill!!"

Marie looked at Brenda strangely and wondered why she would think that.

"Oh, no!" However, if someone paid your son's hospital bill, I am very happy for your family, though."

Brenda looked disappointed. She was back to square one.

"I wonder who it could be? Oh, well, I am sorry to hear about your aunt. Ms. Opal will definitely be missed around our neighborhood for sure!"

Marie smiled and began to speak peacefully, like her aunt.

"Well, I am praying for your son to have a speedy recovery. Unfortunately, I have to move on and tell the next family about my auntie's passing on. Oh yeah, by the way."

Marie pulled out a pen and paper and wrote her number down for Brenda.

"Please, when you come home from here, you and your family call me. As a matter of fact, I want you to come over and help me make some of my aunt's special cookies for the kids around the neighborhood. That is a lot of work for just one person."

Marie looked directly into Brenda's face and at her body language to see if she would come and help.

"Oh, I would love that! I owe that to Ms. Opal. She would always hint for us to come over. She also had a going away party for this one little girl."

"Who, Meagan?"

Brenda looked up to heaven, thinking of Ms. Opal's kindness.

"Yeah, yeah, Megan. She was a sweet girl with a lot of issues. Your aunt loved any and everybody!"

They both put their heads down and tried to stop crying. Toni stepped in and put her arms around her auntie Brenda's shoulders.

"Uh, Ming? I mean Marie."

"Call me either one. I love that name the kids gave me! Plus, it was a special moment with my aunt when she was here."

"Well, I will be there too. To help you make the cookies, if that is, okay?"

Marie hugged them both and answered Toni as she walked away.

"Yes! I would love that. The more, the merrier"

41

Samuel made it to the liquor store. He saw T.J. sitting in the car talking to someone. Samuel tried to slide by his brother to go into the liquor store without being seen. T.J. spoke to his friend Jimmy.

"Yeah, man, it is definitely time for me to change. Basically, what I'm asking is for your help. It's a building I have been scoping out. I think I'm going to go ahead and make an offer on it so I can open this rehabilitation center. So, are you down, man? You going to help me with the inside, right Jimmy. Do I have your support?"

"Man, look, we never knew you had this fancy suit and all this loot! How can we help you? We still broke! We never knew you were made of money!"

"Look here, Jimmy, I am the same person who hung outside that store and would drink. Now the good advice I gave you, you gave me also; wasn't that free and stuck to our soul?!"

"Well, yeah, but...."

"See, no buts, man! I am not here to judge you, or as you can see, I always had money. This money and I haven't ever looked down on y'all before, Jimmy!"

"Alright, T.J., you have a point right there. I got your back, man."

Jimmy looked down in T.J.'s car.

"Now, let me have that bottle in your lap. I will cure your habit for good! Don't restart something you can't finish!"

They both laughed tremendously.

"You always have been slick like Pennzoil, boy!"

T.J. passed Jimmy the bag with the liquor in it.

"Hey, I am not condoning you to stop until you are ready. I will just be here when you are ready to stop, Jimmy. Well, to be honest, I hope it's soon."

Jimmy lifted the bottle and drank, then wiped his mouth with his sleeve before he answered T.J.

"Look here, I got too many bills swimming in my head, and this, this drowns my sorrows for right now. Every time I take a sip, my brain be like, what bill?!"

They laughed. T.J. started his car to leave, not knowing Samuel was in the liquor store.

"Alright, man, well, I will come get you when it's time to get the building started up, and you know I will paint you green. But, I have to go, Jimmy. I have some family issues to take care of right now."

"Well, you know this my second home, so you know where I will be at, man."

T.J. yelled out the window as he drove off.

"See, friends like you let me know money is nothing! Down to earth people with comedy, don't come like you down on Wall Street!"

"Well, alright, T.J., you go ahead show them how it is done. God blessed you to bless us; now go on. You messing up me and Brandy's time."

"Alright, man, I will be back."

Samuel stood at the counter, and everyone who came in line, Samuel let them go ahead first. Ahkili yelled at Samuel.

"Hey! Would you hurry up! I don't know how my uncle put up with you all!"

"Oh, put up with us?! Huh, I know you didn't! With your attitude, I am surprised you haven't got shot yet, youngster!"

"Oh, please! You talking loud and saying nothing!"

Jabeeb heard his nephew arguing. Jabeeb was on a business call, so he ended it to get to the matter at hand.

"Excuse me, I have a situation. Can I call you back, please? Okay, thank you."

Jabeeb hung up and ran towards Ahkili at the counter. Jabeeb didn't see Samuel as he looked firmly at Ahkili, who was still arguing.

"Oh, why don't you just shut up!"

"Stop it! Stop it right now!"

The silence was instant with everyone in the store, except for Samuel.

"Yeah, you tell 'em, boss!"

Jabeeb looked at Samuel, surprised that he was there. Jabeeb knew Samuel only came into his store for an emergency household item, and that was every blue moon. However, Jabeeb knew from talking to T.J. why Samuel was there, and he knew T.J. would not be pleased with Samuel's drinking. Samuel was not as down to earth as his brother T.J., but Jabeeb cared for them both, and he was really concerned with Samuel's safety.

"Ahkili?! How can I continue to let you work for me if you treat most of my customers bad, and badger them up? I told my sister I would look after you! And you will not treat my customers with a callous heart. My customers would be baffled about our heritage because of one person, you, treating them this way!"

Samuel grabbed his drink off the counter.

"Yeah, what he said! You better listen to your uncle, you know baffled means confused, and the way you act, I'm surprised no one has socked you in the mouth yet!"

"I am sorry, Uncle Beeb."

"I will accept your sorry; however, we will practice sensible, not sorry. Our customers are human and our supporters! We should be thankful for the kindness we have. Today could be gone instantly, Ahkili! Tomorrow is not promised, you understand?!"

"Yes, sir."

Samuel smiled in agreement with everything Jabeeb said; however, it would not be Samuel's character unless he made a sarcastic remark.

"You know we need more like you, Jabeeb, a good old fashion whipping for your nephew!"

Samuel laughed hard. Jabeeb stepped down, racing after Samuel to let him know he cared before he took a drink.

"I will be back, nephew. I am going to talk to Samuel, hold down the fort. Correctly!"

"Okay, Okay."

Jabeeb stepped outside in the front where Samuel was.

"So, Samuel is everything okay at the hospital with your family. Oh, wait, or shall I say getting better?"

"You know what? I used to be judgmental towards many people, and you are one of the ones who changed my mind about your kind too."

Jabeeb was very shocked that the sarcastic, rude brother was being pleasant.

"Well, that was nice, Samuel!"

"Yeah, I know you think I am just this rude sucker, but I got a heart. I just have rust around it. People put it there, you know, Jabeeb."

"Well, yeah, I've seen that happen to many! But where is this coming from, my friend? You know, your uh...

Jabeeb paused, not knowing what words to say. Samuel took another sip of his liquor and pointed to his own heart.

"Coming from inside here, but anyway. Thanks for paying my kid's hospital bill."

"No, No, No. I did not do such a thing!"

"Come on, Jabeeb! Nobody has money around here like that to spare but you! So spare the modesty and stop trying to trick me!"

Samuel laughed and took another drink. Jabeeb almost spilled the beans.

"Well, I don't want to say, but your arrogance with your brother needs to change."

Samuel paused, not knowing where Jabeeb was coming from.

"What? Aww, please! Yeah, my brother had a new suit and a car from the insurance when Jade died, and so what! Or wait! Oh, I see, you bought that too?!"

Samuel laughed and slapped his knee. Jabeeb made no sound; he just stared in Samuel's face. Finally, Samuel got the picture from Jabeeb's expression and stood up.

"Wait a damn minute! You mean to tell me...... No! Hell No! That man didn't...... my brother?! Where did he get.....

"While you are trying to collect your train of thought. I am not the one to run my mouth because T.J. may get mad; however, you semi figured it out, plus you need to know! Yes, your brother paid for your son's hospital bill and for your son's friend's bill as well."

There was complete silence for three minutes. However, Jabeeb stayed around while Samuel was in suspense for three minutes. Jabeeb had been around people who drink a lot, and he knew being in shock and drinking sometimes does not go hand in hand for some people.

"Wow! Here I am having all this built-up anger for my brother, for my own selfish reasons, and he is paying my family's bills?! I kicked him out my house several times just because I could, and I talked down to him almost every chance I got! And eighty percent of the time in his face, Jabeeb! I treat outsiders way better than I treat my brother! And I just got the biggest slap in the face right now that my neck about to break! I'll be damned! Now, how the hell will I ever be able to face him and thank him?!"

Jabeeb was very relieved that Samuel knew now. Jabeeb would

never admit it; however, he was happy Samuel received that slap of reality in the face. Jabeeb had a heart, and he did not want to see anybody distraught.

"Well, my friend, take all the time you need to think out here. Is your wife with your son?"

Samuel was so misconstrued. He felt guilty and thankful all once. He was mad at himself for even more reasons now.

"Jabeeb, just stop it! Stop with the nice shit, okay?! Yeah, my son is in the hospital, his mom is with him and.... Go count your inventory or something; just get the hell out of my face, man!

Jabeeb walked away. He knew he would say something harsh to Samuel. However, Jabeeb had respect for Samuel, and eighty percent of that respect was due to his relationship with T.J. So, Jabeeb walked into the store and away from Samuel.

42

T.J. walked into the hospital and sat in the waiting room for a minute to collect his thoughts. Linda, Samantha, and Steve walk into the waiting room. Linda and Samantha saw T.J. and their eyes got big. They just do not know the outcome of what would happen even though Steve cried and poured his heart out. Steve looked at his wife and sister-in-law and gave them the cue to go ahead downstairs. Samantha knew it wasn't his violent look, and she was overjoyed knowing that Steve would stay and talk with T.J. She tried to be nosey and stay also.

"Linda? Let's have a seat and rest."

Linda knew her sister was excited and nosey, so she politely helped Steve and played her big sister role.

"Uh, I was going to get something to eat. I thought you were coming with me."

"She is going with you to grab a bite!"

Samantha knew that was her cue. T.J. looked up and got the hint as well, even though Steve was not talking to him. T.J. figured that now Steve was going to start something up with him, so as soon as the ladies left, T.J. got up buzzed in to go to his nephew's room. Steve placed his hand on T.J.'s shoulder.

"Excuse me, can we talk for a minute?"

"The ball is in your court. What's going on?"

"You know I never been one to, well, to really apologize. But, anyway, you always were the adult in every bad encounter I had with you."

T.J. looked at Steve like he saw an angel come down and touch Steve's body.

"Anyway, to make a long story short, there is no way I should have come off rude to you. And you would think I would come to my senses before my child was laying...

Steve became silent in sadness. Finally, T.J. took over the conversation having sympathy for Steve.

"Look, man, I am not trying to have you rekindle what is already in your face about all this tragedy. But, listen, everybody, I do not care who it is; everybody has a little scandalous in them. Even me and I'm perfect!"

They both laughed.

"No, but seriously, all jokes aside, sometimes serious matters have to show you that a person you hate is not so bad. You really have to realize some people care and want to help you, so trust me when I say no apology is needed. But, you know, just me knowing that you came to your senses for the kids' sake is all that matters to me."

T.J. reached out his hand to shake Steve's hand, and they had a firm yet sincere exchange. Then, Manzel walked into the waiting room. Steve was happy to see Manzel.

"Oh, wow! I really appreciate you for coming; you didn't have to come!"

T.J. looked very puzzled. He knew that Steve displayed a change in his view of Blacks in the last five minutes; however, he didn't see him being nice to another one within the next three seconds. T.J. introduced himself in total shock.

"Uh, uh, I, uh, I am T.J., a neighbor from around the way. You are?"

Manzel smiled and reached out to T.J. to greet and meet.

"Hey, right on, I am Manzel, Steve's mechanic and...."

Steve cut Manzel off.

"And friend."

Manzel smiled at Steve in agreement because Steve never made Manzel feel any other way. Well, at least not in his face.

"Steve, now, is there anything I can do besides the work on your car? You know I am here for your family, and I am willing to help any way I can."

Steve still felt that Manzel paid that hospital bill.

"You know you have helped enough; you not fooling me!"

Manzel worked with Steve for many years, so he knew what Steve was getting at.

"Trust and believe when I say I have the heart, but I don't have the money to pay a high bill, especially a hospital bill at that!"

T.J. became nervous that Steve was lurking to find out who paid the bill, so he buzzed again to go inside Isaac's room. Manzel and Steve shrugged their shoulders, not knowing why T.J. left so fast. But, of course, Steve had no clue; he just figured T.J. was rushing back to see Isaac.

43

Linda and Samantha were at a nearby café, talking.

"Linda, you know what's strange? Who would have thought my husband, my husband, would open up and change his prejudiced ways?!"

Linda leaned in and whispered to Samantha.

"I don't know Ms. every black woman has an attitude."

"Linda, oh please, shut up! Out of all the black women I have encountered, about fifty percent proved me right, but I feel totally different now!"

"Well, good! We all live to learn! I know they feel the same things about our race too. When things happen to you, and you become victim to other races, you cannot help but become distrusting toward that race, no matter what it is!"

"I see my husband is not the only one changing, either.

"What do you mean?"

"Your words, 'my brother,' huh? I have not heard that come out of your mouth in ages!"

"Whatever just finish so we can get back!"

"Stings, huh?"

"Uh, just a tad bit."

They both laughed.

T.J made it into the room. Toni and Isaac were watching television. Brenda looked at T.J., seeing his concern for the children.

"Hey, T.J., you know Isaac is having surgery tomorrow."

"Yeah."

"Yes. I did not know I was not going to pay. The world still has angels out there. Someone paid the bill. I just can't...."

T.J. cut Brenda off. Too many people were mentioning it around him, and he felt someone was figuring things out.

"You know my momma would say, just take a blessing, say thank you, Amen, and keep moving even if you don't know where it came from."

"You know what, T.J., I cannot argue with that wise woman. She was put on this earth before us for a reason!"

"Yeah."

"That man of mines thinks I don't know, T.J., but I know he's drinking."

T.J.'s eyes grew big like headlights.

"Yeah, I feel...."

"T.J., I know how you feel. And that is why I gave you the "that's okay" look at the car. You can't take on a grown man's pain. That pain has been there for years. I know all about Uncle Richard and things. You know what I want you to do for me, T.J?"

"What's that, Bren'?"

"Please, just open up a rehab clinic like Jade wanted you to."

T.J. looked at Brenda, surprised. A few tears dropped out of T.J.'s eyes.

"How did you know she wanted that, Bren'?!"

"Remember you fussed and fussed on her birthday when she finally answered the phone? She was at bingo the year before she died."

"How can I forget? That was when her drinking increased, and I stayed up all night worried, and still, I wonder how the hell she made it home!"

Brenda smiled hard, and tears rolled down her face.

"You have a beautiful home, T.J."

T.J. and Brenda paused in silence for a long time as they just stared at each other.

"Brenda! Are you serious?! You got my wife home safe that night?! And you mean to tell me you knew all this time I had lots of money and all?! Why didn't you say a word about it?!"

"You are my brother despite what you have. And what kind of family member would I be. That does not make me better to throw it in your face. I know you have money, and when your brother comes to his senses a little bit more, you tell him. That is not my place. I want you and your brother to love each other sincerely again. I do not want it to be about what you have. And by the way, T.J., my momma didn't raise no fool. I will never, and I mean never forget what you have done for my son! Now please, please go back and get your brother; I need you all here. And that is Isaac's father. The only father he cares to know. Please go get him, T.J.!"

T.J. always knew Brenda was a good woman, friend, cook, and all; however, by her knowing about his money and always treating him right, and being there for his wife, it was like he saw angel wings with jewelry on Brenda that day.

"Bren'! You are the best thing that happened to my brother and me. I will do what it takes to bring him back."

Brenda knew T.J. got the picture and that she wanted them two to talk.

"Okay, we will be here waiting. Thank you, T.J.!"

They hugged each other tightly. T.J. kissed his daughter's forehead, looked over at Isaac before he headed out of the door. He knew that if Samuel were at Jabeeb's, then Jabeeb would keep Samuel safe. So T.J. headed to get Samuel.

Brenda got a call from her sister, Barbara, letting her know she would be down there the next day and bring Lema.

"Okay, sis. Oh, Lord, Isaac is going to be overjoyed. You know they are like brother and sister instead of cousins, but he needed rest, and you needed to console Lema's soul through all this chaos. Oh, yeah, and you see, Lema was fine. Pat and Ron are a good couple, and they have always been good to us and the kids, so I knew she would be fine there until you arrived. Okay, see you in the morning. Oh, wait! Barbara, I have some bad news. You know Ms. Opal died of cancer. Her niece...."

Brenda was cut off by her sister. Brenda listened to what Barbara had to say.

"Yeah, but please do not tell Lema yet. I want to tell her and Isaac together. Okay, sis, I love you. I will see you tomorrow."

44

At Jabeeb's liquor store, Samuel was wasted and talking out of the side of his neck and to himself.

"Yeah, I know I am worthless, now time to chase waterfalls. Whooo, wee"

Samuel took a drink as a car pulled up to the liquor store. It is a shiny red classic 1967 drop-top Camaro with platinum rims and a beautiful white leather interior. The guy driving the car was playing loud music. Song chorus: *"I will always love my momma; she's my favorite girl"* Samuel rose up from sitting on the curve and started to sing and dance by the driver's car.

"Hey! I always will love my momma; she's my favorite girl! Duh, Duh, Dum, Dun!"

The driver got out of the car. He was a bright-skinned black guy and looked as if he was 26, with short hair, a baseball cap, jeans, jewelry, nice shoes, and a freshly shaved face. He spoke firmly, however polite.

"Can you please step back from my car? The way you staggering, I don't want you falling into my ride, please."

Samuel waved his hand sarcastically at the young man. Then put his finger in the young guy's face.

"Man, please! You got a classic car! That car is classic; that car is fine! Anyway, you look like you what, about twelve?!"

Samuel laughs hard.

"So, you don't know nothing about your classic car, or that song you playing, loudly!"

"Nobody gets at Dub like that, especially today!"

Samuel sarcastically made like he was scared.

"Ooh! I'm scared."

Samuel looked around as if he was talking, and there were a lot of people around him.

"Watch out, it is Dub, and he needs a baby rub!"

Samuel laughed, ran, and staggered back to the ground where he was sitting. He then looked up at Dub.

"And anyway, what you mean today, punk! I got problems you probably don't even know about, young drug dealer. Killing your own people, punk! Now, yea, that is what I said!"

Samuel held his finger up and marked as if he was taking score on a scoreboard.

"Now, that is one for me, Rub, Dub!"

Dub was furious.

"First of all, mutha fucka, I have never sold dope! And while you racially profiling, against your own race, dumb ass. My mom just died! And we have our own business we have been running for 15 plus years now. Since you want to know how I have a nice classic car and clothes! Now, I have a temper, and only my deceased momma could control that! My momma is gone now! So keep talking, she not here to stop me from putting hot led in your ass! I LOST EVERYTHING! EVERYTHING WHEN MY MOMMA DIED!"

Dub grabbed Samuel by his collar and mumbled in his ear.

"That same gun I was about to kill myself with a minute ago in that car will be in your ass! You hear me!"

Samuel was so wasted he was careless with his heart and words and overlooked everything Dub just spoke about. Samuel yanked Dub's hand off of his clothes.

"You better go ahead in that store, Dub! I will holler at you when you come out. You disturbing me and the new love of my lifetime!"

Samuel held up his bottle. Dub walked away slowly, almost inside the store, but he looked back at Samuel. Samuel was still speaking.

"I don't want to talk, and neither do my bottle! And yeah, yeah, kill me! You just another punk! Don't try to tell me you're sad about your momma! Now, my momma, that was a real woman!"

Jabeeb noticed the face of Dub as he stood in the doorway to the liquor store. Jabeeb came from behind the counter towards the door. Dub walked right over to Samuel and punched Samuel's face so hard, Samuel dropped his liquor, and his mouth instantly started to bleed. Samuel tried to grab the bottle pieces but still talking.

"You punk ass bastard! You made me drop my drink!"

"Dub went to the trunk of his car and grabbed his chrome 50 caliber.

"You got me fucked up with somebody who cares! I told you, my momma gone; I don't care about nobody!"

Dub rushed towards Samuel. Jabeeb rushed out the door towards them to try to stop what was going on. T.J. drove up and saw everything. He could not believe what he saw, and it seemed as if things were going in slow motion. Jabeeb jumped in front of Dub.

"Please, Dub, put the gun down. I am sorry for your loss, but this is not what Mrs. Johnson would have wanted, my friend! Please!"

Samuel was still delirious behind Jabeeb. Dub usually respected Jabeeb; however, Dub's temper made his mind blank.

"Nobody going to talk shit about how they think their mom was more real than mines. She not here to defend herself!"

Jabeeb looked back at Samuel.

"Oh, no, come on, Samuel. Why would you say such a thing?!"

Before Jabeeb had a chance to look back at Dub, T.J. yelled out.

"JABEEB, SAMUEL, LOOK OUT!!"

Dub started to fire shots. Jabeeb was hit 6 times. Dub then jumped in his car, sped off, hit a tree a block away, and then shot himself in the head. T.J. jumped out of his car and ran towards Jabeeb.

"NO! NO! NO! SOMEBODY CALL THE DAMN AMBULANCE!"

Neighbors came out yelling all different kinds of comments.

"Oh, hell no! That's Jabeeb on the ground!"

Ahkili ran to his uncle, yelling and crying.

"NO, UNCLE! DON'T DIE! PLEASE!"

Out of anger, T.J. yelled some harsh words to Ahkilki.

"It should have been you! You the asshole! This man hasn't done a thing to nobody! Man, where the ambulance!"

Ahkili cried, and Samuel sobered up enough to feel a lot of remorse and hurt for Jabeeb. Samuel held his lip with his jacket to stop the blood. He cried as well over Jabeeb.

Jabeeb looked at Samuel, T.J, and Ahkili with blurred vision and said his last words.

"Just love one another. Love conquers all."

Jabeeb's eyes rolled in the back of his head then he closed his eyes. Finally, his body became limp, and he died.

T.J. cried out loud.

"NOOOO!"

Samuel cried.

"GET UP, JABEEB. I'M SORRY!"

Ahkili cried.

"UNCLE NO! I NEED YOU! PLEASE, OH, MY GOD, NO!"

All the neighbors cried and moved out of the way because the ambulance was coming through. The EMTs questioned Ahkili and T.J. After which, Ahkili locked up the store. The coroner arrived and zipped Jabeeb in the body bag. The police placed out the yellow tape to secure the scene. Ahkili went to the hospital where they were taking Jabeeb.

45

Barbara and Lema arrived at the hospital. Toni and Brenda left so Barbara and Lema could visit with Isaac before he went into surgery. Lema held her cousin's hand.

"Boy! I was so dang worried! All that blood, shoo! I'm glad you not dead!"

"You?! Me too! But my face hurt so bad, Lema. I'm glad they said they are going to take some frozen pieces out my jaw, though."

Barbara smiled, just happy to hear his voice. She stepped in to correct him. Even though she just wanted Lema and Isaac to have their moment.

"It's fractured pieces, baby. Fractured bone pieces. That is so it will not cut inside more, sweetheart."

Lema held her face and was the normal dramatic Lema.

"Ooh, Wee! Well, I'm going to keep praying, cousin! It is all my fault, cousin. I am the oldest! We shouldn't have sneaked to that store, now look at my cousin and our friends!"

Lema was crying. Barbara had enough of her child feeling responsible. Any of the kids, for that matter. She spoke the truth to Lema under any circumstances, which is why Lema was so strong-minded. She talked to the kids raw and uncut.

"Now, look! That is enough! I will not let you sit here and blame yourself! This is life. I hate seeing my nephew and his friends in this hospital, also! No matter what, something needed to happen to bring all of us families together! With all their judgmental bull with our family and David's!"

Lema did not see any judgmental ways; she was smart, however, still a child.

"Wait. What you mean?"

"Well, if you must know. Some things have been going on, and Isaac's father did not like David's father. David's father did not like your cousin's father because of their misguided judgmental ways!"

Isaac shook his head in disappointment. Lema just brushed off the negative.

"Oh, well, oh, well. David is like my cousin, so I'm still going to talk to him. But I'm not going to disrespect Mr. David, though. And momma, why is Uncle Sam like that?"

"I cannot speak for him, but it doesn't make any sense to me. Let's go, Miss, let your cousin get some sleep."

Lema looked at Isaac, not wanting to leave, but she knew he needed rest. Lema then kissed Isaac on the forehead.

"You are going to be alright, cousin, because I'm going to keep praying! And my momma said, at first, it may seem like something bad going to happen because the devil gets mad when I pray. But then, I get three blessings back-to-back, cousin, because I kept the faith! Right momma?!"

Barbara rubbed Lema's face. She was glad Lema took wise advice and didn't rely too much on her own curious advice.

"Yes, that is correct, sweetheart."

"Yeah, so, see, cousin. I prayed, and two blessings came, and you my third blessing, watch!"

Isaac dozed in and out; however, he still responded.

"Okay, cousin. Thank you."

Barbara and Lema stayed a little longer until Isaac fell asleep completely.

Toni and Brenda became a little restless in the waiting room. They decided to go outside because Brenda wanted to call Samuel. Brenda noticed that Samuel was gone too long, and T.J. was not back at the hospital either. Samuel finally decided to pick up the phone on the last ring. He still had slurred speech.

"Yes, officer."

Brenda, disgusted, moved the phone and stared at it before she placed the phone back to her ear.

"Are you drunk?!"

Samuel started to cry.

"Lord, it's all my fault! I just can't do right by you, or else your son wouldn't be in this situation and...."

Brenda cut him off, angry.

"You judge and cannot stand when Toni is drunk. Now, you drunk, huh?! And what the hell you mean, your son! You never looked at Isaac as not your own. I'm grateful and forget that he is not biologically your son! So, besides that liquor, I smell through the phone, what is wrong with you. Something is really up!"

Samuel busted out crying then he placed the phone down. Brenda heard an officer as he spoke Samuel.

"Sir, you need to come down to the station if you were a witness to anything. Unfortunately, you are in no condition to drive. You need to find a designated driver right now."

Brenda became extremely nervous and yelled so Samuel could hear her.

"Samuel! What is wrong?! Why the cops there?! Put the phone back on your ear?!"

"Bren, babe, so much going on down here! Come get me please!"

"Sir, who is Bren?"

"My wife, my beautiful wife, who I let down."

The officer was friendly and concerned, so he reached for Samuel's phone.

"Can I talk to Bren, please?"

Samuel passed the officer the phone.

"Hello, Bren?"

Brenda wanted to correct him and tell the officer that it was a nickname; however, she just answered because that was not her concern right then. Toni looked so anxious about everything. She was clueless but was eavesdropping tremendously.

"Yes, sir."

"Well, the procedure when a person is intoxicated like this is normally to take them into custody. So I'm going to go ahead take him in and...."

Brenda was hysterical and cut him off.

"No! No! Officer, he is really a good man, and he really not a drunk and...."

"Ma'am! Ma'am! Calm down! I am not arresting him. I noticed your husband has been assaulted, and other situations were going on. I haven't received the entire story. However, I feel he was a witness to a 187 in front of a liquor store. Come down to the station, and we will talk more, alright."

"Okay, I'm on my way right now, officer, thank you. What was your name, please?"

"My name is Officer Gibsy."

Brenda hung up the phone and fell to the ground screaming.

"WHY, LORD! I need you, lord. Oh my God!"

Toni held her auntie tight.

"Auntie! What's wrong?!"

Brenda explained everything to Toni. Toni then grabbed Brenda's face slowly and held it next to hers.

"Auntie, listen. You notice how Marie explained to us how her auntie was smiling until her last breath?"

Brenda shook her head in agreement and wiped her eyes. The thought of Ms. Opal's heart dried some of her tears.

"Look, auntie, let's go see what's going on with Uncle Sam. I am sad for you, and your child may be hurt; I cannot imagine how you feel about that right now, but he is still alive! Uncle Sam may have been beaten badly, but the yellow tape was for another, not Uncle Sam, even though I feel for that person and his family too! I was always told by my mom and dad; everyone has a purpose on earth. Auntie, we are still breathing right now through all our tough times, so we must serve our purpose and read between the lines. What I mean by that, auntie, and like you told me, this tragedy is a wake-up call for us all! I never had to tell you this, I did not feel I had to, but I never looked at you like an in-law. You are a special part of my dad and I's life, and we need you, auntie! Stay strong, please; we are going to get through this! You see, you have angels looking over you. Look how your bill got paid! Every red cent, not half, auntie, all of it!"

Brenda grabbed Toni so tight you would need a vice grip to pull them apart.

"Oh, Toni! I love you so much! You have a heart big as a rich selfish person's ego, you know that?!"

Toni knew what a compliment was, of course, because she received so many like her mother. They both had big hearts. But, Toni was modest like her mom and dad, also. So, she let those things roll off her mind.

"Uh, oh, thanks."

"And I know you knew your dad paid for the hospital bills. So even though it was hard for you to speak of it, I understood what you were saying to me. Yes, he did pay every red cent, and I am truly grateful!"

"Now, auntie, I swear, I did not even know that! Wow, my dad did that?!"

"Wow! What a modest family! He didn't say anything to you. But yes, your dad did!"

Brenda then called her sister and told her everything that was going on.

46

Marie was just finishing up telling David's dad the news about what was going on with her aunt and the things she wanted. Linda and Samantha walked in and looked at everyone's facial expression, which was not so pleasant. Linda spoke up slowly.

"Okay, what did we walk in on? And who are you, sweetheart?"

Marie smiled and introduced herself. She reached out to shake Linda's hand.

"Oh, I am Marie. Ms. Opal's niece."

"Oh, okay, great!"

Linda turned towards Samantha and whispered.

"That nice elderly woman. The one that stays down the street in the middle of the block by you, right?"

"Yes, that was her. Marie, I know we talked early, so what's going on?"

"Well, I wanted to let the boys know that my aunt has passed on and...."

Marie choked up, but she finished what she needed to say like her aunt would have wanted her to.

"Well, may I ask first, is your son going to be okay?"

Samantha looked over at David and noticed he was crying about Ms. Opal. Steve was comforting David and stroking his hair. With everything going on, Samantha had forgotten to share the bad news about Ms. Opal with David and Steve. She wiped her own tears from her face.

Uh, well, it is so far, so good, thank God. I know someone has paid our entire bill in full for his surgery!"

"This hospital is full of blessings and generosity."

"Yes! You can say that again. That beautiful woman opened my eyes with the truth! Ms. Opal was so kind to everyone!"

Linda walked over and stood by Steve.

"Yeah, people like her are here for a reason. Such a tragedy, if I must say so myself.

Even in her grief regarding her son and the sad news about Ms. Opal, Samantha was delighted to see how Linda and Steve were getting along. She looked over at her son.

"David? Son, I really feel it will be okay."

"How, mom, how?! She is gone! We were supposed to make sure she was okay! We promised we would go get her some medicine, now it is too late! Why do things keep happening to us?!"

Linda, Samantha, Steve, and Marie all get big lumps in their throats, and for a minute, there was complete silence.

"Do all of you mind stepping out so I can talk to my son?"

Linda, Samantha, and Marie were all glad Steve took the steering wheel on this conversation. So, they all stepped out.

"Son, look, I'm not a man who even knows how to begin to say I am wrong, but.... I, uh.

David gave his dad an innocent look and wanted to know what was wrong.

"You what, dad?"

"I hid the go-kart, and I feel if it was not for my stubbornness and hatred, you all would not have been in this situation. And I need to go and check on Jerry. I even paid him to move the go-kart into his yard. I have a lot to pay for!"

David was very sad and tried to move around like he was trying to get out of bed.

"Son? Please be still."

"Okay. Well, dad, you said I can talk to you about anything, right?"

"Yes, of course, son, anything."

"Well, I am very mad at you. Well, the one friend that I know really cared about me and made me happy, dad, you hate him! Why?!"

Steve braced himself.

"Trust me, son, when I say I really do not hate him! But, I hate what happened to a family member by someone of the same race as your friend. So, out of anger, it made me despise the entire race."

"Despise?"

"Well, yeah, I forget your age sometimes, son. Despise basically means when you look down on someone or hate someone, which is not a good thing at all. It sounds so unfair, son, but that was my imperfection that I need to correct. Not counting one person for everybody. Now, I wish I could just put all my new positive energy into your legs now, son."

Tears fell out of Steve's eyes, and he laid his head on David's legs, holding them as if he was hugging and embracing them. Then David flinched his legs.

"You felt that!"

"Uh, a little."

Steve passed Samantha and Linda and grabbed a doctor. The doctor, along with Samantha and Linda, ran into the room behind Steve.

"Well, do you need to talk to me as a family, or would you like this young lady to leave until we've finished talking?"

The doctor was referring to Linda.

"No, she can stay. That is my sister she is fine. Now give it to me straight, Doc. We are thankful for a few reasons so we can handle other things if we need to right now. I need to know how my son's status is with his legs and things."

Steve did not disclose the movement he experienced with David's legs. Instead, he wanted to see what the doctor really knew and if the hospital was on top of things.

"Okay, well, we looked over David's x-rays. It is an 85% chance he will be able to walk again. Also, I want you to know a wheelchair is still required. We will give David at least a full year to check on progress. This was really a tragedy that I am sorry your family had to experience, and the process will take a ton of physical therapy sessions. Luckily, he was a little fellow. His bones and other things will heal faster than an older adult."

He looked over at David and smiled.

"So yes, Mr. Smith, you do have some things to be thankful for, and everyone is not as blessed to pull through a situation such as this."

"Yeah, I know what you mean."

"I will come and get David in about an hour. Then, I will need the family to go down to the waiting room in about approximately 30 to 40 minutes, okay?"

Samantha and Steve answered in one accord.

"Yes, sir."

"We thank you."

"No problem. So, I will see you in a bit, okay, buddy? Just hang tight."

"Okay."

The doctor noticed David's long face, so he tried to cheer David up.

"I will take care of you and your Nascar brother, as you call him. We will make sure you two are fine."

David's mood changed, and he lit up; however, he was still worried about Isaac.

"Okay, thanks! But wait. What about my bug friend?"

The doctor looked back at the Smiths, baffled about who David was talking about. Then, finally, Samantha caught on to the doctor's look.

"Oh, yeah, he is speaking of his other friend that was involved in the incident and is here as well."

"Hmm, I was not aware of the third patient. I need to check on that. I was assigned to two boys."

The doctor left the room, and Samantha, Linda, and Steve stood over David. Samantha bent down to kiss her son.

"Okay, babe, we will be downstairs waiting. You are in good hands, and we will pray for everything, okay?"

"Okay, hey, mom?"

Before David got to ask his question, Linda stepped up to David.

"Auntie is going to pull every lemon tree for my lemonade, just for you, nephew!"

David gave the biggest smile ever as if he just had a cup of her lemonade. Steve then stepped in.

"And son, your dad is a man of many mistakes, but trust me, you are not one of them!"

They all gave David a group hug. Then, they headed downstairs to the waiting room; however, Samantha stopped herself knowing her son had a question, like usual.

"Son, what were you going to ask me before your auntie Linda was talking to you?"

"I was just going to say, can we please help Marie keep up Ms. Opal's garden? I feel she will rest in peace if we do."

Samantha got choked up and spoke with a squeaky voice.

"Sure we can, son, now get some rest."

"Okay, mom."

Samantha closed his door, then held onto the door with one hand and covered her mouth with the other as tears unfolded. She regained her composure seconds later and followed the way to the waiting room with her husband and sister.

47

Brenda and Toni arrived at the police station to handle business with Samuel's situation. Toni reassured her aunt that she was there if she needed her; however, she would be downstairs to give them space to talk. As Toni went into the parking lot, she saw her dad. He had changed into different clothing.

"Dad, Uncle Sam was attacked and drinking heavily. The police were involved, and someone was killed. What is going on?!"

T.J. unlocked his car, and Toni got in the car. He explained to his daughter what was going on. Toni became furious.

"This is so damn unfair! How come all the good people have to go first?!"

"I know, babe. Your old pops used to ask that question all the time, but your mom used to tell me, sometimes, God delivers his angels on earth to wake people up. So I just figured maybe he finished serving his purpose down here."

T.J. realized he had put his daughter at ease. However, the realization that Jabeeb was really gone got to him. T.J. proceeded to slam his hand hard on the dashboard.

"DAMN IT! NOT JABEEB MAN! Just not Jabeeb."

They sat silent for a moment.

"Jabeeb was just telling me to open the rehab AAA center that your mom was trying to open up. And here I am about to continue drinking again. He was so good to me, Toni. He did not judge me or say a damn thing! That man was truly a saint; he judged no one, never!"

"Dad, I know this may sound selfish coming out of my mouth, but you have been receiving too many signs lately to do what you were put on earth to do, which is to help people! So please, dad, don't let mama or Mr. Jabeeb down! Oh, yeah, you can dedicate the center in remembrance of both of them! That would make both of us happy. I would love to see it, help, or whatever! That would be so good for the neighborhood also."

"I swear, girl, it is like your mama just jumped down in your body and started talking to me! You are the spitting image of her!"

T.J. grabbed his daughter tight and hugged her like it was her first day at kindergarten all over again. Then the two started to speak about ideas for the rehab center and shared other things.

Brenda and Samuel were about to leave the police station, get Samuel cleaned up, and return to the hospital. When they got to the parking lot, Samuel turned toward Brenda. He had sobered up 90% by then.

"Bren, look, you have been nothing but clean oxygen in this polluted world, you know that?"

"Well, I put a burden on you, which is my son and...."

"What the hell! Where did that come from?!"

"Well, you said I don't need you, and look what I did to your son."

"Really?! Boy, a drunk, ain't...."

Brenda stepped in and put one finger up by Samuel's mouth.

"You are not a drunk, baby."

"Brenda, yes I am! All those years of judging T.J., and here I go! I have got some ugly demons in my past. I keep trying to drown and Bren, they are swimming! I really have to find a rehab to go to, Bren. I have been drinking more than you know, trust that!"

"Well, the first step is admitting. Then, whatever you go through, I am here, babe, seriously!"

"Now, don't you think I know that, Bren. And about Isaac, that boy is my son, and no one can tell me different! So I truly apologize, Bren, I just. I need you, Bren. Be patient with me like you have, and I will follow your model, you know the, you never fail until I stop trying. Okay?"

"Okay, my love, I will trust you. Well, wait, your son and I will trust you with all our heart."

They embraced each other, and as they looked over, they saw Toni and T.J. as they walked up. T.J. spoke about Jabeeb and what his family said about Jabeeb's arrangements. They decided to have Jabeeb's funeral in California instead of his country. That made T.J. and everyone in California happy.

"Little bro, I will spread the word when I consult more with the family and find out the specifics of the funeral. Then I can let everyone know. Hey, is Brenda's sister and little growny, okay? And are y'all going back up there soon?"

"Man, I am about to take a quick shower and go back up there."

Samuel pulled T.J. to the side and whispered talk to him.

"Hey, bro. This Uncle Rob thing really has a demon riding on me. It seems like now that I spoke about it, it brought back memories, and I just want to drink and drink! I need help, man! Is there anyone I can call that you know? Well, I see you cleaned up now. I need to find an A.A. meeting. From the looks of you, I see you must have found one."

"Man, God is good! That was a blessing that you said that. I am opening one up very soon. Now I really have a reason to! To help my little brother!"

Samuel's jealousy kicked in, and he flipped the script. Then, his mood changed, and he raised his voice.

"Oh, here you go, with all the answers. Now you telling me you have the money to open a rehab, just to quote on quote, put your little brother in it, huh? Man, please. I don't need your pity, and I am definitely not your charity case, asshole!"

Brenda and Toni turned around, puzzled.

"Come on, Sam! Stop that!"

Samuel snatched away from Brenda and walked to the car. Then he looked back towards Brenda yelled for her.

"Brenda, come on, let's go!"

Brenda looked at Toni and T.J. Her facial expression apologized to both of them for her and Samuel, even though she had done nothing. Brenda was very embarrassed. At this point, from what her dad told her earlier, Toni felt maybe her dad and uncle would become close. Especially since her God-given cousin was in the hospital.

"Dad?"

T.J. reached for Toni and pulled her into his arms.

"He just not ready, Toni, he just not ready. Let's just go. I know what he is facing, but I believe in my prayers. This, among everything else, is going to push me to what I need and will do.

48

Time passed, and all three boys, Jerry, Isaac, and David, had surgery. Steve and Samantha were constantly busy taking David to his therapy appointments. Linda was supportive and helpful. The funerals for Ms. Opal and Jabeeb were over. Brenda's sister moved in to help her since Samuel's drinking had his focus, and he was gone out of the house more. Jerry's father was building him a bug castle in the garage, and Jerry was in the room asleep. Mrs. Sinclair's client was on the phone, fussing because she noticed Mrs. Sinclair had not been spending several hours with her.

"Okay, now, Ms. Stephanie Mcknight, I truly understand I have not invested as much time with you as normal. Yes, I know sales are down. However, please hear me out. I almost lost my child due to my neglect of his quality time. My child is worth more than hundreds of dollars. Let me ask you a personal question, if I may? Okay, do you have a child? See, you have two! Yes, even though they are grown, they need quality time too. Let me make you a proposal. How about, if you take two weeks and do something with your children, which will allow me to do the same with my son, I will build up your clientele, your money, and throw in an extra incentive."

Mrs. Sinclair moved the phone from her ear because Ms. Mcknight was shouting with excitement.

"Okay, well, I have to go now. Just text me the numbers by tonight from the projections, and everything in two weeks will be fine.

Even though the project only took two days, she was not going to share that with Ms. Mcknight, so she could buy herself some family time.

"Okay, talk to you soon."

Mrs. Sinclair hung up the phone and peeked at Jerry, noticing that he was sound asleep. Then, she went outside and saw Linda, who was looking in the air, thinking. So, Mrs. Sinclair walked to the end of her gate.

"Hey, it's a beautiful night, huh?"

Linda jumped out of thought and looked over at Jerry's mom. She walked out of the fence and right over to Mrs. Sinclair.

"Hey, how are you? So it is, isn't it? Hey, so how is Jerry?"

"Well, Linda, his shoes are tied!"

They laughed.

"All jokes aside, Linda, thanks for helping me recognize that my son was the real importance in my life and...."

"Well yeah, uh, well, I was just...."

"No, please listen. I am a very stubborn and wealthy woman, Linda. So simple things in life that are priceless I tend to overlook. You know, my son even brought what you were saying to my attention. Well, in his own kid kind of way. So, it is like you helped a blind person see again! I was turning into my mom, her childhood issues, and the way she buried herself when she neglected me and did not know it. You are a breath of fresh air! And I thank you so, so much!"

Mrs. Sinclair reached out and hugged Linda tightly.

"I've heard you out, now please, hear me out. And first, let me not be rude and say thank you. Okay, I just did not want to come off rude, and I know you are a good mother. You are doing the best you can financially, and yes, that is important, too. I still have my daughter's pajamas across her bed ever since she passed away. Because a week before she passed, I just... I just miss everything about my child, and I don't want you to miss out on that, you know?"

Mrs. Sinclair's heart dropped. She totally understood now why Linda was so snappy about her and Jerry's situation.

"Oh, I am so sorry. I only had a scare, and I could not imagine how you feel right now."

Mrs. Sinclair ran to the car and got her planner.

"I do not want to ever overstep my boundaries. I just want to express a token of my thanks, so can I, can I um, write down your daughter's birthday, and we can have a block party for her. But wait! Only if it does not bring up any memories, I'm sorry. And may I ask how she died?"

Linda was strong, so she dried up her tears and explained everything to Mrs. Sinclair.

"See, and if you do not mind, we can also do a stop drunk driver's movement, and you can share your story. But, for you to get up and forgive that man, I cannot imagine doing that! I have the best lawyers money can buy, plus the money to pay for the lawyers! I would have requested the gas chamber! You are so amazing!"

Wow! My sister and I were just discussing placing flowers every year on my daughter's grave for her birthday. And to do a drunk driving movement, this is all a blessing from up above!"

"Just do me a big favor, please, Linda?"

"Anything, just name it!"

"Every single time you get upset with me, please let's talk it out because the way you squeezed me so tight. I was glad you were happy but scared of your strength. I rather argue than fight with you for sure!"

"Oh, please. No worries, I will just whip you in Yahtzee sometimes like I do my sister when I am mad at her."

"Okay, it's a date!"

49

Toni and T.J. got an industrial building, and after a while, they got the building all together. T.J. hired a few workers to help get things set up and going. He never forgot where he came from, so T.J. gathered up 7 people who hung with him on the corner. His intentions were to get them focused and show them they could make something of themselves. In addition, he wanted them to know there were other options to solve their problems and issues in a loving way while they tried to get off the bottle. T.J. hired one clean-cut guy from his old college who knew how to get things in order professionally while T.J. handled outside business.

"So, you know I am leaving you in charge? I will be back after a while. I am going to handle some business and retrieve more office supplies."

T.J. walked to the front area of the building with his daughter and stopped. He put his arm around his daughter, then looked around at the facility.

"Ooh, wee, Toni! I just cannot wait to get this place up and running. Your mom is definitely looking down on us, smiling! I truly feel it in my soul!"

Toni was excited along with her dad and happy with what he said about her mother being happy.

"Dad? I cannot wait until the grand opening, and we cut the ribbon!"

The new guy peeked around and made sure that Toni and T.J. had left the building. Peter looked around and saw all the workers hard at work. He looked over at Jim. one of T.J. workers.

"Hey, you?! I'm in charge here; my name is Pete. I need you in my office, now!"

Jim looked at Pete up and down, then back at the other workers.

"Here we go! I knew he was too clean-cut to smell his own piss! Let me see what's up now!"

Pete had already walked away. He heard the workers laugh, so he turned around and looked at everyone rudely. He looked Jim up and down, then turned back and walked toward the office. The workers laughed again as they shook their heads in disgust. Jim got to Pete's office and sat down.

"Hey, No, No, No! Stand, please! The reason I called you in here, you reek!"

"Okay, your point?!"

"The point is you look about 50-55. I assumed you would know how to take a bath. I suppose you haven't learned that yet!"

By this time, T.J.'s other friend, Clyde, was taping the incident outside the door. Clyde had an encounter with Pete once, and he wanted him out of there.

"You rude mother fucka! Yeah, I know how to take a bath, bastard! First of all, you don't know me! You think you better than somebody, huh?! You could have told me more professionally than that, asshole! Second of all, I don't have a stable place. T.J. already told me he would help me get back on my feet, and I could bathe at his crib, and he had some threads for me. If you must know, Mr. Judge Judgmental!"

The phone rang, but before Pete answered, he replied back to Jim.

"Yeah, well, I can't wait until you go to his "crib" homeboy or whatever you call yourself."

Jim spoke loud enough for Pete to hear but not too loud to disrupt the conversation.

"Boy, if T.J. wasn't my boy, I would whip your ass out of your "Threads!" Oh, or whatever you call them!"

Pete rolled his eyes at Jim and took the call.

"A Precious Jade Rehabilitation Center, how may I help you?"

Pete grabbed some paper and wrote some numbers down.

"Okay. Okay."

Jim went to sit down, and Pete shook his head, telling Jim not to sit down. Jim waved his hand to Pete like, whatever, and he sat down anyway.

"Okay, I will try to figure this out and call you back. Thanks."

Pete hung up the phone and plopped in his chair out of frustration. He looked at the paper in his hand, confused. Pete had to figure out some measurements needed for the building. Jim noticed what Pete had to do, so Jim snatched the paper out of Pete's hand. Jim took a glance at the paperwork. Jim figured out all the measurements within 2 minutes and threw the paper back at Pete.

"Here are the configurations for a part of the building."

Jim had one more thing to say before he walked away.

"Oh, yeah, by the way, something reeks on your paper?"

"Yeah, you just touched it!"

"No, your math stinks! You couldn't cut it, huh? Go back to school. Name brand clothes and judging people don't make you smart or better than me, asshole!"

Pete looked down at the paper and could not believe how brilliant Jim was. Then, Jim saw Clyde swiftly walking away from Pete's office.

"Clyde! Clyde! Where are you coming from?"

"Huh?"

"Was you listening?"

"What?!"

"Come on, Clyde, I have known you for 11 years now! You had

that same look on your face when we were looking for the last drop of the 151 we had, and you had drunk it!"

"Alright, man, you got me, but I ought to let T.J. know how that sucka was talking to you!"

"Awe, come on, man, let's get back to work. We are here to help T.J., not him!"

Pete heard the two gentlemen in the hallway, so he came out and set a new rule just to show his authority.

"Excuse me, people, get back to work! And moving forward, your breaks are over at 12:28, not 12:30!"

Jim and Clyde looked at each other and their other friends and co-workers that were around. They shook their heads in disappointment. One of T.J.'s co-workers and friends, Ron, spoke out.

"I have a female friend that would turn that stuck-up cornball out! He needs a reality check and some good loving!"

Everybody working in the facility laughed. Pete did not know why there was laughter, but he proceeded to be rude and yell.

"You all get back to work!"

Jim decided to make fun like he usually did, so he told everybody to say, yes sir, out loud like a choir.

"Okay, y'all, one two three.... "

"YES, SIR!"

Pete smiled and popped his collar.

"Thank you, that's more like it."

Pete walked away. Clyde was furious.

"Oh, hell naw! I'm getting him out of here! I may have been a recovering addict for about two years now, but I know my rights! He is a trip! I am talking to T.J about dude; I'm sorry!"

Jim tried to settle Clyde down.

"Aww, man, don't let him get to you. It is more assholes in the world than good people, so don't let the people, like Pete, get to you. That population is great!"

Clyde was still disappointed.

"Well, I am going to be like the people from Spain back in the day!"

Ron Ron was confused.

"What you talking about, man?"

"You remember they were a small number and won the fight with garden tools. We may be a small number, but I am speaking out!"

Jim laughed.

"You do have a point, Clyde. But I am going to watch out for you on May 5th."

"Why?"

"You may swing a rake at me."

Clyde, Ron Ron, and Jim all laughed.

"You got a point there, man. Clyde, you calm, but you get agitated when you try to get your point across. T.J should know, though. He wouldn't yell at us like angry Pete! Hell, he so down to earth I was shocked to hear he was loaded with money."

Jim pointed at Ron Ron.

"You too?! Tell me about it!"

Clyde shook his head in agreement then they all got back to work.

Brenda sat in the chair outside of Isaac's hospital room, looking out the window, while Lema was in the room with Isaac. Bernice sat in a chair right by her sister because she knew something was wrong.

"Sis, what's on your mind?"

"You know, Bernice, I'm getting sick of every time I become happy; life just shuts me down. I got really blessed with a real father figure for Isaac, then...it must be me."

Brenda puts her head down, frustrated.

"Yeah, it is you."

"What?!"

"Yeah, you bring goodness to everyone you come in contact with. Some people didn't even believe in God until they met you! And yes, some men came and went, but you better believe you left them with a better spiritual sense. Also, look at me. I cannot even direct my next step without calling on you for advice! So I agree, trouble does follow you. You even taught me faith is not easy because you have to work on it! So keep working on that, big sis, and trust, you don't see it, but you will be blessed tremendously for all you do. And the sweet part about you; you are not even looking for a reward."

"Thanks, sis, I appreciate every word; I truly do! But now, I need y'all. People think strong people have it all figured out. Well, that may be true, but we get tired. When we finally have an outcry, people push us away. They think strong people do not feel or experience hurt when they say, I'm scared or not okay. And sometimes we even become clueless, and right now, Bernice, I just don't know how to save my husband's soul."

"You know what, Brenda? I never told you this, but you are strong like Grammy. And you remember what she used to say, you can't do God's work, just keep doing good at being his child, and you will win over people's hearts."

Brenda smiled, reminiscing.

"Yeah, I remember her words completely!"

"So, keep doing your job as the good woman that you are. He will stop drinking and come around, watch. If you stop being there for him, that is when things tend to happen; with no support, people lose hope. And we are here for you, okay, sister."

Brenda's silence and the way she hugged Bernice let Bernice know she understood.

Lema and Isaac listened to music in Isaac's room.

"Hey, cousin?"

"Yeah, Lema."

"Did it hurt after you got your surgery?"

"I don't know, I was asleep, but when I woke up, I felt pain. That did not feel good, and I was sore for weeks. After that, my mama said

I could eat, but I am scared that I still have broken bone pieces, even though she said they removed all of them."

"Yeah. Hey, I'm sure gone miss Ms. Opal. Even though we don't live down here, we staying for a while. Now she not here so we can visit her. We can't even give her her medicine now, Isaac!"

"Yeah. Ms. Opal understood all of us! She loved us, kids. It is like Ms. Opal knew what we wanted before we asked her. She was smart. I miss Ms. Opal, and I love her."

"Yeah, me too. I wonder what Ms. Opal's favorite color was. Maybe we could ask Marie; I know she knows. Then we can put her favorite color flowers on her grave."

"You know what, Lema. Ms. Opal's favorite colors were all the colors!"

"How do you know, she told you?"

"No, she loved all of us children, and we are all different colors."

"Oh, yeah, so true! Well, the flower shop has all different colors and types of flowers there anyway. We have to tell David and Jerry so they can go with us."

Isaac stopped smiling and put his head down.

"Yeah."

"What now? You got me happy now sad all over again. Why did your face change" Are you in pain right now?"

"No, Lema! I just wondered if David would be in the wheelchair forever. I don't mind if he has to be in that chair. He is my friend no matter what."

Lema was now just as sad as Isaac; however, she tried to cheer him up.

"Well, duh! You should be his friend no matter if he is in a wheelchair or not, silly!"

She threw a pillow at Isaac. Isaac smiled back because that was their favorite game. So Isaac threw a pillow back.

"Whatever, big head!"

50

Steve and David came home from David's physical therapy appointment. Steve helped his son get into bed.

"Okay, you all set, son."

David dropped the ball that was in his hand. He tried to catch it before it rolled off the bed; however, he could not.

"Damn it!"

Steve was almost out the door but turned around quickly.

"Son! You want to watch that potty mouth?!"

"Yeah, that is the only thing I can watch. I watched my ball roll because I sure couldn't go get it!"

Steve had the biggest lump in his throat but tried to be strong for his son.

"Son, look, this is a lesson I had to learn to get closer to you, okay? Plus, the doctor said with therapy, this may just be temporary."

David turned his face to the other side of the room, away from his dad.

"Yeah, I know."

Steve felt tremendously guilty. He got up and placed the ball in his son's hands before he exited

"Get you some rest, son."

Steve cut off David's light and closed his door. He then pulled his phone out of his pocket and called Manzel.

"Days and Night Auto, how may we help you?"

"Hey, Manzel."

"Hey, Steve, how's the family?"

"We're hanging in there. Hey, I need a favor."

"Anything, shoot."

"Well, I want to finish putting together this go-kart for David and his friends. I thought we could put a real motor in it. And, and, um."

Steve busted out crying.

"Hey, hey, man, what's wrong?"

"I just feel one hundred percent responsible for everything that happened to my son and his friends."

"Well, why would you say such a thing?!"

Steve explained the entire thing to Manzel.

"Oh! Yeah. Well, the truth is, like my elder family used to say, you cannot escape that, so now you made the 2nd step."

"The second step?"

"Yeah, you got it out with tears. Now, the second step, you can fix things and make it right. The second step is also like saying you have a second chance. So, we have to make the go-kart handicap assessable for your son, also. We have to make it to where the car talks and reminds that Jerry to tie up his shoes."

Manzel laughed but stopped when he realized Steve was not laughing back.

"Yeah."

"Come on, everybody knows Jerry's untied shoes are the talk of the town. I'm just kidding, you know that. You would normally laugh; why you not laughing?"

Then Steve explained the entire situation with Jerry's shoes.

"Wow, yeah, that's not cool. My bad for making jokes about Jerry."

"Come on, Manzel, you didn't know."

"And seriously, who knew that was an attention-getter. All so he could gain his mother's attention?"

"Yeah."

"Well, I got to go. The shop is busy, and I have ignored two phone calls already. I will get right on the go-kart project. We can get more material and start, is that cool?"

"I will work around your schedule because I need your help, but the sooner, the better."

Manzel agreed, and they hung up.

51

Samuel sat on the street corner where Isaac and David first started building their go-kart. Samuel turned up his bottle to get his last swallow of drink. He talked to himself loudly and slurred with his speech. Marie heard him and looked out the window.

"Yeah, son! You can build a go-kart; who am I to say no. I'm just a wretch."

He sang.

"A wretch like me!"

Tears ran down his face as he stopped singing but continued talking himself.

"It's not your fault what Uncle Robert did to me. David and Jerry are your true friends, okay, son?"

Samuel looked up and noticed someone looking out of Ms. Opal's window. Samuel stood up and smiled; however, still in a delirious state.

"Hey! You not dead! Awe, Ms. Opal, I knew it couldn't be true that you gone because you couldn't hurt a fly!"

Samuel swung like he was hitting a fly and then fell straight back on the curve. Marie had just finished a batch of Ms. Opal's cookies. She placed four on a plate and took it to Samuel with some milk in a glass. Ms. Opal taught her there was nothing like milk in a glass.

"Hey. Excuse me. I just finished practicing making a batch of my auntie's cookie recipe. Do you want to try them?"

Samuel stood up, reached his hand out to Marie, and almost stumbled.

"Well, hey, there! It's you again, huh? You're the one who brought me that news about Ms. Opal. Okay, now, quit playing. Now go in there and tell her she was the best person that ever happened to all of us! I'm not prejudiced anymore, okay? I never hated her, and I am trying to drink my demons away. Well, you know the last part, just go get her, please."

Marie had the biggest lump in her throat. This made her so sad as well as happy. Marie had mixed emotions; however, she was very happy about her aunt's effect on people.

"It's going to be okay. My aunt loved you all. Hey, try some cookies. Maybe that will keep a good thought in your head about my aunt and her cookies she used to make for everybody."

Samuel wasn't rude to every person he met; it was mostly his brother. However, he became either passive-aggressive or rude to everyone when he drank.

"Yeah, give me one of those cookies, girl, since you won't listen and go get Ms. Opal out of there."

Marie wanted to respond back; however, her aunt coached her that to love others required patience.

"Have some milk also."

"No, no, I don't think milk going to mix with that 100 proof in my stomach."

Samuel took a bite of a cookie and yelled, startling Marie.

"Awe, Lawd! Oh my God!"

"What?! What's a matter?"

"Go, get her! Now, I know Ms. Opal in there. Nobody knows how to make her chocolate chip cookies, damn it!"

Marie forgot all about being scared, and she became excited that she had almost mastered her auntie's recipe.

"Really?!"

Samuel walked down the street; however, to let Marie know that he cared and didn't mean anything by his behavior, he said something special to her.

"Little lady?"

"Yes?"

"If you let someone put you down, you will stay down. Get up, dust off your own butt because you have to be strong for you!"

"Wow, thank you. I appreciate that!"

"Yeah, I appreciated it too when your aunt first told me that."

He tightly grabbed his liquor bottle walked off. Marie walked away in tears as she prayed out loud.

"Lord, help me, please! This aunt of mine was wonderful. I need you because these are not easy shoes to fill. My aunt was more than good! Please assist me; I am ready."

52

T.J. brought materials back to the rehab and brought them in with a huge smile and pretty teeth. He was intrinsically motivated to do whatever it took to help others. He sat the materials down and looked around the building, satisfied at what he saw.

"Oh yes, it is coming along good, I must say!"

Pete ran out because he heard T.J.'s voice.

"Yes! We must say!"

Jim looked over at Ron Ron and Clyde.

"Hey, y'all, if T.J. smiled, I bet you see Pete's teeth."

Ron, Ron was baffled.

"How is that?"

Clyde looked over at both T.J and Pete; he was baffled as well.

"Yeah, how is that?"

"Pete kissing butt so hard; right up the rear and up to T.J.'s mouth!"

They all busted out in laughter. Ron Ron commented first.

"Now you know you are cold-blooded for that one! For real!"

Clyde agreed with Ron Ron.

"Like a sub-zero fridge, man!"

Pete became furious. He 60% knew the joke was about him, so he became rude and yelled.

"GET BACK TO WORK!"

T.J. looked at Pete and was very disturbed by his behavior.

"Come on now, Pete! That is not how you talk to the workers. Or do you?"

T.J. stared at Pete, disappointed, and waited for an answer. Clyde figured this was his chance to regain respect, so he spoke out.

"He do!"

Pete waved his finger at Clyde.

"Who ask you to speak?! He was talking to me! And all I have done since T.J. has been gone was my professional duties."

(Pete looked to see if he had T.J.'s approval before he continued.

"And that is the least I can say about the rest of you!"

"Yeah, well, I'm a bit professional myself! T.J., can I talk to you in your office, please?!"

Yeah, sure, Clyde. Pete, I'll talk to you later. Confidentiality is a must. No need to talk out here, but in my office, later."

Pete took off his suit jacket, shook it before he put it over his forearm, then pushed his glasses to his face without a worry.

"Yes, sir, T.J.

Clyde and T.J. walked to the office. T.J. sat down but still had an expression of anger.

"Have a seat, Clyde. So, what's going on?"

Clyde was upset and eager to explain.

"Look here, now you know I am not one to snoop, right?"

"Don't make me answer that."

"No, serious T.J., man, look. Okay, when you were out of the office, Pete was way too wrong the way he came at Jim."

"The way he came at Jim. What do you mean?"

"No, man, look, as soon as you left, Pete yelled at Jim and called him in the office and...."

"And what?"

Clyde pulled out his smartphone.

"Awe, come on, man! You going to get me closed down even before I open up. You cannot go around taping people no more, Clyde!"

"Come on, boss man, you have been my friend before anything, just listen!"

"Alright, look, go ahead play it but afterward immediately erase it. I'm trying to share my wealth, and I don't want to end up like 90% of others who try to help their friends and end up in the poor house."

"Okay, T.J.

Clyde let T.J. hear the recording. T.J.'s face balled up like wrinkled foil.

"No. Now, this is not cool at all on any level. Come on."

Clyde felt a little intimidated by Pete's level of education.

"Wait, I'm not scared or anything, but do not tell Pete I said anything. I don't want to lose my job."

"What?! Lose your job?! First of all, I am here to help people who helped me, as well as help people who want to help themselves. Second, you are my friend; I don't care how much education someone has. Common sense is where the smartness lies! And Clyde, since you been here, I've been proud of you. You have been working and have not taken a drink since!"

"Yeah, but T.J., you, you loaded with money, and you treat us like you rubbed your pennies with ours to make a fire. You are truly humble. We never knew you had all this money! So, when you know people who care like that, no matter what, and don't look down on you, you give us hope to one day have the same success!"

"Yeah, well, I owe it all to my wife, Clyde."

"But come on, T.J., good women only attract and gain a humble and real man you know, so you do deserve credit; do not forget that."

"Right on, Clyde. You know she said that before. Clyde, well, let me talk to Pete. And don't worry, I know how to word things, he won't have a clue you told me anything. So why don't you go ahead erase that and go ahead back to work."

'Alright."

Clyde was headed out of the office when T.J. called him back.

"Yeah, T.J.?"

"Thanks, I mean that."

Clyde smiled, threw up a peace sign, and walked off. Pete saw Clyde coming out of the office, so he ran into T.J.'s office. T.J. was still distraught with his hand on his head in frustration.

"Finally! I thought he would never get out of your office."

"Pete, close the door."

"What's up, T.J.?"

"You know Pete, you have a lot of intelligence."

"Yes, I know, and thanks."

"And we haven't seen each other in years since college, huh?"

"Yeah. Uh, so, where is this going?"

T.J. scaled up his tactics.

"No, it is just I need your advice on something."

T.J. leaned over by Pete and turned his nose up. Then he pointed out the door with his thumb.

"What do you think about those guys I hired. You think I made a mistake?"

"Well, now that you mentioned it, yes! For one, Jim reeks of a disruptive odor."

"Uh, huh."

"And that Clyde and Ron, all they do is laugh about nothing like they had a happy pill to go with their "beverage." You know what I mean. No one wants anybody working for their company like that! So, yeah, let's get rid of half of these low-lives and get some real employees up in here. You get it, buddy?"

"You know what? I get it, but it doesn't fit my company?!"

"What do you mean?"

"Well, like you said, hire some real people. Let me tell you, my boys are as real as it gets! Yeah, we are college colleagues, and that's fine, but those guys are understanding, loyal, know how it is to lose and have nothing, and how to fight and struggle to regain. And still, have a smile on their face through all the trial and tribulation they face. Not to mention having empathy for others! Now I will take these paper plates and plastic spoon employees any day before I take your callous silver spoon eating self! And with that being said, polish up your silver spoon and shine your ass right out of my office! And guess what, when my wife died, I was one of them with, as you called it, my "beverage"! And about Jim reeking, your attitude reeks more than his body odor that can be washed away!"

Pete was surprised.

"Hey, but T.J.?"

T.J. waved his hand for Pete to move on.

"Well, if that's the way you want it!"

Pete stormed out of the office and out of the building. Ron-Ron, Clyde, and Jim noticed Pete's anger as he stormed out the door. Jim looked at Clyde and whispered.

"Thanks, man."

"Man, T.J. is alright with me!"

Ron-Ron picked up on the conversation and read between the lines.

"T.J. is real, and that is what it is, which is rare now in this scandalous world. So now, let's get back to work. We can't let our boy down."

T.J. looked in the air and sighed as he sat silent for a couple of minutes.

"Oh, Lord! What, why, and how am I going to do things without my Jade and my former true friend, Jabeeb?! Lord, please guide me. I swear happiness always comes with trials and tribulations."

His phone rang. He answered and it was his sister-in-law, Brenda.

53

Samantha went to check on David. She felt her son's sadness. She cut on the light and saw David's face wet because he had been crying. So, of course, Samantha tried to comfort her son.

"Hey, son, speed racer!"

"Mom, please! You have to love me. That is why you are saying that. Look at me. I'm not a speed racer; I can't walk!"

He turned his face away from his mom. Samantha sat on the side of David's bed and stroked his hair.

"Son, you know we go to church, and the Pastor said God wants us to love him with our own free will.

"Well, yeah, but what does that mean?"

"Okay, what do you mean. I thought I had explained before?"

David remembered his mom explaining; however, he had another question.

"Well, does it mean that God's love does not cost? You all keep saying free will. So, it means we do not have to pay to love God?"

Samantha laughed so hard she cried.

"Never mind, son. I have to tell your Aunt Linda that one when she wakes up! That means to love God because you want to. He does not force us."

"Ooh, I'm dumb!"

'No, you're not! I don't love you because I am your mom. I love you because you are sweet, kind, creative, and I was blessed to have you. I love you being in my world, so when I mentioned your speed racer skills, I meant it!"

David reached up and hugged his mom tightly.

"I love you, mom!"

"Free will, right?"

David smiled.

"Nah, I think I need twenty dollars for that hug!"

Samantha sighed in relief that her son was in better spirits.

"Nah, how about we go to Ms. Opal's and get some cookies for free?"

David frowned again.

"How can she make us cookies if she is dead, mom?!"

"You remember I told you she gave her niece the recipe for her famous cookies!"

David was happy about the cookies but not enthused about Ms. Opal's absence.

"Well, okay, I will be ready when you are. Well, I need your help more, mom. What time do you think we are going over there? Maybe someone can tell Isaac for me. He loved her cookies too!"

"Okay, we will work on that. Go back to sleep."

"Okay."

David laid back down.

The following day at about 10:30, Samantha got a knock on her door. She put on her robe and answered the door. Samantha smiled so hard she showed most of her teeth because it was Lema.

"Hey, Ms. uh, Ms. Samantha."

"Hey, little lady, what's up?"

"Well, my mama said, the gas prices are up."

Samantha laughed hard.

"Okay, sweetie, you here to see David, right?"

Lema spoke in her grown-up way; however, it can come off rude if you do not know her.

"Yeah, but I was saying hi to you out of respect first."

"Uh, okay. Well, just come sit in the living room and let me see if David is dressed."

Okay, I'm fine. I will sit right here.

Lema sat down as Samantha went back to the room. Steve came out to the kitchen to warm some food in the microwave. Then he sat down to eat his breakfast. He was about to put the fork to his mouth when he heard a southern voice and knew who it was.

"Good morning, Mr., I know you 'bout to eat, but my mama said when you come in somebody's house, you suppose to speak even if they don't speak first, cause it is they house whether they like you or not."

Steve remembered how rude he was to Lema, so he started a conversation to redeem himself.

"Well, yep, your mom was right, little one!"

"Oh, my name is Lema."

"I know, I know, it's Lena."

Lema laughed, and Steve looked confused.

"What is so funny about your name?"

"No, it's just that my momma said that kids don't listen and old people forget your name. My name is L-e-m-a, not Lena."

Steve was not so amused, especially since he knew he was part of the joke.

"Well, yeah, you are full of laughter."

"Hey, Mr., you have a nice smile! When I first met you, you had an, uh, let me see. Oh, yeah, like ten angry wrinkles on your forehead."

Steve frowned.

"Oh, really?"

"Yeah, just like that! It is okay, though; I met a man like you. Remember I told you when you did not like me a few months ago?"

"I didn't say that I didn't like you. So why would you insinuate that?!"

Lema's mature mind was so ready to explain.

"Oh, well, because you yelled at me and told me to.... well, let me show you."

Lema illustrated Steve's previous behavior. Lema frowned and waved her finger in the air. Then, in a deep man's voice, she yelled.

"GET AWAY FROM MY DOOR, LITTLE GIRL!"

"Oh, well, I am not a man of many apologies, but I am sorry. Is that okay with you, know?"

"Yeah, that's fine. I liked you even though you didn't like me."

"Why? If someone does not like me. Well, guess what? They would feel my wrath back."

"Well, this man that did not like me; he learned to like me later because I kept speaking to him. He was just like you, angry for nothing. I know he was angry inside. My mama said people who yell at you out their mouth are hot on the inside with anger. So now you cold, huh, Mr.?"

Steve laughed softly; his eyebrow raised, amazed at how bright this little girl was.

"I guess you can say that. You are something else. Can I eat my breakfast now?"

"Uh, I don't mind, Mr. if I was you, I would have ate it a long time ago. It smelled good!"

David pulled into the living room in his wheelchair with the biggest grin on his face. Steve did a double-take at David.

"Hey, Lema!"

Lema ran and hugged him.

"Hey, David. I miss you! Isaac missed you too!"

Tears rolled down Lema's face. Samantha and Steve choked up, watching the children unite.

"Hey, Ms. Opal's niece, Marie, invited us to have some cookies that

Ms. Opal made for us. Her niece invited my mom, my auntie, and Isaac! Are you coming?!"

David looked up at his mom then over at his dad. Samantha spoke up.

"Well, yeah, we will be there in a couple of hours, I suppose."

Lema jumped up and down.

"Yes, ooh wee! I am so happy! I will see y'all soon then. Okay, bye, Ms. Samantha and Mr. Shoo, next time I come over, I may eat some of your daddy's food! That smelled so good!"

Being a southern girl, she loved home-cooked meals more than anything. She was a little bit chubby and not afraid to eat. Steve, Samantha, and David looked at each other then they all laughed.

54

Samuel sat in front of a new liquor store recently built three blocks away from Jabeeb's. Jackie, the new store owner, was a slender oriental man with a strong accent. He came over to talk to Samuel. Jackie loved the money Samuel spent but was tired of Samuel sitting in front of his store.

"Hey, you?! Wake up! You have been here off and on for three days! Go find a shelter!"

Samuel woke up and blocked the sun out of his face as he sat up

"Man, I got a home!"

"I couldn't tell. Go home to it, please!"

"Come on, man. Much as I spend at this store, I paid the rent! You know what? You are nothing like Jabeeb at all, I tell you!"

"And you know what?! I am tired of all of you saying that! If I am so bad, go back and hang in front of his store, now!"

"Ah, please! Don't act like you didn't hear what happened to Jabeeb! Y'all hear what goes on in the U.S. before you even get over here!"

Samuel made a karate move, including the sound.

"Woo- Haa!"

Jackie waved his hand at Samuel in disappointment, and he went back into his store. A short elderly Black woman passing through stood over Samuel, and she blocked the sun.

"May I help you? Well, better yet, thanks for blocking the sun."

"Hey, aren't you Ms. Rose's boy?"

"I thought I remembered you. You were that lady in church who always had a switch ready for the kids! You're name Ms. Lucy, right?"

"No, boy! My name is still Ms. Lucille. I got tired of that Lucy for short stuff. I know someone with a bad rep, and I am in no affiliations with her. Anyway, enough about me, I asked you a question. What in the world are you doing on the ground outside like this?! I know you got a home. Our entire congregation knows Bren! As a matter of fact, one of the church members said Bren was looking for you!"

"Now I remember why I stop going to church, other people. News spread faster than the good word out the Bible in church!"

Ms. Lucille laughed.

"Yeah, well, that may be true, but on that note, you take your tail home! That young boy and woman need you. Here you are feeling sorry for yourself...."

"Oh, no, I'm not...."

"Boy! I don't care how old you are; respect your elders. Now, I wasn't done talking."

Ms. Lucille pointed towards the direction of Samuel's way home.

"Now take your narrow ass home! Since you were little, you wanted to be seen. Be like your brother and worried about what everyone else was doing! You know the one person you never wondered about?!"

Samuel was silent out of respect and fear. Ms. Lucille placed her hand on her hip.

"Well? Huh?!"

"Uh, well, I guess you will tell me."

"You damn right I will tell you! You need to worry about your damn self! I know it hurts but stop worrying about past issues or whatever you going through. It is going to be rough out here. You noticed people who think they got it all look down on people. Then as soon as they struggle, they are jumping off a bridge or going crazy! And you have been blessed with a second chance at life! You are blessed with a wife who loves your dirty drawls, which from the looks of you, they need washing now! And a God-given son who not running in the streets doing whatever like other kids. He could be hanging with the wrong crowds, worrying about being down, and seeing who got five on it. Not to mention getting smart with elders!"

Ms. Lucille snatched his liquor bottle from under him. Samuel jumped up by her face. He stood much taller than Ms. Lucille. She was only 4'11 on a good day. Ms. Lucille got in a boxing stance with one of her short legs behind her, mean-mugging as she looked up at Samuel.

"Come on and leap. I bet you will be limping back like you had three bottles of 151!"

Samuel held his head down and cried.

"Man, you make me miss my momma!"

Ms. Lucille wanted to sympathize so badly with Samuel; however, she had come too far. She had to stand her ground, but she toned it down some.

"Yeah, and my son, Clyde, would have been saying the same thing if I let him stress me out. That is another story. I love you like a son too. That's why I am telling you, you got a lot of love that people wish they had, you hear?! Now get yourself together! By the way, I know you heard about that new rehabilitation center your brother opened up down on Martin Luther King Street. Swallow your pride and go help him; he needs you! The wrong kind of jealousy only makes your days longer. Now use your intelligence, mix them with his and become powerful, like the person that you ignore inside, you hear me?!"

Samuel was still teared up and at a loss for words. He bent down and embraced Ms. Lucille with the biggest hug ever. She embraced him back and hugged him even tighter.

"Now, I don't like the personality of the man at this new store. I try to walk by fast as I can, so I won't lose my religion if he gets smart with me. But I will be coming down here just to see if you are here. And I will run you off the block every time! And if you don't believe me, just watch!"

"Oh, trust me, I believe you!"

They laughed. Ms. Lucille gave her last words as she walked away.

"Okay, God bless you! Because if I see you over here again, you going to need the Lord and five cups of Jesus boy!"

55

T.J. sat in his office, finally able to take a breather, when his phone rang.

"Hello. 24-hour rehabilitation. We are not open; however, we will be soon. How may I help

you?"

There was silence on the other end."

"Hello?!"

"Hey, T.J."

T.J. was a bit confused, but he was still happy as always to hear from his sister-in-law.

"Hey, Bren! How did you get this number? Well, let me rephrase that because you know I don't mind. It is just I didn't give it to too many people and nobody you really know either, so I'm just a little confused."

"Yeah, well, when I went on my search to find your brother, I saw someone who knew you. He said that he was going to work for you soon and gave me the number. Then he walked by me and kept saying, now that is a blessing. Now that is when I was puzzled, but I was glad he was feeling blessed like that, though."

T.J. laughed.

"Let me ask you something? When you walked away, did he look back at you?

"Yeah. What does that have to do with anything, though?"

"That is my friend Ken. Anytime he sees something on any woman he likes, he yells out, what a blessing."

Brenda felt embarrassed.

"Oh."

"Don't worry, I'll let him know. That was a married woman you were talking to, not to mention my sis-in-law. Sorry about that, sis.

"Yeah, that's okay, well, you know I haven't seen your brother in a couple of days. I know he is drunk. But, T.J., I just do not have the energy to tell him to come back home. Then if he refuses, what am I going to tell Isaac?"

"Well, Bren, you know I would go get him, but he envies me for no apparent reason. So, you know he is not going to listen to me either."

"Come on, T.J., I really need you on this one. Now you know you are more of a role model to Sam...."

"Man, Brenda, come on now. Let's keep it real. That man can't stand me!"

T.J., please, just stop it! You know, like I told you, he looks up to you so hard! I am surprised you do not realize that. You are more of a people person, and that is what he envies. Now I love my husband, 200%, but we all know who has the personality and charisma."

"Yeah, he did tell me the same thing. He told me some news that had me shocked, too. Well, let me just get my stuff together, and I will try and find him, okay!"

Brenda exhaled in relief.

"Thank you so much, T.J. If you cannot reach me at home, call my cell because I have to go a couple of places today."

"Alright, Bren."

"T.J., once again, God bless you! I know Jade and Jabeeb are smiling at your progress right now."

T.J.'s soul was at ease from earlier, now.

"Thanks, sis, I needed to hear that, for real! Talk to you soon."

"Okay, thanks."

They hung up the phone. Brenda looked over at her sister after she got off the phone. She wondered why Bernice was dressed.

"Where you going, Bernice?"

"Remember, Lema just got back and said that you said we were invited to Ms. Opal's house by her niece to have some cookies, remember?"

"Oh, shoot! I forgot! Wow!"

"Sis, trust me, I know all that you are going through. You can sit this one out if you want. I will go for the family."

"Would you?! Thanks, Bernice. Let me go talk to your nephew and see if he understands."

"Okay, that's fine. Your niece and I will be in the car waiting for him."

"Okay."

Isaac was tying his shoe when he looked up and saw his mom.

"Hey, mom! You want me to bring you some cookies back from Ms. Opal's?"

"How you know I wasn't going? You heard me? What I tell you about eavesdropping on grown folks conversation."

"No, I wasn't, mom. It's just when you are going somewhere you always do your hair, but you still have your scarf on."

Brenda placed her hand on her hip and leaned on the wall.

"You going to make somebody a good husband one day, boy. You are observant!"

"Is dad mad at me?"

"No, why? Why would you say that?"

"He has not been here in a couple of days, and he is normally always home."

"No, no, son. Everything is fine. He is just collecting his thoughts; he'll be home. I have faith he will be."

Brenda had some doubts even though she was trying to keep the faith. Isaac ran and hugged his mom.

"Okay, mama, I will see you when I get back."

"Okay, Hon'"

Bernice, Isaac, and Lema made it to Ms. Opal's. David, Samantha, and Linda were already there. Every person there, church members, and all that were friends of Ms. Opal were a bit quiet. However, Lema and Isaac talked to David about how they were going to decorate his wheelchair and how they hoped Jerry's mom would bring him. Lema bit into a cookie.

"These cookies taste just like Ms. Opal's. Miss Marie, I miss her for so many reasons!"

"Well, if it's okay with all of your parents, every year, ask can you help me bake some cookies, and then we can take them to the homeless!"

Isaac and David got excited.

"Okay, I'm ready for that!"

"Me too! Ms. Opal always helped people. She would be proud of us!"

"Yeah, so true."

Marie noticed that the adults in the house were very quiet. So, she spoke to break the ice.

"Alright, I'll be back, you all."

Lema answered.

"Okay, Marie!"

Marie surrounded herself on the side where all the adults were.

"Well, eat up, ladies!"

Linda huffed.

"I know I am slim, but if I keep eating up those cookies, I won't be watching my figure; it will be watching me!"

All the ladies laughed. Bernice dug in to get another cookie.

"Well, I will take her share. My figure has been watching me for years!"

All the ladies, including Bernice, laugh profusely. Samantha noticed all the laughter and happiness in the room. So she sparked up a conversation that she had been meaning to talk about since she got there.

"Oh, ladies. They said three more months and David should be walking."

Everyone cheered.

"Wait, I entered him into the Special Olympics in two months. You all can come and bring the children."

Bernice was excited for Samantha.

"Well, we will be there! And I know my daughter will make sure of it!"

Loud laughter came from everyone since they knew Lema's personality. Lema spoke out of turn since she was eavesdropping.

"I sure will be there, mama and...."

"Lema, stay in a kid's place and out of grown folks' business. You are not supposed to be in here!"

Linda laughed.

"I think she is in her place. You have a little grown woman there!"

Bernice leaned over and tapped Linda's knee.

"Tell me about it!"

"Well, I am pretty sure we will support your family, and all come. Where is it?"

"Oh, well, Marie, it will be downtown next to the Convention Center from 12:30pm- 5:00pm. Also, they will have refreshments and donation stands. Marie, why don't you bake Ms. Opal's cookies in tribute to her. I know her church sponsors Special Olympics."

All the church ladies nodded their heads in agreement.

"I did not find out until, until, uh, my son was eligible to become a member. I should have been involved long before that, huh?"

Linda cheered her sister up.

"Oh, Sam, come on. You have always been a sweetheart. We know you mean well even if this had not happened to David! We will support you. And we all must jump in to support Marie. Help bake tons of cookies and take them out there; sugar and chocolate chips!"

There was a knock at the door, so Marie went to answer it.

"Who is it?"

"It's June."

Marie was confused and looked around at everyone to see if they had recognized the voice; however, everyone was just as baffled as she was.

"Yes, June Sinclair."

Samantha jumped up in excitement.

"Oh! Oh, my goodness, it is Jerry's mom; open up!"

"Wow! I only knew her as Mrs. Sinclair the entire time I've known her.

Marie opened the door and gave Mrs. Sinclair a very welcoming greeting.

"Well, hello! Now should I call you June or Mrs. Sinclair?"

"Well, whatever makes you feel comfortable, I suppose. Everyone knows me by Mrs. Sinclair, which is the name I use for business."

"Well, I will call you Mrs. Sinclair also then. It looks like that name fits you."

"Okay, thanks. That is fine."

Mrs. Sinclair kept looking back towards the door to her car. Marie looked back out the door as well.

"Uh, what's wrong?"

"Oh, no, I have to get all the flour and other ingredients out the trunk of my car to donate to you."

Linda threw her hands in the air.

"Well, show us out why dontchu!"

Samantha immediately jumped in. She thought her sister still had a grudge against Mrs. Sinclair.

"Oh, well, I think what my sister means is, do you need help?"

Linda knew what her sister was thinking, so she filled her in that there was no grudge.

Linda walked to the front door.

I'm ready! Where are the goods?"

Mrs. Sinclair clicked the alarm.

"Oh, thank you, the items are in the trunk."

Lema came running out, again not staying with the kids, to ask Mrs. Sinclair a question.

"Where's Jerry?"

Jerry came from behind his mom.

"I am right here."

Everyone looked down at his shoes, and they were tied! Lema, of course, was the one to acknowledge it.

"Oh, hey! You have on new shoes, and they are tied!"

Bernice got up and snatched Lema to the side.

"Hi, I am Lema's mom."

"Oh, hello! You have a wonderful little girl!"

"Oh, you sure about that?!"

Mrs. Sinclair gave Bernice a blank stare.

"No, just kidding. Thanks. Well, come on, have a seat and a cookie. Relax, you look so tense and antsy!"

Linda whispered to Samantha before they went out the door.

"And she wonders why Lema is so outspoken."

Samantha nudged her sister and laughed. Mrs. Sinclair walked in and continued talking to Bernice.

"Oh, well, yes, I stay busy. But I cut my load down a bit so Jerry, his father, and I could travel a little bit to fun places."

Lema got excited.

"Ooh! Ooh! What have you been doing for the summer, Jerry?!"

Lema pulled on Jerry and guided him towards the back with the kids. All the ladies had finished bringing in the items for the party. They filled Mrs. Sinclair in on what had been going on with the invite to the Special Olympics.

56

Steve and Manzel were on the finishing touches of the go-kart they were building. Steve stood back and looked at what they had built with pride.

"Oh, yeah, a masterpiece is among us! What a beauty! What do you think I should call it?"

Manzel was an easy-going guy, so he was very happy; however, nonchalant about the project.

"I'm not sure, Steve; you created most of it. But, I am pretty sure you will come up with a name for it."

"I will call it what we are; I will call it "just us"!"

Manzel instantly noticed the concept from the explanation that Steve told him earlier when he explained why he was prejudiced. Manzel loved the name.

"See, I knew you would find one! Let's go ahead and finish sanding the go-kart down so we can paint it. We have to hurry up so it can be ready for the Special Olympics."

"Alright, alright. I am still puzzled, though, about who paid my son's bill and his physical therapy sessions! Plus, they say Dave is supposed to walk in 3 months, and the Special Olympics is in 2; all of this is crazy to me. Well, hey, I don't know."

"I sense your doubt, Steve. God blessed you, and you did not know where it came from. Sometimes, it is not meant for you to know where your blessings come from. Just keep having faith and let nature take its' course."

"Let nature take its' course, huh?! Thanks for taking care of the bills, Manzel."

"Look, Steve, I am not telling you anymore, man. I did not pay that bill, alright!"

"Okay, okay, I get it! I will just let it go! Well, now I'm thinking whoever did it must have been a long-term friend who cared for me and put up with me for years. I am just definitely flattered! Let's get this project done, then.

Two months passed by, and T.J.'s rehabilitation was up and running well. Brenda was going through the motions with Samuel's drinking. Her sister was still there and a tremendous help while Brenda tried to hang in with everything she was going through with Samuel. Lema, Isaac, and Jerry helped David decorate his chair for the Special Olympics. Once they were finished, Samantha drove David to his physical therapy appointment. When they arrived, Samantha lifted David up to assist him in getting into his wheelchair. Her elbow accidentally pressed into his leg.

"Ouch! Mom, don't press into my legs so hard, please!"

Samantha's eyes grew large like headlights.

"YOU FELT THAT?!"

David looked at his mom, puzzled.

"Yeah, mom."

Samantha latched David in, ran by the entrance doors, and waved down one of the physical therapists. When the physical therapist arrived, she looked at Samantha, frantic.

"What is it? Can I help you with something?"

Samantha whispered in the therapist's ear.

"I need Dr. Zueng, now! "

"Uh, okay, no problem."

The therapist continued to assist David. She was one of the individuals who worked with him.

"Hello, Dr. Zueng. Ms. Smith wanted to see you right away."

Dr. Zueng approached Samantha.

"Hello, Ms. Smith, what's going on today?"

Samantha was pacing while she spoke with Dr. Zueng.

"Okay, now I was helping David out of the car. He felt me press into his leg!"

Dr. Zueng looked at Samantha with a blank stare and a straight face.

"Yes."

"Uh, okay, no, seriously, did he feel that?!"

Dr. Zeung was now aware of why she was excited.

"Oh, yes, no doubt! I looked over his x-rays and charts all last week. As a result, we are placing him on our advanced therapy level, where he could grab onto two bars, then stand, and slowly walk down the bars until he reaches more progress."

Samantha held her hand over her mouth.

"Wow, just wow! What a blessing! I am so prepared for my son to walk again!"

"Well, that is always the part of a good mother."

Samantha looked at him, trying to figure out what he meant.

"Well, you know the good mother and all."

"Thanks!"

"Was you not expecting this?"

"Not this early. However, trust me when I say I am excited and flattered!"

"Well, great. Have a seat, and as usual, we will call you when we are done with David's therapy.

"Okay, thanks."

57

T.J. was on the phone with one of his benefactors for his rehabilitation center.

"Yes. Yes, it is open, but the grand opening party is in 3 weeks. Thanks."

T.J. received another call coming through on his line.

"One second, please, it is my other line. Thank you."

T.J. answered the other line.

"Hello?"

Samuel's voice was raspy as if he had been crying all day.

"Tell me what's next, man, just what is next? I am looking for answers!"

T.J. was overjoyed that Samuel was opening up to him again.

"I am not asking; can I beg you to hold on for one second?"

"I got nothing but time."

T.J. sighed in relief.

"Okay, little bro, one second!"

T.J. went back to the other line.

"Yes, Goet, is it? Okay. Is it okay if I touch base with you later and set a time where we can talk? Thank you. I will call you very soon. Okay, have a good one."

T.J. clicked back over to Samuel.

"Okay, I am back, so what's up?"

"Man, don't get all like you care!"

"Samuel, we had a talk a few months ago. I thought by that sincere talk we had that you learned I care, and we had figured things out."

"Whatever! You the one got it all figured out drunk or sober, sitting or standing, you've been the superstar whether right or wrong!"

T.J. was semi-giving up, feeling this may be a lost battle.

"Look. I will stay out of your way. I know when we had that conflict at your house when I used to drink, I may have said some rude things. And I know for some reason you feel I'm the superstar. So if it makes you happy for me to stay out of your way, then I will. On that note, I love you, and I hope we can reconnect soon. I have to go, Samuel. I can't keep talking if all we are going to do is keep choking at each other's necks."

Samuel knew he needed his brother. He heard the hurt in his brother's voice, so Samuel placed his pride to the side.

"Look, my bad. I just, well, I need you. I know I was disappointed in you for not going all the way to the top in college. But, anyway, clearly, the only reason I waited for you to make it to the next step was that I wait to follow your footsteps in the sand."

T.J.'s heart melted.

"See, now, you a poet! Is that how you snatched up my beautiful sister-in-law?"

They laughed then Samuel dropped his head.

"Nope. I don't know how and why that woman keeps putting up with me."

There was a long pause.

"Hello, you still there?"

"Not really. I just keep going on these binges, man, and I know she tired of me!"

"Listen, Samuel, Brenda is a very good woman. But, trust me, I know, I had one and a hell of a lot of bad ones!"

Samuel went down memory lane in his head with T.J.'s past, then smiled.

"Yeah. I really miss Brenda's spirit."

"I know you do, and you know I know about missing mine and her spirit! But anyway, like I told you before, Brenda is not going anywhere! Brenda is a precious gem. So do not tarnish her and make her lose her value due to the fact that she is so worried and loves you that she drains the love she needs for Isaac, you, and most of all herself!"

Samuel took in every word and dwelt on them.

"Yeah. Man, you said I am just as smart as you, and I need to use my talents. Can I read your step program guide to recovery and come down for a few days, get clean, get a job, basically help you out?

"Little bro, that is more than music to my ears! I would love to have my brother beside me! I have been trying to tell you for years, you are not in front or behind me; we are equal."

"Right on. Well, I'm on my way; I just need to call, Bren. I'm going to wait and tell her about me helping out, but...."

"If, I must say, and I am not overstepping my boundaries, just keep it a secret, and I will surprise her when the time is right with your presence! Is that cool with you?"

"Yeah, I guess, whatever. I'm just trying to get it together for Brenda, my son, and myself. I'm on my way, though."

T.J. smiled and showed all 32 of his pearly whites.

"Come on down, come on down."

58

While Samantha was in the waiting room, she called her sister to share the excitement.

"Would you pick up already!"

"Hello, my sister, whom which will never beat me at Yahtzee."

"Okay, wake up from your dream and listen."

"I never!"

"You never will beat me at Yahtzee, I know; thanks for admitting it!"

They laughed.

"No, seriously, I have something to tell you!"

Samantha explained all the details to Linda about David feeling the pressure in his leg and everything else.

"OH, GOD IS GOOD! Hey Sam, now we have to tell Steve!"

"Well, that is the second reason I called."

"Okay, Steve was making changes and doing good; please, do not ruin my moment. If he went back to his old ways and did something...."

"No, no, nothing like that! I just want to surprise him. When the time is right, I will tell him, okay?"

"Well, damn! This is such good news, and I actually like my

brother-in-law now. But, hey, I understand. But oh, this is such good news!"

"Sis, I love you; thanks for always being there."

Linda cried; however, Samantha did not know. Linda had a good way of containing herself and hiding her emotions at times."

"Awe, come on Sam, you my girl even though you talk a mile a minute."

"Well, uh, void the 'I love you,' that I just gave you then!"

They shared another laugh. When Samantha got home from the physical therapy session, she avoided her husband all night, except for going to bed, in order to not spill the beans.

Bernice, Isaac, and Lema headed home to Brenda's place.

"Hey, you have some nice neighbors, Bren'."

"Yeah, girl, it wasn't like that at first! We had to break down coal to call each other diamonds, that's for sure."

"That's my sister! You always have an inspirational saying, just like mama did."

"Yeah, I wish I had the strength like mama to tell Samuel to go! He keeps coming in and out of this house like he has another woman!"

"You still think that honestly Bren'?"

"Well, yeah, I am tired of him doing that. His lame excuse is that he is working on some project, which is why he is gone so much! He keeps it up; he will need to build him a project!"

"First off, you are too headstrong. You would have definitely known if Samuel was cheating with your dream in the night, self, and our woman's intuition. Plus, he is a new alcoholic drinker right now. You never know; he may not know how to tell you he is going to go drink out of respect for his family."

Brenda deeply thought about it then dropped her head.

"Yeah."

They heard keys. Bernice got up.

"Well, that is my cue. I am going in the room with Lema."

Bernice lifted Brenda's face and whispered before she left the room.

"Talk to your husband."

Brenda shook her head in agreement then waved for her sister to go.

Samuel came in after helping his brother and attending an AA meeting. Samuel tried to ease through the door, thinking Brenda may be taking one of her famous naps. However, as he walked in, Brenda was right there staring at him, her leg shaking and with her arms crossed.

"Hey, babe."

He kissed Brenda on the forehead.

"Yeah, hey."

Samuel frowned and looked at Brenda.

"For real, babe, that's all the reaction I get?!"

Brenda was silent. Samuel put his arm around Brenda.

"Come on, mama."

Brenda gave him the evil eye; however, she loved him so. She just looked at him then allowed him to pull her close.

"Babe, look, I know I have not been here. And I wish I could tell you what project I'm working on, but I cannot. I...."

"I don't care!"

Brenda had a history of being stubborn and silly, like a light switch, and only Samuel knew how to deal with that.

"Come on now, Bren' not today. I need you to care with the kinda project I am completing. I need your moral support like you've been giving me all these years, please!"

Brenda kept looking at Samuel with a straight face.

"Brenda, you the best woman I have ever known! You put up with me unconditionally."

Samuel thought of his brother's words from earlier.

"Woman like you don't come often. I know I have said some dumb things about what kind of father I am. I was just blaming myself. I was angry about the entire incident. And I, I just blamed it all on myself."

Samuel began to cry.

"But I will be damned if I leave out that boy's life under any circumstances! That is my son!"

Brenda felt his sincerity and began to cry as well.

"Okay, but why do you have to be gone so much? I have places I want you to go with me!"

Samuel whimpered, laughed, and wiped his face.

"Where, Bren? Just name it, and I will make it. But I still have to be gone like I do, and trust me, it is not another woman. I know how you think. You are my wife, and I know and value what that means. You know, of course, I see eye candy, but you the only one that provide my eye cavities with your beauty, you understand."

"Yeah, I'm trying. I just feel because I messed up that one time...."

"You did not mess up. I was hanging out, trying to call exes, and doing the most. I yelled at you and more, which hurts me to mention. You had my back, faithfully, one hundred percent! You just got tired and did what anybody might do. I forgave you."

"Well, yeah, I did get tired, and I cheated. That was why I felt when you came home from us fighting that situation with you and that case, we were fighting for you, and you had done the same to get back at me."

"No! You told me what you did, and that was built-up from my bullshit, so it was not the same. I understand, and you told on yourself! Who does that anymore or at all! You gave me an option to walk away. I hated that it was someone I knew that you reached out to. I was pissed, yeah; I just looked at it like it wasn't just you. He was wrong also. And it wasn't like you met him before, but I went to jail fighting for my life. I hated how you two hooked up on the fluke. My situation was not an excuse. I came home and just pursued some dumb shit being a man and not thinking and did not tell you about that female. You found out because God blessed you with dreams and that woman's intuition stuff. See, I was foul because I was sneaking after you gave me an option to stay or go. I was doing foul stuff before I went in and then the last time when I got home. I will not do that again!"

"Be careful saying what you won't do. Temptation is not easy when you are doing good with your woman, and the Halle Berrys and Beyonces start feeling you. When you are single, you can't get a two-dollar hooker to wink at you on the corner!"

They laughed hard.

"You a trip."

"But, yeah, I told you first, then a couple of your family members, and they talked about me like I cheated on them. But they had a right you're their family."

"Please! They need to stay out of it. They were doing the same or worse back then and now. They don't want me to air out dirty laundry. I don't think there is a big enough washhouse!"

"Yeah, well, I overlooked all that. They had a right to talk somewhat, that was foul, and I don't care how much you forgive someone. I know that shit hurt you. I am just glad I am woman enough to admit my wrongs. Can't nobody knock me for that, not even with a Mike Tyson punch! Trust me when I say I know about their dirty laundry too, but I am and always will be on grown woman status, and no need to point fingers. I have a book to finish and business to tend to."

"Woman, this is us in this marriage. Have you cheated on me since we've been married?"

"No! And I will take five lie detector tests!"

"Alright then, let's do us. I forgave you and hope you forgave me. Babe, seriously. When I tell you, you are the scratch-off to my winning lottery ticket. I mean that! Brenda, I sometimes wonder how I even deserve you!"

Brenda smiled so hard her cheeks rose and made her eyes look closed.

"Okay, I will be patient with your project thing, whatever it takes."

Samuel looked into Brenda's eyes, almost in tears. He wanted to tell her so badly; however, he was still in his addiction stages, trying not to relapse.

"Thank you, mama. You just don't know what your support means to me! Goodnight."

He made his way to the room for a shower and bed but stopped and turned around.

"Well, wait!"

"Yeah, what's wrong?"

"Are you coming to bed? Can I hold you? Well, what I'm asking is we good?"

"Let me answer that later. I am enjoying this extra attention right now."

"You are something else!"

59

It was time for David to attend the Special Olympics. David had the support of his mom, dad, Auntie Linda, of course, Manzel, Marie, Mrs. Sinclair, family, and a host of others who knew the Smiths. Manzel and Steve sat next to each other. Linda and Samantha made it their point to greet everyone in attendance and shake their hands. When the games were over, David went down by the host to receive his trophy.

"Now, the moment we all been waiting for. Everyone, please, take your seats."

The host gave everyone a chance to sit down.

"I know as a parent or adult, we wish that all of our special Olympic members could walk, see, or be healed of whatever disability they have. However, we teach our Special Olympic members and staff to be happy and have the faith to keep going. Today we have a new member who is here and very fortunate with a lot of support from family and friends. So let's give a welcoming greeting to David Smith! Come on over!"

Manzel and Steve were closely watching. They were bracing themselves to see what was going on. The host smiled at David, who David rolled himself closer.

"Now, I spoke to this brave young man, and he told me, if he ever was to walk again, he would still attend the Special Olympics every year! I asked him why? David told me that he knows how it feels now to be less fortunate. He feels that is a big reason...."

The host paused to read his cue cards slow as if he was trying to get an understanding.

"His dad now accepts his friends and has become closer to his mechanic. His dad and mechanic built the go-kart together that he was originally against him and his friends making."

The host leaned over to David. The entire audience was silent and wondered what was going on. The host whispered to David.

"Would you like for someone to come down here with you before you get your trophy? I will let you speak on the mic."

"Sure!"

The host passed David the mic.

"Hello, everyone. I would like my Mom and Aunt Linda to come down first."

The audience clapped as Linda and Samantha went on down.

"And then my dad and Manzel, and my best friends Isaac, Lema, and Jerry."

The host took back the microphone, and his eyes got big. He liked what he saw when Samantha and Linda came down.

"Oh, wow, yeah, you two ladies can stand right by me."

The crowd laughed. As Steve and Manzel approached, Steve gave the host strong, aggressive eye contact that could shoot an arrow right through his heart.

"What the hell you mean stand by...."

Manzel tried to stop Steve. He knew where this was going. Manzel tapped Steve and tried to help him calm down.

"Uh, uh."

Steve moved Manzel's hand with aggression.

"You heard him Manzel, I don't need your philosophy or redirection right now!"

Manzel pointed to David and the crowd. The crowd shouted and clapped in applause. David looked at Steve as if he was proud to be his son all over again. Then Steve looked down and saw David walking towards him, staggering but at a steady pace. Samantha and Linda were crying loudly in happiness. Lema and Isaac were jumping up and down with joy. Steve started to cry.

"OOH, MY LORD! OOH! GOD IS GOOD!"

There was not a dry eye in the audience except the host, who took a deep breath of relief.

"OOH, GOD!"

David got closer and was almost there. Linda and Samantha ran to David as Steve and David hugged each other. Samantha and Linda joined in for a group hug. Once they all let go of David, then came Lema and Isaac reached in and gave him the same kind of squeezable hug he had just received from his family. Brenda and Bernice hugged each other as they cried and then ran down. Brenda, Bernice, Linda, and Samantha hugged each other as well. The host's eyes were watery, so he stepped back and allowed Steve to approach the mic. Once Steve stepped to the mic, things calmed down a bit. Everyone was wiping their faces, including the audience, to hear what Steve had to say.

"Um...."

Steve paused for a long time, and Manzel gave him a friendly pat on the shoulder. Then, Steve began to speak again.

"You know we spend our entire lives being mad at a certain person for certain reasons. Whether it is race, background or just a family member, or just ignorant and small life situations. Then we begin hating each other. I really felt I had a right reason for my wrong views, from what happened to my mother by a Black man."

The audience was in awe of what this speech was coming to.

"I was supposed to be upset at something that happened to my mother! However, I was not just mad at the one man, I was mad at every person in that race due to one person, and that was not fair.

Anyway, it took my child and his good friends to show me how wrong I was."

Samantha and Linda started clapping. Next, Mrs. Sinclair and Jerry stood up clapping, then Bernice, Brenda, and the audience followed. Finally, after two minutes, the clapping stopped, and everyone sat back down.

"In saying that, I would like to call another one of my son's friends, Jerry, down here, who taught a grown man like me something. The audience clapped, but Jerry pushed his glasses up and shook his head no. Mrs. Sinclair stood up and guided her son down for support. She knew he was not going to go. Once they were by Steve and everyone else, Steve took the microphone down and walked right over to Lema; however, he faced David, Isaac, and Jerry.

"I thank all of you for being patient with a fool like me! And I am very thankful, all of you are alive with my son! To see my son walk also is truly a day of praise. Kids, I am truly sorry!"

Steve dropped his head and began to cry. Lema first, then Jerry and Isaac stood on each side of David since he staggered and escorted him to his dad. All of the kids group hugged Steve. Manzel took the mic softly away from Steve. Manzel looked up and saw that the crowd had become teary-eyed again. He and the host both had big lumps in their throats.

"Well, friend, I always looked at you for the good encounters we had when we worked on your cars or whatever. I just could tell that there was a ton of bricks somewhere in your life that made the bricks pile up on your chest. God had to show you in some way that they could be removed. I am so glad you were shown through the thing most innocent in this world, kids. Babies and children just come here wanting to love and be loved, no matter if you are big, small, black or white, the innocence of children is they don't see that. Children just want to be loved right. And to those here who may not get the blessing to walk again like David or have a disability that you feel is a discrepancy, it is not! So parents, caretakers, family, friends, whoever, keep the faith, and please do not get discouraged! God has a special gift and place for us all in some shape, form, or fashion! Whether it becomes a lesson learner or a blessing earned, please, be thankful! Thank you."

The audience stood up and clapped for an extended period of time, then sat down. Manzel passed the microphone back to the host.

"Well, I have not been this emotional for a very long time, well, not since my mother passed! I will place some flowers on her grave tomorrow and thank God she gave me life!"

He looked over at Steve.

"And since I still have my life."

(Linda and Samantha quietly giggled.

"So in enclosing, everyone thanks for attending this very special, unforgettable, 23rd Special Olympic Ceremony here in California. Have a safe trip home, and be blessed."

60

A few months passed, and Brenda and Bernice talked in Brenda's living room when they heard a knock at the door. Brenda was not expecting anyone, and she knew that it was not Samuel; he had a key.

"Who is it?"

"It is Lucille."

Brenda looked back at Bernice, and they looked at each other puzzled.

"Lucille?"

Brenda opened the door. Lucille's face looked vaguely familiar.

"Yes, do you have the right house?"

Lucille was nice but spoke firmly.

"Of course, I do. Doesn't Samuel live here?"

Brenda looked back at Bernice, both surprised and nervous.

"Oh yeah, I mean, yes. Is he okay?!"

"As far as I know, yes, he is okay!"

Bernice gave Brenda the eye and hint to let Ms. Lucille come in. Brenda got the hint right away.

"Oh, yes, uh, come in, please."

Ms. Lucille, who was definitely from the old school, noticed Bernice hint at Brenda. So, Lucille was passively aggressive. She spoke on the hint without quote on quote, not speaking on it.

"Yes, thanks! I was wondering when you two were going to greet me in."

Ms. Lucille stepped in, looked around, then sat in Samuel's recliner.

"This is a nice, beautiful, comfy, cozy home, just like I thought!"

Brenda was confused.

"Excuse me?"

Lucille ignored Brenda.

"Yeah, well, I am a long-time friend of Samuel's mother. We attended the same church since your husband was knee-high to a duck!"

Bernice placed her hand over her mouth and silently giggled.

"Well, where is he?"

Brenda dropped her head. She missed her husband.

"Well, he is doing some "project," he said."

Ms. Lucille smiled hard. She knew that the project was in line with following her firm orders.

"Well, why the dropped head, honey?! He is keeping himself busy!"

Bernice crossed her legs.

"Yeah, Ms. Lucille, that is what I told her!"

Ms. Lucille looked over at Brenda and had sympathy for her. Then she looked at Bernice.

"Yeah, uh, what is your name, sweetie?"

"Oh, Bernice!"

"Bernice, you may have told her right, but when you are close to your mate, and they leave longer than what you feel they should, or the time that you are used to, we often first think they want another. That is our human instinct, especially when you are thick as thieves. Sweetheart, you read me?"

"Yes, Ma'am!"

"You ladies cannot be from California! I don't receive yes, Ma'am acknowledgments unless I am back home! Where you two originally from?"

"Oh, we originally from Georgia, Ms. Lucille."

"I thought so. I know this grey hair don't just mean I want to keep up with my age. That is wisdom up there."

She pointed to her hair and laughed. Brenda and Bernice laughed as well.

"Well, how are those boys? You know bad news spread faster than melted butter on bread! Are they okay?"

"Oh, thanks for asking. He is doing fine!"

"And how are the other young ones?"

Bernice spoke up.

"Oh, they are good, also! Thank God!"

"Yeah, thank Him because everything happens for a reason. We here temporarily for a purpose and then gone soon. So, we need to leave a good mark for those to follow. But, my God, these young ones are lost, and it is partly our fault."

"I agree, Ms. Lucille, these kids can say and do whatever now. But what can we do?"

"Read 2 Timothy in the Bible and just be part of the solution and not the problem. You cannot change everyone. The promise land is not promised to everyone. It could be; however, some just will not ever listen! There is some on earth to show us how to be and some on earth to show us how not to be, just plain and simple."

Lucille reached in her purse and passed Brenda some money.

"Oh, no! Is that a hundred-dollar bill?! I cannot take that from you!"

Ms. Lucille went into her firm, motherly role.

"Girl, if you don't take this money, I'm going to shove it in your hand so hard you are going to have fingerprints of dollar bills! Now take it! This is just my token to help you with your family and that baby of yours. I heard your family roots from the deep South, right?"

Both Bernice and Brenda shook their heads.

"Good. So, I know you know it is rude to say no to a gift. It offends people, so here now!"

Brenda looked at Bernice like she would when they were little girls getting into trouble with their mom.

"Uh, uh, okay. Thank you."

"Now, you tell that knucklehead, I said good job on his project and keep it up!"

Ms. Lucille got up and walked towards the door to leave.

"Now, come and lock your door. People meaner than me may just walk in. See you later."

Brenda locked the door.

"Man! She was a piece of work!"

Bernice smiled.

"No, I like her! That was what you call heaven sent! She tells it like it is, and that is rare for somebody to keep it raw and uncut. Gave us what we needed to hear even if it hurt!"

"Yeah, I cannot argue with that, well, with the truth."

61

~

At T.J.'s rehabilitation center, Clyde talked to Samuel, who got on the subject about Clyde's mother Lucille and other serious situations.

"Did my mother rub you the wrong way, man? I know how she can get."

"Hey, I'm here, aren't I? Man, she got the job done; however, she did it!"

Clyde and Samuel laughed as Ron walked into the conversation.

"Yeah, man, Ms. Lucille does not play!"

Samuel got back to being serious.

"So, tell me this, Clyde, with you having a strong-willed mother like that, what made you turn to the bottle. If you don't mind me asking?"

"No, it's cool, man. It was just more than the bottle that made me start drinking. I was a wreck, whether I had a strong mom."

"Really?!"

Samuel looked Clyde up and down.

"You look well, though."

"That is why you don't judge a book by its' cover. Yeah, but I don't regret my past because the Lord does not put anything on you, you can't handle. All the situations that happened to me, so I can help others now. Yeah, I had a good mom, but my mom always told me life was an assignment. So that is why we have to go through things; to help each other before we go."

"Yeah, that mom of yours; that woman tough! And intelligent, though, you cannot take that away from her! What a combination."

"Yeah, I had a good life with my mom. It's just I was hard-headed and selfish before I put God first. Then when I would go through things, I would try to be on cloud 9 and not deal with my problems. I always wanted the easy way out."

"Yeah, well, God definitely has his hand planted on you with a mother like that, and that is for sure! And I am glad she planted her hands on me, also."

Clyde smiled at Samuel, and he noticed Samuel was looking down.

"What's wrong, Samuel?"

"Oh, no, I've been meaning to ask you, what's that book, you carry around with you?"

Clyde was excited that Samuel asked.

"Oh, I'm glad you asked me, man, this book here. Man, I thought he and my mom were best friends. The author's name is Rick Warren. The book is called "Purpose of Driven Life." He keeps it so real it hurts."

"Yeah, well, I agree. Maybe he is related to your mom in that case."

"Man, stall out on moms. Seriously, after I read this book, I stopped being selfish. You have to just accept your purpose in life when you read this. There are a lot of books out there that help people though in some way."

"Yeah, maybe I will read it one day. My wife writing a...."

"A what? Why you stop talking?"

"No, nothing. Let me let my brother know I need to go home. I haven't called her in hours. And I need to check on my niece and sister-in-law. Clyde, I am glad I am getting sober and back to me, but it seems like I am neglecting my family now, man."

"No, that is not it, but I hear you. I am going to get you a copy of this book, okay?"

"Yeah, good looking out, thanks."

Samuel walked over to T.J. and tapped him on the shoulder; T.J. jumped.

"Dang! I see I startled you, huh?!"

"Just a little bit. I was thinking about another program for teenage youths who are on drugs."

"All you have to do is ask Lema, and she would run it."

T.J. laughed hard.

"Yeah, and she would tell those kids off without knowing it, make them think logically and have a solution all at the same time."

"Tell me about it!"

"With her little grown-up self, that is Ms. Growny!"

"Isn't she?! Well, I wanted to talk to you. I think I'm ready for Bren to come on down. Well, I mean, she is in suspense so much I just do not want her thinking I am dipping out on her."

T.J. frowned; however, he would not dare tell Samuel he had talked to Brenda already.

"Come on now, not Bren, she not thinking that is she?"

"Yeah. Well, hey, she is a woman and only human."

"Yeah, you got that right. Women have looks that can make you feel like you came home after the streetlights came on, and you are going to get a whooping!"

"Seriously!"

"Man, one time Jade looked at me, I was like, 'Babe, I only said hi to her'!"

"She good. You told on yourself and only said hi to a female. She had a look that could kill for real then!"

Clyde and Jim knocked then walked in. Jim wanted in on the laughs.

"Hey, we want to laugh too!"

"No, come on, have a seat, man. We just talking about women."

"All hell! Nevermind!"

"Hey, you told us to remind you to call Mr. Goet back."

"Oh, yeah! Shoot! Well, let me take care of this, bro. Let me let you go."

"Yeah, alright. I will see you all in a couple of days at the sobriety grad and official grand opening."

"Alright, take it easy."

"See you, Sammy."

"Hey, you fellas need anything?"

Jim and Clyde looked at each other puzzled, then back at T.J.

"Well, I mean, you know, like materials to finish certain projects or something. The reason I asked is that Naishell is going to grab some materials for me, so we can set up some things for the sobriety certification ceremony."

Naishell was one of Jade's family members who sincerely loved her. Clyde thought for a moment.

"Yeah, we need some. Can you write some down, Jim? T.J., I wanted to give some hand-outs and pamphlets at the ceremony. Did anybody get that together?"

"Yeah, I just hired Jade's relative I was just speaking about. One of her good relatives, I should say. Jade was close to this cousin, and this cousin was always by Jade's side. Naishell is very good at doing things like administrative assistant work. She was going to work side by side with my wife."

"Hey, okay, so I have all the materials we need, and I put down some refreshments I would like.

Clyde shook his head, and T.J. laughed.

"Alright then, man. I appreciate you two sweat and tears, seriously. I have to make this call to Mr. Goet; thanks for reminding me. Jim, you wait in the conference room for me. I will be ready to talk to you be...."

T.J. stopped himself. He did not want to bust Jim out about his hygiene in front of Clyde. So, T.J. made something up since he had already started to speak. However, he gave Jim a big clue but to where only Jim would know what it entailed.

"Uh, so you can fix my shower."

"Oh, yeah, right on! I will wait."

"Hey, y'all need a helping hand. You know I am a Jack of all trades!"

T.J. had to think fast.

"Oh, uh, good looking out, Clyde, but, uh, you work hard. Just go home for the day. I appreciate you to the fullest for everything!"

Clyde smiled and nodded in agreement. He waved goodbye.

62

Samuel got home, and Lema and Isaac were running in the house and playing ball.

"Hey?"

Isaac and Lema did not hear Samuel, so he raised his voice a little more.

"Hey! Hey! Where's your mama at, boy!"

Isaac stopped running so hard his shoes screeched on the floor. Lema looked surprised because she knew she was not supposed to be running in the house.

"Uh, oh, uh, hey, Uncle Samuel!"

"Yeah, hey, sweetheart. Y'all know better."

"I know, I'm, I mean were sorry. I mean, we're not sorry people, but we apologize. Yeah, that's it."

Samuel wanted to laugh at her advanced way of thinking; however, he held it in.

"Lema, come here."

Isaac crept to his room. He knew Lema usually saved them from discipline every time.

"Yes, sir."

Lema moved closer to Samuel.

"Uncle T.J. has a job for you. I will explain it to you later."

"For real, Uncle Samuel! Please just tell me what it is?!"

"We need ideas for our youth and teen program that he thinking about doing."

"Well, I'm 11. Teens?!"

"Yeah, but your attitude and ideas are 27!"

Samuel laughed. Lema just looked at him with a blank stare because she heard that all the time.

"Well, anyway, we will talk later, Lema."

"Okay, Uncle."

Lema ran in the back with Isaac. Bren and Bernice came from the back room. Brenda ran and hugged Samuel, then took his coat to hang it up.

"Hey, babe, I put your food in the oven."

Samuel looked at Bernice then back at Brenda as he was blushing.

"Well, alrighty then! I haven't been welcomed home like that in a minute! Hey, sis!"

Bernice smiled, satisfied that Brenda and Samuel were getting along.

"Hey, there, bro-in-law!"

Bernice headed to the back. That is how humble of a person Bernice was. She did not have any companionship; however, she was not jealous. On the contrary, she loved to see people happy, and she respected quality time between her sister and her husband.

"Alright, I'm a head to bed now."

"Okay, sis, I love you!"

"Love y'all too!"

Samuel gave her a friendly wink saying he loved her back. After that, Samuel and Brenda flirted with each other and played around.

"Hey, sexy!"

"Sam, stop! No, go ahead say it again."

They laughed.

"In a couple of days, I have somewhere to take you. It is a special place to eat."

"Oh, okay, well, what about the...."

"The kids?!"

"Yeah."

"Woman! There you go, Brenda; you do not ever let me take you out without the kids sometimes! I will talk to and pay Bernice!"

Brenda smirked.

"Now what, Bren'?"

"No, it's just, I am tired of my sister being alone. I feel she thinks she is the third wheel sometimes. And we throw the kids on her when she comes from Georgia."

"Bren, no, that is not it. Bernice just smart! Hell, you do not want her to rush to find someone, and he is a senseless fool, right?"

"Yeah, you right, huh."

"Yeah, so don't worry. Bernice will find someone when God wills it. Plus, they have to get past Lema anyway!"

"Yeah, you right. That is a tough little bodyguard! Well, okay then, how should I dress?"

"Uh. Just do you, mama! You always surprise me anyway!"

63

T.J. was back at his house, where he took Jim. Jim was fresh out the tub. He was dressed and sitting in the chair in T.J.'s guest room. Jim started to watch T.V. when T.J. came in and plopped in another seat.

"So, you cool, Jim?"

"Am I? I went from shit to sugar in 2.2 seconds! But, man, this house is beautiful!"

T.J. wanted to tell Jim thank you; however, he was dwelling on how Jade was not there to share the house with him. T.J. was mute, and Jim stared, wondering why T.J. was not just as excited for that big house.

"What man? I heard you."

"No, seriously, I really appreciate you, T.J.! I mean, I literally gave up on myself, almost on life. And people will never understand how down-to-earth you are and how you saved lives! Then when people would look at me, drinking, they didn't see a person that had problems. They just saw in their minds a smelly drunk wasting space on Earth! But not you, man, not you! How can I repay you?"

He looked around the house.

"Well, not literally, but you know."

"It's all good. And I did not get blessed with this until my wife set the foundation. Blessings are not just financial, although it looks and feels good at the time. We have got to put God first, Jim. When I die, I cannot take or spend all this money at the gravesite. But you know what I can do, Jim?"

"What's that?"

"I can leave a mark on how to be. So, what you can do for me, man, is just learn and continue to love! Jim, you are a "somebody" no matter what anybody tells you! I know how Pete can be, and you see how you showed him up on how smart you are without even trying to be egotistical."

"Yeah, that fool needed to be taught a lesson."

"True. And you showed yourself that you could teach it to him. Use that skill without anyone pushing your buttons. Help others pray to God and gain that strength you have that you did not know was there. Find your niche in life; hell, one is math. But that is what you can do for me. Well, not for me, for yourself. Do good, and it may take longer, but good will come back. You see how much Wolverine gets his ass whipped until the end of X-Men. Hell, heroes always finish last; however, when they keep the fight, they win."

Jim wanted to cry, but that X-Men joke cleared it up some, and instead, he laughed and nodded in agreement.

"Hey, man, let me relax then. Get out and let me enjoy my movie. How about that? Am I good at something else now?'

"Oh, okay, I see you. You good at kicking people out of their own places, huh?"

"Amen!"

"Alright, I'm off to bed on that note, but uh, be ready in the morning."

"No doubt!"

The next day night, Brenda and Samuel went on their dinner date. Samuel looked at his watch and noticed that he had one hour until the rehabilitation ceremony. It was a 15-minute drive from the restaurant.

"Alright, Bren', if you don't mind, can you go with me? I have to pick up some paperwork and help T.J. for a quick second. Is that okay?"

Brenda smiled. She loved T.J. like a real brother, and she was glad the brothers were getting along. In addition, Brenda was very appreciative that this project had Samuel slowing down on drinking even though she didn't know how much he was drinking now.

"It is not a problem, I understand. Let's get a doggie bag for my leftover food first and head on out then Hon'."

"Okay."

They head out and to T.J.'s rehabilitation center. Brenda looked up and was wowed by the building and impressed with everything she saw. Brenda and Samuel went inside. Brenda looked around and was wowed again. T.J. saw his brother and sister-in-law and went right over. T.J. hugged his brother tighter than ever and then hugged Brenda just as tight.

"I'm glad you made it to help me right quick."

T.J. gave Samuel a thankful high-five.

"If it is okay with the Queen?"

Brenda was lightly blushing.

"Oh, T.J., stop. You cannot flatter me with the "Colgate's"!"

"Hey, I tried, and I know you have your king here. I don't want any trouble.

He held his hands up in a silly way as if he was a victim. Brenda slapped his shoulder.

"You a mess, T.J.! Where do I sit, silly?!"

T.J. looked at Samuel, happy that Brenda always supported him and now Samuel was back being supportive to him.

"Oh, just sit up front, shoo, you family!"

As Brenda sat up front, she mingled with familiar faces and some she did not know. Then she turned a little to the side and saw Ms. Lucille walking in. Her eyes got bigger than Coke bottles.

"Well, well. Hello lady!"

Ms. Lucille had the biggest grin on her face. Brenda smiled back; however, she was nervous, not knowing if Ms. Lucille would tell her her dress was revealing since Brenda showed a little cleavage. So, she pulled up her dress at the top some.

"Uh, uh, hello, Ms. Lucille."

Ms. Lucille noticed her nervousness. Ms. Lucille knew she could be intimidating at times, so she eased things up for Brenda some.

"Girl, why are you all tense? This is a beautiful atmosphere, as beautiful as you can get. This is really nice in here, and you look like you saw a ghost."

Ms. Lucille laughed.

"Oh, well, uh, I just forgot to tell Samuel you came and checked on him, and tonight we had such a beautiful dinner date, it slipped my mind."

Then Brenda started talking fast and trying to explain.

"And then we stopped by here because....."

"Child, you don't have to explain, and I understand. Husbands think "I do" means you don't know how to live without them sometimes. You were probably due for a dinner date! Plus, you just forgot, everyone makes mistakes or something just slips their minds."

Ms. Lucille leaned towards Brenda's ear and whispered.

"I ain't nobody to be scared of, like that. I am really mushy inside, but that's between you and me! Don't tell a soul, or else I'm a have to kick your ass."

Brenda giggled, then she eased up and made a sarcastic joke back, even though she still respected her to the fullest.

"Okay, uh, that was mushy."

Ms. Lucille laughed then looked around.

"Is there a seat by you?"

"As a matter-a-fact it is!"

They sat down and noticed quite a few people were being seated.

When they looked up at the podium, they saw one of T.J.'s workers move a cloth from a table on the side of the podium. There were a few trophies and certificates on the table. T.J. walked on stage and to the podium. He tapped the microphone to see if it was on.

"Testing, Testing. Can I please get everyone to be seated, please?"

Everyone sat and gave their undivided attention.

"I."

T.J. paused for a very long time. Everyone looked at each other, trying to figure out what was wrong. Jim yelled out from the audience.

"TAKE YA TIME, T.J., SPEAK OUT, AMEN!"

Everybody started to clap. A lady in the audience yelled out.

"There go those "pearly whites," hey now!"

Everyone laughed. Between Jim and the lady in the audience, T.J. loosened up. He took a deep breath and looked up.

"I, uh, decided to open up this rehabilitation center for several reasons. Good friends, good supportive family."

He looked at Brenda and gave her a thumbs up. Brenda smiled and gave him thumbs up as well.

"And most of all. My beautiful wife. This was her dream, and I was going to help her fulfill her dream; however, it was too late, and uh...."

Ms. Lucille cut in from the audience.

"Not too late, you did it, and she is looking down on you smiling!"

The audience clapped in agreement.

"Yes, Ms. Lucille, you're right. That woman was my best friend. She dotted my I's and crossed my T's; she kept me straight. When I just did not see a way out, she really drew me closer to God just with her peaceful presence. That is why I am standing before you all today. Jade helped me become the man I am. When my wife and I decided to build a legacy, we just wanted to help at least one! Just one! And so many of my true friends are here! I had many colleagues in college. Anyway, downright good friends. When you are down and out nowhere to turn, friends are here! Book smart people don't make you smart or care, and street people do not make you dirty and dumb, I'm telling you!"

Audience members shouted as a choir.

"AMEN!"

"Anyway, uh, Jabeeb, uh, used to always tell me how I was good and affected people's lives. And I listened. I didn't take what he said with a grain of salt, and I am not a cocky person because that's not me. However, I was really flattered when he told me that. The reason I was flattered was because in Proverbs. Shoot! I forgot the Scripture; my mom would kill me right now if she was here. But uh, in Psalms or Proverbs, my mom would quote the Scripture to my siblings and me often how it stated, "Let others speak on your good works." Basically, you all know what it is saying. It is better for someone else to say good things about you instead of showing off or bragging about what you do. Because really, if you had to speak on how you helped someone or what you did, have you really helped? Nope?! So, I just wanted to.... let me rephrase that "we" just wanted to spread love and help others. You know, Jade became an alcoholic, upset that her family could never accept her whether she did right or wrong. And when I lost her, I tried the same thing; maybe I could die with her and drown my pain."

At this point, Ms. Lucille and Brenda were in tears.

"But, uh. Do you know what I love about change? Change is good because if no one acknowledges it or you, the fact that you know you can have the power to pray and allow God to help you and you can come as you are, is a good feeling that you have to experience for yourselves. I just cannot explain that good feeling!"

Everyone clapped, and Brenda looked around, wondering why Samuel was not finished and coming to hear this heartfelt speech. T.J. noticed Brenda looking for Samuel.

"Therefore, I am going to stop being long-winded and give you all the reason for this ceremonial season. Today, I have three men here who will graduate with sobriety and hold onto it! I will pass the mic, and uh, they will say a pleasant and brief speech before they receive their trophies or certificates. Alright, so let's give these three men, the first ones at this rehabilitation to graduate from this program, a hand as I call them out."

Brenda focused back on the stage and stopped being rude, looking around for Samuel. So she could give the three chosen guys proper applause at the ceremony.

"1st is Clyde Churchhill."

The audience clapped, and Ms. Lucille stood up, clapped, then sat down.

"2nd is Ronald Watkins."

The audience clapped.

"And last but not least, Samuel Johnson!"

Brenda looked up and opened her mouth so wide you could see the back of her tonsils. A rain of tears came down her face. T.J. looked at Samuel and Brenda smiling so hard. Ms. Lucille placed her arms around Brenda and passed her some Kleenex.

"These three have taken time from their families and have helped me tremendously, day after day with this project."

Samuel looked at Brenda and winked; she cried even more. T.J. looked in the audience.

"Hell, four trophies. Come on up, Jim, you know you also helped with this project! You probably calculated each square in here!"

Everybody laughed and watched Jim as he ran on stage. Brenda had tunnel vision looking only at Samuel now.

"Jim Holdings, y'all! And so, you guys are...."

T.J. stopped talking because Brenda ran on stage and hugged Samuel so tight. The audience was wowed and clapped in happiness for the couple. T.J. just let her stay hugging Samuel. He knew he would love to receive a hug from Jade again, so he understood. A friend of the crew named Keith stood up and spoke.

"Wow, if being clean gets you hugged like that, hey, I have been clean for two days now!"

Samuel yelled back.

"NO, NO, my brother, you have to get your own!"

The audience laughed hysterically. Keith put his hands on the side of his mouth like he was announcing to the audience.

"Okay, you hear that, ladies. I'm getting myself together; I accept hugs!"

The audience laughed hysterically again as well as T.J. and the rest on stage. Then Keith sat down and clapped a high-five with another member at the ceremony.

"Shoo, I need me a good woman!"

"Alright, alright! All jokes aside, we support your hour just like your two days."

The audience calmed down, came back to reality, and clapped in support.

"Also, I want you all to look around, and I want my members from other races that are in A.A. to stand up! Now, before I give up the mic, you see, we are all united. Lend a hand, help a friend, and spread the word. Love is love, and support is support no matter what, here. Okay, on that note, let me pass it on to the fellas to give their speeches."

T.J. stepped off the podium sat by Ms. Lucille. He put his arms around her and pinched her cheeks. He was so excited about all of this, and he knew Ms. Lucille had a part in kicking Samuel into gear. Ms. Lucille smiled and looked up as her son walked up first to speak. Clyde fixed the microphone to his liking, then cleared his throat.

"Well, I was always taught to not sugarcoat anything, and I couldn't if I tried. My Mama right there, and don't let that height fool you. She don't play!"

Jim, Ron, and Samuel yelled out at the same time.

"We know!"

Everyone laughed, and Ms. Lucille laughed and waved her hand at all of them, like go on.

"But seriously, you can have a beautiful parent and take them for granted. You know I came to face my demons when I would sit and blame my mother for every stinking thing my father did when he hurt me. Then when everything blew over and my mother put me in my place, of course; She would grab my face and say, 'You know I understand pain'!" And then she would say, 'And we are all imperfect, and sometimes we end up hurting the ones that are close to us because we know they will still be there, and I forgive you, son!' When she stated that, I knew that having someone constantly fighting life with you and being so spiritual through it all was key. Whether it is your mom or whoever, when they are with you day after day, hand and foot, right or wrong, that makes you yearn to get right! Mama. I know you said we are allowed to do things of our free will, even when it comes to loving God. SO, I thank you for giving me free will to be me whether I make mistakes or not and for accepting me with open arms when I ran back to you every time like the prodigal son! I love you, Mom."

Tears rolled out Ms. Lucille's eyes as she whispered back to her son.

"I love you too, son!"

She hugged her heart and showed him her gratitude. T.J. kissed Ms. Lucille's face.

"You are a wonderful mama Ms. Lucille; I hope you always know that."

Clyde stepped back then Ron stepped up to talk. Ron had a deep voice, so he had to adjust the microphone away from him some.

"Hello, everyone. God is good!"

The audience rang out.

"All the time!"

"So, uh, my story may be a little different from everyone's here, but it all boils down to the same. And that's why we all need to have love for one another, you know. I only have myself and memories of plenty of relatives who passed on and a stepdaughter from my former wife, Linda. Her daughter was killed by a drunk driver."

He thought of his past. Ron showed a picture of Stephanie, Linda, and himself. Brenda's mouth fell wide open, and her eyes grew big when she saw the picture Ron held up of Linda and realized that it was Samantha's sister!

"I was so selfish because I had only her and her daughter and no other family. You would think once she lost her daughter to a drunk driver, I would have stopped drinking. But I was so self-absorbed and had self-pity that I let the devil take control. I even got angry when she had no empathy as to why I was drinking and left me. That was selfish, knowing she had lost her child to a drunk driver, and it kept opening up the same wound over and over again; I would not allow it to close. Do I think God forgave me? Yes, that's why I'm here!"

He looked over at T.J. and spoke directly to him.

"Man, you would sit out there at Jabeeb's with us and help each and every one of us with our problems. With every story we threw at you, you did not judge us even though you had your own problems. I remember I was so drunk, and I told you I'm just a waste to everyone I came in contact with, and that's why I probably lost a lot of family members. You looked at me and told me God bless fools and first sons."

Everyone laughed and cried in the audience. Ron started to laugh too.

"However, the even funnier thing was that T.J. did not know I was both, the first boy in my family and a fool!"

Ms. Lucille threw her Kleenex box at Ron and started laughing with the audience. Ms. Lucille yelled out.

"You're keeping it too real now, but keep it going!"

Ron continued.

"But, I am getting myself together. I prayed and asked God to forgive me for all my sins. I accepted Christ, and I still pray for my ex-wife often. It's just I am so glad I have my spiritual family because love is not just bloodline for biological families. Whether you believe it or not when Jesus died on the cross. The blood was poured out for us all, and I am glad he embraced and blessed me with you all. Thank you."

Everyone gave applause, and Ron stepped back to let Samuel speak. Samuel still had his arm around Brenda, so she walked to the mic with him and adjusted it. Samuel paused as he looked at his brother. So long that everyone looked over at his brother also. Then Samuel Samuel began to speak to the audience.

"You know we all noticed something today up here while we were receiving our awards. And that is with addictions; there is sometimes selfishness. You know I have never seen the good in me, and I always second-guess my talents."

He looked over at Ms. Lucille. She nodded her head for him to go on. Samuel continued.

"I tried to live my life through my brother all the time. You see, my brother was this professional professor, very street smart and book smart, got all the looks from the ladies also. I went through three tubes of toothpaste at night trying to get my teeth as pretty as his!"

The audience laughed.

"But when my brother faced his own issues and didn't finish being a professor, I treated him...."

Samuel paused and put his head down.

"I treated him like a dog! But I tell you what, not once did he not stick by my side! I just had this desire to make my brother into what I wanted him to be, and that's all because I wasn't happy in here."

He put his hand over his chest.

"Plenty of times, I turned my brother away from my door. I would disown him at times, and why you may ask. I was jealous. It seemed like he had it all, and I had nothing."

He looked over at his wife.

"God blessed me with a beautiful wife and a step...."

He stopped himself.

"I mean, son. My brother would tell me over and over again how I have a beautiful wife. Even though he lost his better half and was clearly grieving, it took a lot of guts to still be happy for others. My brother always knew the right words to say when you needed him. And he would not throw in the towel once he decided to help someone. I kept a family secret for over 30 years that I didn't even reveal to our mother. God rest her soul. Because she was on her deathbed then, and we were really young. I just wanted to enjoy every breath she took and not worry her. When I revealed my secret to my brother, he made me feel even lower."

The audience mumbles.

"I know you are like, how was that? Well, through all I had done to him, he had a right not to care about what I told him. But what happened? He listened, he cried with me, and still left his door open 24 seven like 711! I just thought of Jabeeb when I mentioned 7-Eleven."

Everyone in the audience put their heads down, remembering how much of a good soul he was.

"I would like to say God bless Jade and Jabeeb; they were definitely guardian angels to a lot of people, including us! And T.J., my jealousy is in control. I am willing to help you now instead of harm. You have the intelligence and charisma, as well as the patience to keep this empire and other projects going. You know I almost lost my son, and he almost lost his friends. I just wanted to turn the bottle, to drown my sorrows, and I blamed myself for it all because I had so much hatred from my past tragedy and how I treated my family. I am saying this before you all today to let you know, life is all about change. Some learn sooner than others; however, I hope all of you in this room pray for God to help you with the things you cannot control. Hold your head up, and don't allow bigger tragedies to happen because you ignored blessings and signs. If you can't handle your temporary job here, how will you receive your eternal job in heaven?"

Everyone stood up and applauded. T.J. went on the stage, and Brenda stepped back and gave his brother their moment. T.J. and Samuel hugged real tight and cried. T.J. wiped his face and started to speak.

"If you all were wondering if I'm a punk, thanks to my brother, these tears show that I am! Wow!

He looked at Jim to grab the mic, but Jim shook his head no. He humbly chose not to speak. T.J. continued.

Before I give these ribbons and trophies to our rehabilitated individuals here. I would like Ms. Lucille to come up to the stage so she can read the plaque we have on the wall."

Ms. Lucille grabbed the mic and began to speak.

"Now, I don't know why he asked me to read it. I have four eyes."

She pushed up her glasses.

"Well, Ms. Lucille, we have some Windex in the back."

Ms. Lucille laughed.

"All right, boy! Keep it up!"

She walked over and read the plaque.

"Okay, it says in loving memory of my wife, Jade Johnson, and my friend, Jabeeb Muhammad. May God continue to bless others to leave a mark and have a sincere heart to care for someone like these two important people left for us!"

T.J. thanked Ms. Lucille then he had Samuel, Clyde, Ron, and Jim walked over to another door. There was a gold ribbon tied in front of it.

"Now, for my last and final surprise before I close the ceremony, would you all please stand up?"

Brenda looked at Ms. Lucille as to what was going on. Everyone else looked puzzled. Once all the guys cut the ribbon, they opened the door.

"Also, welcome our new soup kitchen for the homeless in the community!"

It was such a big soup kitchen, like never before. Once they walked in, there were servers and a big dinner waiting for all the members at the ceremony to break in the new kitchen for the homeless!

This is the end of this book; however, it can be your beginning!

Shannika is a fighter, overcomer, and a down-to-earth lover of diversity. She acknowledges that her strength comes from God, and she is willing to share that strength with anyone in her path. Her motto in life is to pray then jump headfirst, and the good and bad, the smart and dumb mistakes will separate themselves. That determination helps her fight for the underdog. A product of the foster-care system, she was almost a high school dropout and told she was not smart enough for college. However, she returned for her diploma and later received her bachelor's degree at 40.

Shannika loves who she is and encourages others to share in that confidence no matter their background. There will be more to discover about this new author because this will not be her last book, screenplay, and/or whatever she decides to write. The blessings never end. Stay-tuned!